THE UNBOUND QUEEN

A Novel of The Four Arts

M.J. SCOTT

emscott enterprises

PRAISE FOR M.J. SCOTT

The Shattered Court
Nominated for Best Paranormal Romance in the 2016 RITA®
Awards.

"Scott (the Half-Light City series) opens her Four Arts fantasy
series with the portrait of a young woman who's thrust into the
center of dangerous political machinations... Romance fans will
enjoy the growing relationship between Cameron and Sophie,
but the story's real strength lies in the web of intrigue Scott
creates around her characters."
—*Publishers Weekly*

"Fans of high fantasy and court politics will enjoy The Shattered
Court. Sophie is such a great heroine..."
—*RT Book Reviews*

The Forbidden Heir
"This story was packed with action, political intrigue, scheming,
and high stakes."
—*Alyssa - Goodreads reviewer*

"This is a marvelous book. The world building is unique and complex. The characters are well developed and likable and there is intrigue for days. If you've read the first book in the series it only gets better in this one."
—*Lissa - Goodreads reviewer*

"'Forbidden Heir' is a great rarity: a sequel that I liked better than the original book."
—*Margaret - Amazon reviewer*

Fire Kin
"Entertaining...Scott's dramatic story will satisfy both fans and new readers."
—*Publishers Weekly*

"This is one urban fantasy series that I will continue to come back to...Fans of authors Christina Henry of the Madeline Black series and Keri Arthur of the Dark Angels series will love the Half-Light City series."
—*Seeing Night Book Reviews*

Iron Kin
"Strong and complex world building, emotionally layered relationships, and enough action to keep me up long past my bedtime. I want to know what's going to happen next to the DuCaines and their chosen partners, and I want to know now."
—*Vampire Book Club*

"Iron Kin was jam-packed with action, juicy politics, and a lot of loose ends left over for the next book to resolve that it's still a good read for series fans."
—*All Things Urban Fantasy*

"Scott's writing is rather superb."
—*Bookworm Blues*

Blood Kin

"Not only was this book just as entertaining and immensely readable as Shadow Kin—it sang in harmony with it and spun its own story all the while continuing the grander symphony that is slowly becoming the Half-Light City story. . . . Smart, funny, dangerous, addictive, and seductive in its languorous sexuality, I can think of no better book to recommend to anyone to read this summer. I loved every single page except the last one, and that's only because it meant the story was done. For now, at least."
—*seattlepi.com*

"Blood Kin was one of those books that I really didn't want to put down, as it hit all of my buttons for an entertaining story. It had the intrigue and danger of a spy novel, intense action scenes, and a romance that evolved organically over the course of the story. . . . Whether this is your first visit to Half-Light City or you're already a fan, Blood Kin expertly weaves the events from Shadow Kin throughout this sequel in a way that entices new readers without boring old ones. I am really looking forward to continuing this enthralling ride."
—*All Things Urban Fantasy*

"Blood Kin had everything I love about urban fantasies: kick-butt action, fantastic characters, romance that makes the heart beat fast, and a plot that was fast-paced all the way through. Even more so the villains are meaner, stronger, and downright fantastic—I never knew what they were going to do next. You don't want to miss out on this series."
—*Seeing Night Book Reviews*

"An exciting thriller . . . fast-paced and well written."
—*Genre Go Round Reviews*

Shadow Kin

"M. J. Scott's Shadow Kin is a steampunky romantic fantasy with vampires that doesn't miss its mark."
—*#1 New York Times bestselling author Patricia Briggs*

"Shadow Kin is an entertaining novel. Lily and Simon are sympathetic characters who feel the weight of past actions and secrets as they respond to their attraction for each other."
—*New York Times bestselling author Anne Bishop*

"M. J. Scott weaves a fantastic tale of love, betrayal, hope, and sacrifice against a world broken by darkness and light, where the only chance for survival rests within the strength of a woman made of shadow and the faith of a man made of light."
—*National bestselling author Devon Monk*

"Had me hooked from the very first page."
—*New York Times bestselling author Keri Arthur*

"Exciting and rife with political intrigue and magic, Shadow Kin is hard to put down right from the start. Magic, faeries, vampires, werewolves, and Templar knights all come together to create an intriguing story with a unique take on all these fantasy tropes. . . . The lore and history of Scott's world is well fleshed out and the action scenes are exhilarating and fast."
—*Romantic Times*

Wicked Games
"Extremely engrossing book with great world building, captivating characters and a sizzling romance to top it all off. The chemistry between the protagonists is very steamy as well. I NEED the next one!."
—*Cherylyn - Amazon reviewer*

"A little bit different to the norm in this genre. MJ Scott has

written a rattling good yarn that keeps you engrossed from start to finish.."
—*Andew - Amazon reviewer*

"'This book is a bit like Ready Player One with witches. The premise is really unique and fascinating and I fell in love with the characters. I really want the next book in the series right now..."
—*Lissa - Goodreads reviewer*

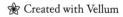

For the Aussie firefighters who are awesome and brave and unflinching and all the things true heroes and heroines should be.
And Vivienne who is also a very good egg for supporting them via the Authors for Fireys auction!

ACKNOWLEDGMENTS

There were times when I thought this book was going to defeat me. But thanks to all those who kept asking me about it and those who kept telling me I could do it—you got me to the end. Big smooches to my lovely Mum and to my tireless crit gals and writer pals. And the non-writer pals for rolling with weird writer friend. Extra big smooches to Sarah Mayberry for helping me unstick the start with her brilliance.

Once again, I have to thank Katie Anderson for her beautiful covers for this series. She is a talented talented gal!

The last few years have been crazy and we seem to be stuck with that rollercoaster for a bit longer. Thank you also to all the writers and creators bringing some escape to our lives and I hope this book brings some escape to some of you too.

Onwards we go...

Deep the earth
    Its harvest life
    Bright the blood
    Sharpest in strife
    Swift the air
    To hide and fool
    False the water
    The deadly pool

CHAPTER 1

There was most likely a correct and tactful answer to give when faced with an emperor offering you a crown, but Sophie Mackenzie couldn't, at that particular moment, think of one.

"Your Imperial Highness, you cannot expect me to answer that," she blurted, knowing, even as the words tumbled from her mouth, that it was precisely the wrong thing to say.

The implacable expression on the face of Aristides Delmar de Lucien, Emperor of Illvya, indicated that he very much did expect her to answer the question. What's more, that he expected her to say "yes." Possibly while groveling in gratitude.

She wanted to flee, not grovel.

Fleeing wasn't an option. Groveling, she couldn't stomach. She focused instead on trying not to let the horror she felt show on her face as she watched Aristides to see what he might say next.

Perhaps to him, his offer wasn't so outrageous. After all, he was an emperor. Descended from a family of conquerors and overseeing an empire that stretched across a continent. It was entirely possible that he'd grown blasé about changing the course of a life with a simple word.

But no matter how powerful the emperor, there was one key difference here. The Anglion crown he dangled in front of Sophie was hardly his to offer.

And it definitely wasn't Sophie's to take.

No. Anglion had a queen—the queen Sophie had served as lady-in-waiting—and to suggest any course of action that would deny that the throne belonged by right to Eloisa was the very definition of madness. Madness Sophie had no desire to take any part in.

The silence in the throne room stretched thin and thoughts of fleeing once again flashed through her head like lights glinting on a broken mirror. But the guards—not to mention the Imperial mages present—would stop her before she'd taken more than a few steps if she tried to run.

Besides, she and her husband, Cameron, needed Aristides's continued friendship. They'd survived another assassination attempt tonight. The emperor had made it clear he wouldn't brook another such attempt. But if he withdrew that protection, then they would be fair game for anyone who viewed her as dangerous to try again to kill her.

So far, it had only been Anglions who had threatened her. But she had no doubt that some of those assembled in this throne room disliked her as much as whoever it was orchestrating the Anglion attacks did. Some of them would probably be far happier if she was now down in one of the emperor's dungeons like Sevan Allowood.

Sevan, who had tried to kill her, who'd called her a traitor. She still didn't entirely want to believe that she had become a person that others wished dead, but it was true.

So no, she couldn't afford to offend the emperor.

Instead she had to stand there and try to behave as though Aristides had said something perfectly reasonable while she frantically tried to work out how to avoid giving the response he clearly expected. Acid gnawed at her stomach, making it difficult to think.

The emperor's face changed from implacable to displeased, but he didn't speak. The weight of his gaze was as heavy as the silence that had descended over the room, and Sophie had the odd sensation that she and Aristides were the only ones present who were actually breathing.

Certainly the sound of her breath and the rise and fall of air through her lungs were almost the only things convincing her she wasn't actually dreaming this whole disastrous audience.

"What I mean, Your Imperial Highness," she said, aiming for a tone that was polite but firm. The way that Domina Skey or Queen Eloisa or even Madame Simsa would deliver the words. None of them were women who uttered the word "no" with anything other than complete certainty that those listening would respect their wishes. "Is that I do not want the crown of Anglion." She'd never had any desire for power. She had spent most of her life so far down the line of succession—thirty-second in fact—that there had been no reason to ever contemplate such a possibility. Now that she stood dangerously high in the ranks of Anglion heirs, she still didn't want it.

Aristides shifted his weight, straightening on his throne. "Lady Sophia, we do not always get what we wish in life."

A ridiculous statement from a man who did get nearly everything he wanted. Should Aristides decide that a change of rule in Anglion would best benefit Illvya and the empire, then he clearly expected that she would be happy to comply.

She doubted many people had ever won a battle of wills with Aristides, but in this situation, she had no alternative but to try. For one thing, declaring a desire for the Anglion throne could only increase the number of people who might wish her dead. She'd survived an assassination attempt in Anglion and another here in Illvya. Not to mention being left with no choice but to bond with a sanctii—a creature she had been raised to believe was a bloodthirsty demon—to protect herself.

She'd been lucky to survive thus far. Why, in the name of the goddess, Aristides thought she would want to paint an even bigger target on her back was beyond her.

She wanted nothing more than to be left in peace. To find a way to build a life with Cameron that didn't involve such things as assassins and political plotting. Yes, she would like to return to Anglion if she could do such a thing safely, but she had begun to accept that going home might never be possible. Exile was preferable to possible death.

"Forgive my bluntness, Eleivé," she murmured. "You took me by surprise." If he took offense to her refusal, Aristides might well become the most immediate threat to her wellbeing.

"Does that mean you agree?" Aristides asked.

"It means that I need time to consider. Surely you can grant me that? There is no urgency in this matter, is there?" Granted, the messages sent from Queen Eloisa had been less than friendly, and the Anglion delegation who had carried them here had included Sevan, but that didn't equate to an immediate need for the emperor to act. At least, she fervently hoped not.

The emperor didn't answer immediately. Her heart pounded, the beats filling each passing second in greater and greater numbers.

[Come?] The voice in her head was rough and deep, and, for a moment, Sophie wasn't sure what she was hearing. But the faint chill that ran through her in the wake of the word made her realize it was Elarus. The only thing she could think of right now that might make this situation worse was the appearance of an overly protective sanctii.

[No!] She hoped Elarus would hear her. The bond they'd forged was brand new, and formed in haste, and Sophie really had no idea about how to use the knowledge of water magic the sanctii had gifted her with. It was still mostly a swirling mass of words and ideas in her mind that she couldn't make head nor tail of. She had no idea at all if she could control Elarus. Who was another reason that Aristides's proposal was nonsensical.

In Anglion, the familiaris sanctii were feared and reviled as demons, the water magic required to bond with them strictly taboo. Anglion accepting a water mage for their queen was less likely than Sophie suddenly sprouting wings and flying back to the island nation that was her home. And Cameron's. She glanced sidelong at her husband, standing rock still, barely breathing; so fierce was the strength of his attention on the emperor.

Years as a blood mage and a member of the Red Guard—the Anglion monarch's personal guard—had honed his instinct to protect. To fight when needed. But he couldn't fight now. She squeezed his arm and waited for the emperor to speak. Around her, the members of Aristides's court who had witnessed his offer and the attack that came before it waited also, staying silent though Aristides had proposed an action that was tantamount to war.

Amongst those standing to one side of Aristides's sunburst throne stood Imogene du Laq, the Duquesse of San Pierre. She didn't look in the slightest bit tense, though her expression was solemn. Then again, she was a soldier, of a kind. An Imperial mage. Perhaps she would welcome the opportunity for a war. Perhaps they all would. Or perhaps they thought that they could take a country as small as Anglion easily enough. Though not without some degree of death and destruction. Which would mostly rain down on Anglion heads.

Aristides cleared his throat, breaking the chill-inducing path of Sophie's thoughts and returning her attention to him.

"I grant, Lady Scardale, that it has been a trying day. And yes, the need is not yet at the point where action is unavoidable."

She tightened her grip on Cameron's arm as the sudden relief sweeping through her threatened, for a moment, to buckle her knees.

A reprieve. Though there was no way to tell how long it might last. Sevan was currently being interrogated by whomever it was that Aristides used to drag information out of his prisoners.

Whatever Sevan had to reveal would have an impact on the emperor's plans. Was it wrong to hope he would say nothing?

Or at least stay silent long enough to let her decide how best to approach resisting the emperor's plans should he decide to pursue them.

She tilted her head forward and let those treacherous knees carry her down into a curtsy. Cameron waited until she was safely upright again before he offered a bow.

"Your Imperial Majesty," he said. "As you say, this day has been both trying and long. I would like to take my wife back to the Academe. After all, we both have classes to attend in the morning."

The quirk to Aristides's mouth made it clear that he was well aware that this was Cameron making a strategic withdrawal from the field of battle. But, for once, it seemed that the emperor was willing to leave the discussion unresolved. He inclined his head. "Of course, Lord Scardale. There will be many opportunities to continue this conversation in the coming days and weeks."

Sophie managed not to wince at this pronouncement. Leave now, worry about the future later. She'd reached her limit for dealing with politics for one night. The thought of returning to the relative safety of the Academe, crawling into bed, and pulling the covers firmly over her head was more appealing than almost anything else she could imagine right now.

So she added a second curtsy to Cameron's murmured, "Thank you, Your Imperial Majesty," and tried to keep her pace to sedate rather than frantic as they left the throne room.

"He cannot be serious!" Cameron slapped the wall near the door of their apartment, sending a surge of power into the wards. The impact that echoed back up his arm and sent a twinge across his forehead did nothing to reduce his fervent desire to hit something. Possibly someone. Aristides came to mind. Sadly, the emperor was off limits. He scowled at the wall, flexing his stinging hand, and turned from the door as the wards flared into place, ensuring no one would be able to hear them. He'd held his tongue during the carriage ride back from the palace—treasonous plots not being something it was safe to discuss in public—but they were going to talk about it now.

"The man is insane."

Sophie stood near the end of the bed, untying her cloak. The shadows under her eyes spoke of creeping exhaustion. He should let her sleep. He should sleep himself. But not until they dealt with what had just happened at the palace.

"Not insane. Merely used to getting his own way," Sophie said.

Did she think that made Aristides's suggestion any less ridiculous? "You are *not* going to agree to this. It would be madness." There was no escaping the fact that Sophie stood high in the line of succession, but to actively try and take the throne from Eloisa? That went against every oath he had ever made. He—or they—might be exiles, but that didn't make them traitors.

"Did I do anything back there to make you think I disagree with you?"

"You didn't say 'no'," he said, the words sharper than he'd intended.

Her lips pressed tight for a moment as though she was biting back a response, but then she lifted a brow. "Can you tell me how I was supposed to do that without angering Aristides?"

He threw up his hands. "Not offhand, no." Which was part of the reason he was so furious. The emperor had very neatly sprung a trap around them.

Sophie tilted her head. "All right. Then we're agreed. There was no way to refuse back there. So how about you stop looming and scowling, and we talk about what we are going to do?" She sank onto the end of the bed and patted the quilt beside her. "Come and sit down. I don't want to have to explain to the healers if you collapse."

"I'm not going to collapse," he muttered.

"It's been a busy day," she said. "Explosions, assassination attempts, sanctii, emperors. If you don't need to sit down, how about you come over here and let me lean on you? I, for one, am exhausted."

Guilt flashed through him. She looked exhausted. But she clearly wasn't going to rest until he did. And she wasn't the one he was angry at. He pulled hard on the reins of his temper. It didn't help much. But the worry in Sophie's eyes pulled his focus. He lowered himself onto the bed beside her and pulled her close. She laid her head against his shoulder with a sigh, but the tautness in her body told him she wasn't relaxed. He doubted either of them would be able to rest until they finished this conversation, and he needed rest as much as she did. His recently healed head was throbbing with each beat of his heart.

"We can't let Aristides do this. It's madness," he said.

"I agree. The question is, what do we do to stop him?" Her fingers tightened around his. "Perhaps we should have returned to Anglion." Doubt quivered through her voice.

"That is no more a choice than agreeing to what the emperor wants," Cameron said sharply. In fact, it was a worse choice. He pressed a knuckle to the side of his head where the throbbing was worst. The two of them going back to face Eloisa's wrath without the protection of the emperor and the might of his army was tantamount to suicide.

Sophie straightened, sliding away from him on the bed. "What then? Do we stay? Try to change the emperor's mind?"

If only he knew the answer to that question. In truth, he couldn't see many good options. "That seems best, for now."

"For now?" Sophie's brown eyes widened. "For how long? And if that doesn't work, then what?" Her brows drew in. "People who want to put themselves totally beyond the emperor's reach usually try for Anglion. We can't do that."

"It's a big empire," he said. "There have to be places we could hide. Go unnoticed. Your Illvyan is good now and only getting better. It's a possibility."

She didn't look as though she agreed with him. He wasn't sure he agreed with himself, which made it hard to fault her doubt.

"Wouldn't they come after us? Track us? They have sanctii. Sanctii can find people."

The pain in his head bit deeper. "Do you know that for sure? They can find their own mages. That doesn't mean they can find anyone else." He still knew next to nothing of water magic. But Sophie had bonded with a sanctii and that sanctii had apparently provided her with the knowledge she needed to be a water mage the fast way. The dangerous way. His stomach clenched at the thought. Henri Martin, the Maistre of the Academe di Sages had been horrified at the risk Sophie had taken, letting a sanctii dump magic into her mind with no idea what she was doing. "Does it?"

Sophie's frown deepened. "I'm not sure." She grimaced, digging her fingers into the back of her neck. Maybe her head hurt as much as his. "We could ask Elarus."

She said it easily, as though it was perfectly normal that she now had a sanctii to call on. He'd started to grow accustomed to being around sanctii during their time in Illvya, but apparently he was still Anglion enough to feel a flash of fear at the thought of his wife summoning one to their rooms as matter-of-factly as calling for one of the Academe maids.

"Now?"

Concern flashed through her eyes. Then changed to resolution. "We need to know."

"All right." He took her hand again. Watched as she closed her eyes and felt a tiny spark of power through their bond. Then the sanctii—Elarus, he had to get used to using her name—appeared in front of him. He managed not to flinch.

"Thank you," Sophie said, looking at Elarus.

"You need help?" The sanctii's head turned from Sophie to

him, her large black eyes somehow assessing. He stared back, trying to commit her features to memory. Elarus was taller than the male sanctii and her skin darker, shaded in charcoal and black rather than the stonier grays of the male sanctii he knew. She allowed his inspection for a few moments, then turned back to Sophie.

"Help?" Elarus repeated.

Sophie cleared her throat. Glanced at him briefly, then continued. "We have a question."

"Ask."

"Can sanctii track people? Find someone across a distance?"

"Find you," Elarus said. "Always."

"But what about others?"

The sanctii lifted a hand. "Some. If know their magic."

"You can follow someone's magic?" Cameron asked.

"If it is known," Elarus said slowly. "Some easier than others." She pointed between Sophie and Cameron. "You two would be easy. Because of that."

That? Did she mean their bond?

Sophie's face fell. "Our bond? That makes us easier to find?"

"Not common," Elarus said. "So, yes."

"I see," Sophie said slowly. "So, someone who knew us could find us by looking for the bond? You or Ikarus or one of the other Academe sanctii?"

"Not needed for me," Elarus said. "The others, likely."

"What about people who aren't mages?" Cameron asked.

Elarus shrugged slowly. "Soldiers. Trackers. Empire has many." Her tone suggested such things were unimportant.

"But sanctii can't track someone without magic?" He pressed.

"No," Elarus said. She tilted her head. "No...song. No joining to the power."

The power? Did she mean the ley line connection?

"What if someone you knew changed their magic somehow,"

THE UNBOUND QUEEN 11

Sophie said before he could ask another question? "Could you find them?"

"Change how?"

"I don't know," Sophie said. Her gaze was fixed on Elarus "What if they added a bond? Or broke—"

"No!" Cameron interrupted her.

She still didn't look at him. "Elarus? Would that work?"

"It doesn't matter if it would work because we're not doing that," he said. He reached for Sophie's hand. Elarus's hand shot out and caught his wrist before he could touch her. There was a flash of near chill when her fingers closed around him, and then it faded to just rough skin gripping tightly. He froze.

"Elarus, let him go," Sophie said. "Please."

The sanctii's eyes were deepest black this close. And they looked angry. Her grip didn't loosen.

"Elarus, it's all right. He wasn't going to hurt me. It was a disagreement, nothing more."

Elarus made a disbelieving noise, but then she released him. He pulled his arm back but schooled himself to make no other move, keeping watch on the sanctii.

"Sophie?" he said, slanting a quick glance sideways. "Is everything all right?"

Sophie nodded. "Elarus. Thank you, that's all we needed to know. And you never need to worry about Cameron. He'd never hurt me."

"Safe?" Elarus said.

"Safe," Sophie agreed. "Always." She moved closer to Cameron. "Thank you."

Elarus gave Cameron another look, the moment stretching uncomfortably. But apparently, she was satisfied because the next moment she vanished.

Sophie shivered and sagged back down onto the bed.

Cameron joined her. "That was...interesting."

"It's new," Sophie said. "And I think she was upset earlier, when we were at the palace."

"Was she there?" Cameron asked.

"She spoke to me," Sophie said. "I don't know how close she was."

That was hardly comforting. But getting used to Elarus would take time. Right now, making sure they would have that time was more pressing. "So, no running, then," he said.

Sophie straightened. "That's not what she said. We could—"

"We're not breaking our bond," Cameron said. "It's not an option."

Sophie gripped his hand. "I'm not saying I want to. I'm saying we need to consider it. If it would give us a chance to get away. To be free."

"No." How she could even think such a thing?

"Listen to me. It wouldn't mean we're not married. It wasn't part of our wedding." She squeezed his hand together. "It doesn't change how we feel about each other. And if we had to—"

"We don't even know if we could break it," Cameron interrupted. "We don't even know how we formed it in the first place."

"Elarus said she could," Sophie said quietly. "When I bonded with her, she asked if I wanted it still."

"You didn't mention that."

"I kept it. There was nothing to tell." She lifted one hand and gently pushed his face around to face her. "I know you don't like this idea, but we need options. This is an option. A chance. One we might need. If it let us get away, to stay hidden, then it would be worth it. It wouldn't have to be forever. So, be angry with me, but I'm going to talk to Elarus about this some more. See what she knows. So, if it comes to the worst, we can get away. Body and blood. Whatever it takes, yes? To stay safe. To stay together?" Her eyes searched his face.

She was right. He hated it, but she was. But that didn't mean he was ready to accept it. Not just yet. He leaned down, pressed his forehead to hers. "Body and blood. But we can discuss this further tomorrow. I need to sleep. So do you. Or there won't be enough of either of us left functioning to do anything at all."

She breathed out a sigh. "Sleep sounds good."

More than good. The call to lie down and simply not be for a while was hard to resist. But he forced himself up, helped Sophie with her dress and managed to discard his own clothes before he crawled into bed and curled himself around her, breathing with her while he still could.

CHAPTER 2

Surely she hadn't been asleep long enough for it to be morning? But the morning sun slanting over Sophie's face as she squinted one eye open told a different story. Definitely morning.

Cameron didn't stir beside her as she eased upright. She listened to his steady breaths, trying to shake the fog from her brain. A smart person would go back to sleep, but as her mind started to whirl through all the events of the previous night, she knew she wouldn't be able to.

She slid free of the sheets and found a robe. Her stomach rumbled as she slipped it on carefully, still watching Cameron to make sure she didn't disturb him. He needed sleep to finish healing. She, if she wasn't going to sleep beside him, needed a bath. And then tea. Lots of tea. Perhaps some food, though she wasn't entirely sure her stomach wouldn't rebel if she ate. And then, she needed to talk to Elarus.

Half an hour later, she'd not long settled herself at one of the smaller tables in the dining hall with a tray of tea and plain toast, when Willem, one of the younger students, darted into the room, his expression turning relieved when he spotted her. The boy's pale curls bounced as he half jogged toward her, his face flushed in a way that suggested he had been running before he'd reached the hall.

Her stomach, which she'd only just managed to convince to contemplate the toast, tightened again as he reached her.

"Good morning, my lady," Willem panted.

She made herself smile. "Good morning, Willem. What brings you here at such a pace?"

He glanced at her and for a moment, his eyes widened as his gaze flicked between her collar and her face.

Her hand flew up to her neck self-consciously. She reached for her new student robes after her bath. The ones Madame Simsa had given her the night before, after she'd bonded with Elarus. The ones that carried both the blue of water magic and the brown of earth at the collar.

The Academe was a difficult place to keep a secret, but apparently Willem hadn't yet heard the news of her change in status.

She braced herself for the seemingly inevitable question, but the boy, after a second quick glance, seemed to recollect that he was there for a reason.

"A message from Madame Simsa, my lady," he said. "You are to see her at the training rooms immediately after breakfast."

She'd been right, then. No rest for the wicked. Though she'd been expecting the summons to come from Henri, not Madame Simsa. She'd bonded a sanctii without training or permission. She'd managed not to kill herself or go crazy in the process, but based on the reactions from the Illvyans the previous evening, that had been pure dumb luck.

The Academe wasn't going to risk her getting into still more trouble. She'd expected a lecture from Henri Matin, but apparently the Maistre had assigned the task to Madame Simsa.

She poked at the cooling toast on her plate, pushing the pieces around, appetite completely vanished. Madame Simsa had already made it clear that she thought Sophie was foolhardy beyond belief for bonding with Elarus. It seemed unlikely that their coming encounter would be pleasant. She was starting to forget what pleasant encounters were like.

"My lady, are you all right?" Willem asked, frowning down at her with worried blue eyes.

No. But Willem couldn't know that. She couldn't tell him the truth about what had happened at the palace or how she felt. The only one she could share that with was Cameron. And even then, she wasn't sure she wanted to let even him know exactly how scared she was. She'd burdened him with enough. So she would keep going, keep pretending she was perfectly fine. Until she was.

She lifted her tea. Sipped it. Found a smile. "Yes, Willem. I'm all right." The bell that signaled the end of breakfast began to chime above them. "You should get to your lessons."

Tea sloshed uneasily in Sophie's stomach as she reached the training rooms at the far end of the Academe's grounds where she usually took her lessons with Madame Simsa. She'd stretched her breakfast out as long as she dared past the ringing of the bell, drinking nearly the whole pot, and walked as slowly as she could, but now there were no more ways to put this off.

The door of the room they most often used stood open. Madame Simsa was probably already inside. And hovering outside the door was only going to delay the inevitable.

"Come in, child." Madame Simsa's voice came from inside as though she could read Sophie's thoughts.

"Coming." She hoped her reluctance wasn't quite so obvious to Madame as it sounded to her. As she stepped toward the door, a sudden caw—accompanied by a whistling feathery rush of air —made her pause. Tok settled on top of the open door, wings spreading as he found his balance and cawed again. The sound was more subdued than his normal greeting.

"Hello, yourself," she replied giving the young raven a smile.

She hadn't seen the bird in the last day—not that she'd had much time to think of him—but earlier when he hadn't been waiting for her outside her apartment, she'd started to wonder if the bond with Elarus had somehow scared him off. But apparently her feathered swain was made of stouter stuff than that.

"Stop talking to that bird and come inside," Madame Simsa called. The snap in her tone was fierce. Sophie looked up at Tok, who settled his wings with a movement that looked peculiarly like a shrug. Apparently he agreed she should get this over with.

She tugged at her robes, then stepped inside, telling herself it was foolish to feel nervous as she closed the door. She knew this room. For the last few weeks, she had spent a good part of most of her days here having lessons with Madame Simsa.

Small, and not exactly luxurious—built to resist magical mishaps rather than for the comfort of whoever might be working within its thick walls—it had grown familiar. She knew where the small drafts came from on windy days and which of the small windows had a latch that resisted being opened after it had rained. Knew that the chair on the far side of the small table wobbled slightly and the one nearest the door didn't.

She'd grown comfortable with it and with the woman giving her lessons. But today, she wasn't sure Madame Simsa would be in the mood to be comfortable.

The older mage stood by the table, leaning on her cane, her silver hair twisted back into a severe arrangement. Her robes gleamed softly in the lamplight, revealing the subtle rainbow sheen on the surface of the black cloth. Behind her, her sanctii, Belarus stood sentry, his gray face settled into the unreadable mask that Sophie had come to think of as normal for sanctii who were on duty with their mages.

His black gaze met hers, but his expression didn't change. Nor did Madame Simsa's. The sanctii hadn't often taken part in their lessons. But Sophie was less concerned with Belarus being in the room than she was with the fact that there was a fourth to

their party. Henri Matin, Maistre of the Academe di Sages, stood
by Madame Simsa.

His sanctii, Martius, was nowhere to be seen. Which was a
small mercy. The training room was small—lacking space even
when it was only Sophie and Madame Simsa. Adding in one
sanctii and one additional human made it distinctly cramped.
Two sanctii, and the potential for damage they represented,
would be pushing her nerves to its limits.

Sophie curtsied briefly to the mages, but before she had
barely opened her mouth to greet them, Madame Simsa pointed
to the middle of the room.

Apparently there was to be no polite small talk to begin the
session today.

So be it. Sophie moved to stand at the spot indicated, unsure
if there was any significance to the precise location. Other than,
perhaps, making her feel like a child being called to confess some
wrongdoing. She straightened her shoulders and faced the
mages. Perhaps what she'd done with Elarus had been foolish,
but she'd had good reason. They could argue with her about
those reasons, but she didn't think they could actually undo the
bond.

Nor, when Aristides was still interested in her, would they
banish her from the Academe. So, they had to teach her. Or
show her how to use what Elarus had given her, which was
perhaps something slightly different. Admittedly they could
make the lessons unpleasant, but she could deal with unpleasant.

Madame Simsa regarded her for several seconds, then tapped
her cane on the floor. "We shall begin. Tell me what you know
about water magic."

False the water, the deadly pool, floated through Sophie's head.
An old, old Anglion rhyme but one that probably had no
meaning to an Illvyan who hadn't been raised to believe water
magic was heresy. "Divination, deception, destruction,
demons." Perhaps not much better than the rhyme in terms of a
tactful response, especially the last word. Illvyans found the

term "demon" rude. They called them sanctii. Or used their names.

But those four words neatly summed up the little Sophie had been taught about the fourth Art back in Anglion.

But her Anglion indoctrination was no longer all she knew. Now she had all the knowledge Elarus had given her. And though that was mostly a swirling weight in her head, she had the vague sense the words she'd used weren't completely wrong. Though not the whole of it.

"Anglions." Madame Simsa thumped her cane on the floor once again, and Belarus turned his gaze to her for a moment before resuming his study of Sophie. "So blinkered." The cane jittered in an irritated staccato. "So. We'll start with the basics."

Sophie hid her instinctive wince, schooling her face to bland. The thought of cramming still more information into her head— or making sense of what had been crammed there by Elarus— made her temples throb. She'd done little else but scramble to learn what she needed to know since arriving in Illvya. But, she had asked for this. She had bonded herself with Elarus to protect herself. She needed to learn to use the weapons she'd acquired. Safely. "Whatever you think is best, Madame."

That earned her another quick tap of the cane. "If you'd thought more about what might be best before you behaved so recklessly, then we wouldn't be standing here, would we? But as you, Lady Scardale, are apparently determined to do things your own way, what's done is done. Thus, we begin. Demons." Her gaze narrowed at Sophie. "As a first point on that subject, I do not expect to have to remind you again, not to refer to them in that manner. You survived the first test of a sanctii. You didn't kill yourself forming your foolish bond. Best you not aggravate the sanctii you have paired yourself with by being ill-mannered. Given the irregularity of your bonding, who knows what could happen should she decide to teach you a lesson."

"I—" Sophie closed her mouth. She hadn't thought of that. Madame Simsa was correct. Elarus had done the binding not

Sophie. Normally a mage bound a sanctii—or the sanctii agreed to be bound—and the mage controlled the bond. With Elarus, anything might be possible.

Madame Simsa's cane rattled over the floor again. "So. Let us see what you can do with it. Call your sanctii, please."

At that request, Belarus pressed his mouth closed. Sanctii didn't have terribly expressive faces but unless Sophie was mistaken, what Belarus was expressing right now was distinct disapproval.

But she didn't have time to wonder why. Not with Madame Simsa standing there, steely eyed.

"Yes, Madame," she said. She closed her eyes.

"Keep your eyes open," Madame Simsa snapped.

Sophie obeyed. "Does that make a difference?"

"It's not a good habit," Henri interjected, his tone somewhat friendlier than Madame's. "You may have to call your sanctii when you are under threat. The last thing you need if you're facing down some danger is to have to close your eyes to make contact. That could get you killed."

There was no arguing with that. Sophie kept her gaze firmly on Madame Simsa while she fixed her thoughts on her sanctii.

[Elarus?] She paused, trying to work out how to politely phrase her request. After the reminder that the usual constraints may not apply to her bond with Elarus, polite seemed prudent.

[Yes?] The response came before Sophie could shape the next thought. The sanctii's voice seemed stronger here than it had in the palace.

[Would you mind joining me please?] That was polite.

No answer drifted into her mind, but before she had time to worry whether she should have tried a command after all, Elarus appeared by her side, her arrival accompanied by a chill that rolled through Sophie like a sudden dousing of ice water.

"Here," Elarus said. Behind, Madame Simsa, Belarus folded his arms, eyes narrowing.

"Thank you," Sophie said, smiling at Elarus before focusing back on Madame Simsa. "Was that correct?"

Madame Simsa cocked her head. "It was effective, therefore it will do. For now. So, that is something you can do." She looked at Elarus a moment, lips pressing together, and then she lifted her cane and pointed to the table. "Sit."

Sophie moved to the wobble-free chair and settled herself. Elarus followed and resumed her position by Sophie's side. The chill of her presence had lessened, but it still felt somewhat like sitting by a large block of ice.

To avoid thinking about it, Sophie turned her attention to the table. It was bare other than for an empty white china bowl and a lidded metal jug. Her stomach sank. She recognized the bowl and jug for what they were. Anglions weren't taught much about water magic, but they were taught that the arts of divination water mages practiced were part of the reason they were banned.

"You want me to try scrying?" she asked dubiously. From time to time Anglion earth witches showed a small talent for foreseeing, but generally such visions were unpredictable, coming to the witch rather than being sought deliberately. Eloisa was rumored to have that power though Sophie had never seen her use it.

Water mages used scrying to deliberately try to see things hidden or yet to be. She clamped down on her instinct to refuse, ignoring the bone deep mistrust of water magic that had been drilled into her. Water magic had not harmed her yet. But she needed to be honest. "There is little talent for foretelling in the witches in my family." And none she'd seen in her own earth magic.

Madame Simsa dismissed this objection with a curt wave. "That is not this. True, the goddess seems to sometimes send hints of the future to earth witches, and there are some in the temple who seem to be granted more than hints from time to time, but scrying is a different art."

"Shouldn't I learn the theory first?" Or start with something simpler. Like scriptii—the runes water mages used to embed their spells in objects enabling them to be triggered later. Not that that was necessarily a simpler concept than scrying, but a scriptii was a tangible thing. Sophie could understand it. Touch it. It seemed more likely a place to start than trying to see the future.

Henri smiled at her briefly. "This is a preliminary test only. Scrying is a skill that takes time to master."

Madame Simsa tsked. Unlike Henri, she seemed in no mood to indulge Sophie's nerves. "Open the jug and fill the bowl."

The jug was cool to Sophie's touch, and the liquid that streamed from it was black as ink. Maybe it was ink. The smell was astringent, not entirely unfamiliar, but she couldn't quite place it. Still, she took care not to spill any as she filled the bowl nearly to its rim.

As she settled the jug back onto the table, Elarus stepped closer. The sanctii peered down into the bowl and made a noise in Sophie's head not a million miles away from the "tsk" that Madame Simsa had uttered. The similarity was amusing enough that it distracted Sophie from her nerves as she stared down at the dark liquid.

[Smells.] Elarus offered silently.

[Yes.] The scent didn't seem to be dissipating even though the usual drafts wafting through the nooks and crannies of the walls were stirring the air inside the room. The acrid note tickled Sophie's nose and she risked a quick rub. Sneezing into a bowl of goddess knew what probably wasn't the best plan.

Maybe Elarus knew what the fluid was. Or maybe not. Sophie had no idea if the sanctii had ever been bound to another mage. Something to add to the list of things Sophie wanted to discuss with her.

Until she could, she had no way to gauge if Elarus might be familiar with the tasks the mages would be setting Sophie in her lessons. Maybe it was for the best. She didn't want Madame

Simsa and Henri to think that she was learning from Elarus rather than them.

She lifted her head. "What do I do now?"

"Look into the bowl. Think of someone important to you. Like your husband," Madame Simsa said. "Focus on him. Then see if you see anything."

"As easy as that?" She doubted it could be so simple.

"This is merely a test," Henri said reassuringly. "Just try, Sophie. Let us see what happens."

No further guidance seemed to be forthcoming.

Sophie bent her head back to the bowl. Tried to see nothing but the black liquid and to think of nothing but Cameron. At first she felt foolish; no sensation, bar the odd feeling her eyes were going to cross, manifested itself to tell her she might be doing something right. She blinked and stared harder at the small black circle, her fingers digging into her palms as they curled with the force of concentration.

Still nothing. But then, as she was about to give up, the surface of the bowl rippled so softly it was barely a movement. Rippled, then lightened. She caught a glimpse of something that might have been Cameron's face—or might have been mere wishful thinking—before the bowl suddenly cracked into four pieces and the black liquid flooded across the table, a good portion of it spilling into her lap before she sprang back from the table and out of the way.

"I think," Henri said, as Madame Simsa tsked and Sophie tried to shake the liquid from her robes before it could soak through to her dress, "that perhaps we may need something larger to try that again."

Madame Simsa shot him a surprised look. "Do you think that wise?"

"The girl has power. She needs to learn to use it. And I don't want to spend a fortune on scrying bowls before she does." Henri nodded at Sophie. "And I suspect it might be easier on her clothing."

"Well. We shall see," Madame Simsa replied. "Now?"

Henri nodded. "That seems prudent."

Sophie had no idea what they were talking about. "Can someone please tell me what is happening?" She tried to keep her tone polite, but more than a hint of exasperation escaped her control. Or perhaps that was exhaustion creeping through.

Perhaps she could plead fatigue before the lesson continued. But she wasn't sure she could calm the thoughts spinning in her head if she lay down. And if she gave them free rein, she might be pulled down into the whirlpool they created and never escape. Empires. Kingdoms. Power. She wanted none of it.

She'd watched many people vying to grasp power during her time at court. She was yet to find anyone who could teach her how to avoid it.

"We need a bigger vessel for your practice," Henri said. "Something you are unlikely to shatter."

In Sophie's mind Elarus made another noise not a thousand miles away from "tsk." Hopefully that didn't mean the sanctii thought larger might not be better. Exploding things left and right didn't seem like it would be helpful in convincing the Academe that their bond wasn't a mistake.

"I'm game if you are," she said to Henri, trying to sound enthusiastic.

After a short break to dry her robes off, Sophie found herself trailing Madame Simsa and Henri through the Academe grounds. They wound up in a part of the complex that she was unfamiliar with.

Henri opened an unassuming door in the side of a building and led them into a hallway. They walked for maybe a minute before they turned a corner and passed through another door, which led to a staircase. When Henri began to descend, she wasn't entirely surprised. Water magic seemed to have an inherent secrecy. Not the kind of thing you practice out in the open. Or maybe that was her Anglion prejudices again.

She was surprised, however, by how far down the staircase

went. She had always vaguely assumed the Academe would have a basement level or two, much like any grand house she'd ever been in, but she hadn't thought much more about it. But they had descended farther than that, and with each flight of stairs, the wards layered over the walls and floor grew thicker. Whatever was beneath the school, the mages didn't want it found easily.

The brightening pulse of power from the ley lines below them told her she was quite some way beneath the earth by the time the stairs ended in another doorway. This one was less unassuming. The wood was blackened with age and banded with iron wider than Sophie's outstretched fingers. Two massive locks sealed it in place, the security they provided supplemented by the wards writhing over the door.

Anyone who passed through this door would have to know how to do so safely. Madame Simsa lifted a hand. The wards faded, then vanished. Henri drew a set of keys from the pocket of his robes. He opened each lock in turn, his body blocking Sophie from seeing exactly which keys he used.

No one volunteered an explanation as to where they were, as she followed Henri, Belarus, and Madame Simsa though the door. Elarus brought up the rear. Not long ago the thought of having a sanctii anywhere nearby had been one of Sophie's worst nightmares. She wasn't sure what it said about her, or what the last few months had been like, that she now found Elarus's presence at her back almost comforting. Almost.

She stepped over the threshold and into darkness. She couldn't tell how large the room was or see Henri and Madame Simsa. She blinked rapidly, hoping her eyes would adjust. The space felt big. And it was cold, colder than the stairs they'd climbed down, colder than the sanctii chill behind her. The air smelled damp. Not the stagnant neglected scent of long-standing water but the damp of a brook running through a forest. Clean damp. Was there a water source here below the Academe?

Earth-lights flared to life around her. Colored spots whirled across her vision, making her eyes water. She wiped them on her sleeve, blinking again as she shielded her eyes with one hand. When she could see again, the room resolved into something closer to a cave. The walls and ceiling were natural stone that curved and flowed into each other. In the center of the space was a body of water. Outside she might have called it a pond. Roughly thirty feet across. But down here, the water looked as eerily dark as the liquid they'd used upstairs, the reflected glow of the earth-lights catching slow ripples on the surface, and pond seemed too tame a word.

"Is that for scrying?" she asked, nerves making her throat catch.

Madame Simsa nodded. "You shouldn't be able to break this one."

Sophie studied the water. A rough, stone-edged teardrop, it seemed almost as though it was a natural depression in the earth. The narrowest end was closest to the door. That seemed like the logical place to stand if she was to attempt to scry again. She wasn't going to voluntarily immerse herself in the inky darkness. Hopefully standing would be all that would be required.

Not waiting for yet another order from Madame, she moved to the edge of the water, keeping her feet clear of the lip of the stone as she breathed slowly, pushing the fear away. She wanted to learn this magic. She *had* to learn this magic.

The water moved slowly, and she let her gaze follow the lines of reflected light, trying to clear her mind as she had in the practice room.

Think of Cameron. That was what Madame Simsa had told her to do.

At first all staring at the water and trying to conjure Cameron's face seemed to do was rouse every other worried thought in her brain. The emperor. Anglion. Her family. The future. Elarus. But gradually, as she breathed in the cool damp air, her mind began to ease, the thoughts slowing, as though synchronizing with the patterns on the water. The glimmering light and the dark water blurred and shifted. Then faded away. In their place, she saw Cameron. Sleeping in their bed in their room upstairs, the rise and fall of his chest reassuring.

Safe.

But even as she thought the words, the image changed again. Cameron. Awake. Standing next to what looked like a mast, his expression urgent and alarmed. Before she could try and take in what was in the rest of the image, it blurred again. And again. A series of images ran though her head. A chain, heavy and black. Her mother, red eyed and exhausted. The palace at Kingswell, part of the tower rebuilt.

A horse rearing.

Then Domina Skey, smiling coldly before her lips parted to speak.

Sophie flinched from the image, and it changed again. A giant tree rose before her, strong and tall and lush, its leaves dazzling green. She didn't recognize the species but the sense she had was one of peace. Of rightness. Until her gaze moved down and she saw a body beneath the tree, beneath the ground, in fact, as though it floated in the earth itself. A woman, red hair loosened and rough with dirt, face covered with black lace. The tree's roots pierced her body, as though they fed from her. Some were pale and white, but others were darkening, near black.

That seemed wrong. But there was no time to contemplate what it might mean before the vision shivered, narrowing in on the body. The lace covering the woman's face dissolved and Sophie was left staring in horror at Eloisa. The queen's face was peaceful but starting to decay and sink into nothingness.

"No!" The scream of protest was instinctive. The revulsion was enough to break whatever state of mind Sophie had fallen into, and she blinked and found herself several paces from the edge of the pool, cold and shivering.

"What did you see, child?" Madame Simsa said. "You cried out."

"I—" Sophie hesitated. The shock of seeing Eloisa's face was still echoing through her, fear speeding her heartbeat. And, on the heels of fear, caution. "I'm not sure."

"You must have seen something," Madame pressed.

"I think I did," Sophie said. "Cameron asleep, maybe. And then..." she paused again, sorting through the tangle of images in her head. "My mother, I think. She was crying. That's what startled me. I was thinking of Cameron. I wasn't expecting to see anybody else." That much, at least, was the truth.

"It is only natural that you think of those closest to you," Henri said. "It is a common thing, among beginners."

"Is what I saw real?" Sophie asked. Her voice quivered, and she rubbed her arms, fighting off the lingering fear and panic the vision had left in its wake.

Henri hitched one shoulder. A very Illvyan gesture. "It is difficult to say. You are untrained. And not all who do water magic gain much from scrying. There is a skill to it that can be learned, but like most things, some have more aptitude than others and will have greater success. What you saw may be true. Or it may merely be a fear lurking in your mind that you have brought forward. The only thing that will tell is time itself."

Not a helpful response. Sophie stared down at the water warily. What she had seen had felt completely real. Felt like truth, of a kind. But she didn't think Eloisa lay buried beneath a tree. The emperor would surely be hustling Sophie back to Anglion on the next possible ship if there had been even the slightest hint that the Anglion throne stood empty.

So perhaps the image was merely a reflection of fear as Henri suggested. Her mind behaving as it would in a dream whilst she had been in the trance.

Based on what Henri was saying, there was no way she would know for sure other than to let time pass and see what happened. Not a terribly useful form of magic, in that case. Though maybe more experienced water mages were better at knowing if what they had seen was real or not.

[You have knowledge] Elarus's voice in her head was soft. [You know water magic. I gave you knowledge.]

[Yes. But I need to know how to use that knowledge.]

[I can show.]

Sophie was glad the sanctii was behind her and couldn't see the wince that flickered across her face at the suggestion. She'd gotten herself into enough trouble already. The Academe had been her sanctuary, and they were already unhappy about her bond with Elarus. If she suddenly started going against Henri's warnings and using the magic she'd been granted without knowing the risks, then who knew what might happen?

Nothing good, she suspected. And contemplating that set of unpleasant possibilities only made her acutely aware of her lack of sleep. For a moment the room wavered around her, and she took an involuntary step forward.

Henri stepped forward and caught her arm, steadying her. "Sophie? Are you unwell?"

"Tired," she confessed. "Perhaps the scrying...."

"It is tiring at first," Madame Simsa said. "Like learning anything new. But you should practice."

The hairs on the back of Sophie's neck lifted at the thought, and she almost took a step back. She wasn't ready for another vision.

Not until she knew more about what the first one might mean. She had let the Academe and everyone else in Illvya tell her what to do for weeks now since they had arrived. She valued what they had to teach her and the refuge they offered. However, if she didn't start to stand up for herself, then she was going to become a pawn in the game of power here, as she had been in Anglion—a prize to be owned and controlled. And while she might not have any desire to be a queen, she also knew that she had lost any taste for being the lowliest player on the field. Her powers were valuable to the Illvyans.

She was valuable.

So, she should value herself.

"Not today," she said, drawing herself up to full height, which was somewhat taller than Madame Simsa. "Enough for today. I will return tomorrow, and we can continue, but for now, I want to rest. And see how my husband is recovering."

Madame Simsa lifted one gray eyebrow, but the objection that Sophie expected was not forthcoming. "If you must. But we will start again in the morning. Straight after breakfast."

Sophie nodded. "Yes, Madame." She hurried for the door before anybody could change their mind.

CHAPTER 3

By following the glow of the earth-lights and her sense of the direction guided by the ley lines, Sophie found herself back above ground quite quickly. Elarus had followed her from the scrying room but had vanished as Sophie began to ascend the stairs. As much as Sophie still wanted to talk to the sanctii, she was glad to be alone for now. She needed to breathe and shake off the lingering unease from her vision. And then she needed to sleep to shake off the bone-deep weariness that had made every stair she climbed feel like half a mountain.

As she stepped out of the building, she realized she didn't know exactly where in the grounds she was. But there was a path cutting across the small swathe of grass and she followed it until she came to a well-oiled iron gate and found herself nearly at the Academe's main entrance.

The hum of people and carriages and horses from the street was unexpected and she halted, startled by the sudden change. It was the first time she'd been near the front gate unaccompanied and the temptation to open it, step into the stream of people and vanish for a few hours—or even forever—flared like a quick-struck match. A few steps and she could disappear. Find herself a new start and an ordinary life.

But the thought guttered as quickly as it had sparked. Even if she had thought that vanishing might be truly possible—that what Elarus had told them the night before was wrong and that the empire's mages couldn't track her magic, there was Cameron. Who she could no more leave behind than she could her own right arm.

She started to turn toward the front door, intent on joining Cameron in bed and going back to sleep, when a carriage clattered up to the gate. The pair of jet-black horses pulling it snorted agreeably as they came to a halt. The carriage door banged open and a cheerful, "Lady Sophia, just the woman I was looking for," came from the gloom within.

Sophie turned back, heart sinking, to see Imogene du Laq descending from the carriage, waving off the attention of the driver who had leapt down to assist her. The duquesse smiled at Sophie, one hand straying up to pat the expertly piled riot of black, brown, and red curls on her head.

Sophie curtsied. "Your Grace, good morning."

Imogene flipped a hand. "My, so formal. Good morning, yourself." Then she grinned, deep blue eyes flashing. "I hope I haven't caught you about to make a run for it?" She raised a brow. "That was quite the spectacle in the throne room."

"Spectacle is one word for it," Sophie agreed. Not the one she would have used, but there was nothing to be gained from correcting the duquesse before Sophie knew why Imogene had come to see her. "But no, I wasn't planning to run."

"Not without that handsome husband of yours, at least. That would be a mistake for any woman." Imogene grinned again. "But let's not stand on the street talking, when we could be comfortable inside."

～

Cameron submitted to Rachelle's probing fingers with gritted teeth. His head no longer felt like he'd been kicked by a whole herd of horses as it had the night before—thanks partially to the healer's services—but the bruises were still tender.

"Do you have a headache?" Rachelle asked, fingers pressing a path across his right cheekbone.

"Nothing of any significance." He felt only half-awake, but he attributed that to the fact he had yet to eat that day or have anything civilized like tea to clear the fog from his brain. He wasn't entirely sure what had jolted him awake earlier. He'd tried to go back to sleep at first but had given up when the memory of the previous night had rushed back, the shock of it enough to drive him from bed.

He'd found a note slipped under the door, instructing him to present himself for an examination at the healers when he woke. His aches and pains had been enough to convince him that would be a good idea, and he'd made his way across the Academe to submit to their ministrations. Maybe not at his best, but alive.

Rachelle made a humphing noise under her breath but didn't reply, merely pressed harder on the highest point of his left cheek. He winced.

"Sore there?" She pressed again.

This time he managed not to react because he'd been expecting the pain. Why healers insisted on prodding a man's sore bits over and over was something he'd never understand, but he was used it. Serve in the Red Guard long enough, and it was impossible not to become far too familiar with healers. "Some?"

Her humph was louder. "Lord Scardale, I appreciate that you are a blood mage and a soldier and a man, but if you have half a brain left after being tossed onto the street from an overturned carriage as you were, I trust that you are sensible enough to know that it is wise to speak truth to healers. We can't help you if you don't."

Clearly he wasn't going to get away with anything less than a full accounting with this particular healer. "It's sore," he admitted. "Not overly so. I had a broken cheekbone once. This doesn't feel like that."

"Nor should it after the effort we put into you last night," Rachelle said tartly. "But that is good to hear. Maybe we can speed this process up, given you are accustomed to minor wounds and injuries. Does anything else hurt in a way that would suggest something unusual to you?"

Did emotional pain count? His head didn't ache from the carriage accident, but his mind spun as though he was still tumbling through the air.

Aristides had offered Sophie the throne of Anglion. She had refused—thank the goddess—but he doubted that would be the end of it. He'd only known three monarchs in his lifetime. One king and one queen and now, one emperor, but even from such small acquaintance, he'd learned that those who reached the highest seats of power were generally used to getting what they wanted.

And determined to walk the paths they decided should be walked to get it.

Clearly Sophie was a path Aristides was considering taking to reach whatever destination he had in mind for Illvya's relationship with Anglion.

Making the game that Cameron and Sophie were caught up within ever more dangerous. And he had no idea how he was to see her through it safely. Staying seemed risky. Fleeing—after what Sophie's sanctii had told them last night—didn't seem to be an option.

But if he told that to Rachelle, she would probably think his brains had been rattled too hard by his accident. He doubted the emperor's offer would become public knowledge terribly quickly. The only ones in the throne room when Aristides had so casually offered to place a crown on Sophie's head had been members of the emperor's inner council and his court mages—and Henri Matin of course. He couldn't see how any of them could benefit by leaking the information and tipping the emperor's hand before he made his play.

Cameron needed to keep his own cards close to his chest. "Nothing unusual," he said to Rachelle. "I'm fine."

"You're not fine. A head injury, even one tended to quickly and healed, is not to be underestimated, Lord Scardale. You need to rest for the next few days. Maybe a week. I will inform M'sille Marignon that you are not to train with the blood mages until I tell her otherwise. If you get pains in your head or your eyes or any numbness in your face, then you should come to me immediately. Understood?"

It would be easiest to just agree with her. Not necessarily comply if it became necessary to disobey her orders, but he'd never found much profit in arguing with healers. It always resulted in finding yourself confined to quarters until they were satisfied that you weren't going to do anything idiotic and make things worse.

He wasn't exactly sure how he might be confined to quarters here at the Academe but given the number of mages far more skilled than he that filled the place, he didn't think it would be overly difficult. He couldn't protect Sophie if he was unable to leave their apartment.

"I understand," he said, aiming what he hoped was a trustworthy smile at the healer. The effect might have been slightly lessened by the loud rumble that issued from his stomach as he started to slide down from the stool he'd been perched on during the examination.

Rachelle finally smiled at the sound. "Well, that at least I can offer a quick solution to. I recommend the dining hall. Immediately."

~

Sophie preceded Imogene into the Academe, not exactly sure

where to take her. She didn't want to wake Cameron if he was still sleeping. Somewhere in the buildings were private parlors students could use to study or socialize. But Sophie had yet to have time for the latter and, for the former, she'd used the libraries. The result being that she wasn't entirely sure where the parlors were.

The simplest solution would be the dining hall, where at least there would be food and tea. But simplicity came with no privacy. Taking tea with an Imperial mage could only set tongues wagging. Perhaps the best approach would be to find out what Imogene needed to discuss before deciding where to hold the conversation.

"Do you have a message from the emperor?" she asked. She hoped not. A summons from Aristides so soon was unlikely to be good news.

Imogene shook her head. "No. I came to see how you are. There has been much...excitement in the last few days, and while everyone is busy figuring out the political ramifications, they tend to forget that there are people involved in these small dramas."

Sophie didn't for one second believe that Imogene wasn't also calculating the political ramifications. One didn't become the wife of a Duq and confidante to an emperor without considerable skill in the game of power. Nor was Sophie sure assassination plots and attempted suicides should be described as 'small' dramas. Though maybe, in the day-to-day politics of the Illvyan court and the empire, they were. But still, perhaps that view was overly cynical, and she should accept concern where it was offered.

"Shall we have tea, then?" Sophie said. "There will be some in the dining hall. And food, if you are hungry." She wasn't entirely certain how much time had passed during her lesson, but the dining hall catered to the sometimes-irregular hours kept by the students and maistres. There were set times for breakfast, lunch, and dinner, but in between there were always tea, chilled drinks, and various simple dishes—soup and sandwiches and stews and such—to fill the bellies of those who may have missed a meal. Magic, after all, took energy to work, and mages and witches generally had hearty appetites.

But Imogene knew that, she realized. Imogene had been a student here once.

"Tea would be most welcome," Imogene said. "We've had so little rain recently that the streets are filled with dust."

There wasn't a single speck of dust on the stark black fabric of Imogene's uniform or her gleaming black boots. Perhaps dust didn't dare sully the boots of Imperial mages? They hadn't taken more than fifty steps towards the dining hall when a squawk and a hiss of feathers in the air alerted Sophie that Tok had tracked her down once more. The raven swooped over her head, then alighted on the nearest earth-light.

"Hello to you, too," Sophie said, which earned her another caw. She shook her head at the bird. "There's no need to take that tone. I was having lessons."

Imogene watched the exchange. "I didn't realize you had taken a petty fam," she said, nodding at Tok.

"I haven't," Sophie said. The words "not yet" hung on the tip of her tongue, but she held them back. After bonding with a sanctii, there no longer seemed much reason to avoid Tok's pursuit. After all, a demon put her so firmly beyond the pale in Anglion that a bond with a familiar couldn't do any more damage. But she wanted to be certain. A petty fam couldn't be put aside, and she didn't want to cause Tok harm. She needed more time for things to settle before she decided once and for all. "Tok is just curious. He would make a good spy."

"As would most ravens," Imogene said.

"Do Imperial mages take familiars?" Sophie asked curiously.

"Some do. But there are risks, of course, if one is in battle. To leave a familiar behind is hard. To take one into a fight is to risk them being hurt or worse. And then there is the hurt done to them if their mage is killed. Personally, I feel it unkind." She smiled up at the raven. "Though you are a handsome breed. I'd look quite good with a raven on my shoulder. Don't you agree, Sophie?"

"Raven feathers would go nicely with your uniform." Sophie echoed Imogene's smile, happy to take the conversation back to something more frivolous. Something safer. "You could set a fashion in court."

"I can just imagine it," Imogene said, rolling her eyes. "It's bad enough when the court goes through animal crazes. Two winters ago, half the ladies were carrying small dogs in enormous fur muffs to keep their hands warm. I'll admit the creatures were sweet, but the palace did begin to take on a distinct scent of dog on rainy days. Ravens don't smell, I suppose. But they do shed feathers. And one can imagine that if the court adopted ravens less smart than those bred here, there would be other messes as well. That would not be received kindly. For one thing, the clothiers like Helene would quite likely go on strike if they learned that the ladies were submitting their creations to claws and bird droppings."

Sophie laughed. Imagine Helene Designy's face if Sophie proposed such a thing. Though if she did decide to take Tok on, she might have to. Her clothing would need reinforcement. Of course, without the Academe footing the bill, she doubted she would be shopping at the Designy's establishment any time soon. "Best not to risk it," she said. "Though, you know, Madame Simsa has a monkey, not a bird."

Imogene pulled a face. "Monkeys were a craze four years ago. Tiny golden things from Silaria. It's a small country in the far north." She added the explanation when Sophie shrugged at the mention of the name. "They had a distressing tendency to steal any shiny object they came across. And some of them *bit*." She eyed Tok. "Ravens also like shiny things. The court would have to spend half their days trying to determine whose bird had made off with whose earrings or necklaces or hair combs. Which might keep them out of trouble, I suppose. But no"—she shook her head—"there is enough monkey business at the palace without adding more animals to the mix." She glanced at Sophie. "I imagine the Anglion court is much the same."

"Well, I don't think there was ever a craze for monkeys." Anglion, being one small island, didn't have the same variety of wildlife that the empire did. "But intrigue and trouble enough, I guess."

"It does make one wonder why people can't just get along." Imogene shrugged one shoulder. "But power is what it is. So, let us turn to more pleasant things. Like tea. Which seems a more immediate priority than trying to understand courtiers and their games."

That would take more tea than the Academe could hold. Possibly more tea than the empire could produce. They commenced their journey to the dining room once more, Tok flying ahead, alighting now and then on handy surfaces when they fell too far behind for his liking.

The level of noise from the dining room as they approached it was minimal, which raised Sophie's hopes that it would be mostly deserted and that she and Imogene wouldn't attract much attention.

She wasn't expecting to see Cameron seated at one of the tables, his plate stacked high with sandwiches.

He caught sight of her, eyebrows lifting as he spotted Imogene, and lifted a hand, smiling as he beckoned them over. He stood, too well-mannered to do anything else, as they approached, but he didn't let go of the half sandwich in his hand.

Sophie's stomach rumbled as the smells of the dining hall registered with her nose. It had been an age since her lack of breakfast and her stomach had apparently decided that food trumped nerves for now.

"You should be in bed," she said as she reached Cameron.

He leaned down and kissed the top of her head. "Don't fuss. I woke up. I've been to see the healer, and she cleared me for such dangerous activities as eating." He looked past her. "Good morning, Major. Or is it afternoon?"

"Afternoon," Imogene said, and Sophie blinked. She hadn't thought as much time as that had passed. The trance that had brought her visions had seemed to take only seconds, but maybe it had been much longer?

"Ah," Cameron said. He pulled one of the chairs out and gestured for Sophie to sit and then did the same for Imogene. "No wonder I was hungry." He nodded at the plate of sandwiches. "The kitchen made those for me. You're welcome to share, if you want to eat. Can I get tea for you both?" He already had a cup by his plate, a small pot on the table beside it. Not enough for three.

"Tea would be lovely, thank you," Sophie said. She reached for a sandwich, then belatedly wondered if Imogene was happy to sit with Cameron. But the other woman seemed unperturbed as she also took one of the sandwiches and bit into it.

The first bite of bread and cheese and the spicy relish the kitchen here made only seemed to amplify Sophie's hunger, and she had to remind herself to eat like a lady and not wolf the whole thing down and reach for more. She chewed as slowly as she could bring herself to, swallowed, and then put the sandwich down despite the protests of her stomach. To distract herself, she watched Cameron make his way across the room to the counter where the kitchen staff took orders.

He walked smoothly, not limping or giving any other sign that he'd been hurt, but she still couldn't bring herself to look away.

"He seems to have recovered," Imogene said. "You don't need to worry."

Sophie's cheeks went hot. Was she that easy to read? "I wasn't worrying."

"My dear, if you want me to believe that you need to learn to keep a straighter face. Granted, you manage most of the time, but your eyes give you away around that one." Imogene tilted her head in Cameron's direction. "It's a weakness."

"He's my husband, am I not supposed to care?" Sophie

retorted, the words sharper than she intended. She took another bite of her sandwich. Perhaps hunger was making her ill-tempered.

"You can care. But it isn't always politic to show it. The default assumption of most people is that marriages such as yours and mine were arranged. That they are alliances of mutual benefit, not emotion. Give them a notion to think otherwise, and they begin to wonder how they can exploit that emotion."

"Do you pretend not to like your husband in public?"

"Oh no, they know I am fond of him. Besides, we have been married a long time. People have learned it is not wise to try such games with us. But you, you are new to court. They haven't figured you and your place out yet."

"Given I have no place at court, I don't see why they would be concerned." Not the truth and Imogene's immediate arched eyebrows told Sophie that Imogene knew it. But she didn't want to talk politics. "Besides, our marriage *was* arranged. Which I'm sure the court knows. But that doesn't alter the fact that we are strangers here and that Cameron is the person I know best. It would be odd if I weren't concerned about him, would it not?"

Imogene gave a quicksilver shrug. "Perhaps. I was only offering advice. But I should remember that you have spent time in a court before." She paused a moment. "Though you must remember that this court is not that one. And that your status has recently changed. I would imagine, even if you were back in Anglion, now that you have moved so high in the ranks of succession, your experience there would be quite different to what it was before."

Sophie's shoulders slumped. The food had curbed the edge of her hunger, but it did nothing to defeat the sense of overwhelming exhaustion. She hadn't asked for any of this. She wanted desperately to just wake up and be Sophie Kendall, unimportant lady-in-waiting, again. But that would mean life without Cameron. Life married off to some other lord who would feed off part of her power. So, perhaps no easier a life than this one. She closed her eyes briefly against the wave of fatigue.

"Perhaps the one you should be concerned about is yourself," Imogene said softly.

Sophie opened her eyes, puzzled. "I'm fine."

"You look exhausted, child." Imogene said. "Black is well enough for those robes you wear, but it does you no favors under your eyes."

"I need to catch up on my sleep. The last few nights were eventful."

"More than eventful, I would say. But that is what I came to talk to you about."

"What is?" Cameron's deep voice came from behind Sophie. "Is there something on your mind, Major?"

Imogene smiled, her expression brightening as Cameron placed two steaming cups of tea on the table. "Nothing official, Lord Scardale. Quite the opposite in fact."

"Oh?" Cameron settled himself back into a chair. Sophie found herself watching him again, searching for signs of discomfort.

"I had a thought this morning that perhaps you and your wife might appreciate some time away from the city. My husband's estate is only a few hours from Lumia. Perhaps a few days there might be good for us all. Give everybody some time to think and come to more reasoned plans."

"You don't agree with the emperor's...." Cameron paused, glancing around. There was nobody seated at the closest table, but when he spoke again, his voice was softer. "The emperor's approach?"

Imogene blew on her tea, then sipped and swallowed before she set the cup down. "Let us say only that I am never in favor of rushing into things without careful consideration. Aristides was in a temper last night. Such decisions should not be taken out of anger. If you are out of the city for a few days, somewhere where he knows you to be safe, then he will have time to reflect more carefully. Our estate is guarded, and it seems unlikely that anyone connected to the Anglion delegation would know where it was or that you were there. And you and Sophie would be able to rest for a time. I'm sure the Academe has done nothing but fill your days with lesson upon lesson since you first arrived. Hard work may be a virtue, but it must be balanced with some pleasure."

"Pleasure hasn't been high on the list of our priorities," Cameron said.

"And you are wise to secure yourself a place here," Imogene said. "But most of the Academe's students have weekends off. I'm sure Henri would not object to you leaving for a short time if he knew you were going with me."

Sophie wasn't so sure about that. Imogene was an Imperial mage. She had trained at the Academe but then chosen to leave it for the court. She and Henri were mostly polite in their dealings, but it was clear their relationship was not entirely friendly.

"Besides," Imogene continued, "I doubt Henri approves of what Aristides asked of you in the slightest. You are too interesting a pair of mages for him to want you to slip beyond the Academe's influence. He will see the wisdom of me taking you out of the emperor's immediate path for a time."

Cameron frowned, obviously weighing Imogene's words. Sophie knew she should be thinking more carefully about the offer too, but mostly she just wanted to say "yes." To get away, to get beyond the limits of the Academe, and the city. To spend some time somewhere quiet and peaceful with no lessons, no politics—other than Imogene and the Duq—sounded wonderful. And, she couldn't help but think, somewhere where there might be an opportunity to get a better idea how they might get away from Lumia, should things come to that point.

"Who else would be there?" Cameron asked.

"No one," Imogene said. "Other than my husband and the household. I'm not suggesting a house party, my lord. It's far too early in your life here in Lumia to subject you to that. A few days respite in the country was all I had in mind."

Sophie met Cameron's gaze. What was he thinking? What would he think if he knew what she was thinking? Oh, to be able to speak to him silently in her mind as she did Elarus. But for now, she would have to wait and hope he didn't object to the idea. After a moment, he raised one dark brow briefly but nodded.

Sophie turned her attention back to Imogene. "It's an extremely kind invitation. Getting away from all of this would be wonderful." Hopefully she sounded as though there was nothing more than a relaxing sojourn in the country on her mind.

"Do I detect a 'but' in that response?" Imogene asked.

Sophie shook her head. "Not on my part. I'd love to do it. But I'm wondering if we will be allowed to go." Not all she was wondering, but Imogene was not the person to confide in. The duquesse was friendly to them, yes, but Sophie had no doubt that Imogene's ultimate loyalty was to Aristides.

"Leave that part up to me," Imogene said with a flick of her hand that seemed to indicate that she didn't foresee any obstacles in getting her own way. Perhaps being both a royal mage and a duquesse gave her an advantage not available to mere mortals when convincing the Maistre of the Academe and the Emperor of Illvya to go along with her plans.

"You don't foresee any objections?" Cameron asked, sounding doubtful.

Imogene tossed her head. "Objections there may be. However, I will point out to those who voice them that they are wrong. You are both safer out of sight for a time. Besides which, the emperor should be turning his attention to the investigation into exactly what has gone on with the Illvyan delegation for the next few days at least."

And what if he discovered something that made him even more determined that Sophie should take the crown? Sophie bit her lip. If that happened, then being away from Lumia might become their best chance to disappear.

"Well, if you can manage that part, then I'm sure Sophie and I would be more than pleased to accept your kind offer," Cameron said, his tone more enthusiastic. She didn't look at him. Didn't want any hint of her racing thoughts—and her desire to know what he was thinking—showing on her face.

Imogene lifted her tea and toasted him. "Excellent. I will speak to Henri and others on the matter as soon as possible. I'll send a message when we can make plans that are more certain." She put down the cup and rose. Cameron stood too. "In fact, I will make a start now. I'm sure you both have classes this afternoon. The Academe was always diligent in keeping its students occupied."

Sophie didn't correct her on that matter. Thanks to her standing up to Madame Simsa and Henri, she had a free afternoon now, and she wanted to spend it with Cameron, not Imogene. They'd had little enough time to simply be since they'd been married. She would steal moments with him where she could.

"Thank you again for the invitation," she said, rising and bobbing a quick curtsy. Imogene was after all, a duquesse and the ins and outs of court protocol had been so thoroughly drilled into Sophie that it was difficult to break herself of the habit here at the Academe where it seemed that rank from the outside world played a pale second to the hierarchy of power.

"Do not even think of it," Imogene said. "It is perfect to have an excuse to get away from court myself without having to invite all of one's closest acquaintances and enemies."

Which was a more perfect description of life in court than Sophie had ever heard before. She had to suppress a laugh. "We look forward to your message, then."

CHAPTER 4

"Do you think we'll be allowed to go?" Sophie asked, reaching for a sandwich. Cameron still stood, watching Imogene making her way out of the dining hall.

"I think she must be extremely persuasive when she chooses to be. And I don't think she'd get much argument from Henri about removing you from Aristides's immediate reach. The sticking point will be the emperor, not the Academe, I'd imagine. But then, Imogene seems to be close to Aristides. I doubt she'd waste any of her good standing with him proposing such a thing if she didn't think he would agree." Cameron sat again, swigged tea.

She hadn't thought of that. Which was yet another sign that making her a queen was a stupid idea. Sophie had had her time at court and had training in Anglion history and politics, but she didn't always see every political angle to any given transaction. Cameron, with his extra years at the palace—not to mention being the son of an erl and a soldier trained in strategy—thought about such things automatically. As someone fit to be queen would.

"I hope you're right," she said, looking down at her plate. The ache in her belly had eased with the food, but the fatigue burning at the edges of her brain was as strong as ever. But she couldn't rest. She needed to talk to Cameron about whether they should use the opportunity Imogene had dropped into their laps.

"Getting *away* from Lumia would be wonderful." She couldn't risk saying anything more explicit in the dining hall but wanted to see if Cameron was thinking along the same lines as her. But his face gave away nothing to suggest he was strategizing.

"I can't disagree with that. But we will have to wait and see." He leaned back, wiped his mouth with a napkin. "Do you have to return to your lessons? I assume that's where you were?"

"Yes. But no, I don't. I told Madame Simsa and Henri I needed the afternoon to rest."

He straightened. "You were with both of them? What exactly were you doing?"

"Having my introduction to water magic. Supposedly. Though there was some lecturing to begin with."

Cameron's mouth quirked. "Well, I can't say I disagree with that either. You—"

Sophie cut him off with a raised hand. "You cannot possibly have anything new to say on the matter. Let's change the subject."

"How about I won't mention—" He paused and glanced around. "Is she here?"

"Who? Elarus?" She had no idea. Should she have an idea? Perhaps that should be a question to start her lessons with tomorrow. How to know if one's sanctii was nearby when they are invisible and silent. "I don't know."

He didn't look particularly reassured by that information. "All right. I'll make you a deal. I won't fuss about her if you don't fuss over me resting."

That was cheating. "Elarus didn't hurt me. You had a carriage fall on you."

"How much would you care to wager, oh wife of mine, that

your Elarus is more likely to have longer lasting repercussions than my carriage?"

She stuck her tongue out. "I'm not going to answer that. And I reserve the right to fuss if necessary."

"If that's what you want. But if you can, I can." His brows drew down. "And, I have to say, you look tired. What exactly did this lesson involve?"

No one was close enough to overhear them. "Scrying. Or attempting to."

Was she imagining things, or did he flinch? Fear of water magic was as ingrained in him as it was in her. After her experience this morning, she couldn't say she could blame Anglions for banning it.

"Did you see something?" Cameron asked cautiously.

"I'm not sure," she replied, equally cautious. "Nor am I sure that it's something to discuss here."

His expression grew more discomforted. "Then perhaps we should return to our rooms?"

She wanted to sleep. More, she wanted Cameron's body curled around hers, holding her safe. But she also wanted to be away from the Academe. She didn't want to talk about her vision anywhere there could be mages or sanctii to overhear. So she had to convince Cameron. "It seems a waste. I have no lessons. You have no lessons. Perhaps we could do something together. Outside of the Academe."

"I'm not sure that's advisable." He had his soldier face on.

"The Anglion delegation must be back on their ships by now, at least those whom the emperor isn't interrogating. If those ships are still in the harbor, then I'm sure they are under as much surveillance as the emperor can muster. We must be safer now than we were yesterday."

"Assuming they don't have any fellow conspirators in the city."

"We can't hide away forever." The words were bolder than her heart felt, but she knew they were truth. If they were to make a life here—if Aristides gave up his madcap plan and they were allowed to just be Sophie and Cameron—they couldn't live in fear. They could have done that back in Kingswell with far less trouble.

"Not forever. But staying out of sight for a few more days might be prudent."

He was right. But the walls of the Academe felt as though they were shrinking toward her. She needed to breathe. But Cameron clearly wasn't going to agree to leave if he thought they would be at risk. She thought for a moment. Somewhere safe. Somewhere peaceful. Somewhere she would be able to think for a moment. Shake the fear the vision had conjured and regain some clarity. "We could go to one of the temples. That should be safe enough."

"What do you want with a temple?" Cameron said. He didn't sound enthusiastic. He'd attended the weekly rituals with the court back home, but she'd never really discussed his belief with him. Perhaps blood mages didn't have the same direct sense of the goddess as earth witches did.

But she missed the ritual of it. Domina Gerrard, who she'd met at the temple near Helene's store, had been kind. Meeting her had been a first step in restoring the part of Sophie's faith that had been damaged by Domina Skey. The temple here in Illvya was different. They wouldn't expel her for being a water mage for a start.

More importantly, there had been familiarity in the small temple, in the smells and sounds of it, and the welcome from the dominas. A hint of home. "I miss it," she said simply. Truth enough.

He raised a brow, but his expression softened. "Not the temple by the palace, I presume?"

"Goddess, no," she breathed. That particular temple was the center of the worship of the goddess in the empire. She had no desire to mingle with the adepts there. If they were anything like those who served the goddess at the Kingswell temple, then politics would be as central to their lives as religion was. No, thank you. Nor did she want to go anywhere close to the emperor. "I was thinking of the one near Helene's. It would be somewhere safe to...talk about things."

His brows rose higher. "I see." He tilted his head, studying her, worry clear in his eyes. She knew he wanted to ask her more. But he seemed to understand her reluctance to speak here.

"I'd have to ask permission to take one of the carriages," he said.

If they asked, they could be refused. "Or we could ask Willem if there's another way. There must be transport for hire."

"That requires money."

"We have some, don't we?" Cameron had managed to find a money changer on one of his earliest ventures into the city and change a few of their Anglion coins.

"Some. Do we want to spend it on this?"

A reminder that they hadn't been able to bring much with them. So far they'd been fortunate, and the Academe had not asked for any sort of payment for their food and board, but still, they should be prudent. They'd need all they had if worst came to worst.

She hesitated. "What about a portal? It seems logical that there would be one near the temples."

"Portals make you unwell."

"Not for long."

Cameron sighed. "You really want to go, don't you?"

"Yes. And if you don't want to stay, you could leave me there for a time. If you wanted to explore...the city more." She knew the restrictions on their movements chafed on him. Knew he was probably dying to know if the Anglion ships were still in the harbor.

"I'm not leaving you alone." He squared his shoulders. "Let me speak to Willem, he may have some ideas."

"Don't do anything that would get him in trouble," she said. The younger boy was somewhat in awe of Cameron and eager to please. She didn't want him doing something to aid them that would only rebound on him.

"It's either him or ask Henri," Cameron said. "Pity your new...friend can't take us there."

Sanctii moved between places in a manner that no one quite understood, appearing out of thin air and returning to the same. As far as she knew, it wasn't a service they could offer to humans.

"She may know something of the portal system," Sophie said.

"I don't think sanctii use portals," Cameron said.

"No, but they spend time in this city. They live a long time. She probably knows more than we do." She had no idea if that were true. But the sanctii had found her at the palace, on the streets when the carriage had been ambushed, and here at the Academe. She obviously knew something of Lumia. Sanctii might not be quick tongued in human speech, but they were in no way stupid.

"Can you call her?" Cameron asked. Then seemed to think better of it. "No. Don't. It would be better not to have her show herself here where we have an audience."

"I'm sure the word has already spread," Sophie said. It seemed the moment she and Elarus had bonded had been noisy. It had woken most of the mages in the house. The rumor mill had no doubt taken care of the rest of them and the students who were yet to manifest their powers. "And sanctii are not unusual here."

"True. But people don't seem to bring them to meals. If she comes here, it will guarantee that people pay attention to our conversation. Let's go back to our room."

She couldn't fault his logic. And it was pleasant to walk back through the halls with her fingers twined in his. More than pleasant. If she hadn't suspected she would fall asleep the moment she let herself lie down on a bed, she might have been tempted to come up with another way to spend their unexpected afternoon.

But when Cameron carefully locked the door to the apartment before taking up a position in front of it, as though he wasn't sure whether he might face invasion or need to be able to make a fast retreat, all Sophie's amorous inclinations died.

"Might as well get this over with," Cameron said.

Sophie hesitated. Before this morning she hadn't tried to call Elarus deliberately. Hopefully her success in the practice room wasn't pure chance. She remembered Madame Simsa's instruction to keep her eyes open and tried to focus on the memory of the sound of the sanctii's gravelly voice. [Elarus?]

[Yes?]

[Could I talk to you for a moment, please?]

[Talking now.] The sanctii sounded faintly amused. Maybe. Sophie needed far more experience speaking with sanctii before she would lay any claim to being able to interpret the slight variations in intonation in their voices. Henri spoke to Martius in the sanctii tongue sometime, a language that sounded like shovels scraping over snow, harsh syllables and near growls. Goddess, was she going to have to learn that too?

Or could Elarus do what Martius had done when he had performed a reveilé to improve her Illvyan and gift her the language? Sophie didn't think Elarus had done so as part of their bond. No phrases sprang to mind. [I'd like to talk to you in person.]

She waited for the sanctii's response. Instead a sudden chill rushed over her skin and Elarus appeared at the foot of the bed. Sophie flinched but managed to stifle the accompanying squeak of surprise. She had to get used to sanctii movements.

"Hello, Elarus," she managed over the sudden pounding of her pulse in her ears.

The sanctii nodded, dark eyes focused on Sophie. Then her gaze moved to Cameron. "Mate," she said.

"Husband. Cameron." Sophie said. She turned to Cameron, angling her face so Elarus couldn't see and mouthed, "Say something."

Cameron swallowed. "Hello, Elarus," he said, echoing Sophie's own words. "It's nice to see you again. And thank you.

For the help with the carriage." He bowed slightly, then straightened. "I didn't get to say that last night."

"Yes," Elarus said. "I help."

Hardly the most illuminating response. Sophie turned back to the sanctii. "We are very grateful—*I* am very grateful." Somewhere in her brain, something stirred in the knowledge of water magic that Elarus had planted there. Something about rituals and correct forms of address. But she and Elarus weren't bound in the usual way, and she'd heard Henri and Madame Simsa speak normally to their sanctii and ask them questions. She doubted there was any real risk in talking to Elarus as she would any other person. "Can we ask you some questions?"

"Question of what?" Elarus said.

"About Lumia," Sophie said. "And the portals. Do you know about those?"

The sanctii tipped her head. "Humans use. Not sanctii."

"But you know where they are?"

That got her a nod rather than another sentence. "Is there one near the temple in Isle de Angelique?"

Elarus nodded "Why temple?"

"We want to pay our respects to the goddess," Sophie said.

"Water mage," Elarus said.

Was the sanctii's tone sharper? "Yes, but I am also an earth witch. I was raised in the temple."

"Human goddess, not sanctii goddess."

Did the sanctii have gods? Another thing she didn't know. or have time to ask about. "I'm not asking you to come with us— we only need to know about the portal. If you know this, it would be helpful to us."

"I can give map," Elarus said.

Give? The last time Elarus had given her something it had been the bond. Which had come with pain. Having experienced a sanctii sharing information in that way twice now, she had no desire for a repeat performance anytime soon. "Can you show me the symbol? Draw it?" Each portal location was keyed to a unique glyph. The right symbol was all they needed to travel from the Academe to their destination.

The sanctii held up her hand. Her fingers were long and thick and moved slowly as she flexed her hand. Not exactly designed for wielding a pencil. "No draw."

"Can you show me a picture the way same way we talk when we are apart?" Sophie asked. "Not a gift. Can you send me an image of something you see or have seen?"

The sanctii considered. "Maybe." The crags in her forehead grew deeper, which Sophie thought was probably a sanctii frown. Or a sign of concentration, perhaps.

[This.] Elarus' voice was in Sophie's head again. Her voice and, for a second, a flash of something that might have been a feather. Or a fern. A stylized curve of darkness edged in light. It vanished before Sophie could quite make it out.

[Almost. Can we try again?]

The flash came again. Slightly longer. A curve with a spiral at one end and smaller arcing curves coiling in the from the spine of the line. It was vague but portal symbols were designed to be distinctive. Sophie was sure if she saw the one that corresponded to the image Elarus was sending that she'd know it.

[Thank you.] She paused. "How do I say thank you in your language?" she asked aloud.

The sanctii blinked. Then said three slow syllables. Even spoken at that pace, they sounded impossible, but Sophie cleared her throat and attempted to repeat them.

One side of the sanctii's mouth lifted.

Sophie grimaced. "That was terrible, wasn't it?"

"It was," Cameron said. "You sound like you need oiling. No offence, Elarus."

Elarus blinked again. "If wish speak sanctii. I give."

Ah. That was confirmation of what Sophie suspected. That water mages acquired the language via magic rather than by hard work and study alone. "I think we will wait until the Maistre says that would be the right thing to do before we try it."

Elarus looked past her at Cameron. "You?"

He held up his hands. "I will wait for the Maistre too. Besides, I'm not a water mage."

"Mate," Elarus said and looked back at Sophie, dark eyes unreadable. "Learn."

Sophie wasn't sure that Cameron would be taking marriage advice from a sanctii. If marriage advice, it was to suggest that the husband of a mage should learn the sanctii tongue. Nor did she know if learning it was something expected of him.

"I have to learn it the human way," Cameron said.

"Humans slow," Elarus said.

"Yes, we are," Cameron agreed. "It's probably because our brains are smaller than yours."

Elarus's mouth curved again. Cameron, it seemed, was amusing.

Sophie tried the phrase again. It didn't sound any better. But she was trying. "We should be going, if we want to get to the temple," she said. "We'll need to be back for dinner if we don't want to raise any alarm bells."

[I come?] Elarus said.

[Do you want to?] She didn't know if a sanctii could enter a temple. In Anglion, the temples burned salt grass and the walls were blessed annually with seawater. There had been salt grass in the temple in Isle de Angelique, but who knew if they blessed the walls. Probably not, given the Illvyan acceptance of sanctii. Then again, perhaps such things weren't enough to repel a sanctii. They could be mere ritual. Used by the Anglion temple to reinforce the fear of water magic. After all, sanctii were claimed to be able to rip humans limb from limb. That had to be a bloody process, and there was salt in human blood.

[Safety.] Elarus replied. [I watch.]

Having a sanctii accompany them through the streets of Lumia should ease Cameron's concerns for their safety, even if he wasn't yet used to Elarus. The added element of protection that a sanctii could provide had been a large part of the reason why she'd agreed to the bond. Elarus had proven several times already that she was prepared to act to protect Sophie and Cameron. Sophie wasn't entirely sure what the sanctii gained from the arrangement they had, but that was something to concern herself with later. For now, she would take the safety Elarus offered.

"Elarus is coming with us," she said to Cameron and went to gather her things.

CHAPTER 5

The short journey through the portal left Sophie feeling vaguely ill. But the queasiness wasn't as severe as usual. Perhaps water magic helped in that department? Still, she took a moment to breathe deeply as they left the portal vestibule and Cameron consulted their map.

[Elarus?]

[Here.] The sanctii hadn't chosen to be visible but it was a relief to know that she was nearby. Sophie couldn't feel an immediate chill, so she didn't know how close Elarus might be, but distance didn't seem to be any particular challenge to their connection. Close enough to come to their aid, should they need it. Hopefully they would not.

The temple was only a block away, and Cameron set a brisk pace, keeping himself between Sophie and the road. Isle de Angelique wasn't thronged with people at this time of day, and few people they passed offered as much as a glance or a polite smile. They walked past rows of near-identical red brick buildings, all with neat iron fences and doors painted dark blue or black or gray. Brass plates near some of the doors proclaimed them to be the offices of businesses of one kind or another. But most of the buildings offered no clue as to what might go on beyond the doors.

As they approached the temple entrance, Sophie felt a sudden breath of cool behind her. [Elarus? Is that you]

[Yes. I wait.]

[You can't go in?]

[Can. Boring.]

Well, that answered that question. Sophie had never considered boredom might be an affliction the sanctii suffered from. They lived such long lives, maybe it was inevitable. Was that why Elarus had been drawn to Sophie? Because she was interesting? She should try harder not to be. [All right. Stay close.]

She turned her attention back to the temple door. The only difference between it and the others they'd passed was that this one was marked with the quartered circle of the goddess.

"You know that's strange, don't you?" Cameron said.

"What's strange?"

"You get this odd look on your face when you're talking to her. At least, I assume you are talking to her, and you haven't adopted a habit of pausing to daydream at random moments." He sounded half-curious, half-amused.

"Yes, we talk."

"Strange," he muttered again, but then he shook his head. "Let's go inside."

Elarus or no Elarus, he clearly wasn't comfortable with them being on the open street.

They stepped into the foyer of the temple, an empty white-walled room lit by hanging lamps. Across the room, a larger door with a more elaborate symbol of the goddess barred the entrance to the temple itself. Sophie's gut twisted uneasily as she reached the door, and she hesitated.

"Sophie?" Cameron said.

She shook her head. It was nothing. She was overtired. Some time spent here in the peace and quiet of the temple would do her good. Give her time to think. And then, to talk with Cameron.

Pushing the odd sensation of doubt away, she went through the door.

She had a few moments to take in the temple itself, the stained-glass circles in the ceiling, the neat fires with the offering baskets of salt grass stacked before them. But as soon as the scent of the grass filled her nose, she suddenly saw Eloisa again, lying bloodied and decaying beneath that vast tree, threads of something black and rotten twined around her, through her. Spreading down into the roots of the tree itself. Nausea spiked, and she doubled over, fighting to banish the vision.

"Sophie!" Cameron's arm came around her.

[Help?]

[No. Thank you.] She didn't think a sanctii appearing in the temple would aid the situation.

"Lady Scardale, are you unwell?" Another voice came from somewhere to her right.

She couldn't lift her head to see who it was, the nausea still burning her throat.

"Fetch water." A third voice entered the conversation. There was a quick beat of retreating footsteps, then returning ones. As the fear and pain retreated, Sophie began to straighten.

"Are you all right?" Cameron demanded, blue eyes anxious as they searched her face.

"Sip this." A metal beaker of water appeared in front of her face. Sophie took the cup and drank gratefully before looking up to meet the amber eyes of Domina...Gerrard, that was it.

"Are you feeling better, Lady Scardale?" Domina Gerrard asked. "Here, sit." She motioned to the nearest bench of those surrounding the offering fire.

Sophie did as instructed, then sipped more water.

"Has your wife been ill, my lord?" Domina Gerrard asked.

"No," Cameron said. "Though she was tired, earlier."

The domina's dark brows drew together, one hand twining

around the long black braid that fell over her shoulder. She opened her mouth, then closed it, then opened it again. "There's no chance she is with child?"

"Sophie?" Cameron's voice cracked on the word, though she wasn't sure if it was in alarm or surprise.

Did he want children? Another thing they hadn't talked about. It was expected that royal witches would continue the bloodlines. She thought back, but no, she'd had her courses as usual over the time since they'd been married. Besides which she knew the herbs that the ladies in court recommended to prevent any surprises. Cameron must understand that they were currently in no position to bring a child into the world. "Um, no. I don't think so," she managed.

Disappointment fleeted across Cameron's face before he schooled it back to something more controlled.

The domina nodded. "All right. I can call for a healer, if you wish."

"No," Sophie said. "I am beginning to feel better. Perhaps it was a delayed reaction to the portal, after all."

"You came via the portal?" the domina asked. "Not in a carriage?"

"It seemed a nice day for some exploring," Cameron said smoothly.

"Of course," the domina said, though she frowned.

It was probably foolish to hope that the news of the emperor's offer hadn't filtered back to the Illvyan temple. Or that they had been given instructions on how to deal with Sophie should she appear again. Last time she'd been here, she'd told Domina Gerrard she was Madame Mackenzie but as Domina Gerrard had called Sophie Lady Scardale, she clearly knew their true identities. "Does portal travel always make you unwell, my lady?"

"Yes," Sophie said. "But I thought I had escaped the worst of it this time."

"Such things can be unpredictable. Especially if there are other factors to consider."

Was that a polite way of letting Sophie know that, yes, the domina did know about Elarus?

"So it seems. I'm sorry to have caused a disturbance," Sophie said. She had recovered enough to scan the temple. It was empty. It seemed the people around Isle de Angelique stayed off the streets and away from religion at this time of day.

"We are always glad to aid those in need," the domina said.

Was Sophie imagining it or was there an extra emphasis on "always." A message? Perhaps. But deciphering it would have to wait. She'd come here for some peace, not more intrigue. Perhaps that had been a foolish hope.

And it seemed a lost one now with the echoes of the vision still sharp in her mind.

"Perhaps we should return to the Academe," Cameron said. "I'm sure we can hire a carriage."

"I'll be all right. I'm feeling much better." The nausea had faded to almost nothing. She wasn't looking forward to stepping back into a portal, but they had agreed to saving their money. Besides, she didn't think it was the portal that had made her so ill. "I'd like to stay. Make an offering."

Cameron pursed his lips, looking as though he was going to object.

"It would be better for you to sit a while longer anyway, perhaps," Domina Gerrard said softly. "A swaying carriage is not always pleasant if one is feeling unwell. If you like, you could come back to our quarters behind the temple. We have tea and food. Nothing grand, but they might help. Then you can make your offering and return to the Academe once you are feeling fully recovered."

"Thank you," Sophie said. "If it's not too much trouble, some tea would be nice." Even though accepting the offer killed any chance of talking privately here with Cameron. She snuck a glance at him. He still didn't look pleased, but she didn't think he would argue with a domina without more cause than this.

"We are here to give aid and guidance to those who seek it," the domina said. "And, as you can see, you are not taking our services away from anyone else. Besides which, there are four of us here today. Our devout, Sera, can tend to the offering fires and anyone who comes in." She looked down at Sophie. "Do you feel able to stand yet?"

"Yes," Sophie said. She rose carefully. The room didn't spin nor did her stomach rebel. She took a relieved breath. Cameron extended his arm, and she curled her hand around it, squeezing gently to reassure him that she was fine. He smiled at her.

Domina Gerrard walked slowly, pointing out offices, a small room for more private devotions, and a staircase that led upstairs to the living spaces used by the devouts and priors on duty. The rest of the temple complex was as simple as the temple itself. White-washed walls, plain dark wooden furniture. Rows of earth-lights hung on the walls. Bowls of flowers graced some of the tables, placed in front of simple statues of the Great Tree or the goddess herself. Offerings of another kind.

The familiar scents of a kitchen, bread and herbs and wood smoke began to replace the smell of salt grass and incense before they reached it.

The kitchen was also simple. A large wood-burning stove, along with racks above a fireplace to allow for additional cooking, several large sinks, rows of shelving, and another door that Sophie assumed led to a pantry or cold storage. A large, well-worn, and well-scrubbed wooden table stood in the center of the room, flanked with eight chairs.

"We have a dining room," Domina Gerrard said, "if you prefer something more formal. But for tea and such between our usual mealtimes, we usually sit here."

"Do you have a cook?" Sophie asked, curious. This was a small temple, but at the city temples in Kingswell, the dominas had servants, aided by the devouts in training—or those who might have earned themselves some disapproval from the domina in charge.

"We have someone who comes in and makes bread each

morning and prepares what we need for our meals. Depending on what those might be, she starts them, or we cook ourselves. With only a few of us here at a time, we don't need much help." As if to demonstrate her point, she busied herself at the stove, moving a kettle onto one of the hotplates and stoking up the fire. That done she unearthed tea and dark green earthenware mugs from various cabinets. While she was occupied, Cameron grimaced at Sophie.

"What?" she mouthed.

"We should go back to the Academe," he mouthed back, but before he could press the point further, the domina returned to the table, a tray of sliced bread in one hand and plates in another.

"Something plain may settle your stomach, Lady Scardale."

"Please, call me Sophie." The bread did smell good, fresh and light somehow. She took a piece and a plate. Then, because both the domina and Cameron were watching her, she took a careful nibble. "It's delicious. Cameron, you should try it."

"I have jam. Or cheese, if you would prefer, my lord," Domina Gerrard said.

Cameron waved her off. "No. Thank you. Tea will be fine. I had lunch rather late today."

Before the domina could respond to this, the kettle started its whistling song and she turned back to the stove.

"Why do you want to go back?" Sophie mouthed at Cameron, but he just shook his head and pointed at the piece of bread. She rolled her eyes but took another bite.

"Tea," Domina Gerrard said, coming back to the table with three mugs that steamed and gave off a faintly sweet, faintly minty smell. "Mint and dried alen berries and a touch of ginger and honey. Soothing to the stomach."

"Do you have a garden here?" Sophie asked. Most temples in Anglion did. Earth witches were good with plants and coaxing things to grow where they usually wouldn't.

"A small vegetable garden. A few herbs in pots. We haven't

much space. The mint is ours, but the alen berries and ginger come from the larger gardens at the temple near the palace. The honey is from bees at our branch house."

"What's a branch house?" Sophie hadn't heard the term before.

Domina Gerrard cocked her head. "You don't have them in Anglion? They are larger properties where the devouts go for a time for instruction before joining a temple. Priors and dominas also rest there if they are unwell or can go for special periods of devotion or training. Older members of the community, who may want to step down from active temple life and prefer not to return to their families or home countries, retire to them. Sometimes they have orphanages or such attached. We farm what land we can there with the help of some of the people who live in wherever is the closest town or village. We have one here, a few miles to the east of the city. There are several herb farms in the area and our honey is considered particularly fine."

Sophie blew on the tea and then sipped it. The taste was an odd mix of cool and warm and sweet, and yes, something green beyond the obvious notes. "In Anglion, such things are generally done in the larger temple complexes," she offered. "Though I believe the temple has properties it farms. Some people leave them land as a bequest."

"Yes," Cameron said. "My squad used to stay at temple estates sometimes. Cleaner beds than inns, though not always particularly fancy ones. But I guess the temple here must have more people to train. And to serve."

"We do our best," the domina said. "The empire is large, and there are many beliefs in many countries, but the message of the goddess is one we try to share. And, of course, there are always earth witches who prefer to serve a higher purpose." She sipped her own tea, amber gaze resting steadily on Sophie.

"We must all find our own path," Sophie replied blandly. Going into the temple as a domina was never an option that had appealed to her. Nor had it been a choice she could have made.

She'd been raised to be the wife of a nobleman, her bloodlines supposedly too valuable to lose, regardless of whether she manifested.

"And what do you see your path being, Sophie?" Domina Gerrard asked.

"All I ever wanted was to have a family. A simple life," Sophie said. "I hope that will still be what I can achieve."

"An admirable goal," the domina said. "But sometimes the goddess puts your feet on another road. I imagine you didn't envision yourself spending your life in Illvya even a few months ago."

"No. But now that I'm here, I don't see why my life should be greatly changed. Cameron and I are content to live quietly." She squeezed his hand, the one where her ring circled his finger. Body and blood, they'd sworn. So far there'd been too much blood for her taste.

"I see," Domina Gerrard said.

But she seemed to think better of pressing the point. If she had been charged with encouraging Lady Scardale to serve the emperor's schemes, should Sophie happen to pass through this particular temple's doors again, she apparently wasn't going to rush her fences. "Was there something in particular that brought you here, today?"

"We had a rare block of free time in our schedule," Cameron said before Sophie could answer. "We have missed our devotions and thought it would be good to take the time to renew them. Sophie told me of your welcome when last she was here. I wanted to see the temple for myself." He straightened in his chair, a move that subtly reinforced his height and the breadth of his shoulders. Not a threat, rather a signal of protection. A reminder to the domina that if the temple was involved in any attempts to manipulate Sophie, then there was Cameron to get around first.

Had it been Domina Skey, who headed the temple in Anglion, sitting across the table, she would have been uneasy with him playing things this way but the temple here in Illvya had shown no signs of aggression. Indeed, Domina Gerrard had told her more about the history of the temple in Anglion than Sophie had ever learned while she lived there. She took a few more sips of her tea. Her stomach had eased, and she felt normal again. "Perhaps we should make an offering. We must return to the Academe before long."

"Of course," the domina said. She collected the mugs and plates, tidying everything away. Which made sense if they lived without servants. Deal with the mess now, or deal with it later; it would have to be dealt with eventually.

A thought that cut far too close to home.

They returned the way they had come. Sophie paused before one of the statues of the Great Tree, taken by the play of light on the beautifully carved pale wood. The vast tree grew from a disc that represented the world. The disc itself had been carved to show the roots of the tree twining through it in intricate flowing patterns. She reached toward it, then pulled her hand back, unsure if it would be right to touch it.

"Ah. That one invites touch, doesn't it?" the domina said. "Are you drawn to the tree, my lady? The heart of the world?"

"I've always liked the image," Sophie admitted. "The roots of the goddess, holding the earth true for us, her power above and below." The ley lines were said to be the gift of the goddess, running between the roots of the tree, providing her power to those who could reach it. Maybe that was why the vision of Eloisa lying beneath a tree had been so disturbing. There had been no light. No power. No ley line. Only darkness and corruption.

"I have always found it a comfort," the domina agreed. "There is a magnificent depiction of the tree at the temple near the palace. A beautiful window in stained glass. Glasswork has been an industry here in Lumia for a very long time. Our artisans are thought to be the best in the empire. The tree is one of their masterworks. You should go and see it."

Was that a suggestion based on Sophie's professed interest in the symbol of the tree or a less than subtle hint that Sophie should pay her respects to the palace temple? For now it seemed wisest to pretend she had no idea it could be anything other than the former. "I will try," she said. "I have little free time at the moment."

"I'm sure Maistre Matin and the others with calls upon your time cannot quibble at you spending some of it in devotion."

The domina's tone was steelier. A shade too close to the sorts of tones Sophie had been used to hearing from the Anglion dominas. A hint of command, rather than suggestion. "I will see what can be arranged," she said, intending no such thing. If the temple here was beginning to want to play politics with her, then she was staying as far away as possible.

CHAPTER 6

Cameron helped Sophie settle into the seat of the hired carriage before taking the seat opposite her. He thumped on the wall behind him to tell the driver to move off but kept his eye on Sophie's face. Despite her insistence that she no longer felt ill, she looked paler than she should, and tired.

"So," he said when the carriage was moving through the traffic and he was satisfied that the driver wouldn't overhear anything they said despite the lack of wards. "Do you want to tell me what really happened back there?"

Sophie's eyes widened. "What do you mean?"

"I mean that I don't think you had portal sickness. Did you?" Even though he was sure he was right, he'd insisted on taking a carriage for their return journey. Not only to spare Sophie any further discomfort but because this was a conversation he preferred to hold outside the Academe.

"I—" Sophie started, then hesitated. "I'm not sure," she said eventually. "It could have been the portal."

"I don't think it was," Cameron said. "Because when you doubled over, I felt something through our bond. And that's never happened before when I've been with you going through a portal." The sensation hadn't been strong. A brief tug on the link they shared. A flare of connection that had faded as fast as it had bloomed. Or maybe he had been too busy focusing on Sophie to really pay attention. Come to think of it, it had been much like the sensation that had woken him that morning. "What happened in the temple? And does it have anything to do with whatever happened in your lesson this morning?'

Her mouth dropped open. "How did you know about that?"

Damn it. He hadn't wanted to be right. "What happened?"

"At the temple or at the lesson?"

"Start with the lesson. Taking things from the beginning makes things easier, I find."

Sophie twined her hands together, her fingers restlessly playing with the ring she wore. His ring.

"Sophie," he said. "Talk to me. I'm not angry. Just worried."

"I told you, they wanted me to try scrying," Sophie said.

"That sounds like leaping off a cliff before you can even walk," Cameron said. There were many reasons why water magic was reviled in Anglion. The power of the sanctii was one. The power of water mages to glimpse—and try to manipulate—the future was another. The thought of Sophie using such powers was...unsettling.

"They said they were trying to see what I could do already," Sophie said. "They made me call Elarus first."

"Ah. Yes. Elarus." He glanced around. "Is she here?" Sophie claimed to be able to feel water magic—and sanctii—by the chill that accompanied them. But if it were true, then it wasn't something he shared through their bond. He'd felt a chill perhaps when Elarus had touched him but nothing more. It was difficult enough being in Illvya knowing that there were sanctii at the beck and call of the water mages. Knowing that Sophie now had one, a sanctii who might easily choose to be invisible or incorporeal—he didn't know exactly which it was the sanctii did—while accompanying his wife made the back of his neck prickle uneasily.

Sophie's face went blank in a way he was starting to recognize as her talking to the damn demon. He supposed he would get used to the idea in time, but for now it was a complication.

"She's watching, but she's not in the carriage," Sophie said.

Watching? What did that mean? He rolled his shoulders, trying to relax. Granted, it was some comfort to know that Elarus was with them and that she would protect Sophie if needed, but still, it was a queer sort of comfort. Besides which, now he had to learn about water magic. He was fairly certain he had no talent for it himself, but he needed to understand how Sophie's bond with the sanctii worked.

He could feel Sophie through the bond he shared with her. Now that Sophie had showed him how. She was simply there, like a melody in the back of his mind or a distant pleasing hum. Something he had become used to. He rarely felt more than that unless Sophie did something big with her magic.

He'd felt the joining with Elarus clearly enough. It had been hard to miss.

But he didn't feel the sanctii though, or any change in his connection to Sophie. Whatever bond Elarus had formed with Sophie seemed separate to the one they shared. Did Elarus feel Sophie? Know when something was wrong? Or did she actively watch? From this realm? From the demon realm? Not knowing made him uneasy, like there was a weakness in his defenses, like a squad missing from formation. He wouldn't know how to factor Elarus into his plans until he knew how the bloody water magic worked.

More goddess-damned study.

It was all they had done since arriving in Illvya. His skull was crammed full of more new knowledge than he could handle, and it still wasn't enough to keep Sophie safe. Not when he was dealing with emperors with wild schemes, assassins, and goddess-damned demons. Who, in this bloody country, weren't so goddess-damned after all.

A soldier's job was to defend. As was a husband's. He was going to his damned job.

He rolled his shoulders a second time. Focus on the task at hand. Then go onto the next thing. The immediate problem was what had happened to Sophie. She was watching him, muscles tense, eyes wary.

He hated that she looked that way. That she had anything to worry about. That he couldn't fix it all for her.

"All right. So, what happened next? You attempted to scry?"

"They wanted me to try," Sophie agreed. "We were in the practice rooms. I was using a bowl filled with ink—I think it was ink—but when I tried to scry the bowl broke."

"Broke?"

"Cracked into pieces," Sophie said. "I think I used too much power."

His brows shot up. Breaking bowls sounded like blood magic. Something that, technically, Sophie shouldn't be able to do. Was this another complication of their bond? Or something water mages did as a matter of course? "And then?"

"They took me to a room beneath the Academe. There was water there, a...pond, no, a reservoir of some sort I suppose it is," Sophie said. "I don't think there's a river under the Academe, but I didn't ask where the water came from."

At this point nothing about the Academe should surprise him. "Water mages need water, I guess," he said. Worry about the source of the water later. If there was some sort of underground river or even pipes feeding it, he'd like to know how and where. He'd devoted quite some time to understanding the layout of the Academe, though he hadn't been able to scout all the rooms and buildings yet. He'd known there were basements. He hadn't known there was water. Water needed entry and exit points. Something to consider should they need to leave the Academe in a hurry.

"I tried scrying again. Using the reservoir."

That seemed...advanced? Not the first time his lack of knowledge of water magic was going to trip him up. Maybe the size of the surface used didn't matter. Maybe Madame Simsa and

Henri had only taken Sophie to this underground whatever-it-was to make sure there were no more exploding bowls. But something in his gut told him that power amplified in odd ways. Blood mages could strengthen their magic with blood or strong emotions. Earth witches were always strongest with their feet on the earth itself. He had no idea what those who used the Arts of Air called upon to amplify their powers, but it seemed logical that for water mages, water would be the element that applied.

"What happened the second time?" He asked.

Sophie closed her eyes briefly. "I saw...something."

He waited. She didn't seem keen to tell the tale, but he needed to hear it. Particularly if it was causing her ongoing harm by triggering attacks like the one she'd had in the temple.

"I saw you, at first. You were sleeping. That was all I was trying to see. You. But then...there were other things."

Her voice had gone quiet. Not a good kind of quiet. More the "I don't want to remember this" kind. The same tone he'd heard men use after they'd been through a battle or killed someone for the first time.

"Tell me," he said gently. If he'd learned anything from the Red Guard, it was that those who kept such things to themselves —the experiences that had frightened or scarred them—those were the ones most likely to break in the end. And Sophie wasn't going to break as long as he had breath to hold her together.

"I saw darkness. Pain. Mama crying. And Eloisa—" she broke off, biting her lip.

"Eloisa?" Every muscle in his body tensed. The first time Sophie tried to scry, and she saw the queen that Aristides would see her overthrow? That couldn't be good.

"She was dead. Or looked dead. Buried beneath a tree, rotting. It was—" Sophie sucked in a deep breath, let it go shakily as her body shuddered. "It was wrong, Cameron. Terribly wrong."

"But it might not be real," he said. "It was your first attempt. Perhaps you saw Eloisa because she was on your mind."

"Why would I see her dead?" Sophie whispered. "I don't wish that on her."

Cameron shifted in his seat. If Aristides ever forced Sophie down his mad path, then it was entirely possible that Eloisa's death could be the outcome. In Anglion history, not many overthrown monarchs survived. Eloisa's own family had taken the throne by force.

But perhaps they did things differently here in the empire. After all, Aristides couldn't be everywhere in the continent at once. He needed people in place to rule for him. Perhaps he worked with those he conquered. And that added more Illvyan history to the list of things he needed to learn. "Maybe not dead. Maybe it was a symbol. It was a vision, after all. What did Madame and Henri say?"

She shook her head, the light coming through the carriage window glinting redly over her hair. Redder than ever. Though, in several places he fancied it was growing darker than before. Chloe de Montesse had hair like flames and night, a record of the magics she had used once upon a time. It marked her as a stranger, a refugee, and one to be distrusted in Anglion. Would Sophie's hair eventually tell that same story?

"I didn't tell them," Sophie said. "I said I saw you. I didn't mention Eloisa. I didn't want them telling Aristides. Not until I know more about what it might mean."

Logical. With the emperor's offer hanging over her head—an offer that Henri Matin had witnessed—it would be foolish to announce that her very first vision had showed the Anglion queen lying dead.

"What did they say about scrying? Is it always true what you see?"

"No. They said not."

He blew out a breath, not entirely comforted. "Then it could be nothing."

"Perhaps." She looked unconvinced. "Perhaps. But when I stepped into the temple, I saw it again."

He'd been expected her to say it. But that didn't mean hearing it didn't chill his blood. "Saw what exactly?"

"Eloisa. The tree. The darkness. It turned my stomach."

That much had been plain. "But you weren't trying to scry then."

"No," she said. Her knuckles were white as she toyed with her wedding ring. "So why would I see it again? If it's not true?"

"I don't know," he said. "Usually I would say you should ask somebody, but I agree that it doesn't seem like the safest thing to share." He paused. "Damn. This is where we need Madame de Montesse to talk to." Unfortunately Chloe—Henri's daughter—was an ocean away in Kingswell. He didn't know for sure that she was a water mage despite the colors in her hair. Her father was, but as an Illvyan refugee in Anglion, she'd never advertised what skills she might have in arts other than earth magic. And she didn't even use that. She owned a magical supplies shop near the port, but the temple would not have allowed her to do more. But she'd been raised and trained in Illvya. She could have helped them.

"There's always Elarus," Sophie said tentatively. "She may know." She glanced around, as though half expecting the sanctii to appear.

Cameron hesitated. He'd rather understand more about Elarus and her motivations for wanting to bond with Sophie before relying on her for anything as potentially dangerous as this. "I—"

Sophie sighed. "You're going to say we should do some research, aren't you?"

"I think we should proceed carefully. We don't want anything to force the emperor's hand at this point. So I'd rather understand what your vision means before anyone else finds out about it."

"I agree." Sophie bit her lip. "We need to talk about options again. If this could force his hand, we need to make a decision."

"We're not going to break our—"

Sophie stopped him with a finger to his lips. "Let's not say not. Not yet. We need to talk about it." She cupped his cheek. "I know you don't like it. I don't either. But we need to consider all our options."

He pressed his hand over hers. He'd sworn to keep her safe. So she was right. "All right. But not here. Once we're back in our rooms."

~

Sophie braced herself as they passed through the doors of the Academe. When they'd first arrived in Illvya, its walls had offered protection. But now, as things became more complicated, they were starting to close in.

More rules. More expectations. More obligations. Each one narrowing down their future to a pattern that may as well have been the bars of a prison cell.

Unless she and Cameron could find another pattern for themselves. She knew he didn't want to run. Or at least, not if the only way to do it safely would be to break their bond. But she was starting to think they had no choice. His hand was clasped around hers, his grip almost painfully tight as they headed for their rooms. But they were only halfway there when Lia and Magritte rounded the corner.

"Sophie," Magritte called, pale blue eyes lit with curiosity. "Where have you been? We missed you in lessons today."

Magritte had not yet manifested, but she was always one of the first to hear any gossip in the Academe. Was she fishing for confirmation? Sophie was glad she was no longer wearing her new robes. Her new status would be public knowledge soon enough, but right now she didn't want to be interrogated all over again.

Which was only one more reason why she would be a bad queen. Queens were supposed to be good at politics and subterfuge and dissembling. To enjoy them.

"I was not feeling well earlier," Cameron's voice came smoothly from her side. "Sophie stayed with me."

Magritte raised one brow. "That is unfortunate. Though, you must be feeling better to have left the grounds." Her tone was arch. The blonde was not exactly Sophie's greatest admirer. Her manner had thawed some from their first meeting back on the first morning they'd arrived at the Academe, but she still held an air of being distinctly disgruntled that an upstart Anglion refugee had attracted so much attention within the school.

What she might say if she knew of the emperor's offer didn't bear thinking about.

"Rachelle thought some fresh air and sunshine might do me good," Cameron said before Sophie could think of how to politely get rid of Magritte.

"Healer's orders. It's best to follow them," Sophie added finding her tongue as Lia tilted her head at her as though silently questioning what had really happened. Unlike Magritte, Lia did have her powers, and she might have felt the bonding last night. But if she had, she held her tongue, merely glancing sideways at Magritte with imperfectly concealed exasperation.

"Have you come from dinner?" Lia asked. The summer sun was starting to lower, the light through the windows falling golden across the patterned tiles on the walls.

"No," Sophie said. "Is that where you're going? Aren't you going to study?" She really didn't want to have to wriggle out of an invitation to join the two girls for dinner.

Lia grimaced. "Eventually. But I'm starving. Early dinner for me tonight. I swear Maistre Jordain spent an hour on one single day four centuries ago where, as far as I can tell, not much happened other than the investiture of a new librarian here at the Academe. After that I need food—preferably dessert — before I can even think of opening another book." She smiled. "You could come with us. We can tell you what lessons you missed today and what you need to catch up on."

The very thought made Sophie's head throb. She opened her mouth to decline, but Cameron beat her to it.

"Perhaps at breakfast," he said smoothly. "Unfortunately I have been confined to quarters. More rest after my outing. The healers said they would send our meals to our room."

Magritte shuddered. "I hope it's not their famous healing broth. I had that a few months ago when I was unwell. It was..."

"Terrible?" Lia suggested.

"Exceedingly dull," Magritte corrected. "Like the blandest chicken soup you can imagine."

"I'm sure Rachelle won't starve us. After all, I'm not sick, and if she has any understanding of men, she should know that he would have no shame in stealing some of my food if he was hungry," Sophie said.

"Not all of it," Cameron protested, with a smile. "But you are smaller than me." He squeezed her hands, perhaps wanting her to keep up their pretense of normality.

She summoned a smile of her own. "Yes, but you've lazed around all day. I studied this morning."

"You did?" Magritte pounced on that tidbit of information. "You weren't in our lecture on distillation of herbs. Did you have a special lesson? Something to do with the commotion last night, perhaps?"

Magritte might be disagreeable, but she wasn't stupid.

"Was there a commotion?" Sophie asked, widening her eyes.

Magritte narrowed hers in response. "You know there was. It's been the talk of the—"

Her words cut off with an "oof" as Lia jabbed an elbow neatly into her ribs. Her blue eyes slitted with displeasure.

"Sophie doesn't have to tell us where she was," Lia said. "And whatever happened last night, she is free to discuss it or not as she chooses. Either way, if Cameron is unwell, we should leave them in peace, Magritte. Come along, I'm hungry. And don't you dare say that I'm always hungry, that's impolite."

"You are always hungry," Magritte said, still looking annoyed. "Telling the truth is not impolite."

"And they say the islands are uncivilized," Lia said, rolling her eyes. "Telling the truth can be most impolite. Especially when it is unnecessary. Now, come along. Perhaps a piece of cake will sweeten your mood. I'm sure I smelled lemon cakes when I passed the dining hall earlier. You know they always go quickly."

"Yes, you wouldn't want to miss lemon cake, Magritte," Sophie said, hoping the lure of a favorite dessert would tempt Magritte away from further questions. "But, you will have to excuse us, we must return to our apartments. We will see you at breakfast, perhaps."

She nodded at the girls and tugged at Cameron's hand, beginning to walk. Which was perhaps, no more polite than Magritte, but if they didn't move, they would be having the conversation forever.

"They know," she said softly as they reached the bend in the corridor and turned right toward the final staircase that would take them to their apartment.

"About Elarus?" Cameron said. "Well, yes. No one here would think bonding with her should be secret. Which is why Madame Simsa gave you those new robes."

"What if they know more than that?"

"I don't think that's likely," Cameron said, "Not yet." He spoke in a low tone. They were alone on the staircase, but of course, that only meant that there were no other mages. There could be ten sanctii listening to their conversation and neither of them would know it. She felt no chill on her skin, but that didn't necessarily mean they weren't being watched.

"Things will change once people know," Sophie said. They reached the door to the apartment.

"Things have already changed," Cameron said, holding the door open. "What matters is us, not what others think of us."

That wasn't entirely true. Yes, they could hold to their own picture of what their life should be. But unless they took action to bring that picture to life, then what others thought of them—what they thought she and Cameron should be—would be the only thing that mattered. She locked the door and laid a hand to the wards.

When she lifted it again, she hoped Cameron wouldn't see that it trembled. "I want to ask Elarus more about hiding our magic."

Cameron scowled. "You mean ask her about breaking our bond."

"Yes. So we can decide what we want to do. Imogene wants to take us out of the city. That seems like a chance."

"A chance to run."

"At worst. At best, a chance to find out more about what the country is like outside the city. Where we might get away should it be needed."

"We might not need to," Cameron said. He moved closer, held out a hand. "Aristides might calm down if Eloisa does nothing more to provoke him." He stared down at her. "Your hands are shaking, love. Come, sit. You're upset. This vision of yours—"

"Visions," she corrected.

"Visions. They've spooked you."

"Yes." She didn't bother to deny it. Cameron wrapped his arms around her, and she pressed her cheek into his chest, trying to breathe him in, let the bone-deep sense of safety he always gave her wrap around her. But it didn't ease the knots writhing in her stomach. "I don't know what they mean but I don't like how they felt. I don't like any of this."

"So you want to run?"

"Maybe. I want us to be free, don't you?"

"I want us to be happy. I want you to be happy." He kissed the top of her head. "So call your demon, and let's ask her more questions."

The conversation went quickly at first. Elarus confirmed what she had already told them. That she could remove their bond, which would make it difficult for a mage to track them. News that made Cameron's face darken, though he held his tongue.

"How long would it take?" Sophie asked.

"Fast," Elarus said. "You want?"

"No! Not now. We're just interested."

"Is it noisy?" Cameron interjected.

Elarus tilted her head. "Noise?"

"The mages here all felt when you and Sophie did what you did. There's no point breaking the bond if doing so would alert every mage nearby that something was happening."

He was right, of course.

"No noise," Elarus said. "Breaking is different to bonding."

That didn't lighten Cameron's expression any. "Could you make the bond again?"

Elarus shook her head slowly. "Human thing. Not sanctii."

"We can do that part ourselves," she said. "We did it once before."

"We can hardly roll you over a ley line just as your magic manifests a second time," Cameron said.

"We would work it out, together." Now wasn't the time to bring up again that one reason to break the bond would be to let them separate for a time, to hide more easily apart. Now wasn't the time to continue this conversation at all, if she was any judge of Cameron's temper. She would ask Elarus what she knew about visions in the morning. Right now Cameron needed sleep. As she did. And food. Or food and then sleep, she didn't really know or care which order.

She thanked Elarus and the sanctii disappeared.

Cameron stared at the spot where she had stood, a muscle ticking in his jaw.

"Do you want to eat or sleep?" she asked.

"Is this conversation done?"

"For now," she said. It was the best she could give him. "Unless you want to keep going?"

"Goddess, no," he said. He pressed his thumbs to his temples. "Food. I need food."

That solved that problem. She crossed the room and used the charm to summon a maid.

Cameron excused himself to go and wash up before dinner. Or to go and curse somewhere she couldn't hear him perhaps.

She sat by the fire to wait for him, resisting the urge to lie down on the bed. If she did that, she wouldn't wake until morning.

The doorbell chimed not long after Cameron returned, and she opened it to find one of the kitchen maids with a fully laden trolley.

"We hadn't ordered anything yet," she said, confused.

"No, my lady but the healers sent a message to say if you hadn't by the time the main hall was served, then we were to send some. We were getting ready to bring this to you any way. There is a tea for Lord Scardale that he is to drink. In the blue pot, my lady."

"All right, thank you." She stepped back to let the woman in. As the trolley rumbled forward, a familiar squawk came from the corridor and Tok landed on the floor a few feet away from the door. He squawked again and then hopped to Sophie's feet and pecked at the hem of her dress. "Caw."

"Hello," Sophie said. Which earned her another peck. She twitched the hem back. "Don't do that. I'm sorry I haven't been here today, but look, I'm fine." She bent down and stretched a finger toward the bird. He tapped it with his beak, then rubbed his head against it, the movement oddly cat-like. "You go to bed, Tok. They will be wondering where you are. And we aren't going anywhere tonight."

The bird looked back down the corridor and spread his wings, ruffling his feathers.

"You go have your dinner. I'm going to have mine." She rubbed a finger down his back, and he leaned into it again. He was getting harder to resist. Perhaps she should ask Madame how one went about bonding a petty fam. In a few more days. After everyone had time to calm down about Elarus. Though, if she and Cameron decided to leave.... Perhaps not. "Go on now," she said gently, trying to ignore the sudden pang of sorrow at the thought she might have to leave Tok behind.

"Persistent beasties, aren't they?" the kitchen maid said from behind her. "They come around the door to the kitchens, begging for scraps. We're not supposed to feed them, the Master of the Ravens doesn't like it, but we do sometimes. Better to have them on your side, I think."

"Yes," Sophie agreed. She straightened, and Tok squawked again. She shook her head at him. "Go. I need my dinner. You need yours. I will see you in the morning." She smiled at the kitchen maid. "Thank you for bringing the meal."

"My pleasure, my lady." She looked down at Tok. "If you come with me back to the kitchen, I can find you a treat before you go back to the tower. Cook was making pate earlier. I'm sure there were liver scraps. The raven master won't know."

Tok clicked his beak enthusiastically and launched himself into the air, disappearing down the corridor.

Sophie laughed. "Liver seems popular. I must remember that."

"Is he to be your fam, my lady?" the maid asked curiously.

"Maybe," Sophie said. "We shall see."

The maid nodded. "These things take time. And I must be on my way. If he gets to the kitchen before me and starts annoying the others, they'll shoo him off, and he'll come back to bother you. Then we'll both have the Master of the Ravens looking for our heads."

"We wouldn't want that," Sophie agreed. "Thank you again."

When she went back into the room, she found Cameron, damp hair shining in the firelight, arranging plates and covered bowls and baskets on their small table.

"The tea in the blue jug is for you," Sophie said. "Rachelle's orders."

Cameron eyed the jug dubiously. "I might start with food," he said. "In case it's one of those healer teas that tastes like three-weeks-dead carrion."

"As long as you drink it eventually," Sophie said.

"Rachelle wouldn't know if I tipped it out the window," Cameron offered, looking unenthusiastic.

"I wouldn't be so sure about that," Sophie said. "Besides, you need to drink it. I want you at full strength in case I get the urge to have my way with you."

He laughed and held out one of the chairs for her. "That's an incentive I cannot resist."

Hunger kept them silent for the next twenty minutes as they made short work of the food, which Sophie was pleased to see included several pieces of the lemon cake Lia had mentioned.

She was devouring a slice when the chimes sounded again. "What now?" she muttered through a half-full mouth.

Cameron shrugged and went to the door. There was a quick murmur of voices, and then the sound of paper tearing after the door closed again.

"A note from Imogene?" Sophie asked, still intent on finishing her dessert.

"No," Cameron said and something in his tone made her look up.

"Who then?" She asked.

Cameron held out the piece of paper, and she saw the heavy wax seal on the bottom. The cake turned to stones in her stomach.

"The emperor," she breathed.

"Yes." Cameron said. "We are summoned, it seems." His tone was grim, and she regretted that more than the cake. She didn't want to be the wife who brought that sound to her husband's voice.

"When?" Perhaps it could wait to morning. If it could, then it couldn't be bad news, could it?

"Now," Cameron said.

CHAPTER 7

The emperor stood with Imogene, Colonel Perrine—the chief of the Imperial mages—and another tall blond man Sophie judged to be somewhere around thirty. His face was handsome—strikingly so—but coldly stern as he gestured at a piece of paper that lay on the table behind them. The other three didn't look pleased with what he was saying.

All four looked up when the servant cleared his throat and said, "Lord and Lady Scardale."

"Your Imperial Majesty," Sophie said, dipping into a hasty curtsy.

"Lady Scardale," Aristides held up a hand. "Lord Scardale. If you could wait there." He turned back to the blond man and motioned for him to continue. Imogene broke away from the group to join Sophie and Cameron.

"Major," Cameron said. Imogene didn't quibble about his choice of address. So. They were here for a matter where she was an Imperial mage, not a duquesse.

"Lord Scardale, Lady Scardale." Imogene nodded. She stood in front of Sophie, partially blocking her view of the emperor and his companions.

"Major du Laq." Sophie bobbed another curtsy before she

realized that perhaps she shouldn't if Imogene was using her rank, not her title.

Imogene's mouth twitched, but she made no comment.

"What's going on?" Cameron asked in a low tone shaded more toward demand than question.

"His Imperial Majesty will tell you shortly." Imogene's blue eyes were sympathetic, but her face stayed impassive.

Cameron frowned. "Can you at least tell us who that is with the colonel?" He gestured to the three men standing by the table.

Imogene's mouth flattened. "That is Lucien de Roche. As of a few months ago, also the Marq of Castaigne."

"Oh? And what does he do when he's not being a lord?" Cameron asked. Imogene turned toward the emperor, leaving Sophie with a clear view of the man.

He wore Imperial mage black, like Imogene. The Imperial mages held ranks within the emperor's army, but Sophie didn't know what all of them were. Or if there were any special ranks for mages. Imogene was a major and wore golden suns on her collar as badges of that rank. Whatever insignia decorated the marq's collar was done in black, and from this distance, merged with the fabric so she couldn't determine its shape.

"Lord Castaigne is a Truth Seeker," Imogene said.

Truth seeker. The way Imogene said those words suggested they were a title, not a general description of the man.

"What is that exactly?" Sophie asked quietly. Lord Castaigne glanced over briefly but turned back to the emperor when Aristides said something Sophie couldn't quite make out. Whoever he was, he looked immaculate, black clothes unwrinkled and unstained, long boots gleaming. His blond hair, ruthlessly tamed into a queue, also spoke of control and restraint. The only thing out of place in the severe angles and planes of his face, were his eyes, a curiously smoky shade of green that stood out against his pale skin even at a distance. A color that seemed somehow too wild when compared to the rest of him.

Imogene turned back and gestured for them to all move farther away. Sophie followed her. Until the emperor decided to include them in the conversation, there was nothing to do but wait. Better to spend that time finding out whatever information Imogene was free to share with them.

"Truth seeking is an unusual talent," Imogene said, her right hand toying with the buttons of her severely tailored left cuff before stilling again. "They are illusioners, but they work with the judiciary and the military in matters of crime. People call them the emperor's all-seeing ravens. They can monitor interrogations or help...facilitate a confession."

"Torture?" Sophie swallowed. She'd been under no misapprehension as to what was likely to happen to Sevan when he'd been dragged out of the throne room by the emperor's guards.

"Not exactly," Imogene said. "Not *bodily* harm." Her lips pursed. "But they can show things to a prisoner that might persuade them to cooperate."

"Such as?"

"Images of the crime. Images of their likely fate," Imogene said. "Whatever may work. But truth seekers also somehow know when someone is lying. It is not a common talent. Some say they have the sight, as water mages do. Lord Castaigne has a reputation for being *very* good at his work. They say he never gives up. Can never be swayed. Some might call it ruthless."

There was an edge to her voice. Whoever this lord was, Imogene did not appear to approve. Given she herself was an Imperial mage, a major at that, and the wife of one of the most powerful duqs in the empire, Sophie was hard pressed to imagine what a truth seeker might do that Imogene might disapprove of.

On second thought, she was better off not trying. She had enough to worry about without letting her imagination add to the list.

"This is about Sevan, then?" she said. What else might someone with the abilities Imogene had described, be doing for Aristides that could possibly concern Cameron and her?

Imogene's brows lifted. Sophie's jaw tightened. *Illvyans*. Just because she didn't want a damn crown for herself didn't mean she was stupid. "What else could it be?" Sophie said, voice sharper than strictly polite.

Aristides had said that he would question Barron Deepholt and James Listfold before putting them on a ship back to Anglion. They might have had something to tell that might be relevant, but she didn't believe they had any part of Sevan's plot.

Hopefully Aristides had treated them with some degree of care, with respect to their diplomatic status, if nothing else.

Roughing up an ambassador was not the done thing. Of course, Aristides might consider himself above such trifling concerns, but she hoped—for the barron's and James's sakes— that he had not completely lost his senses. She had no fondness for the barron, but James was part of Cameron's family. His sister-in-law's brother.

But before Imogene could respond, the emperor said, "It seems we are at an impasse. Thank you, Lucien"—in a somewhat disgruntled tone—"Let's get this over with."

Sophie, Cameron, and Imogene all turned. Besides, the emperor, Colonel Perrine was rolling up the piece of paper they'd been studying, though something about the expression on his face made Sophie think that perhaps he'd rather have been tearing it to pieces. She suppressed the shiver that threatened to crawl up her spine despite the overly warm room. The emperor's expression spoke of news that was unpleasant, if not outright awful.

Aristides beckoned. There was no choice but to obey the summons. Cameron moved closer to Sophie as they walked to the table.

"Lord and Lady Scardale, this is Lucien de Roche, Marq of Castaigne," Aristides said, his words somewhat brusque.

The emperor was in a mood. Sophie braced herself, then remembered she should be curtsying to Lord Castaigne. His rank of Marq was equivalent to Cameron's Barron, but it was still polite to curtsy when being introduced.

But before she could, Lucien bowed. A brief but perfectly executed movement that suggested he was impatient with the whole business. Sophie kept her response along the same lines. Now that she was closer, she could see that the insignia on his collar was a stylized bird. An all-seeing raven?

"Lord Castaigne was supervising the interrogation of your Mestier Allowood," Aristides continued.

Was? Sophie swallowed, stomach suddenly far beyond cold. "I see," she managed. "I assume if you have brought us here, Your Imperial Majesty, then something has happened? Did Sevan confess?"

"Not exactly," Lucien said. His voice was deep. And grave. A serious voice to go with the serious-looking man. "He was not entirely coherent. Whatever the poison was that he took, it did some damage before the healers arrested its progress."

"He must have told you something, or we wouldn't be here," Sophie said sharply. Aristides's brows lifted, but he stayed silent. Sophie ignored him. The man had offered her a crown. If she was to have any hope of him taking her refusal seriously, she needed him to know she wasn't a pushover. Not a pawn for him to place as he pleased. Of course, it was a fine line to walk between that and not making him think that she was fierce enough to hold a throne.

She turned her gaze to focus solely on Lord Castaigne. Whose expression was unreadable. This close, she saw that his collar wasn't empty but that the insignia pinned there was the same black as the material. Two black circles. They were engraved but she couldn't tell what the design might be. "Did he say anything?"

"He did. But, as I said, he was somewhat incoherent. We were hoping that perhaps you and Lord Scardale may have an easier time understanding what he may have been talking about," Lord Castaigne said.

"Can't you ask him?" Cameron cut in.

Lucien's lips pressed together briefly. "I am afraid not. The poison had weakened him. His heart gave out in the end. My condolences."

Sophie shuddered, bowing her head. Poison? Or what the Illvyans had done to him? Poison was a convenient sort of excuse for a dead prisoner. Particularly one who'd been under interrogation. Sevan Allowood had tried to kill her. She'd wanted him punished, yes. But she hadn't wanted him dead.

Unlike whoever had sent him to kill her, who seemed not to have cared if Sevan died in his attempt. Her fingers started to curl, and she relaxed them with an effort. She might not have wanted Sevan to die, but she was rapidly developing a desire for the person behind his efforts to do so. Painfully, if possible.

They clearly didn't care much about the fate of anyone who got in their way. Only about achieving whatever mysterious goal they were trying to achieve. Aristides called it manipulating the succession in Anglion, but Sophie didn't know if it was that simple—if one could call playing games with kingdoms simple. Why bother killing her if it was simply about the crown? She had removed herself from eligibility in the eyes of most Anglions, if not by the letter of the law, by coming to Illvya.

"What about the others in the delegation?" she asked. "Did you ask them about what Sevan said?"

"They claim to have no insights. Lord Castaigne tells me he believes them," Aristides said, frowning. As though he was annoyed by the marq's assertion but had no reason to challenge it. Which was something to remember. That this truth seeker's word was accepted by the emperor it seemed, even though Aristides didn't like what Lord Castaigne had to say.

She didn't much like it either. "Are—"

"You used your...talents on them, my lord?" Cameron interrupted.

Sophie recognized the quiet anger underlying his words,

knew the thought of James being hurt in any way would make him sick. As it did her. She swallowed, hard.

Cameron trusted James—believed that it was James who'd tried to warn them that the Anglion delegation may be treacherous—but more than that, James was family. Someone who'd done nothing to deserve being dragged into this mess. Other than be connected to Cameron by marriage. The only reason for him to have been sent on the delegation was to see if family loyalties would lure Cameron home where simple duty could not.

Lord Castaigne cocked his head, as if acknowledging the challenge in the question. "I am a reasonable judge of character, Lord Scardale. And my profession brings with it a certain skill at recognizing the truth when I hear it, even without using my magic," he said calmly. "We questioned the other members of the delegation at some length, but it wasn't necessary to encourage them any farther than that."

He sounded as though he was telling the truth. Sophie hoped he was. He had no reason to deceive them, after all. It wasn't as though they were in any position to challenge the emperor's authority to do precisely as he liked with prisoners under his control.

"If they couldn't tell you what Sevan was talking about, what makes you think that my husband or I would know more?" Sophie asked. "Neither of us knew him well."

"It may be that you cannot, Lady Scardale," Lord Castaigne said. "But I would not be fulfilling my responsibilities if I didn't use all the sources of information at my disposal in conducting this investigation."

Something about his dispassionate tone grated. It was obvious that here was a man who had a mission and a duty, one he would fulfill or die trying. The kind of man who perhaps would have been better following a religious path. Full of zeal and convinced he was justified in doing whatever needed to be done to serve his purpose. But his purpose wasn't the glory of the goddess or doing good. No, his purpose was truth. In the service of the emperor—or perhaps in service of that concept alone.

It would be more than satisfying to tell this cool Illvyan lord that she wasn't at his disposal. She clenched her teeth against the urge. That would be stepping over the line she was trying to skirt. Lord Castaigne was clearly a force in the emperor's court. Not to mention, possibly the reason Sevan was dead. It would be foolish to take him as merely the perfectly calm and perfectly presented Illvyan nobleman he appeared to be. She would give him no reason to need to use his talents on her.

"Of course," she said, striving for a calm tone to rival his own. "We will tell you what we know." It wasn't a lie. She didn't think they knew anything that would help. She wished she knew more about his powers. Did he always know if someone was lying or did he have to intentionally use his magic?

Lord Castaigne nodded. "Then if you would be so kind." He nodded toward the table where a small pile of neatly inked papers lay. "Those are the records of the discussion with Mestier Allowood. Read them, please. See if anything makes sense to you."

Sophie would rather have picked up a snake. Her skin crawled as she reached for the first paper. Sevan had been unpleasant in real life. She had no desire to read the words he'd uttered between attempting to kill her, then himself, and then finally dying.

But she did it anyway. She drew a breath to steady herself and began to read.

The words were Anglish, which made her wonder who had been recording the conversation. Someone with a good ear for the language, it seemed. The words were disjointed and rambling, but they sounded like an Anglion speaking to her. Like Sevan, even.

The first few pages were repetitive, with Sevan denying his guilt and the right of the questioner—Lord Castaigne presumably—to question him. The interview seemed to have taken place over nearly a full day, with the times neatly recorded. What did the gaps in time represent? Had Sevan been unconscious or raving or had the Illvyans been doing things to him that they didn't want documented? She steeled herself to read on. With each successive page, Sevan's words grew more confused.

More denials. But in between those, pleas. And sentences that were completely out of context. Mentions of names Sophie recognized as his cousin, the late Baron Nester, and if she was remembering rightly, another man, Sevan's father. A snippet of description of a house beside a stream—his home perhaps? Her eyes stung as she read on. She blinked hard against the tears. She would not cry for a man who had tried to kill her. Who thought her a traitor and an abomination. But the words he'd spoken vibrated with pain and despair. Sevan was not much older than her. Or *had* been not much older than her. Because now he was dead.

On the second to last page, there were several lines that came from temple services. "O earth, rise to keep me" and "glorious merciful lady." But the rest descended into single sentences and then single words. Nothing that made any sense. Whether the poison had made him incoherent or the pain of torture, she saw nothing that might give any hint of whose orders he had been following.

The final words on the page, halfway down were "Please. The root." Then there was nothing more. She dropped the paper back on the table and stepped back, rubbing her hands down her skirts as though she could wipe the sense of Sevan's desperation from her body.

"Sophie?" Cameron said. "Are you all right?"

"Lord Scardale, I would prefer you to read the papers yourself before you discuss anything with your wife," Lord Castaigne said.

"And I don't care what you prefer," Cameron said. "My wife is distressed."

She swallowed, struggling for composure. She didn't want to

break down. She wanted this to be over with. For it to be over with, Cameron needed to read Sevan's testimony. Then they would answer Lord Castaigne's questions and leave. "Cameron. It's all right. *I'm* all right."

The blaze in his blue eyes told her he knew she was lying. Lord Castaigne would know as well. But, if he did, he made no move to relieve her distress in any way. "Do as he asks," she said, raising her chin. "Then it will be over."

Cameron watched her a moment longer, as though reassuring himself that she wasn't hurt. Then he reached for the papers. The minutes while he read seemed to stretch interminably, the room deathly quiet other than the sound of paper rustling as he let each page fall back down to the table when he was done.

As the last one fell, his mouth twisted as though he felt the same distress she had. He backed away from the table and put himself between her and the truth seeker.

"There's nothing in there that makes any sense to me," he said, directing the words to Lucien.

"Nothing?" Lord Castaigne's tone was skeptical.

"I recognized the names he mentioned," Cameron said. "His cousin. His father—I think."

"Yes," Sophie agreed before Lord Castaigne could swing that cool green gaze in her direction. "Those were the only two names I knew. And there are two lines that come from temple services." She repeated what they were. "The rest...the rest meant nothing."

"Not even the last?" Aristides asked.

Sophie shook her head. "No. I'm sorry but no."

Lord Castaigne's eyes narrowed. "You have no idea at all?"

She forced herself to meet his gaze. "I suppose it could have a religious meaning to him. Sevan was a devout man. To him a tree would be the symbol of the goddess. Perhaps the root could have something to do with that. But it's not a term commonly used in our observances in Anglion."

"No," Cameron agreed. "It's not. Perhaps you could ask the

dominas here if it has any significance. But I can't tell you any more than that, and I imagine Sophie can't either."

Lord Castaigne's expression eased. "Thank you for telling the truth, Lord Scardale. What you have said is consistent with the other Anglions. So it corroborates my conclusions."

Sophie let go of a breath she hadn't realized she'd been holding.

Aristides's lips thinned. His mood did not seem to be improved by this turn of events. "So we know nothing more about whoever was controlling Mestier Allowood than we did at the beginning." He tilted his head at Sophie. "It seems I owe you an apology, Lady Scardale. I promised you answers. Which I cannot provide. Not yet." His gaze flicked toward Lord Castaigne, and Sophie's lungs tightened again. If the emperor demanded, the other Anglions could be questioned—or tortured—further despite this truth seeker's decree that they had not been involved.

"No one could have foreseen that Sevan would die, Your Imperial Highness," she murmured, hoping it was a suitably soothing statement.

"Do you not want to know who wants you dead, Lady Scardale?" Aristides asked.

"Of course, I do. I want the truth. However, Lord Castaigne has said he does not have that for us tonight."

"Yet," Aristides corrected.

Sophie shook her head. "You cannot torture a truth from a man who does not know it, Eleivé. If you believe your Lord Castaigne can do as he says, that he knows the truth when he hears it, then you must believe what he is telling us now. That the other Anglions do not know. You must let them return home."

"To carry the tale of the failure with them. If whoever was controlling Mestier Alloway learns of that tale, what will they do next?"

She lifted her chin. "Perhaps they will realize that I am no threat to them while I am here in Illvya and leave it at that."

He shook his head. "Do you really think that is likely?"

"I do not know. But if James and the barron return and report that I am consorting with Illvyan mages, then I will be tainted in the eyes of most Anglions. That must surely reduce whatever threat whoever is doing this thinks I may pose."

"Perhaps," Aristides said.

"We can only hope, Eleivé."

She didn't know if he would share that hope. Not if he still wanted an excuse to invade Anglion. But she wanted him to see that she preferred to be left in peace. It might not sway him but...she had to try.

"It grows late, Your Imperial Majesty," Cameron interjected. "Was there anything else you needed us for? My wife needs her rest."

"Your wife is not the one recovering from an injury, my lord," Aristides retorted.

"Yes," Cameron said blandly. "I need my rest, too."

The emperor's eyes flicked toward Imogene. "Major du Laq tells me she wishes to take you away to her estate for a time."

"Yes, your Imperial Majesty," Sophie said. "It is most generous of her to invite us. I would like to see more of Illvya."

"You wish to go?" Aristides pursed his lips. "I am not sure it is wise."

Sophie's heart sank. Would he refuse? Keep them hemmed in here in Lumia? Did he suspect that they may try to run?

"Our estate is quite safe," Imogene said. "It hardly seems likely that any Anglion agents would be able to follow Lady Scardale there. Our people would be quick to notice strangers."

Sophie tried to ignore that part. They would deal with how they might get away—if they chose to leave—when they got to Imogene's estate. The more important thing was to convince Aristides to allow them to go. "It would be nice to get to know the country beyond Lumia," Sophie said. "As it seems likely we will be staying awhile."

"Is that a polite way of saying you have had enough of the capital and politics, Lady Scardale?"

"I'm not sure there's a polite way to answer that question, Eleivé," Sophie replied, lifting her chin, and sending him the sort of smile she used for court banter. She didn't want him to think she was overly eager to leave.

Aristides smiled. "And what will Maistre Matin have to say?"

"If you give permission, then I'm not sure he can say anything," Imogene said. "I'm not proposing to kidnap his Mackenzies for months, just to give them a few days away from Lumia. Henri can wait to continue their education."

The emperor made a vague noise of agreement. "I suppose that you will continue to ask me until I agree?"

"You know me, Eleivé," Imogene agreed with one of her brilliant smiles. "So, you may as well say yes."

The emperor snorted. "What about you, Lord Castaigne? Are you sure you will not need the Scardales again?"

The truth seeker shook his head, blond hair gleaming in the lamplight. "I believe my work is done, Your Imperial Majesty. There is nothing more for me here."

Aristides still didn't look pleased, but after a long moment, he nodded. "So be it. Imogene, proceed with your plans. Just keep me informed."

CHAPTER 8

"We need a plan," Sophie said as they watched the carriage the emperor had sent them home in move off down the street. She hadn't been willing to say anything in the carriage—who knew what means the emperor might have to spy on them there—but now they were home. And running out of time. She didn't know exactly what had her feeling so uneasy, but the sensation had only increased with each passing minute since they'd left the palace.

Cameron reached for her hand. "Sophie, love—"

"We need maps and clothes and—"

"Sophie, slow down."

She tugged her hand free. "No. We don't have time. Imogene could arrive in the morning and want to sweep us away. We have to be ready."

He frowned, then gestured toward the front gate. "This isn't the best place to discuss this."

"I know. But we're running out of time. We need a map. You go to the library and—"

"We don't even know where the estate is," Cameron objected.

"Then we'll ask. We have the perfect excuse." She headed for the door, not waiting to see if he followed her. The first person she saw in the hallway was Willem, seated on a bench near the door, nose deep in a textbook of some kind. "Willem! Just the person I need."

She summoned a smile as the boy looked up. "The Duquesse du Laq has been kind enough to invite Cameron and me to visit her estate. Do you think there might be a map of it in the library? I'd like to know what sort of a place it is. So I can bring the right clothes for whatever we might do there." She hoped Willem didn't remember that she and Cameron had arrived virtually empty-handed.

Willem snapped his book closed. "Yes, my lady. There are atlases in the library that show many parts of Illvya and the empire." His brow wrinkled. "The du Laq holdings are north from the city. I'm sure we could find something." He focused his gaze on Cameron. "Do you want to go now, my lord? It's not yet that late."

"Perhaps—" Cameron started to say, but Sophie interrupted.

"Yes, he does." She pushed Cameron in Willem's direction. "Go on."

"No, he doesn't," Cameron said, a growl edging the words. Willem looked slightly alarmed, and Cameron softened his expression as Sophie glared at him, willing him to do what she said.

"Willem, I will meet you there," Cameron said eventually. "I will need to fetch a notebook from our rooms. I won't be long. Come along, Sophie. I don't want to keep Willem waiting."

He hooked an arm through hers and set off, leaving her little choice but to go with him. They made it back to their rooms in record time, and Cameron closed the door with a firm thump.

"You need to take a breath, love," he said. "Or tell me why you're suddenly in such a rush." His eyes widened. "Did you have another vision?"

A vision? "No."

"Then tell me. Do you definitely want to try and get away when we're with Imogene?"

He didn't sound sure. Was she crazy? Rushing where there was no need? Perhaps she was, but insanity didn't trump the anxiety coiling through her. "I think we should, yes."

"Do you want to tell me why?"

"It's just a feeling," she admitted.

"A feeling about what?"

"A feeling that if I asked Aristides if he intended to see me on the throne of Anglion in front of Lord Castaigne, and he said 'yes,' then Lord Castaigne wouldn't find that to be a lie."

"I didn't hear him say anything that makes me think he's about to act immediately. And he was angry about Sevan. If he didn't let that sway him, then he strikes me as a man who takes his time."

"So you think I'm wrong?"

"I don't know," Cameron said. "But if this is what you want, then I'm willing to try. But even if we can get away—and there is no guarantee of that—they may find us. Bring us back. That might leave us in a worse position."

"Or we might get away. If we can stay hidden long enough, then Eloisa will lose interest. If she loses interest, then Aristides has no reason to move against her."

"There are a lot of 'ifs' in all of that."

"I know. But unless you are determined not to try, then I think we have to. Which means you should go meet Willem. And I should find luggage." They'd arrived with their belongings in two small bags. And while they may indeed have to sneak away from the du Laq estate with the same two bags, they couldn't arrive there with only those.

"Luggage?"

"Trunks. That kind of thing. They won't suspect that we have anything in mind if we arrive with more trunks than two people could possibly carry."

Cameron's mouth twitched. "You realize we probably don't own enough clothes between us to fill that many bags?"

"That's my problem. Maps are yours. So go. For all we know, Imogene could arrive in the morning and want to leave. Tonight might be our only chance."

"Are you having second thoughts about this?" Cameron asked, not sure what was causing the hesitation in Sophie's voice. Their departure for the du Laq's estate had been delayed a few days when Imogene had claimed she had business to attend to. She had then dragged Sophie off to the clothiers for yet more clothes provided by the emperor. An apology Aristides had said, for the attacks they had endured. Cameron had spent time with a tailor himself. Between them, they would have no trouble filling a pile of luggage big enough to satisfy Sophie's plan.

Their spare time between that and lessons had been spent in the library, trying to learn more about the countryside around the du Laq's estate along with more of the geography of the empire, and holed up in their rooms, having long discussions about options. Sophie had become more and more tightly wound with each day that passed, though she put on a good face whenever they weren't alone. She had seemed near-desperate to leave. But now, as they were finishing packing before their departure in the morning, she was oddly reluctant.

"No-o-o...." Sophie met his gaze but her hand twisted nervously in the skirt of her dress.

"That doesn't sound like certainty. We don't have to do this. We can go with Imogene, enjoy a rest in the country, and then come back and deal with what comes next."

Her mouth twisted. "It's just...." She trailed off again, looking down at the trunk at her feet.

"Just what?" he prompted.

"You'll think I'm being silly."

"Sophie, love. You are many things, but silly is not one of them." Maybe that wasn't strictly true. When he'd first become aware of Sophie at court, when she'd been one of the laughing, decorative, noisy group of ladies-in-waiting surrounding Eloisa, he'd assumed she was like most of them, a girl with fashion, romance, and ultimately, marriage on her mind.

The life the court ladies led was geared toward amusement. Not through any fault of their own, he saw now, but because the court at Kingswell didn't offer many options for high-born women. Even amongst Eloisa's ladies, the impression he'd formed of Sophie was of a young woman more quiet and serious than some of the others, but she'd still been part of the fizz of smiling females who served the crown princess. He had been focused more on Eloisa than any of the women who surrounded her all day.

But now he knew her. Every day, knew her deeper. Learning her in his bones. She had a keen sense of humor; she enjoyed herself when she could—even though there had been scant opportunity for that since they had married. But she was the opposite of silly. She was serious. Focused.

"Tell me," he said gently.

"Imogene has been kind to us. I know we don't owe her anything, but we will be leaving her to deal with some nastiness when we leave." Sophie flipped the trunk closed, and sat on it, shoulders slumped.

He hadn't expected that to be the objection. Guilt? Was that all there is. "I think Imogene is more than capable and can take care of herself."

"I don't want to make more enemies."

"Neither do I. But the Illvyans will be unhappy if we leave. We can't change that. So it has to be a price you are willing to pay." He moved behind her, pressed his thumbs into the tense lines of her shoulders. "I will admit, when we first were invited, I hoped it might be a way for the two of you to become closer. You should have friends."

"I have friends here. Lia. And Willem."

He didn't think that was quite the same. She'd been part of a band of women at home. He didn't know which of the ladies she'd been particularly close with, but she had to miss them. The students at the Academe that she was starting to form friendships with were nice, but they had less in common with Sophie than someone like Imogene. Sophie was part of the royal line. She knew aristocrats. She knew courts. She knew how they worked, even if Illvya was an unfamiliar one. Imogene also knew court life and its intricacies. But perhaps that was not to be. Nor would their connections to any of the people they'd met in Illvya get a chance to develop into something stronger. They'd be leaving them all behind.

"I'm not sure Imogene would want to be my friend anyway," Sophie said. "Any more than I'm certain we can fool her for long once we are alone with her. She's smart. Intimidating."

Another emotion he hadn't anticipated.

Not because the description of Imogene was incorrect, exactly, but Sophie had served a princess who'd become a queen. Eloisa had never been a shrinking violet. A mere duquesse shouldn't daunt anyone who'd served her.

"Intimidating how?"

"She's just... so sure of herself. She's a mage, she's beautiful, she's one of the emperor's favorites. She's one of *those* women." She waved a hand irritably. He pressed his thumbs deeper, willing her to relax.

"Those women?"

"Good at everything they do. All the time. Like Beata. No faults."

Lady Beata Talley, Eloisa's chief lady-in-waiting was a formidable woman but hardly without faults. She was far too fond of rules and her position for a start. Imogene du Laq didn't strike him as being the kind of stickler Beata was either. "I'm sure Imogene has plenty of faults," he said.

But he understood what Sophie meant. Imogene was

extremely competent. But most of the women at the Academe were extremely competent. Illvya gave its women room to excel at more things than marriage and motherhood.

"There are plenty of people who would say you are very good at everything you do, too," he said.

"Me?" Sophie craned her neck around, eyes wide. "I've done nothing but make one mistake after another. I broke the one rule I was supposed to follow, ruined everyone's plans for me, nearly got killed—twice—and had to flee from my country to live with our deadliest enemies."

None of those things were her fault. But she blamed herself, he knew. And he didn't know how to ease her guilt.

"To be fair," Cameron said, trying to ease the mood. "If you have to flee from Anglion there aren't many other places to go to other than toward our deadliest enemies."

She twitched out from under his hands, turning on the trunk to fix him with an irritated glare. "It's not funny."

"Not funny that we only have deadly enemies everywhere else in the world? It is somewhat funny, if you stop to think about it." He hadn't really, before now. Back home, the fact that Anglion needed to be protected at all costs from the empire had seemed like a matter of life and death. But really, repel all invaders was a ridiculous policy for an island kingdom. Once upon a time, when Anglion had had water mages of their own, perhaps it made sense. But now, without the strength that sanctii could add to their defense, if Aristides really wanted Anglion, Cameron couldn't see any way that the Anglions would be able to stop him.

"*You're* not funny," she said grumpily.

"You are. And that is only one of many things you do so well," he countered. "You're an earth witch. And a water mage. You formed a bond with me that no one quite understands. You've been a model student in a new country where you barely spoke the language. You have the respect of your teachers, and you've attracted a sanctii to your side. You're the woman who an emperor looks at and sees a potential queen."

Her eyes turned flinty. "I rather suspect the emperor sees a pawn."

"And is he right about that?"

"No." It was nearly a snarl, and he smiled.

"Well then, if Aristides doesn't intimidate you, I don't see why Imogene should."

"I didn't say he didn't intimidate me, just that he was wrong."

"He's human. So is Imogene, I'd imagine. You're more than a match for her. Besides, she has no reason to suspect we want out. If she did, she wouldn't have invited us."

"Aren't you concerned about what advantage she might be trying to gain from us?"

He nearly smiled. Sophie liked to think she didn't play political games, but she didn't miss much. He shrugged. "Maybe she isn't trying for anything. Maybe she is offering genuine kindness."

"Which we will reward by using her." Sophie sighed. "But I doubt it's that simple. She will be considering all the angles to getting to know us. It's what you do when you have her rank and her position. So we can't assume she wants nothing from us."

"No, but I'm not sure what we have to offer her in terms of advantage—not to mention that we won't be around to be used —so I don't think you should worry about that. It's not as though she can do us any harm while we are her guests. The emperor didn't take it kindly the last time someone tried to hurt us."

"Maybe he's the one who wants us out of the way," Sophie muttered. "And it's more convenient to have us vanish in the countryside."

"It seems a convoluted way to go about it. He could have disappeared us at any point up until now if that was his endgame. Besides which, he has a purpose in mind for you. He needs to keep you safe."

"Until he realizes that I really don't want to be queen."

"We'll be gone by then."

She looked unconvinced. "There are other people who want me out of the way. Imogene could be in league with one of them. The crown prince, for instance. He seems to despise me. He practically dragged me across the dance floor at the ball to make me dance with Sevan."

"Alain is a troublemaker. The kind of eldest son who makes his father wish for a change in birth order." Cameron agreed. "But Sevan failed, and the emperor has made it clear that you are under his protection. I don't think Alain's likely to try anything. He's not as smart as Aristides, as far as I can tell. And he knows he has siblings who could replace him if he stepped out of line. Besides he's past thirty."

"What's that got to do with anything?" Sophie asked.

"They stuff us full of military history in the guard," Cameron said. "If a prince is going to try to overthrow his father, he usually tries to do it quite young. Older men who try for power are usually not directly in line for that power to begin with."

"Men like Imogene's husband?" Sophie said.

"I've heard no rumors that the duq is anything but loyal. Aristides isn't a tyrant or a bad ruler. Illvya has relative peace and stability. Why would the duq risk his current position?" He plucked Sophie off her perch on the trunk, gathered her into his lap on the end of the bed. Her body was tense in his arms, but she didn't try to wriggle free. "You can think of a thousand problems to worry about, but you'd do better to focus on what we want. We go with Imogene. We spend a few days working out the best way to leave. Then we leave, if that's our final choice."

She shivered. "You make it sound easy."

"It may not be. But so far, we've mostly succeeded at the hard things. I have faith in us."

～

When the sound of the carriage changed from the soft swish and rumble of the paved roads to the crunch of gravel, Sophie jolted awake.

"You dozed off," Cameron said as she lifted her head from his shoulder, blinking groggily.

Damn. She sat up, stretching surreptitiously to ease the stiffness in her neck. How long had she slept? So much for her good intentions to pay attention to their route along the journey.

They had left Lumia shortly after dawn. She'd managed to make polite small talk with Imogene as they'd rattled away from the Academe, but her stomach had churned with guilt and anxiety. The Academe was the closest thing she currently had to a home, and she might never see it again. Never see Henri or Madame Simsa. Or Tok. Or any of the others who'd been so kind to them.

They'd stopped along the road at a *calle*, as the Illvyans called an inn, to break the journey and have something resembling a light second breakfast. She remembered climbing back into the carriage again but then. . . nothing. "I'm sorry. That was rude of me."

But Imogene, seated opposite, merely smiled. "Further proof that you need the rest we can provide."

"We should thank you again—" Sophie began to say, but the carriage began to slow.

"Thank the goddess, we are here," Imogene said, shifting forward on the seat. "Welcome to Sanct de Sangre."

Sophie pulled back the shade from the window—Cameron must have closed it while she had been sleeping and peered out. She'd prepared herself for a grand house, but the building that confronted her was closer to a palace.

Pale gray and white stone formed towers and wings and arched rows of windows. A flag, bright gold with a sea blue star above a red heart supported by two gauntleted hands, fluttered over the massive portico. The duq's coat of arms, presumably.

The house itself was too large to reveal much of the grounds around it from the carriage's current angle, but there were definitely gardens on either side, bleeding into woods and hills in the distance. She knew from the maps they'd found that several small towns and villages were somewhere beyond those hills. Whether or not they would be able to get to one of them was another matter. As was the question of whether any of them had portals. Cameron hadn't found any sort of guide to portals beyond the city.

The house drew her attention back, the sheer size of it demanding focus, as they came to a halt on a strip of blinding white gravel opposite the portico that sheltered the front door. Sophie shielded her eyes from the sun and tried to count the windows to get some idea of exactly how big the house was. But she lost count when the front doors opened and a small army of servants, clad in a more subdued version of the blue on the flag, marched out and headed to the carriage.

The man leading the charge wore a long jacket in the same blue and matching trousers rather than the breeches the servants wore. The jacket was frogged in gold and silver, suggesting seniority, and his straighter-than-a-flagpole posture hinted that he might have been a soldier many years ago when his hair hadn't been gleaming white as it was now. He stopped a few feet away from the carriage and began directing the others with a brisk series of orders.

Men moved to hold the horses, others to gather the luggage, and the final two, who were dressed only a fraction less magnificently than the man—what was the word in Illvyan, a seneschal? —giving the directions stepped up to the door, one unfolding the steps and the other swinging the door open before stepping back to hold it in place.

At that, the white-haired man stepped up to the door and bowed. "Welcome home, Your Grace," he said and held out a hand.

Imogene rose from her seat, took the proffered hand, and descended from the carriage briskly. "Barteau, how good to see you." She turned back to the carriage and waved a hand. "These are our guests, Lord and Lady Scardale."

"Lady Scardale." Barteau bowed deeply, then straightened and held out his hand again. Sophie, after Cameron made no move to go before her, rose and allowed herself to be helped down the stairs, blinking against the brightness of the day. Barteau guided her to Imogene's side, and then turned and bowed again.

"Lord Scardale," he said as the soft squeak of carriage springs and a crunch of gravel told Sophie that Cameron had joined them. Barteau stepped back to allow the other two servants to raise the stairs and close the door once more before he inspected the luggage racks as though to satisfy himself that nothing remained to be removed, before issuing another order to the driver who urged the horses forward in response. The carriage began to roll away. The servants carrying their small mountain of luggage were disappearing in a neat procession back to the house.

Sophie had spent much of the past three days being fitted and poked and prodded and more than once accidentally jabbed with pins. Helene had presented her with more than a week's worth of clothes-day dresses and evening gowns and riding habits and such—with the promise that more would be awaiting her when she returned. Another thing to feel guilty about. Hopefully Aristides would still pay the clothier if Sophie didn't return to collect the fruits of Helene's hard work.

Somewhere carefully buried in one of the trunks were the small bags she and Cameron had arrived in Illvya with. They'd fill those with what they could when they left, including some of the trims from Helene's beautiful dresses. Lace and gold work and beading was expensive. They could sell it to help fund their flight.

But as much as she was dismayed by the thought of the gowns going to waste—and somewhat concerned by the underlying message that Aristides thought she needed a much grander wardrobe—the part of her ingrained in the need to put on a display in court was glad she wouldn't be wearing plain gray wool and cotton while spending time with Imogene. Who had brought with her more trunks than Cameron and Sophie combined.

As the carriage turned out of sight around the house, Barteau brought his attention back to them. "Your Grace, His Grace is inside. He was finishing up some business when the outrider came with the message you were arriving."

"Of course he was," Imogene said, but she sounded happy, not annoyed. "Did you prepare the Lily Room for our guests?"

"Yes, Your Grace. All is ready."

"Excellent. I don't know what I would do without you. You go on ahead, I will show our guests the way."

The seneschal smiled, bowed, and then turned on his heel and strode away.

Imogene took a deep breath, shaking out her skirts, while regarding the house with a look of deep satisfaction. "I propose that we go inside, refresh ourselves, have lunch, and then we can enjoy the rest of the day."

"That sounds perfect," Sophie said. The meal they'd had at the calle felt like a distant memory. Cameron was looking around, getting the lay of the land, as was his habit in any new place, but he smiled his acquiescence.

"Then let us proceed," Imogene said. She set off across the expanse of white gravel, moving at a brisk pace. In her deep pink dress, she stood out against the house like some sort of exotic plant in a formal garden. But no doubt she was part of the landscape here.

Sophie studied the house as they followed Imogene, trying to take it in. It had four floors in all, and she counted at least thirty windows across the front of the second floor before they got close enough that she would have had to crane her head back to keep counting.

Clearly a house built to awe and intimidate. It was also a

house built over a ley line, she realized as she stepped onto the steps leading up to the door and power thrummed deep below her feet. Perhaps if she had been paying more attention, she would have felt it earlier. But there was no time to do more than register the ley line's presence as Imogene ushered them inside.

The entrance hall—though hall seemed too small a word— was as grand as the house's exterior. It was roughly circular with doors to the left and right. The latter stood open, revealing glimpses of a corridor. At the point of the circle opposite the front door, a double staircase rose, gleaming white marble stairs and bannisters curving around and up in an elegant arc.

After all the color she'd grown to expect in Illvyan buildings, the stark white—only accented by the sun falling through a round window at the peak of the dome room—was dramatic. A frame for whoever stood in the hall to greet guests.

Certainly Imogene's dress and the blue of the footmen's livery, stood out. As the initial dazzling impression settled, Sophie noticed that the walls—also white—weren't as plain as they first seemed. There were carvings running in fine bands up to the base of the dome, which was also paneled with carvings. She couldn't make out the detail from where she stood, and it would be rude to make a closer inspection. Perhaps she would get a chance to satisfy her curiosity later.

Before she could decide exactly how she might go about that, the door to their left opened. Imogene turned as a veritable giant of a man strode through, his dark clothing and hair making him stand out like a roiling storm against the white marble.

"Imogene, you have returned to me," he boomed as he crossed the room and bent to kiss Imogene's cheeks before embracing her.

She laughed as he released her. "How could I stay away? Every minute without you is endless."

That made him laugh—an inside joke perhaps. Sophie recognized the expression on Imogene's face as she smiled at the duq.

And the one he gave her. There was love between them, not just affection and alliance.

"But we are being rude. You must greet our guests." Imogene turned back to Sophie and Cameron, gesturing the duq forward. He closed the gap between them in two long strides.

"Sophie, my husband, the Duq of San Pierre," Imogene said. "Your Grace, Cameron and Sophie Mackenzie, Lord and Lady Scardale."

Sophie stared up at the man, momentarily lost for words. She had never really thought about what Imogene's husband might be like, but she hadn't been expecting this mountain of a man. His Grace, Jean-Paul du Laq, Duq of San Pierre had to be close to seven feet tall. Well, perhaps not quite that. But he beat Cameron, who was well past six feet. And, while Cameron was broad-shouldered and strong, the Duq was a veritable wall of muscle topped with dark hair that looked like it would curl wildly had it not been caught back in a queue, and deep gray eyes that reminded her of the color of a sword blade.

Formidable. That was the word that immediately sprang to mind. Maybe it came from having generations of ancestors who must have helped the various emperors build their empire, cutting down enemies and riding off to battle in far-off lands. That had to favor the survival of the biggest and strongest men born into the family. Men who had built and held this vast house, and the no doubt equally extensive holdings that surrounded it. Men of substance. And size.

The duq did nothing to make himself appear smaller. Which was only to be expected of a man of his rank. He filled the space he occupied in the way she was familiar with from the higher nobles in the Anglion court. But there was an extra edge to Jean-Paul. Illvyan duqs held military ranks and the man held himself like a soldier, his alert stance akin to Cameron's.

A silvery scar carved a line down the right side of his face—in the process somehow only improving the rugged handsomeness of it—so she had to assume he had taken that duty seriously and not stayed out of the line of fire. Not a man to underestimate. Another complication to factor into their plans.

"Your Grace, I am very pleased to meet you," she managed, recollecting herself. Imogene smiled a smile that was close to a smirk, amusement clear in her blue eyes.

"And I you, Lady Scardale." The duq returned in a voice that brought to mind low, rolling thunder. Deep and musical. Commanding. "My wife has told me much about you." He turned his attention to Imogene a moment, a smile that was skirting the edge of wicked flashing across his face as he gazed at her.

Imogene's smile widened and she raised one eyebrow. Sophie couldn't help smiling at the two of them, taken again by their obvious delight in each other. Imogene had spoken of being fond of her husband, but Sophie had assumed they had still married for convenience or political ambition and perhaps that affection had grown from that. If that was the case, then it was clear that Imogene, like Sophie, had been a winner in the marriage lottery. If, of course, the Duq was as pleasant on the inside as he was on the outside. And if the emotion they were displaying was real. It was always possible that the two of them were brilliant actors, their show of harmony honed over years of palace intrigue. But somehow Sophie didn't think that was the case.

"I must apologize, then, Your Grace. That must be extremely dull," she said.

The duq's attention came back to her. "On the contrary, Lady Scardale. Your adventures are quite...diverting." One side of his mouth lifted lazily. It only emphasized the fact that Imogene had chosen a very handsome husband. One who obviously knew how to use charm when it suited him.

But at court, one learned not to trust charm for what it appeared to be. And Sophie wasn't sure she liked his tone. Or that she should trust a man who thought that kidnapping attempts, assassination plots, and sanctii were diverting, no matter how much he might seem to be in love with his wife. Something to remember. She needed to keep her wits about her.

"I'm sure they have been exaggerated, Your Grace," she said.

"I hope not," he said, smile broadening. He turned to Cameron. "Lord Scardale. It seems you have been blessed, as have I, with an interesting wife."

"I count myself fortunate for it," Cameron said neutrally.

"Better than someone only interested in clothes and embroidery," the duq said, and Imogene rolled her eyes.

"Name me one woman you know who is only interested in clothes and embroidery," she said dryly. "Really, Jean-Paul, you will make the Scardales think you are a clod-mannered military oaf."

"Am I not?" Jean-Paul grinned.

"That remains to be seen," Imogene said tartly. "Be nice."

"My apologies, Lady Scardale," Jean-Paul said, though he didn't sound contrite. "I was only teasing."

"No apology required. Thank you for the invitation to stay," Sophie said, falling back into the safety of court manners. "Your estate is beautiful."

His smiled turned from amusement to genuine pleasure. "It is our honor to welcome you here, my lady. And thank you. Sanct de Sangre—both the house and our land—has been in my family for generations, and we are proud of it. But I'm sure Imogene will give you the full tour." He bowed briefly. "Unfortunately, I have business to complete this afternoon. Please, make yourselves comfortable and I look forward to getting to know you both better this evening."

"As do we, Your Grace," Sophie said. Which earned her another slightly unnerving smile.

The Duq stepped forward and kissed Imogene's cheek. "Until tonight, wife."

"Yes," Imogene said. "Go do your dull duq things so that we may enjoy ourselves later." Dimples flashed in her cheeks as she smiled up at her husband.

"And you try not to succumb to the temptation to bore our guests with your pet projects. Show them around. Perhaps you should go for a ride. It's a beautiful day." He nodded his head again at each of them and then turned on his heel and strode off.

Imogene watched him for a moment. Then turned back to Sophie in a swirl of skirts. "Do you ride, Sophie?"

"Yes, I do." She rose up on her toes a little, unthinking. The thought of getting out into the countryside they'd traveled through in the carriage and feeling space and air around her was tantalizing. More importantly, a ride would be a starting point to exploring the estate and how they might leave it. Her gaze traveled to Cameron. Who probably should be resting. He was still recovering, and if they did get a chance to run, he needed to be as healthy as possible. He would never say he was tired and leave her and Imogene to ride on their own through country he didn't know, no matter how many grooms or household guardsmen the du Laq's may have to accompany them. So perhaps it was safer to stick to the plan. Play at having nothing more on their minds but relaxing as they got the lay of the land. "But maybe tomorrow? I'm somewhat tired after the journey. And I would love to see the house and gardens first. They look so beautiful."

Hopefully Imogene was as proud of Sanct de Sangre as her husband seemed to be.

To her relief, instead of looking disappointed, Imogene looked delighted at the prospect. "Then a tour it should be. But first we must get you settled. And eat. Our cook here costs me a fortune, but she is worth every penny. I stole her away from the Marquioness of Ferrier, and she still hasn't forgiven me."

That remark could have fallen from the lips of any of Sophie's friends amongst the court ladies back home in Anglion. Sophie's smile froze as a stab of longing pierced her. Oh to be home. Or even, to be here under no false pretenses and perhaps just spend time with Imogene. Make a new friend. But that was not to be.

If she didn't want to fall into line with Aristides's plans, then she had to make her own move. Get away.

Imogene was part of the emperor's court—and one of his confidantes. It would be a mistake to trust her and cruel, perhaps to befriend her only to betray her trust. But it was tempting. To simply try to *be*. To enjoy the moments as though there were no greater concerns in her head than what dress to wear to the next ball and whether Imogene's home was suitably impressive.

"My mother always said a good kitchen is the key to a happy home," she said, trying to push down the whirl of competing emotions. "I don't think she ever had need to lure a cook away from another position, but I don't doubt she would have done so in a heartbeat." A small exaggeration. The Kendall estate wasn't a grand one, and the servants were more like family. Their cook had been firmly in charge of the kitchen for as long as Sophie could remember, and it would take something truly dire for her parents to replace her. Not least, because her food was delicious.

"Good meals definitely help keep husbands happy," Imogene said, slanting a glance back at Cameron. "And it doesn't hurt to have the best to make all your friends jealous." She grinned. "All while feeding them such delightful meals that they can't risk annoying you in case you cut them off from their supply of lemon cake. My husband would write poems to our cook's lemon cakes if he had a literary bone in his body. Speaking of which, we should feed yours. If he is anything like me, then he must be starving after that journey. As you must be."

"I am," Sophie admitted. "So, by all means, let us eat. And then you can show us this glorious house."

CHAPTER 9

S everal hours later Sophie wished she hadn't been quite so enthusiastic about a house tour. Not that the house wasn't magnificent, but it was magnificent and *huge*. Her feet were beginning to ache as Imogene led them down yet another staircase, opened yet another door and announced, "The ballroom."

Sophie stopped a few steps into the room, dazzled, aching feet forgotten.

The ballroom's walls were huge mirrored panels. Everywhere she looked, her reflection looked back, a thousand dizzied Sophies, looking startled. Unlike the ballroom at the palace, there was no break in the mirrors. They covered the walls from floor to ceiling. She tried to imagine the effect when the room was full of people moving and dancing and couldn't decide whether that might be beautiful or overwhelming.

It would be spectacular but must also feel like being surrounded by an endless press of people. The thought made her uneasy.

"The servants hate this room," Imogene said, sweeping a hand at the mirrors. The movement, echoed by the Imogene reflected in each glass pane, was like a ripple in the world.

"If I had to clean all that glass, I'd probably hate it too,"

Sophie said, lightly, trying to focus on the real person, not the images. "It reminds me of the ballroom at the palace."

Imogene sniffed. "Yes. They copied this from what I've been told. But showed more restraint."

"It's—"

"Somewhat overwhelming," Imogene said before Sophie could finish her sentence. "Not precisely my taste. The ballroom was renovated by Jean-Paul's grandmaman at hideous expense. It was a marvel of its time, to have so many flawless mirrors made. I don't dare suggest we change it." She studied her reflection, lifting a hand to pat a loose curl back into place. "But that doesn't mean I don't do my best to cover some of the mirrors when we host a ball."

"It must be spectacular by lamplight," Sophie said tactfully.

Imogene smiled. "As long as one hasn't over indulged. Then it tends to make one feel a tad seasick." She glanced at Cameron who stood behind Sophie. The mirrors showed Sophie his politely interested expression. He'd been politely interested for most of the tour, asking the odd question about paintings or sculptures or strange artifacts but mostly letting Sophie and Imogene talk uninterrupted. She assumed he was trying to fade into the background so he could study the house, but she feared Imogene would think he was bored.

"But we mustn't continue boring Cameron," Imogene said, confirming Sophie's fear. "This room is also one of the quickest ways to get a good view of the rear gardens." She crossed the room, heels tapping on the intricate parquet floor. It was only when Sophie got closer to the far wall that she realized a section of it was made of mirrored doors. Imogene pushed two of them open.

"Come," she said over her shoulder. "We've spent enough time indoors."

Sophie agreed. After Lumia, the fresh-scented country air was nearly intoxicating. The immaculate gardens that she suspected lay beyond the doors weren't exactly virgin country, but they were uncrowded by buildings and people. Her view of earth and sky and plants would be uninterrupted. She hadn't been an earth witch long, but she'd been raised in the country, and she missed it. Even without the pull of the ley lines and all the growing things, she would have been eager to be outside.

She stepped through the doors onto a paved terrace.

The movement and colors of the tiles caught her attention, and she paused to admire the artistry that had created the elaborate floral mosaic. Then she lifted her head, saw the view laid out before her, and gasped.

The gardens of Sanct de Sangre were vast. Immediately before them, formal beds and hedges circled statues and fountains, bisected by pathways that traced precise lines and curves around them and the perfectly green grass. These flowed into lawns and rows of tall trees that offered glimpses of woods nestled at the base of hills. The placement of the groups of trees seemed too perfect to be natural. Had it all been sculpted by human hands?

How long must that have taken? She'd seen some beautiful gardens before—the palace at Kingswell had served generations of earth witches after all—but this one was breathtaking. How many gardeners—and earth witches—did the du Laq's command? And if these were the gardens, what was the rest of the estate like?

And just how big was it?

How far to the nearest town or village? Too far to go on foot in a night, to get away in the space of time they might have before they were missed?

She didn't look at Cameron. It was too soon to panic. They would think of something. There would be a way. For now, she should focus on Imogene, find out what she could from her.

"Imogene, this is astonishing," she said, sweeping her arm at the vista. "I've never seen anything like it."

Imogene's smile widened. "Thank you. The grounds might be my favorite part of the estate. The du Laq's have had quite a few earth witches in the family, and most of them seem to have a talent for gardening. When Jean-Paul's grandmaman wasn't buying acres of glass, she was most often ordering a small battalion of gardeners about."

"And you? Do you continue that tradition?" Growing up on the estate with her mother—an inveterate gardener beyond the need for the herbs and vegetables that filled their kitchen gardens or the crops that grew in the fields—had instilled Sophie with a definite fondness for gardens. Though the Kendall's rambling flower-and-herb-and-vegetable-filled garden probably would have fit a hundred times over into the grounds here. Of course, the du Laq's could hide the rambling purposeful parts of the garden such as herb and vegetable gardens out of sight.

"I do my best. Jean-Paul has more talent for gardening than I," Imogene said. "But it is not something he has much time for."

"I would imagine not," Sophie said. If she had grown up in a place and family as elevated as the du Laq's, it was unlikely her parents would have had anything to do with the grounds beyond discussing plans with the stewards and servants who would do the actual work.

It was difficult to dispute the path the goddess set for you, but maybe Jean-Paul would have been happy as a gentleman farmer or gardener.

"This way," Imogene said. "We will head toward the stables."

Their progress wasn't fast. Sophie kept stopping to admire the beds of flowers, the statues, the ponds and streams and fountains. The ley line ran through the garden, and the combination of the strength of its power and the life force of all the plants made her senses tingle.

"The earth is strong in you," Imogene said, pausing beside her. "You have that distracted look out here. Jean-Paul gets the same way."

"He has earth magic?" Sophie asked, startled. She hadn't

made the connection when Imogene had mentioned the duq's fondness for gardening.

"Some. Some blood as well. He is not particularly strong in either, but the du Laqs make up with brains what they lack in magic. And they tend to marry those with power where they can."

"Was your marriage arranged?"

Imogene laughed "No. We were quite the scandal. We met at court, a few years after I first joined the Imperial mages, and that was it. At least for us. Jean-Paul's father was less convinced. I think he may have preferred a daughter-in-law without a sanctii."

"He didn't approve of water magic?"

"He had someone else in mind, I believe. There were objections. And my family was nothing special. We were comfortable enough but not of the nobility. The du Laq men have sometimes married witches and commoners in the past but rarely water mages. To be fair, there are less female water mages to begin with."

"There are?" Sophie hadn't realized. Between Madame Simsa and Imogene, she hadn't noticed a lack of female water mages.

"Yes. And fewer of those, as it is with the men, who choose to attempt a sanctii bond."

Was it rude to ask more? But Imogene was offering the information freely. "What made you decide to—" She wiggled her fingers in the air.

"To bond?" Imogene said. "I wanted to advance as a diplomat in the Imperial mages. I had no talent for blood magic or the Arts of Air to speak of, but a sanctii is an asset in an army."

"Yes," Sophie said. "And did you see the empire?"

"I saw my share. But then I met my husband. He was happy for me to stay in the service, but I didn't want to leave him for weeks or months at a time, so I stopped going on diplomatic missions. But the emperor has found me useful, and I have found other interests in the service to keep me busy."

Interests like the navire d'avion that Imogene had showed them in the palace? "Perhaps you should have been an engineer, not a soldier." To imagine a ship that sailed on air as the navire was intended to do, required an engineer's brain, surely?

Imogene flashed a smile. "My father *was* an ingenier. Eventually he owned one of the largest firms in Lumia. But he didn't travel much. He stayed home and ran his business. I wanted more than that. Or I thought I did. I seem to be becoming more my father's daughter these days. A Mage ingenier. Though still a solider, I suppose. Not quite the duquesse anyone expected, I think. But Jean-Paul held firm against his family. Thankfully his father came to like me well enough before he died, and Jean-Paul became the Duq."

"A successful outcome from a difficult beginning," Sophie said, stroking the leaf of a cirrus bush, feeling the small pulse of life force in the plant.

"Yes. Something I think you have some experience with?"

"Some," Sophie agreed. She looked at Cameron waiting for them about thirty feet away. She didn't want to discuss exactly how he had come to be her husband with Imogene. "But we should go on."

Imogene tilted her head toward Cameron. "Lord Scardale is an impatient man?"

"No." Sophie shook her head. "But I would like to see more of your estate. Enjoy the time we have here." The more ground they could cover, the better.

"We'll head to the stables, then," Imogene said. "The best way to see the outer grounds and the estate is on horseback." She paused, eyeing Sophie's dress. "I know we said we'd ride tomorrow, but can you manage in that rather than a habit?"

"Yes. My habits are cut for me to ride astride, but I can use a sidesaddle in this." The gown she'd changed into was one of Helene's simpler designs made of fine dark blue wool. It should stand up to a ride. "But I would like to see how Cameron is feeling. He is still recovering from the accident." Not that she thought that would stop him. Stubborn man.

Imogene nodded, then called to Cameron. "Lord Scardale, do you think you could manage a short ride? I don't want to waste this lovely day. But only if you are not tired from our journey."

Cameron raised his eyebrows and started walking toward them. "I'm fine, Your Grace. My wife worries over much.

Imogene looked pleased. "Good. The stables are this way."

The stables were no less grand than the house. Indeed, the large building looked as though it had been built from the same stone. Four wide sets of doors marched across the breadth of its front wall, standing open to the warmth of the day. Their elaborate brass handles sparkled in the sun. From inside came the sounds of horses and murmurs of voices.

"Is your sanctii close by?" Imogene asked, halting before they stepped onto the stone paving that surrounded the stables.

"Elarus?" Sophie realized she hadn't thought of the sanctii's whereabouts since they had left Lumia. "I don't think so, why?"

"Some of the horses are nervous around sanctii. Including two of our prize stallions."

"They're not used to Ikarus?"

"He generally stays unseen if he is anywhere near me when I ride. My own horse doesn't mind him, but it's kinder not to frighten any of them needlessly."

"I can ask her to stay away," Sophie said. At least, she hoped she could. Hoped that Elarus had followed them, as she had agreed to do. The bond between a water mage and a sanctii was supposed to be unbreakable—other than by large bodies of salt water such as the sea that lay between Illvya and Anglion. But the knowledge Elarus had gifted her told her that huge distances strained the bond and made it chancier that a sanctii might hear their mage call for them. Most water mages, from what Sophie could tell, made sure that their sanctii moved with them, though Sophie wasn't entirely sure how that worked. But they would need Elarus's help when they left. Better to know she was close.

"That may be wise." Imogene said.

[Elarus, are you here?]

[Close,] came the reply. [Need?]

[No. I'm fine. But Her Grace would prefer you to stay away from the stables.]

The sound that came next in her head was definitely a snort. [Don't need horse.]

[Nevertheless, horses can be scared easily. Please don't go in there.]

The next sound was closer to a sniff that seemed to suggest that if Elarus wished to see the stables she was perfectly capable of avoiding terrorizing the horses. [Horses not interesting. Do not need to see their house.]

That gave Sophie pause. What exactly *was* Elarus finding interesting on the estate? If indeed, she was within the grounds. Close was somewhat of an indefinable concept when sanctii could blink in and out of sight and place in an instant. But if Elarus was engaged in exploring the estate, Sophie had to trust she would be careful. Elarus knew that Imogene had a sanctii. Hopefully that would stop her from doing anything that might cause offence or trouble.

[Thank you. Perhaps we can speak later.]

[Perhaps.] Elarus said, the tone almost amused, which only reminded Sophie again of her need to understand their bond better.

"She will stay away," Sophie said to Imogene. Cameron, standing behind the duquesse, raised one brow. Perhaps he hadn't been considering Elarus's whereabouts either.

"Thank you," Imogene said. She led them to the second door from the right of the stables and into a long corridor lined with stalls. Horses poked their heads over the doors, watching them approach. They looked sleek and expensive.

Rows of long narrow windows sat high in the walls and also ran along either side of the beamed roof, giving enough light for her to see the horses' eyes turning toward them, ears flickering with curiosity. Huge lanterns, currently not alight, hung between the rooftop windows and an earth stone sat in a sconce next to each stall's doors.

They weren't more than a few feet into the building when a man wearing a version of the du Laq livery more suited to the stables—buff breeches, long boots, and a loose coat and shirt in the family blue—came striding up to meet them.

His dark hair was graying, but his face looked young as he smiled and bowed quickly to Imogene. "Your Grace, welcome home."

"It is good to be back, Norris," Imogene replied. "In fact, I find myself eager to see how things have gone along since I was here last. Can you saddle Pom for me, please? And this is Lord and Lady Scardale. They need mounts."

Norris fixed dark brown eyes on them. "My lord, my lady, welcome to Sanct de Sangre. Do you ride often?"

"Often enough," Cameron said. He glanced down at Sophie. "But perhaps it would be best to give us a couple of your quieter horses. That way everyone can be at ease."

It was the right response, judging by the smile that quirked Norris's mouth. "As you wish, my lord. Your Grace, if you go through to the mounting yard, we'll be with you shortly."

Their progress down the stable was slow. Imogene stopped to scratch the noses of the horses who whickered for her attention as she passed, telling Sophie and Cameron about each of them as she fed them lumps of sugar. The sweet steamy grassy smell of the horses was a familiar one that brought another pang of homesickness to her throat. She pushed it away, focusing on Imogene's words.

By the time they reached the far end of the stable and walked back outside, Norris and two other grooms stood waiting for them with three horses. Norris held a massive gray with a white nose and a matching white star. The horse stretched his neck forward and snorted at the sight of Imogene, dancing in place, which earned him a quick murmured "wait" from Norris. The other two—white-footed bays several hands shorter than the gray—didn't make any fuss.

Imogene went to the gray and patted his neck. "Pom. Behave, you wretch." She looked back over her shoulder. Pom snorted again, tossing his head.

"He doesn't look much like an apple," Cameron observed.

Indeed, the name seemed unsuited to the giant horse who gleamed with health, the shine of his coat outlining every muscle. Mountain, perhaps? Or something aggressive and masculine like Cannonball or Steel.

"He wasn't always this big," Imogene said. "When he was born, he was quite scrawny and his star"—she reached up to scratch the round white mark on Pom's forehead—"looked quite like an apple. So we called him that. It stuck. We didn't know quite what to expect from him back then. His dam was a warhorse. We bred her to one of our stallions but then discovered her in her field the next day with another—one of Jean-Paul's racers who was quite the escape artist back in his day. Meaning we had no idea who this idiot's father was at first."

"I take it, it was the warhorse?" Cameron asked. The horse flicked an ear in his direction, then pulled his head down to nudge Imogene's pocket.

"No, he's actually smaller than he should be if that were the case." Imogene produced a sugar lump and gave it to Pom. "And not nearly mean enough. Besides, he's the spitting image of the racer. He was one of the few grays we had at the time. When this one's coat began to lighten, it solved the mystery. Jean-Paul was quite irritated. It's not a cross there is much demand for. But Pom and I got along, so I kept him."

Smaller than he should be? The horses the Red Guard rode in Anglion were bred for strength and speed, but they weren't as large as Pom. She tried to imagine a whole squadron of men mounted on horses even bigger than the gray charging as one toward an enemy. A frightening image.

She glanced at Cameron, but if he was thinking along the

same lines, he gave no sign of it, his expression admiring as he
watched Pom. It was silly to be worried about Illvyan warhorses
anyway. The scariest thing in any Illvyan force attacking an
enemy would be the sanctii, not the horses.

"But enough about this reprobate. He will be better for some
time out stretching his legs." She held out a hand to Norris who
handed her Pom's reins. "Norris, why don't you introduce Lord
and Lady Scardale to their horses?"

Norris did just that. Sophie was brought over to the smaller
of the two bays. Norris had obviously noted her dress and the
bay wore a sidesaddle. "This is Chennei, Lady Scardale. He won't
give you any trouble."

The Illvyan vocabulary in her head informed her that
Chennei was a type of tree. She had no mental image to go with
the word, but if the horse was named after a tree, she hoped it
was a good sign that he was the solid and sensible type. She
spent a minute or two getting to know him, feeding him an apple
Norris gave her, then allowed the groom to help her into the
saddle.

Imogene and Cameron mounted—Sophie had heard the
groom tell Cameron that his horse's name was Samuel—and
Imogene nudged Pom forward. The gray moved off eagerly, and
Sophie barely had to touch her heels to Chennei's sides before
he followed. Imogene kept Pom to a walk and then a trot as they
moved clear of the stable yard and headed away from the
buildings.

When they passed into a section of the grounds that was
more park than gardens, Imogene let the gray have his head. The
resulting gallop through the grounds was exhilarating. Sophie's
horse gave no sign of wanting to race, though he was keen
enough to run with the others, and he responded to her slightest
touch of hand or leg so she was able to relax and enjoy the sheer
thrill of speeding over the land with nothing but the pounding of
hooves beneath her and the wind in her face filling her head.

Eventually the horses slowed, Pom apparently having worked

off enough energy to be happy to continue the rest of their tour at a more sedate pace.

The day was sunny and warm, and it was pleasant to ride through pretty countryside and listen to Imogene tell tales of life here. She had seemed such a creature of the court and the city back in Lumia that it was hard to reconcile the understanding of Imogene she had gained there with the mistress of the estate on display here. But Imogene was clearly proud of Sanct de Sangre and the life that she and Jean-Paul provided for the people who lived and worked on their lands, and the facts and figures she was providing about the estate seemed to roll readily off her tongue.

Cameron joined in the conversation, but Sophie could see he was paying close attention to their route. They passed fields and woods but nothing like a village. Not even much hint of a road bigger than a cart track.

They rode for maybe an hour before returning. Grooms appeared as soon as they had clattered into the mounting yard, but Imogene waved them away, slipping down from Pom with ease. Cameron dismounted, handed his reins to a groom and then came to help Sophie off Chennei's back.

He looked happy after the ride and kissed her fast before turning back to take his horse. "Show me where his stall is," he said to the groom. "I like to see to my own horses."

The groom's eyebrows lifted, and he glanced past Cameron to Imogene, who nodded.

"These three are all stabled close together," the groom said. "If you'd follow me, my lord."

Sophie surrendered Chennei to a second groom but followed along behind Imogene and Cameron. Settling the horses back in their stalls took time. Imogene stayed with Pom and spent a few minutes brushing him. Sophie did the same. She'd taken care of her share of horses growing up, and the familiarity of the task was soothing.

By the time Imogene appeared in the doorway of Chennei's stall, he was more interested in the contents of his feed trough than with Sophie's ministrations. She left him to it and joined Imogene outside the stall. Cameron was still in with Samuel; she could hear him murmuring to the horse and laughing softly.

"He like horses, your husband," Imogene observed.

"He does," Sophie agreed. She hadn't known quite how much. The most time she and Cameron had spent together with a horse had been when they had fled Kingswell after the attack. Not exactly a pleasure ride through the country. "He grew up in the north. There are long distances to cover up there. And they breed good horses." She glanced toward the stall where Cameron was. The ride had been enjoyable, but she was eager to talk to her husband and find out his thoughts on what they'd seen. "Should we get back to the house?"

"No. Let him have his fun. Jean-Paul would say it's a good sign that a man insists on taking care of his horse."

"So would my father. My mother too, I think." Sophie stretched cautiously, trying not to wince. As much as she had enjoyed the ride, now that it was over, her body was reminding her how long it had been since she had been on a horse. Come to think of it, the most exercise she got these days was walking the halls of the Academe. Perhaps she should ask to join the blood mages' training classes. They seemed to be keeping Cameron in shape nicely. She however was definitely out of it. She was going to be sore in the morning, if not by dinner.

"Are you feeling stiff?" Imogene asked. "Was the ride too long?"

"Not at all," Sophie said. "I enjoyed it thoroughly. But yes, I confess that I am feeling it now. I haven't ridden in some time."

Imogene made an apologetic face. "I'm sorry, I should have thought. I was enjoying myself. It has been over a month since I last was here. You can bathe before dinner. That will help."

"I look forward to trying out that tub in our suite," Sophie said. "I think I could swim in it or near enough." The suite that Imogene had given them was several times larger than the rooms she and Cameron shared at the Academe and about a hundred times more luxurious. The bath was enormous. More than large enough to soak every aching muscle she might possess and Cameron's at the same time.

"I may have something even better than that," Imogene said with a smile.

"That is hard to imagine," Sophie said.

Imogene's smile widened. "You don't need to imagine." In the distance a bell began to chime, and her smile faded. "But perhaps that will need to wait until tomorrow. I hadn't factored the ride into my timing for this afternoon, and you will scarcely have time to bathe and change for dinner as it is." She turned to face Cameron. "Lord Scardale, I assure you the grooms will take good care of the horses. And they will be here in the morning if you wish to ride again. But we must return to the house."

Cameron came out of the stall, his expression reluctant. Enjoying himself, Sophie thought. Stealing a moment of peace before they had to upend their lives once more. Perhaps imagining what their lives could be. A house in the country, tending the land, and raising a family was the sort of dream she'd always had for her life after marriage. The sort that Cameron might have also imagined for his life after he retired from the Red Guard. If they ran, it would a life nowhere near as grand as Imogene's, but perhaps they could still find a smaller, simpler version of those dreams.

She hoped so.

But to get to those dreams, they needed to get away. So they had to survive the next few days here with Imogene without giving themselves away

Starting with dinner with the Duq.

CHAPTER 10

"My lady, could you turn your head to the right, please?"
Sophie obeyed Mari's request, turning her head to the left to give the maid better access, and tried to hide her impatience with the whole process. She'd only had a few minutes alone with Cameron before Mari had arrived to help her dress for dinner. Not enough time for him to say anything more than he needed more time scouting the estate before they could make a move. So they would continue on. Be proper guests.

After being at the Academe for weeks, she had gotten used to wearing simple clothes and doing her own hair—though she mostly left it to do whatever it pleased—and not having servants to help her dress or be present most hours of the day. Compared to the fishbowl experience of being one of Eloisa's ladies, where there was rarely any time unobserved by servants or guards or both, she'd found it a relief. A return to something closer to how she had grown up.

Simpler was easier.

But there was nothing simple about the deep green bead-encrusted gown that lay in a carefully laid out gleam of satin across the bed where Mari had placed it after bringing it back from being ironed and steamed. Nor was there anything simple about the intricate structure of curls that Mari had spent more than thirty minutes already on coaxing Sophie's hair into.

Anglion women favored braids and curls, often wearing their hair long, but Mari had pulled a face when Sophie had suggested leaving her hair down and Sophie, recalling how Imogene and the other ladies she'd seen at the emperor's ball had worn theirs, had decided it would be wisest to give the girl free rein.

Now, staring at herself in the mirror while attempting to keep still as Mari wielded heated iron tongs with total concentration, she hardly recognized the woman in the mirror. Mari was talented. As elaborate as the style was, Sophie had to admit that her hair looked beautiful. Every curl and roll and tuck seemed to highlight the deepening red shades of Sophie's hair. She could barely see any of her original brown left. No one would be left in any doubt that she was an earth witch now.

Mari pinned the curl she had been working on into place with a satisfied sort of noise and then stepped back and turned away to place the tongs over the tiny brazier she was using to heat them. Sophie tilted her head to get a better view of her hair and then froze. There. Just below her right temple where the hair usually hidden from view was exposed by the elaborate curls. Was that a patch of...black?

She leaned closer, not quite daring to touch the spot in question in case she ruined Mari's work. But, no, it wasn't a trick of the light. There was definitely a darker patch of hair, the color beginning to flare from the roots.

Her heart began to pound. But why?

She'd seen Chloe de Montesse's hair. She'd seen Imogene's. She knew what happened to the hair of men and women who wielded water magic.

She'd known this would happen to her eventually. Silly to be surprised.

But, as she analyzed the emotion coursing through her, she recognized not surprise, but fear. Apparently she was still Anglion at heart. Because her instinctive reaction to seeing the signs of water magic—something that would see an Anglion woman exiled or worse—beginning to stamp themselves on her body made her tremble.

There was no hiding what she had done. No hiding the choice she had made. Like the red glow from her earth magic, once that black streak lengthened and was joined by others, no one could mistake her for anything other than what she was. She shivered, then tried to ignore the fear. It didn't matter if people knew she was a water mage here in Illvya. Illvyans didn't care.

"Are you cold, my lady?" Mari asked, turning back with newly heated tongs in hand. "I'll be finished in a minute and we will get you into your beautiful dress, but I can fetch you a shawl if you need one now."

Sophie took a breath. Nothing to be afraid of. She had chosen this. Become a water mage to keep herself safe. She would use that same magic to get herself away from Aristides's grand plans. She had to be what she had chosen. "I'm fine, thank you," she said firmly. "Finish your work."

Cameron paused as they reached the door to the parlor where one of the servants had ushered them. Sophie, at his side, stopped beside him. She tipped her head up to him carefully— not wanting to dislodge her artfully arranged hair he imagined— one eyebrow lifting as though she was asking him why he'd hesitated. The truth was, he wasn't entirely sure.

He'd been looking forward to dinner; the ride and the time outdoors had left him starving. And the tea they'd found waiting for them back in their suite hadn't really done much to fill the hole in his stomach. The time on horseback had left his still healing ribs twinging, and Sophie had insisted on trying some of the earth magic healing she'd been learning on him while they'd had a hurried discussion. It had mostly eased them, but then the damned maid and valet had appeared and their preparations for dinner had turned into an elaborate ritual, which didn't give him enough time to think.

He'd bathed and shaved and been fussed over as the valet helped him into clothes the man had selected, all while he'd been trying to think how he could get to see more of the estate. Find their route out. The best he could come up with would be to try and charm Jean-Paul into taking him on a tour in the morning. Hopefully the man was a hands-on sort of landowner rather than one who sent his stewards out with orders.

By the time Sophie had reappeared, gowned in green with her hair piled high, he'd been ready to gnaw one of his arms off, his gut churning with both hunger and nerves.

Though the sight of her had been a distraction, a different kind of hunger roaring through him to temporarily quell his stomach.

Helene Designy deserved every penny of whatever the emperor had paid her to produce Sophie's wardrobe practically overnight. The green satin dress was the color of the deepest heart of an unfurling leaf. A secret, subtle, shade that made Sophie glow.

Her skin gleamed golden, the arch of her neck bared by the way her hair had been piled into curls coiling around her head. The gown plunged low, hugging her torso and emphasizing her breasts. She wore a simple fine gold chain and the bronzed pearl earrings he'd given her on their wedding night.

Beautiful. Beautiful enough that he'd wanted to tell Imogene and Jean-Paul that dinner could wait and haul her off to bed.

But he'd controlled the urge. Limited himself to one hard, fast kiss, careful not to spoil the effort she had made in dressing. He'd seen her dressed in court finery more times than he could count, but tonight she seemed to have reached a new level of beauty. Maybe it was the touch of sun on her skin or the shade of the dress. Or maybe it was knowing that this could be one of the last times he'd see her in such a gown. They wouldn't be consorting with nobility if they left. They would find a quiet, backwater sort of town and live simply.

But to get there, they had to get through this dinner. He had to build a connection with Jean-Paul. Imogene was one thing, but her husband was another entirely. The man was an unknown quantity. Powerful. Rich. Ambitious. A man who was, perhaps, not entirely unlike Cameron's father.

So, maybe not completely unknown after all. Though, it was to be hoped that Jean-Paul had some of the redeeming qualities Cameron's father had lacked. But still, Cameron was the son of an erl and now brother to one. He knew better than to keep a powerful host waiting. Too many of them would take it as an insult.

He hoped that Jean-Paul might prove to be different, but his aim was to make the man like him, not antagonize him. So why was he hesitating in the doorway now like a raw recruit called in front of his commander?

In truth, he had no idea. Maybe it was reluctance, after the afternoon of freedom, to step back into the fray, and focus on protocol and position while trying to understand yet another unknown Illvyan who could prove to be friend or foe.

Of course, when he had been a raw recruit back in the Red Guard, his squad leaders, sergeants, and everyone else at each step up the chain of command had relentlessly drilled one thing into their skulls.

That information could keep you alive.

That informed decisions were often better decisions.

That yes, sometimes there was no way or no time to get good intelligence before you could act, and in those moments, you just had to throw your dice and hope the goddess smiled.

But at all other bloody times, the soldier who was prepared— the one who took a moment to think things through and gathered intelligence where he could—was more likely to live. Of course, they also spent a lot of time teaching him to obey orders without hesitation. The two things hadn't always gone hand in hand, but he'd learned both lessons. There was no one here to give him an order, which left him with using his head. Starting with walking into this room and trying to get to know Jean-Paul du Laq.

"What shall we toast to?" Jean-Paul said more than an hour later as Sophie settled herself into a chair at the vast dining table in the du Laq's lavish dining room.

So lavish they were actually outnumbered by the servants— four footmen and Barteau himself—who were moving sound-lessly around the room, filling water glasses and wine goblets with precise and practiced movements. The dining room was not mirrored like the ballroom, but there was enough gold and gilt and silver to glitter in the lamplight and reflect the images of the men in their blue livery onto unexpected surfaces. Sophie looked up from where she'd been caught by one of the reflections in the gold-filigreed candlesticks in front of her to smile politely at Jean-Paul.

"The emperor is the usual way of it, my dear," Imogene said from across the table. She was seated next to Cameron and across from Sophie who was on Jean-Paul's right.

"What the emperor doesn't know won't hurt him," Jean-Paul said with a smile.

It seemed a jest. But Sophie didn't know the man well enough to know for sure. She hoped it was. The last thing they needed was to land themselves in the middle of some wrangle between Jean-Paul and Aristides.

"Behave or I'll have Barteau cut off your wine," Imogene said, lifting her glass. "You don't want the Scardales to think you were raised by wolves."

Jean-Paul laughed at that. "Not many would argue that my father didn't have a touch of the wolf about him. Scary when he showed his teeth. But, all right, wife. I'll behave." He raised his own glass, the delicate goblet looking small in his huge hand. "To Aristides. Long may he reign."

"To Aristides," they all echoed. Sophie took a cautious mouthful of the straw-colored wine. Imogene had already pressed several glasses of campenois on them while they had waited to go in to dinner. There had been small tidbits of food to go with the wine but not enough to soak it up. She needed to eat before she drank much more if she was to keep her wits about her.

She'd no sooner had the thought than a footman appeared on her right and placed a small plate in front of her. It held an array of exquisitely arranged vegetables. Not exactly the sort of food to soak up excess wine, but no doubt it would be the first course of many if the du Laqs ate the same way the emperor did.

She selected the correct fork and began to eat. Several courses followed in rapid succession. Soup. Then fish. Then lamb with an unfamiliar red berry sauce. Then a tartly herbal sorbet. She managed to avoid drinking more than a sip or two of wine with any of them.

When the next course was placed in front of her, she had no idea what the food on it actually was.

"Have you not had periven before, Sophie?" Imogene enquired as Sophie regarded the pale green china set before her dubiously.

The shape of the...object...on it looked something like a large quail or small pigeon. If one had removed their legs and wings. But quail or pigeon didn't come coated in a hard, red shell like the kind that coated the kessil crabs fished along the southern coast of Anglion. Though crabs had legs and segments in their shell that offered some sort of access. She raised her gaze to Imogene. "No, I haven't. I don't think we have it in Anglion."

"You're in for a treat, then," Imogene said. "It's a delicacy. They're found only on certain parts of the eastern coasts. It takes a long time for them to grow big enough to catch. Luckily they can be transported live or we'd never get to taste them here.

They're something like a lobster but even better." She picked up the large knife by her right hand. "There's a trick to getting into them, though." Her head bent as she studied the creature as though mentally dissecting it.

"Or there's the easy way," Jean-Paul said.

Sophie turned her head to him. "And what would that be, Your Grace?"

"Simple. You just have to be ruthless, Lady Sophia." He grinned at her, picked up the periven, and tore it in two with one determined wrench of his hands. The pieces hit the plate again with a thud. The scent that rose from the gently steaming white flesh revealed in the shell was not that different to crab.

"It smells delicious, does it not?" Jean-Paul said, dipping his hands into the finger bowl immediately presented by the closest footman and then drying them off.

"Really, Jean-Paul," Imogene said, pointing her knife at him and wagging it disapprovingly. "You're not in a barracks now. I'm sure Sophie wasn't raised to eat like a soldier."

Jean-Paul shrugged. "Maybe she should try it. If Aristides wants to put her on a throne, she's going to need to learn that ruthless has its place."

Sophie's jaw tightened. They'd come to Sanct de Sangre to avoid this conversation. "The emperor has no need to interfere with Anglion. I don't think I'll be wearing a crown any time soon."

Jean-Paul shrugged. "My lady, I hope for your sake—for all our sakes, as it would avoid a war—that is true. But Aristides is the living definition of ruthless when he sets his mind to something. If he sets his mind to your country and its throne, you would be wise to learn from him."

"Does power always have to be ruthless?" Sophie asked, curious as to what the duq would say despite her dislike of the topic. Though, pursuing it in this direction at least led away from Aristides's ridiculous proposal. And the fact that she wouldn't be taking any part in it. Jean-Paul was a soldier. A nobleman. He'd grown up in an empire, not a small island country. He had a wider perspective than hers.

Jean-Paul's expression turned contemplative with a hint of approval. As though he appreciated the question. "I think power has to be prepared to be ruthless, to maintain its hold. To make those who wield the power believe in it. It can't be ruthless all the time or ruthless only to serve the interests of those who hold it, or it descends to tyranny and madness. But sometimes a ruler must make decisions that will inevitably harm some while benefitting others. They have to ensure those decisions are accepted. In peace, perhaps this is a quality rarely called upon, but I don't think we're talking about peace here, are we, Lady Sophia? If Aristides acts, it will be war. It might be short. But war, nonetheless. War is about survival."

She didn't want war. She didn't want any of it. Perhaps Jean-Paul was right. She needed to be ruthless to get what she wanted. "This war would be about greed, it seems to me. Illvya and the empire don't need Anglion. And, it's Sophie, not Lady Sophia."

He tilted his head. "Is it now? But I agree, we don't. Which makes me wonder exactly what game Aristides is playing. My emperor is not a stupid man, my lady. If he does this, he will have good reason to think it is the right path to pursue."

"I'm sure there are those who would call him a tyrant. Him and his family." She saw Cameron frown slightly but lifted her chin, even as she wondered why she was baiting Jean-Paul. "They have taken what belongs to others."

"But they rule fairly," Jean-Paul countered. "And your queen's family did the same. Took the crown. Cut your country off from the rest of the world because of a belief—or fear—perhaps. That takes a large dose of ruthless in itself." He considered her over his glass, the deep red of the wine casting splashes of red light over his face, the shade too close to blood for comfort. "You have some of that blood in your veins. So perhaps you won't need to work very hard to find some ruthlessness if you need it."

Across the table from her, Cameron had gone still, one hand resting on the knife beside his place, eyes fixed on Jean-Paul. Her husband, she knew, could be ruthless when he wanted to be. When he was protecting what was his.

But right now was not the best time to demonstrate that fact.

Right now, they were supposed to building an alliance of sorts, if they could. Cameron wanted more information out of Jean-Paul. Information they needed. She put down the fork she hadn't realized she was still holding and picked up the periven. With one quick twist, she dismembered the poor thing, much as Jean-Paul had. "I'm generally considered to be a quick study, Your Grace," she said with a smile, letting it fall back to her plate precisely as he had. She smiled, not turning her head as the footman offered her a bowl and towel for her hands.

The laugh that echoed across the room as she wiped her hands clean, broke whatever tension there had been floating over the table between the two men. Cameron blinked and eased back in his chair, looking down at his own periven. Beside him, Imogene lifted her glass in a small toast, tilting it in Sophie's direction.

Sophie's head was pleasantly fuzzy from the wine and the excellent food. The dinner, after Jean-Paul had decided to drop politics as a topic of conversation, had been delicious and, she thought, successful. Cameron and Jean-Paul had gotten along, diving deep into a discussion about the estate and what was farmed there. She'd listened with half an ear but also talked with Imogene about the local families and the gardens.

Now, standing by the open windows, looking down at the darkened grounds and breathing in the cool scent of night-damp grass and flowers, sleep seemed impossible. She should be tired after the long carriage journey and the tour of the grounds and riding. It had been quite the day.

But instead she felt a distinct urge to try for yet more physical exertion. There were no other guests. They had virtually the whole of the wing where their suite was located to themselves. The occasional servant might pass by, but there was no one else within earshot. No one next door as there was at the Academe where, despite their aural wards, it was sometimes hard not to be aware of all the other people living under the same roof.

The Academe was similar to the palace at Kingswell in that regard. True privacy had been in short supply.

But not here. Here was the closest that she and Cameron had been to being truly alone at any time other than those few hunted days they'd spent hiding in the countryside after the attack on the palace. They hadn't known each other at the beginning of that time. They had come together in an accident of magic and passion during it. They married after it, still not knowing each other.

But she felt she knew him now. Knew the depth of the man, solid down to the bones of the earth. Rooted like the tree of the goddess. Offering his strength to her when she needed it even though she still wasn't sure why he had chosen to do so. Other than the undeniable fact that there was still magic and passion between them. And from that beginning, their marriage was starting to grow roots of its own, giving them a solid place beneath them forged by everything they had been through.

For everything they were yet to navigate.

Cameron. Her husband. Who would have stabbed a duq without blinking earlier today if he'd decided that was the best way to keep her safe. The girl she'd been back in Kingswell probably would have found that thought horrifying. But now, she found it...reassuring. And very attractive, goddess help her.

Cameron, who would turn his world upside down once again for her when they left.

Cameron, who she loved.

So. It seemed to her that the best use of their time alone, and this perhaps final interlude of luxury and safety, involved the two of them, the ridiculously large bed in their bedroom, and far fewer clothes than either of them were wearing now. She turned away from the window, one hand stroking the chain at her neck.

Cameron sat by a small table where a selection of liqueurs and more campenois had been laid out for them when they'd returned to the room. He hadn't poured himself a glass. Instead he was watching her.

The weight of his gaze across her skin was headier than any of Imogene's wines.

She watched him watching her, hand still moving slowly along the chain, fingers drifting down to where it led toward her décolletage. His eyes followed her movements, the blue of them deepening with each passing second.

She let her hand fall, took a step toward him.

He smiled. "Thirsty? Can I pour you a glass of something?" He swept his hand toward the collection of crystal decanters.

"Not thirsty," she said. Took another step. "I think there's been enough wine today."

"Sleepy, then? It's been a long day." He leaned back in the chair further, tugging at his cravat.

"I find myself strangely awake." She reached up and undid the necklace. Slid the chain from her throat and let it fall to the carpet. "How about you?"

He smiled slowly. "I seem to have found my second wind. So how are we going to occupy ourselves?"

"Right now, I lean toward taking off our clothes and putting that great big bed over there to good use."

Cameron tilted his head, considering. "I think we should definitely get to that part eventually."

Her breath caught. "Eventually?"

"We have the whole night." He patted his lap. "But first, I'd like you to come over here and let me investigate that very distracting frock for a time."

Her pulse was starting to beat heavy in her ears. "You like my dress?"

"I do. Helene is worth every last penny that Aristides paid her."

Sophie swished the skirt slowly. "It's a big dress. That's a small chair. How will I fit?"

"I'm sure we can work something out. The chair feels quite sturdy to me."

"You get to explain to Imogene if you're wrong."

"Imogene can afford all the chairs she wants. And I don't want to talk about Imogene. Or Jean-Paul. Or any Illvyan either of us knows. I want to kiss you. It feels far too long since I did."

"You kissed me before dinner."

"As I said, far too long. And that was deliberately sedate, polite kissing. I didn't want to muss you."

"It didn't feel that sedate." She smiled at him.

"Then imagine how much better it will feel when I'm not worried about mussing you."

She pursed her lips, pretending to think about it. "I don't know, as you said, this dress was expensive. I don't want to ruin it."

"I'll be careful with the dress."

"And with me?"

"Do you want me to be careful?" His eyes seemed blue like oceans, luring her in.

"Not particularly."

His smile widened. "Well, I aim to please. Come here, Sophia. I want to touch you." His voice went low, rumbling through her, setting nerves awake in its path. Her legs felt strange as she walked to him, desire pulsing through her. She stopped when the edge of her skirts brushed the toes of his boots.

He spread his legs wider.

"Closer." Another step had the fabric of her skirt billowing onto his lap.

"If I come much closer, I might smother you."

"Oh, I don't know about that." He grabbed two handfuls of fabric and start easing the yards of fabric up. Soon his hands found her thighs. Helene had included underwear that was a froth of lace and satin and silk. Insubstantial. Designed to be seen.

Designed to be taken off. His hands slid higher. Found the edges of the lace and the ribbon that bound it to her waist and worked it free with a few quick tugs as she stared down at him and his blue eyes burned up into hers.

The underwear fell to her ankles and she stepped out of it as Cameron's fingers began to slowly stroke her inner thighs, sending ripples of heat both down her legs to weaken them and up to pool between her legs.

Her knees began to tremble, and she swayed forward.

"Stay still," Cameron said, his tone low and rough. The sound of it did nothing to help her regain control. But she wanted to find out what would happen if she did as he said, so she sucked in a breath and braced her muscles, fighting not to move.

His fingers moved higher, brushed the crease in her thigh and then paused again.

"Legs wider, love."

She didn't have to be asked twice. She widened her stance. He murmured approval, his eyes dropping briefly as though he wished he could see through the layers of cloth that hid his hands from view. But he didn't seem to need to be able to see what he was doing to wreak havoc with her nerve endings as his fingers drifted oh-so-slowly upward.

Too slowly. She wanted his touch and a small moan escaped her.

"Impatient. I like that," he said approvingly. "But don't move. Or I'll have to slow down."

She bit her lip, fighting the urge to give up the game, tear his breeches open, and ride him, but that would spoil the fun. Cameron smiled and his fingers settled along her inner lips, stroking and skimming but missing the place where she throbbed and ached for him.

"Does that feel good?"

She nodded, wordless as he teased her.

"Let's see if we can make it better still."

She knew the tone in his voice, knew the longing and heat in it, urgent as her own. But as she stared down into his eyes, she felt the lash of heat, spill into something bigger. Something deeper. "Take me to bed, Cameron."

His fingers stilled, eyes not leaving hers, drowning her in blue as always. "Impatient, love?"

"I just want you."

"Then you shall have me. He pulled his hand free, and she moaned again, a small whimper of frustration as he rose, lifting her from her feet to carry her to the bed and set her down at its foot.

His fingers made short work of the tiny buttons that fastened the dress, and he pushed it down off her shoulders impatiently, working at the ties on her petticoats. As the layers of fabric pooled around her knees, leaving her standing in her corset and little else, the air cool on her skin as he shucked his clothes.

Naked, he pressed a kiss into the curve of her neck. "Helene's dress was exquisite, love," he said. He stepped closer behind her, the heat of him palpable even though he wasn't quite touching her. "But you're more beautiful like this." His hand traced down her spine. "So beautiful I sometimes can't believe you're mine."

Mine. The word sank into her skin, blazing through her. She shuddered and felt her knees give way again.

But Cameron's hands caught the sides of her waist, kept her upright. The weight of his cock pressed against her.

"I am," she managed, swaying, trying to get more of him.

"You are. Body and blood. Mine to hold."

"Yours to have," she gasped, pulling him back toward the

bed, desperate for him. To have his arms around her and his body over her. To have him inside her.

He settled himself at her entrance, and the wicked pleasure of it blurred her vision. She bit her lip, focused only on him.

"Yours to have," she repeated.

"Exactly," Cameron agreed, his grip tightening on her hips as he lifted them higher. He thrust home, hard. Exactly as she needed. Showing her she was his. And he was hers. That they were together. That he loved her.

She rocked from the force of it, but his hands held her still—his fingers biting into her skin—and the feel of him sliding so fast and strong into her was dizzying. She moaned, needing more even if the sensation was perilously close to the edge of pleasure.

She shouldn't like it, but she did. Loved the strength and power of him as he worked her. Loved knowing that all that strength and power was driven to such hunger by her, could be brought undone by her as she was undone by him.

The bed creaked beneath her, but she couldn't bring herself to care about Imogene's furniture. There was only Cameron and the power of him as he loved her until she was gasping his name with each thrust and writhing up to meet him as the pleasure built and built pushing her further into the place of only him and only now.

Until finally he whispered, "Now, Sophie," and she crashed through the peak of it to the place where everything went away.

CHAPTER 11

B y the time Sophie and Cameron made it to breakfast the next morning, she was sure they were horribly late. But Imogene was sitting in the sunny room the footman showed them to, reading a letter and sipping tea, a neatly sliced apple on the plate in front of her. In a leafy-green day dress, she looked perfectly relaxed.

She looked up and smiled as they entered. "Good morning. Did you both sleep well?"

"Very, thank you," Sophie said. She pressed her lips together to stifle a yawn. She had slept like the dead when they'd finally slept. But they had only finally slept a few hours earlier.

She took the chair the footman held out for her and then reached for the tea that had appeared in her cup before she had barely settled herself. It was difficult not to drain half the cup in one go. She restrained herself to one large swallow before she resumed conversation. Across from her, Cameron had no such scruples, lifting his cup for a refill already.

She hid a smile. "Has Jean-Paul finished breakfast already?"

Imogene nodded. "The man wakes abominably early. But he'll be back for more tea shortly. He likes to get out in the gardens first thing, then come back and eat again before he deals with whatever else his day holds."

She'd hardly finished her sentence when Jean-Paul strode in. He was dressed simply in breeches, a white shirt, and a well-worn and rumpled dark-brown linen jacket.

"Scardales. Good morning," he said before kissing Imogene's cheek. "Anything interesting in the post, wife?"

She shook her head. "A letter from my sister. Some from other friends. Nothing of note to report in any of them. Tea?"

"Tea and food," Jean-Paul agreed. "Jasmine had her puppies this morning. Six of them. Etienne came and fetched me." He turned to Cameron. "One of our best hunting hounds. Always a relief when the whelping goes easily. Do you hunt, Cameron?"

"I did when I was younger," Cameron said. "There's not a lot of opportunity in the capital, and being in the Guard didn't leave me with much free time."

"Well, that's hunting a different kind of beast," Jean-Paul said. "Depending on the state of politics at any given time, I suppose." He grinned as one of the footmen placed a gigantic plate of buttered toast and bacon in front of him.

"What do you hunt in these parts?" Cameron asked.

"Some deer, some boar. There are a few small predators around that can cause issues. Cats and mere-wolves and such. Though my gamesmen take care to keep those under control. It's not really the season for game at the moment. Everything's in breeding mode. But we could ride out today if you want. Take some of the dogs and let them stretch their legs. See what trouble we can find." He forked up bacon, chewed, swallowed. Washed it down with nearly an entire cup of tea. "Let Imogene and Sophie have some time together to complain about us behind our backs."

Sophie tried not to grin at Cameron. The offer to explore with Jean-Paul was exactly what he'd hoped for. A chance to find a way for them to leave. She drank tea to hide her excitement.

"Have you been doing things I need to complain about

again?" Imogene inquired. "Sophie and Cameron haven't been married long enough to start annoying each other. They're still virtually newlyweds."

"I'm sure you'll think of something, my darling," Jean-Paul said, refilling his tea. "What say you, Cameron? Shall we ride?"

Cameron looked over at Sophie. "Do you mind?"

She shook her head, knowing he was only asking to seem polite. Both of them wanted him to go. "No. You enjoy yourself. I'm not sure I want to spend more time on a horse today." Her body, when she had rolled out of bed had let her know that between the long carriage journey, the riding, and her night with Cameron, she had perhaps, overdone things. Even if some of the aches and pains were the good kind.

"Excellent," Jean-Paul said. "Then let us finish eating, and we can be on our way."

After the men had left, Imogene stacked the pile of mail by her plate, then looked across to Sophie. "I take it from your comment about not wanting to ride today that you are perhaps feeling sore from yesterday's ride?"

"I confess I am. I am out of practice, it seems," Sophie agreed. She soaked for a time last night and this morning, but there not even Imogene's sybaritic bath could perform miracles, it seemed.

"Then I know how we will start our morning," Imogene said. "The boys will be gone long enough. We have plenty of time to enjoy ourselves. Finish your breakfast. I need to take care of a few things with Barteau, but I'll come and find you after that, and we will laze like experts."

Sophie finished eating and then wandered back out to one of the portrait galleries, studying the paintings. They were a lengthy series of large, dark-haired men like Jean-Paul and the women she assumed were their wives, along with various children, horses, huge shaggy golden hounds, and small black curly-haired dogs all posed in various degrees of luxury inside or around Sanct de Sangre. She didn't spot Imogene or Jean-Paul amongst them, but the fashions shown in the pictures didn't look current to her eyes. Perhaps the more recent family portraits were hung elsewhere.

"Admiring the ancestors?" Imogene asked as she joined Sophie before Sophie had made it even halfway down the gallery. Apparently her business hadn't been lengthy after all.

"They are a handsome lot."

"Mostly, yes. Though some of them were thoroughly unpleasant if the history books are telling the truth."

"I suspect that's true of most noble families," Sophie said. "The kind of people who are always meek and mild and kindly aren't the type to seize power for themselves."

Imogene lifted a brow. "I suppose not. But I like to think, on the whole, we do good for our lands and the people who live here."

"I'm sure you do," Sophie said. She nodded up at one of the portraits. "I wonder if they felt they were doing the right thing. They all look so sure of themselves."

"It's a family trait," Imogene said wryly. "The du Laqs, in my experience, do not tend to lack confidence. I could give you a long list of who is who and what they each did, but I'm sure the Academe is already ensuring your head is thoroughly stuffed with more new information than you need. So I will not force the adventures of my husband's family on you. They will keep." She studied Sophie a moment, expression serious. "I know they have taken you in and I understand that you must feel grateful, but you do not need to do everything the maistres suggest, you know. No one can study round the clock, but *they* will let you work yourself into the ground if you're not careful." The emphasis on "they" reminded Sophie that Imogene and the Academe seemed to have an uneasy relationship.

"I have a lot to learn," Sophie said.

"And time to learn it, one hopes," Imogene said. "I can understand your desire to find your feet in a new place—I remember being an eager young student there myself—but you have to pace yourself. The Academe is another place full of people who don't lack in confidence and think they are doing the right thing. They've done their share of manipulating power for what they saw as good over the years, too."

There was a hint of warning in her voice.

"Makes you wonder how many of them were right," Sophie said. "From Jean-Paul's family or the Academe. Or your emperors. Or the Anglion nobles." So many people who had made choices that in turn had affected the lives of thousands-or tens of thousands or more—of others. The weight of those decisions. How did you bear it if it went wrong? How did you decide that you were the one to choose in the beginning?

She couldn't imagine it.

"That's far too complicated a question for so early in the morning," Imogene said. "Jean-Paul's dinner conversation has rubbed off on you. You need the antidote. I shall do my best to take your mind off such things for the next few hours. You came here to rest. Aristides will not be pleased if I return you to the city more exhausted than you left."

He'd be less pleased when she didn't return at all. She smiled to hide the thought. "You're very kind," she said. "And you're right. Rest sounds just what I need."

Imogene smiled. "Then you will enjoy this, I believe. Come with me."

They left the house and entered the gardens, taking a different path to the one they had the day before. They hadn't walked more than one hundred feet when Elarus appeared, winking into existence in the center of the small lawn they were crossing. Sophie stopped short, startled. Then flinched despite herself, when Ikarus appeared behind Imogene as well.

She didn't know how tight a rein Imogene kept on her sanctii —no way of telling if he had come of his own volition or if Imogene had summoned him in response to Elarus appearing.

Ikarus wasn't doing anything overtly threatening—though right then she had to fight down her instinctive Anglion reaction to see it—but his black gaze was fixed firmly on Elarus.

Imogene was watching both of them. And her, Sophie fancied.

Sophie pasted a smile on her face, acting as though nothing was wrong. "Elarus, good morning."

Elarus inclined her head. But didn't speak.

"Was there something you wanted?"

"Looking," Elarus said. "No more."

Imogene made a noise that may have been a cough or a stifled squeak of surprise. Ikarus folded his arms. In the bright morning sun, the darkness of the skin of each sanctii only served to underline their size and strength. Even though both of them stood motionless, there was unmistakably tension between them.

Sophie wasn't entirely sure what to do to ease it. Without really thinking, she sent her awareness down into the earth, trying to locate the ley line. It might do no good at all if the two sanctii decided to clash, but it made her feel slightly better. She reached for a casual tone. Imogene hadn't moved, maybe it was best to proceed as if everything was normal.

"We were just going to..." She paused, looking to Imogene. "Where exactly is it that we are going?"

"The *bain-sel*. To soak those sore muscles of yours." Imogene hesitated, glancing over her shoulder at Ikarus. "But the sanctii don't join us there."

A salt bath? Sophie didn't know what that was. But Ikarus made a grunting noise of agreement at Imogene's announcement.

Elarus tipped her head to the side, considering him. "Wet. Don't need wet."

Ikarus huffed.

Elarus stared at him. There was a long pause, broken only by the sounds of the breeze moving through the trees in the garden and the falling songs of the birds in the branches above.

[Elarus] Sophie said cautiously in her head. [Is everything all right?]

[Yes]. Elarus replied. [Wet no good. I will stay. But I watch.]

Well, that was clear as ash. But for now it seemed a good thing if the sanctii kept to herself.

[All right. We'll talk later, if you like.]

[Yes] Elarus said. Then she vanished as quickly as she had appeared. A few seconds later, Ikarus disappeared as well.

Imogene released a breath in a long careful-sounding sigh. "Sophie, you may need to be careful about that."

"About what?" Sophie asked, still not entirely sure what had just happened.

"With your sanctii doing as she chooses. I had heard your bond with her is different, but it might be safer to retain the illusion of control."

Where exactly had Imogene heard that? "Why? Aren't Illvyans used to sanctii?"

"They are used to water mages with bonded sanctii who appear to be obeying orders. Who *are* obeying orders," she amended. "But Illvyans have a healthy respect for what a sanctii can do. They have heard the stories of sanctii gone rogue, as Anglions have. So it would be more comfortable for everyone if you keep things...somewhat normal."

"That would be easier if I had a better idea what normal was," Sophie said.

"I imagine it would. But we can speak more in the bain-sel." Imogene glanced around as though fearing they might be overheard. "It will be easier there. Come."

She set off at a brisker pace, her green dress swishing over the grass. Sophie followed behind, still confused. The building that Imogene led her to was a long, low box built from the same gray stone as the main house. There were no windows and only a single door painted what Sophie was coming to think of as du Laq blue. It reminded Sophie more of a smoke house or storage shed than anything else, but she doubted Imogene had dragged her across the garden to show her sausages and hams.

When Imogene withdrew a key from her pocket and opened the door, a waft of warm air hit Sophie's face, carrying with it a smell almost like the sea. Curiosity rising, Sophie followed Imogene inside and found herself in a small room, tiled in shades of blue and green, the colors flickering under the light of a bevy of lanterns.

Imogene turned and closed the outer door, locking it again before tucking the key away. Then she pressed her hand to the inner door and Sophie saw wards flare to life beneath her touch.

"Don't worry," Imogene said when Sophie raised a brow. "The servants have a key for emergencies. But this prevents unexpected interruptions. Follow me."

She opened a door in the far side of the room, freeing an even warmer gift of air. The room they stepped into was so unexpected, Sophie stopped where she was, too enchanted to do much more than stare. Communal baths weren't used in Anglion, other than the ritual baths in the temples. But the size of the bain-sel was beyond even the scale of the temple bath where Sophie had been bathed before her Ais-Seann rites.

In fact, it wasn't only one bath. Four—no, five—bodies of water were spaced over the softly sparkling white tiled floor. The largest was bigger than any bath Sophie had ever seen. It had to be nearly forty feet long and half that wide, a rectangle of softly, steaming water that appeared dark blue thanks, she had to assume, to being tiled in that color. At the farthest end of the room, past the large pool, was another square pool about ten by ten feet and closest to where they stood, three, well, perhaps they could truly be called baths, though they were large enough for two or three people to share comfortably. Two of them had towels neatly stacked on their edges, along with baskets holding soaps and various glass bottles. Lanterns hung from the ceiling in rows, the light dancing over the water. The walls were as white as the floor tiles and between the water, the soft layer of steam in the air, and the lanterns, the whole room almost glowed.

"Imogene," she breathed. "This is...magnificent." Or decadent, perhaps. The sort of place where one of the fabled Illvyan courtesans Anglions told tales about might relax.

"It is all rather overindulgent," Imogene said. "But that doesn't mean we shouldn't indulge." She gestured toward the end of the room past the largest pool. "There are two dressing rooms there. You can undress, there are robes if you wish. We wash and soak in the small baths—then you can swim in the larger one if you like. The square one isn't heated. It lets you cool down if you grow overly warm." Sophie was only half paying attention. The thought of sinking into hot water unto her neck sounded so tempting, she didn't want to wait any longer.

"Why don't you go and undress?" Imogene said. "I'll meet you back here."

Sophie did exactly that, disrobing in record speed, glad that she'd insisted that Helene make day dresses and under clothes that she could remove herself. The sort that would be useful when they ran.

She was lowering herself into one of the small baths when Imogene reemerged from the other dressing room, wearing a light muslin robe.

"Not too hot?" Imogene asked as she walked to the bath next to Sophie's, stopping at the other end so she was facing Sophie rather than sitting beside her.

"No." Sophie sank deeper into the water to prove her point. Then decided to go all the way under. She surfaced again, groping for a towel to dry her face, eyes stinging unexpectedly. "Salt water?" she asked when she could see again.

"Yes," Imogene said. She didn't offer any further explanation.

Sophie closed her eyes and leaned her head back against the tiles, feeling the tension running out of her muscles. There were no sounds to distract her other than the lap of the water and Imogene's soft breathing, and she let her mind drift, not wanting to think any more. There would be time enough to think when Cameron returned. It was only when she realized she was in danger of nodding off that she forced herself to open her eyes.

The walls almost sparkled in the flickering lamplight, as though there were tiny crystals embedded in whatever the white material was. "This is lovely," Sophie said. "So peaceful."

"Peaceful and *private*," Imogene said. "That was the reason the bain-sel was built this way."

"This way?" Sophie said. The warmth of the bath was soothing all her aching muscles. And the salt added a sensation of weightlessness to the warmth. The combination was like being rocked in a perfectly soft warm bed and it was difficult to concentrate and not let herself lean back and doze.

"It's not just the water that is salt, Sophie. The walls are made from salt bricks."

Sophie's eyes flew open. "Salt walls?" How? Was that even possible? But she had seen salt transported in large blocks some-times. There was no reason why they couldn't be used for walls in theory. But, in practice, water dissolved salt. "Don't they dissolve in the weather? Or from the steam?"

"Over time, if left alone they would, yes. But the walls are several feet thick and the baths are lined," Imogene said. "It's expensive to maintain, but it's secure. The sanctii won't come in here. More to the point, nobody can send one in here. Not with this much salt. No one can eavesdrop. The emperor has a room lined with salt somewhere beneath the palace. Not baths, a council room. But I've never seen it. Such places are proof against sanctii but not against other forms of espionage or loose tongues. I'm not sure they're of great use for keeping secrets, if you are dealing with large groups of people who might be able to subvert a ward or don't know how to hold their tongues. Nor does the emperor have a sanctii he might wish to avoid from time to time. I suppose if a water mage went rogue, it might come in useful to hide in."

"Do you sometimes want to avoid Ikarus?" Sophie asked, curious. "Don't you trust him?"

"I trust him," Imogene said, with a shrug that sent the water rippling. "But sometimes it is nice to know that you are truly alone." She grinned at Sophie and swiped a hand over her face where steam—or maybe sweat—was starting to bead at her hairline. "Jean-Paul and I come here from time to time."

Sophie hoped the heat already in her cheeks from the bath hid her blush. She wasn't a stranger to women chatting about such things—you couldn't be one of a dozen ladies-in-waiting who lived in each other's pockets for several years without becoming familiar with the way women talked together. But she still didn't know Imogene terribly well. And Jean-Paul, hardly at all. She didn't necessarily want to know about the intimate side of their marriage. She definitely didn't want to talk to Imogene about Cameron in the bedchamber.

"Did Jean-Paul build this?" she asked, waving a hand at the room to change the subject. She reached for one of the bars of pearl-white soap piled on the edge of the bath. Her fingers closed over the bar, but it slipped through her wet hand and flew into the air. Directly toward Imogene's face. Without thinking, Sophie flung out a hand. And the soap...stopped. Not caught. At least not by her hands. Instead, it hung in the air like an unlikely butterfly.

Her mouth dropped open as she contemplated it for a long moment.

A discreet cough from Imogene made her look up.

Imogene's brows were arched, her eyes wide. A minute ago her skin had been as pink as Sophie's from the heat, but now she looked somewhat pale. "I don't think you ever did tell me what happened after the carriage accident." Her tone was very...careful.

"Elarus came. She helped me," Sophie said, too distracted by the soap hovering in the air in front of her to wonder why Imogene was asking. The longer she stared, the wobblier it became until it suddenly dropped into the water with a splash that sent salt water straight into her mouth. She spluttered and coughed. "Damn." She found the soap near the bottom of the bath and held it firmly while she put it back where it had come from.

"Helped you how, exactly?" Imogene asked. Through the steam, her eyes were suddenly intent. A cat watching a mouse she hadn't quite decided what to do with.

Sophie's neck prickled. Weren't they supposed to be relaxing?

"She lifted the carriage." Sophie sank lower in the water. She didn't really want to remember the horrible moment when she'd realized that Cameron was trapped beneath the carriage and that the men who had tried to kidnap her could return at any second and kill them both. The sensation of feeling like a fox in a snare, waiting for the hunters to close in, was one she tried hard to forget even though it seeped into her dreams sometimes. She shivered despite the warmth of the water. "I pulled him free."

"Lifted it herself or by using magic?" Imogene asked.

Sophie tiled her head. "I'm not entirely sure. The whole thing is a blur. Why? Is it important?"

"Yes," Imogene said bluntly. "What you did with that soap...floating it. That is not a common thing. Not for you to do it so easily." She caught her lip between her teeth. "We know sanctii can lift things when they choose, but it is not an ability they can share easily with their mages. Some water mages have been able to move small things in such a fashion with the help of their sanctii. Those who are most skilled usually also have some blood magic. Which makes sense given that it is blood mages who usually have the ability to move objects. But I understand it is quite fatiguing. And usually a skill acquired after many years of practice. Do you have any blood magic, Sophie?"

Sophie blinked. *Damn. And more damn.* She didn't want to tell Imogene her secrets. She had used Cameron's blood magic before. Not intentionally, but she had done it. But she wasn't sure if that was something she should reveal.

"Maybe? I'm not sure." Prevarication. She hoped Imogene wouldn't see through it.

"Or perhaps, if you share an augmentier with your husband, you have it through him?"

Triple damn. Imogene knew too much. Bloody Illvyans. "I've been told that it is possible that I could," she said cautiously.

"Can you lift the soap again?"

She didn't want to try. Imogene's interest was making her nervous. "I don't know how I did it the first time."

"Try to think."

Sophie reached for the soap. Placed it on her palm. Stared at it wondering if she should actually try to do as Imogene asked or not. Perhaps, until she better understood why Imogene was so interested it would be better to not...or to merely give the appearance of an attempt perhaps. But then again, Imogene could see her connection to the ley line, if she wanted. She would be able to tell if Sophie wasn't actually trying to use her magic.

She touched the soap with her free hand, considering before letting that hand sink back into the water. Then stared at the soap hard, reaching for her magic. But she hadn't been lying when she said she had no idea how she had floated it and the soap stayed stubbornly in place even when she tried to direct a careful flow of magic toward it.

She let the soap fall into the water. "It would seem not."

Imogene frowned. "You did it once."

"And perhaps, in time, I might be able to work out how. But not today, it seems." She shrugged. "It's not important, is it?"

"Sophie, you made something hover in the air. Without a sanctii," Imogene said, sounding exasperated. "Of course it's important."

"Why? You said the sanctii could do it anyway."

"They can't do it surrounded by salt water. Or over salt water," Imogene said. "After all, if the sanctii could make things fly through the air over an ocean, the history between our two countries would be entirely different. Anglion, I imagine would either be part of the empire or perhaps ruling it herself."

"I don't understand." She didn't want to understand. Because she was afraid she'd unwittingly stumbled on something that would only make her of more interest to the emperor.

"Flying machines are something that our mages who have a bent towards the work of an ingenier have been considering for a long time...so far no one has succeeded in finding a method that's sustainable. Humans find it tiring to lift anything of any size. Sanctii can't do it over the ocean, so while they can assist with some distances—if they choose to and if their mages can tolerate it, it hasn't been successful. You've seen my navire."

"Your ship of the air," Sophie said. No. Imogene's ship that *should* fly through the air but didn't. Her ship that needed to magic float. Magic that didn't yet exist. "Oh."

"Oh, indeed," Imogene said. "How to fly the navire is the missing piece of the puzzle."

"A ship is a lot bigger than a piece of soap." Sophie's mouth was suddenly dry in a way that mere ingestion of salt water couldn't explain. "Or even a carriage. And I can't even lift the soap twice. What makes you think I can lift a ship?" Or fly that ship over an ocean, which is what had to be the ultimate goal. Would that be a way to transport sanctii to Anglion? If they could travel far enough above the ocean, with their mages, would they be able to make the journey?

A force of Illvyan army supported by water mages and sanctii would be as close to unstoppable as anything she could imagine. Anglion had nothing to stand against it.

If she had had any lingering doubts that she and Cameron needed to disappear, they melted like soap bubbles touching the ground at that realization.

"Indeed. And perhaps my suspicions may be unwarranted. But you are an unknown quantity. You are not bound like Anglion earth witches usually are. You have the *augmentier* with Cameron. That flows both ways, not only serving him. Which, if I understand the matter correctly, is the way that such things usually work between Anglion lords and their wives. And then there's your sanctii. You didn't do that in the usual way either. So what I am forced to wonder, Sophie, is what else you can do that isn't in the usual way?"

At her words, Sophie went cold despite the steaming water surrounding her. She was struck by the thought that perhaps Imogene's invitation hadn't been so altruistic after all. After all, the woman was a mage and a soldier and ingenier. She had to have had this in the back of her mind—that maybe she could put Sophie to use—even if she hadn't known about the carriage.

She ducked back under the water, buying time to think. Was she being paranoid? Or right to be wary? Or maybe the truth lay somewhere between those two options. Imogene was a servant of her emperor. Not to mention a mage searching for a solution to the challenge of how to make her precious navire a workable tool.

But Sophie wasn't going to be a tool.

Her lungs began to inform her it was time to breathe again, and she resurfaced, pushing her dripping hair back from her face. "I'm not sure there is anything else." She stared down at the bar of soap, resting on the edge of the pool, avoiding Imogene's gaze. Who knew that a bar of soap could turn into such a tangle of complications? But it had.

So it wouldn't do any good to let Imogene think she was weak. "But you're not exactly in the usual way yourself, are you? How many Imperial mages are married to duqs? How many duquesses are ingeniers? Or favorites of the emperor?"

"More than you might think when it comes to that last one," Imogene muttered.

"But you're the only one I've seen with him with any regularity."

"Because when it comes to you and your husband, the emperor's concerns are diplomacy and magic and power. That intersects with my role in the Imperial mages."

"Queen Eloisa's father used to say that diplomacy is merely war getting the lay of the land."

Imogene wrinkled her nose. "He sounds like a cynic."

"You don't agree?"

"I think that it is better to try means other than force for two nations to coexist."

"But that has hardly been the policy of your emperors, has it? I mean, one doesn't build an empire by asking your neighbors politely to let you take over?"

"The empire has been formed for quite some time now. I wasn't involved in forming it, but I have a duty to help it run smoothly."

"Yet, Illvya still has an army, despite having run out of places to conquer."

"To maintain the peace."

"That doesn't sound far off war getting the lay of the land." She skimmed a hand over the water's surface, restless. Unhappy to be having this conversation even if she needed to hear it. Needed to know what she was avoiding. "After all, your navire d'avion, that is a tool of war, is it not? What are the uses for such a thing in times of peace?"

"Transportation," Imogene shot back. "If my calculations are correct, it will move faster than a ship traveling by sea or the fastest fabriques the Mage ingeniers have yet devised. If we can work out how to make them fly easily, then people would be able to travel far more easily."

"Is that what the emperor wants?"

"It is our experience that those who experience other places, other ways of living, who can adapt are those who begin to see the benefits of the empire over the old ways of viewing everyone who is not of your country or kin as the enemy." She raised her chin. "You should understand that. Your country is isolated. You were told the empire was a place of nightmares and terrors and untold depravations. Why? To keep you fearful. To keep you controlled."

"To keep us free."

"Really? Free for what? To live your life confined to one small island? To have your magic bound from you? That does not seem like freedom to me."

Sophie opened her mouth to reply, then closed it again. What exactly was the counterargument to that? And if she couldn't think of one, what did that tell her about Anglion? That perhaps the court and the temple there were no better than Aristides and his line? She didn't know. She frowned down at her hands, seeing the faint hint of wrinkles forming on her fingertips. "Perhaps freedom is different for someone who comes from a line of conquerors."

"You come from a line of conquerors yourself," Imogene retorted. "You are in the line of succession for your throne. Your queen's forebears overthrew others to take that crown. They did things that probably even the history books don't mention. That blood runs in your veins. So the only difference might be that I am perfectly clear how things are run here in Illvya. And in your country, it's all still shrouded in mystery."

"You may understand how things are run here, but does someone not in the court? Not a mage? I'm not sure that Illvya is any easier to understand than Anglion."

"At least we don't lie to women about their magic."

CHAPTER 12

Sophie opened her mouth to retort, then snapped it shut. It was an accusation she couldn't refute. "Just because Anglion has faults, that doesn't mean Illvya is perfect," she said eventually.

"No," Imogene agreed. "No country is. But do you think you could return to Anglion and live as you did before? Restricted to only earth magic. Knowing your sisters and daughters and friends would never be able to reach their full potential?"

"I—" She hesitated. "Perhaps not. But I don't think Aristides is overly concerned with the welfare of my countrywomen."

"Is change not a worthy goal?"

"Change comes at a cost," Sophie said. "And war is too high a price to pay."

Imogene's lips pressed together. "Do you think your country-women would agree?"

Sophie sucked in a breath. "I don't know. But I know it's not my place to make that choice for them. Neither is it Aristides."

"How can they choose if they do not know the truth?" Imogene pressed.

Sophie shook her head, anger flaring. "As I said, that is not my place to decide. And, I believe this has turned into exactly the kind of conversation that I came here to get away from. If you'll excuse me, I believe I would like to return to the house." How long could Cameron be? Goddess grant that he returned with the knowledge they needed. Because they had to leave now. If Imogene got Sophie back to the city and told the emperor about the navire, they would never get away.

Imogene's expression eased. "You're right. I apologize. I did not mean to press you. I was hoping we could get to know each other better. I have grown used to arguing about politics. It is a fault."

Sophie managed a smile, trying to bring her temper back under control. She had to keep Imogene on her side until Cameron returned. Until tonight or the next night when they could leave. "Well, if we are to know each other, then perhaps it is best if we know each other's faults." She held up a hand. "But I am growing wrinkled. So perhaps we should return regardless."

"Go ahead. Ring for Mari if you need help dressing," Imogene said, waving toward the stairs as they walked back into the house. "We'll have some tea and decide what to do after lunch when you come back down."

Sophie forced a smile. Tea. More time for small talk of the kind that had gone so badly in the bathing rooms? Please let Cameron and Jean-Paul return before then. Imogene had showed no signs of the tension that had descended between them in the bain-sel while they had dressed and walked back to the main house, but Sophie was less sanguine about what the other woman may be feeling in private.

Still, maybe with some time alone to wash the salt from her skin and dry her hair, she would come back down and the awkwardness between them would have faded, and she could pretend that everything was normal once more. "Thank you, tea would be perfect."

She made her way back to her suite. At least the bath in the bain-sel had loosened the aches in her muscles. Pity that the relaxation that it should have brought had been ruined by their argument.

It was tempting to just hide away once she'd closed the door behind her. But she suspected that Imogene would come looking for her if she didn't return, so she quickly filled the bath and rinsed the salt from her skin and hair. Wrapped in fine linen towels, she sat at the dressing table, gazing into the mirror. Her reflection offered no insights or answers, revealing only that her skin was heated, lending a flush to the gold and that her eyes were somewhat shadowed, showing the aftereffects of the late night. "You're no help," she muttered to herself and reached for one of the cut-glass jars of perfumed balm lining the table.

As she rubbed it into her skin, she thought about what Imogene had said. About Anglion. And the navire. About war.

She couldn't let it happen. They had to get away. She should talk to Elarus. Let the sanctii know of their plans, so she would be ready to help.

But before she could call Elarus, there was a knock at the door and Mari entered, bobbing a quick curtsy before informing Sophie that she had been sent to help her dress.

The sound of voices drifted up as Sophie descended the stairs half an hour later. Mari had combed out her hair and twisted it into a more elegant version of Sophie's usual braids before selecting a dress. Sophie hadn't needed her help and wasn't exactly sure why Imogene had sent the maid when Sophie hadn't asked for her, but there had been no easy way to send her away. So no conversation with Elarus.

She paused on the landing and listened. Male voices. Had Cameron and Jean-Paul returned early after all?

The prospect quickened her step. But it wasn't Cameron and

Jean-Paul standing in the entry hall, but two men dressed in familiar black uniforms, their faces serious as they spoke with Imogene.

Who turned at the sound of Sophie stepping onto the marble tile.

"Lady Scardale," she said and the formality in her voice brought fear to Sophie's stomach.

"Your Grace," she said, keeping her voice calm. "Has something happened? Who are these men?"

Imogene grimaced briefly, the expression gone before Sophie was sure that she had seen it. Her face was carefully polite as she turned back to the two Imperial mages. They looked quite young to Sophie's eyes, one blond and one dark, both of them blank faced and not giving anything away. The dark-haired one stepped forward and nodded at Sophie.

"Lady Scardale, I am Lieutenant Vermier. We have brought a message from the emperor."

"A message for me?"

That earned her another nod and a small bow. The other mage reached into black leather satchel hanging from his shoulder and withdrew an envelope. Sophie didn't reach immediately to take it, and after several seconds passed, Imogene plucked it from his grasp. She turned the envelope over and Sophie caught a glimpse of the now-familiar emperor's seal. She fought the urge to put her hands behind her back and refuse to read the damned thing.

Because she was suddenly certain that whatever it contained, she had lost her chance to run. Aristides wouldn't send soldiers for anything minor. Goddess, she wanted Cameron.

"Thank you, Lieutenant," Imogene said. "One of the servants will come and show you both to a room. You can eat and refresh yourselves while Lady Scardale reads this."

Lieutenant Vermier frowned, brown eyes displeased. "We were told the matter was urgent, Your Grace."

Imogene frowned back at him, her expression far icier than

his own. "I believe that's Major du Laq to you, Lieutenant. I appreciate your urgency, but my husband and Lord Scardale are currently out riding on the estate so no matter what this letter contains, no one will be doing anything until they have returned. I suggest you take the opportunity to rest." It was clearly an order, not a suggestion.

The lieutenant's frown didn't ease, but he nodded reluctantly and then saluted. "Yes, Major."

Imogene crossed the room and tugged the bell pull discretely placed at the side of a grand portrait. When a servant appeared, she gave a few quick orders and the two mages followed the man out of the room.

After they had left, Imogene turned back to Sophie, holding out the letter. "Do you want to read this here or go into one of the parlors?"

"I don't particularly want to read it at all," Sophie said, trying to sound halfway calm.

"It may be nothing," Imogene said.

"Does the emperor often send two Imperial mages to deliver a message when it's nothing?" she said, and the words came out more harshly than she had intended. "I'm sorry," she said immediately. "I didn't mean to be rude. I—"

"We'll go into the garden room," Imogene said smoothly. "I've already sent Ikarus for Cameron and Jean-Paul. Hopefully they haven't ventured far and will be able to return quickly. We may as well be comfortable while we find out whatever this holds," She waggled the letter. "Come along."

Sophie followed her, and in less time than she would have liked, was seated on a silk sofa in a beautiful room that smelled of flowers and sunshine. But it could have been a stone in the middle of a desert for the all the attention she had for her surroundings. Imogene had placed the letter on a small table in front of her, and it sat there, looking too innocuous for something that she knew for certain held news that was pulling her back to the snare of fate awaiting her in Lumia.

Eventually, not wanting Imogene to think she had lost her
wits, she reached for it. The wax seal yielded to her fingers and
she withdrew the heavy paper, heart pounding.

The letter when she unfolded it, was short and to the point.
She had no idea if the heavy black script was Aristides's own
hand, but the bold signature undoubtedly was. *Aristides*. Nothing
else required. The name was enough. He was the emperor. He
was to be obeyed.

She held it out to Imogene, hoping her hand didn't shake.
"The emperor requires us to return to the city," she said. "Immediately."

Imogene scanned the letter herself, her gaze moving rapidly
down the page. "He gives no reason."

"I'm assuming that's because the reason concerns news he
does not wish to convey in a note. Nothing good, I'm sure." She
folded her clammy hands then, clasping them tightly as fear
rasped its way from her stomach to dig claws into her throat.

Imogene nodded and put the letter back down on the table.
"I could lie to you and tell you not to worry, but that would be
disingenuous. But until you know exactly what the news is, I
would suggest that you try not to let worry become anything
greater. So. We return. I will get the servants to pack your things
and ours."

"You're coming with us?"

"The lieutenant also passed on a request that Jean-Paul and I
should accompany you."

"Then you already knew what this contained?" Sophie
nodded at the letter where it lay. A simple piece of paper
shouldn't be frightening, but she had to fight the urge to throw it
into the nearest fireplace. Not that she could pretend that she'd
never received it with Lieutenant Vermier and his companion
waiting to escort them back to Lumia.

"I knew you were wanted back in the capital. I didn't know
what else Aristides might care to tell you."

"Well, it seems as though he didn't care to tell either of us anything more," Sophie said. "Which I can only think means nothing good. Especially if he sent soldiers to make sure that we obey and return."

"He sent the soldiers with a *chargeurre* to make your return faster," Imogene said.

Chargeurre. She frowned. In Anglish, that would be something like war carriage. But like with chennei, she had no mental image to go with the definition. "What's a charguerre?"

"A type of fabrique used by the army. Faster than a normal carriage."

One of the army's conveyances. What did that mean? What could have happened to be so urgent? "And how many men come with it?" It was a pointless question. There was no way to flee now. That knowledge sat like a stone of ice in her stomach. But she couldn't help asking.

Imogene shook her head. "There are only two. Lieutenant Vermier is a Mage ingenier. He knows how to drive the charguerre. It is normal for a Mage ingenier to travel with a backup, that would be the sergeant. Do not imagine you are under any kind of arrest. Aristides is not known for his patience. He will be thinking of speed, not anything else. He knows you have a sanctii. If he was going to try and force you back, he'd have sent more than two men."

"Perhaps he was relying on your sanctii being able to control mine."

Imogene grimaced. "I doubt it. Please don't waste energy inventing dangers where none exist. Focus on what you can control. Which, for now, is packing and making sure we are ready to leave as soon as possible when our husbands return."

"They've been gone for several hours already, that could take a while."

"As to that." Imogene concentrated for a moment. "Ikarus says that they are already returning and are about an hour away. That doesn't leave us much time."

Sophie and Cameron's luggage wouldn't take that long to deal with, not with Imogene's army of servants to pack. But packing would be a distraction at least. Imogene was right. She could waste energy panicking now or try to keep calm until she knew what had happened. There was no doubt in her mind that something had.

If she knew more about scrying, perhaps she could try and see, but as it was, the thought of another uncontrolled vision taking her and showing her death and rot again made her stomach churn. Nor could she afford the weakness—or worse—that seemed to follow in a vision's wake.

No. Better to stay busy.

"All right," she said. "I'll return to our suite. If you send a maid, I'm sure we can be packed well inside an hour."

"I can send more than one," Imogene said. "It will take no time at all. I'll send someone with food. The men took luncheon with them so hopefully they will have eaten, but you should eat. Lieutenant Vermier will be eager to leave once Cameron and Jean-Paul return. Even with a chargeurre, it's still several hours journey to return to Lumia."

By the time Sophie left her suite again, close enough to an hour later, and followed the small parade of servants carrying her and Cameron's luggage back downstairs, she had managed to stomach some tea and sandwiches. The maids hadn't allowed her to assist them so, other than changing her dress to one more suitable for traveling, she'd had nothing to do but try to choke the food down and worry and regret that they hadn't been brave enough to try to get away sooner.

Logically she knew they hadn't had the knowledge they needed to pull it off. But her heart only saw the freedom that had slipped from her grasp.

Imogene stood in the entry hall talking with Barteau. Thankfully the two Imperial mages were nowhere to be seen.

"Ah, good," Imogene said, catching sight of Sophie. "Cameron and Jean-Paul have returned to the stables. They'll be with us shortly. Which means we can be underway soon." She turned back to Barteau. "Is everything ready?"

"Yes, Your Grace. We will send on whatever else is needed with the carriage. It will only be a few hours behind you."

"You're not taking your carriage?" Sophie asked.

"The chargeurre will hold us all. I'm hardly going to leave you to deal with the lieutenant or Aristides alone. Jean-Paul won't want to be left behind either. The charguerre can take all of us and is faster than any carriage." She tilted her head. "So we will endure the journey together."

"Endure?" What did that mean? Was Imogene worried about the conversation turning awkward again?

Imogene smiled. "Sorry, I am being overly dramatic. Charguerres are not my favored mode of transport. They are noisy and not usually built with luxury in mind. Comfortable to a degree, but nothing more than that," Imogene said. "The speed can take some getting used to when they really get going. The scenery whips by with no chance to take it in."

Sophie hadn't considered what it would be like to ride in a fabrique. She'd seen the fabrique carriages in the streets in Lumia, but there they had traveled at the same pace as the rest of the traffic.

"What does everyone else on the road do?" she asked.

"Gets out of the way," Imogene said with a shrug. "That's the benefit of the noise, plenty of warning. But the chargeurre is also designed to be able to navigate rougher terrain than a carriage. It can go around obstacles if needs be." She shrugged. "It is the lieutenant's problem to manage but don't worry. I've ridden in them before and never come to any harm." She frowned. "Do you know where Elarus is?"

"I haven't seen her," Sophie said, then flushed. "I didn't think. I should speak with her, let her know that we are returning to the city."

"Yes. She and Ikarus can return via their own means. Six humans will fit but adding two sanctii would make it a squeeze."

Noise came from behind them, and Imogene looked past Sophie's shoulder. "Good. Here comes Jean-Paul and your Cameron."

Sophie whirled to see Cameron striding toward her. He enveloped her in a hug, murmuring, "It will be all right, love," in her ear before he released her and said hello to Imogene.

"I'm sorry to cut your day short," Imogene said.

"I think the fault for that lies with Aristides, not you," Cameron said, voice tight. "If what Ikarus told us was correct."

"Yes," Sophie said, trying to ignore the sick feeling in her stomach. "It was. We've been summoned. We have to go back."

Cameron took her hand and squeezed it quickly. A small comfort, but she had to let him go again soon enough as the level of activity turned into a whirlwind. Cameron and Jean-Paul disappeared to change and returned just as the lieutenant and his sergeant re-emerged, accompanied by the same servant who'd escorted them away earlier. After Imogene told him they were ready to leave, he led the way out of the house to the charguerre.

The—machine? creation?—she wasn't entirely quite sure of the correct term for a fabrique—looked distinctly out of place on the pristine white gravel of the driveway. It bore a passing resemblance to a carriage in that it had four sides and a roof and wheels, but that was about all it had in common with the luxurious and elegant conveyance they had travelled from Lumia in.

The fabrique was larger and looked like an iron box designed by someone with no regard for any sort of harmony to the eye. Plain, unrelieved matte black, other than the small windows and the imperial crest painted in gold on the door, it seemed to squat in place, heavy and ungainly. The wheels—four of them on each side—were much wider than a normal carriage's.

If she hadn't known what it was, she would have perhaps guessed that it was a wagon for rubbish collection. Something so mundane, that no one had cared what it looked like.

But no mundane wagon would have four fabriques harnessed in front of it where horses or maybe an ox or two should have stood.

The fabriques looked nothing like the faux horses that pulled carriages through the streets of Lumia. These were larger and stronger and squarer. Perhaps what you'd get if you crossed an ox with a horse and then tried to fashion an imitation of the offspring from steel and iron. Though they weren't as graceless as the carriage, the lines of their jointed limbs suggesting strength and some degree of agility.

But they stood, black and perfectly motionless under the blue sky. Clearly machines. The only sign that they might be able to do more than stand there forever like sculptures was a faint hiss of steam seeping from their mouths.

"Impressive, aren't they?" Imogene said. "The soldiers call them *fer taureaus*."

"Yes," Sophie agreed. Iron bulls. It seemed a fair description. It didn't entirely encompass the unsettling creatures but seemed a good name for something that looked like it could put its head down and charge through any obstacle with ease. Subtlety apparently wasn't the Imperial army's strength. Perhaps that made sense. If you were trying to overwhelm an enemy with your might and power, no point calling your weapons names that didn't invoke those things.

"Does the army have many of these?" Cameron asked. He took a half step closer, his soldier's curiosity getting the better of him perhaps, but then seemed to think better of it and returned to Sophie's side.

"Not many yet," Imogene said. "It takes certain talents to make them and certain others to be able to pilot them successfully. A combination of blood magic and air for the latter. A few other things for the former. But the ingeniers and mage ingeniers who make them are becoming more skilled with time. You've seen the horses in Lumia. Those are simpler than these. These came from the same principles. But they are...improved."

The fer-taureaus didn't look more complicated than the fabrique horses, which were far more lifelike. So "improved" in this case probably meant that there was some form of weaponry built into their bodies or that they themselves could be used for more than pulling a charguerre.

Sophie expected Cameron to continue with another question. But he stayed quiet. Perhaps he thought that Imogene would refuse to answer. After all, he was not part of the Imperial army and the fer-taureaus—and what they were capable of—had to be classed as military secrets.

"They don't look fast," she observed. "They must be heavy."

"They are fast enough," Lieutenant Vermier replied. "I will have you all back in Lumia in two hours, my lady."

That hardly seemed a selling point, but there was no point in dampening the obvious pride in his voice. She eyed the charguerre warily. It didn't become any prettier with further inspection, and even if she had wanted to return to the city, two hours seemed alarmingly fast. It had taken five hours for them to reach Sanct de Sangre yesterday.

"To that end," Lieutenant Vermier continued, "We should be underway." He swept his hand toward the charguerre, clearly wanting them to climb aboard.

Sophie froze in place, unable to move. She didn't want to comply, though she knew she had to eventually. To hide her reluctance, she pretended to study the charguerre.

Rather than a seat at the front of the thing, where a driver would normally sit behind horses, there was another smaller iron box mounted in front of the larger one. Big enough to fit two men, she judged, and the long window that bisected the wall of the smaller box seemed to confirm that yes, this was where a driver and companion would steer the contraption from. She supposed it would be useful to be protected from the elements and stray tree branches or such at head height if one was traveling faster than a normal carriage.

Jean-Paul was the first to move toward the charguerre. "Let

us not waste time," he said, waving them forward. He was no longer the smiling relaxed man from breakfast. Now, with his hair tamed and face serious and voice stern, he was every inch the duq. The lieutenant bowed, crossed to the charguerre, pressed a hand to the seal on the door, and stepped back as it swung open.

"If you care to enter, Your Graces, my lord, and my lady."

Sophie let the du Laq's go first. Not only out of respect for protocol and precedence, but because she wanted to delay as long as possible before climbing inside.

"Sophie?" Cameron offered his arm. She took it, holding it more firmly than strictly necessary. "It's all right, love."

It was a kindness of him to try and reassure her, when he had to be as furious and scared as she was, but she wasn't reassured. They had lost their chance to be free of Aristides. And whatever the news that waited for them in Lumia was, it wasn't going to be good. Only fear of having a repeat of what had happened back in the Academe with her visions and fainting prevented her from throwing caution to the winds and trying to scry and see what that might be.

Instead she could only hold onto Cameron and pretend that she was calm.

[Elarus?] she said as she stepped into the charguerre. [You will follow?]

[Follow] came the reply clear as a bell in her head. [Keep safe.]

The reassurance was a small comfort. But only for an instant. Before she realized that the fact that she found a sanctii comforting was yet another sign of just how strange and unpredictable her life had become.

And that it was most likely about to become stranger still.

CHAPTER 13

The charguerre might be faster, but apparently "faster" did not come combined with "more comfortable." The metallic clank of the taureau's hooves hitting the road, the shuddering of the charguerre itself, and the bouncing of gears and springs as it jolted over the road rattled Sophie's bones. The seats were nowhere near as comfortably padded as those in the du Laq's carriage. The ingeniers had tried to compensate by providing leather straps on the walls and roof for the passengers to grip, but they did little to alleviate the rough ride.

The tension that the bain-sel had soaked from Sophie's bones was back in full force. Unless the roads improved, she would be one big ache by the time they arrived back in Lumia. If Aristides's soldiers commonly traveled any sort of distance in these contraptions and were ready to fight upon arrival, they must be made of sterner stuff than she was.

The creak and clatter of their passage also cut off any opportunities for conversation. If there was any sort of aural ward around the charguerre to spare the passengers from its noise, the lieutenant hadn't bothered to activate it.

With no chance to plan for what might be to come, or even to discuss the possibilities with Cameron, Sophie spent the time fighting rising panic. The discomfort of the journey was some distraction, but by the time the charguerre entered the gates to the palace grounds, she was weak-limbed with fear.

They continued past the palace itself and shuddered to a halt beside some sort of barracks complex farther back in the grounds. A few seconds later, the door sprang open.

Jean-Paul climbed out silently, followed by Imogene who winced slightly as she rose from her seat.

"Sophie? Are you all right?" Cameron asked quietly, squeezing her hand. She wasn't, but she didn't see that made any difference to what might come next, so she swallowed, summoned a weak smile, and nodded, not trusting her voice.

Cameron's eyes narrowed but he didn't press, simply squeezed her hand one more time, fingers stroking hers before he let go and followed the du Laqs out.

Tempting as it might be to stay in the charguerre and let the taureaus carry her off again, that would only be delaying the inevitable. Sophie took a deep breath, steeled her knees, and rose as Cameron turned from where he stood outside the door to offer his hand. Her muscles were stiff, but she managed to descend to the cobbled yard without stumbling, which she counted a small victory.

A waiting servant took them to a carriage that drove them back to the palace. It seemed strange to ride when they could have walked the distance in ten or fifteen minutes, but apparently the emperor was not to be kept waiting.

Louis, Aristides's seneschal, met them at the palace. His manner gave no hint as to what might be waiting for them. He wouldn't have told them if he knew, she supposed.

The lack of any familiar landmarks as they walked through the palace made her suspect they were not returning to the throne room. Whether or not that was a good or bad sign remained to be seen.

Aristides wasn't alone in the room Louis delivered them to. Sophie hadn't expected him to be. King Stefan had rarely held an audience with no advisors or witnesses, and Eloisa had followed his example. But, of the five people in the room with the emperor, the only familiar face was Colonel Perrine's. She thought two of the men standing with the emperor had been in the audience chamber where Aristides had offered her the throne. But she didn't recognize the third, who wore a sober dark blue jacket and pale gray breeches. A heavy golden chain hung around his neck, ending in a pendant ringed with gold and diamonds. Some sort of badge of office?

The sixth occupant was a woman dressed in temple robes. She had striking red hair threaded with silver, and she inspected Sophie with eyes the color of spring leaves. Her expression was kind, but somehow aloof. This, Sophie had to assume, was Domina Francis, the head of the goddess's temple here in Illvya.

"Your Graces," Aristides said. "Lord and Lady Scardale. I apologize for cutting your entertainment short."

"What happened?" Sophie said, her nerves suddenly breaking through her tightly held composure. Protocol could go to ashes. She wanted to know now, not after a round of useless pleasantries and introductions.

Aristides didn't immediately respond. As the silence grew, he studied her, as though trying to make up his mind about something. "Lady Scardale, I appreciate that you must be anxious," he said eventually.

"If you didn't want us to be anxious, you would have told us more in your letter, your Imperial Majesty. For you not to say anything more means either than the news is bad or you are secretive for your own purposes. I assume it's the former?" She stared back at him, not shifting her gaze. Yes, the man outranked her, but she was damned if she was going to let this drag out.

If he wanted her to believe that he thought she should be a queen, then he was going to have to treat her like a queen. As someone deserving of his respect and his assistance. An ally rather than a mere minor foreign noble he could maneuver as he saw fit in his games of empire.

"It is," he conceded with a nod. Around the room, the shoulders of most of the others lowered a fraction as it became clear that the emperor wasn't going to take her to task for her breach of etiquette. To Aristides's left, the domina's expression had turned somewhat assessing.

"I will not draw this out, Lady Scardale. It seems the Anglion delegation found fair winds and made good time on their return to your country. It seems also that Queen Eloisa was decisive in her reaction to the news that you did not wish to return. Late last night an Anglion ship arrived and another envoy came ashore, bearing a new letter from your queen."

"A letter for me?" Sophie asked.

"A letter for me," Aristides corrected. "Though you and your husband feature heavily. In short, Lady Scardale, I regret to inform you that your queen has made another demand for your return and informs me that she is holding members of both your families as surety for your compliance with her wishes."

"Who?" Cameron demanded from beside her, and the word was closer to a shout than a tone suited to the emperor's audience chamber. Sophie bit back a cry of her own. All she could think was *She dares?* The notion swiftly followed by a tide of incendiary rage that shocked her with its savagery.

Elarus blinked into sight beside her and Aristides's hand curled at his side.

Colonel Perrine stepped between the emperor and the sanctii, one hand lifting towards Elarus.

"Sophie," Imogene said urgently. "Send her away."

Elarus's head turned to study the duquesse, but she made no other move.

"It's all right, Elarus," Sophie managed. "There's no danger."

[Angry,] Elarus said and the word seemed to echo around Sophie's head.

[Yes, but that is not something that you need to worry about. Please. You are making people nervous. I will be all right. If I truly need you, I will call you.]

Elarus grunted but vanished again. There was a collective whoosh of air in the room as several of the counselors released their breath at once.

Apparently unexpected sanctii could make even Illvyans nervous.

"*Who*," Cameron repeated. This time his voice was softer, but the anger that thrummed beneath the words was as deep as Sophie's own. She could feel him through the bond, a flare of red incandescent fury. Dangerous emotion for a blood mage. But she was in no mood to soothe his anger away. All she could do was try to not feed his to a higher pitch with her own.

She reached for control, for reason, trying to lock down the emotion. "I would also like to know the answer to my husband's question." Her voice only quivered slightly on the final word, and Aristides nodded at her, approving her control. The motion was slightly jerky, suggesting he wasn't as calm as he appeared either.

His eyes flicked down to the paper in his hand and he began to read off a list of names.

She could have guessed most of them. Yet each one sank like a dagger into her heart, pain driving deeper with each syllable. Her mother and father. Cameron's mother. James and his wife. Not Liam. Apparently Eloisa wasn't yet so far gone to try and arrest one of her erls with no evidence of wrongdoing. The final name on the list was Chloe de Montesse.

That snapped Sophie back out of her daze. "Chloe? Why?"

Aristides shrugged. "Your queen neglected to provide any explanation as to her choices. I take it these are people close to you?"

Sophie bit back a retort. She didn't believe for a second that Aristides didn't know who each of the Anglions named were. No more than he could claim to be ignorant of who Chloe was. He knew far too much about her and Cameron not to know who their families were. Even if he hadn't paid close attention to the far ends of the Anglion line of succession before she'd arrived in Illvya, she couldn't imagine he hadn't availed himself of the resources he clearly controlled in Anglion to find out everything he wanted to know as soon as possible after they had landed in his lap.

"My parents. Cameron's mother. His brother-in-law, as you know." Not her brothers, thank the goddess. Or Cameron's other brother, Alec and his wife, for that matter. It seemed Eloisa may only have swooped on those who had been in Kingswell itself when claiming her hostages. Though she could have added to the tally after penning the letter. Hardly any time could have passed between the Barron Deepholt and the rest of the original delegation returning with her refusal and the second ship setting sail with this new demand.

Or Eloisa could be lying about who she had under her control. Though that made no sense. If she held the most powerful cards—their parents—already, there would be no point to hiding the fact she also held others.

She was trying to make them fall into line and obey her. She wasn't going to expect them to do anything else, not with their families at stake.

What else could they do, in her mind? It wasn't as though they had any idea where Eloisa might be holding her hostages. The traditional place that nobility who fell afoul of the Anglion crown were kept was the east tower of the palace. The Doom, as it was known, though its official name was the Crown's Fist. The members of the court called it the east tower when they couldn't avoid mentioning it at all.

Name aside, it had been damaged in the attack on the palace. But Eloisa had other prisons at her command. Or she could have locked them up in any one of half a dozen or more properties she owned in Kingswell.

Besides which, they were here in Illvya, not in any position to mount a rescue mission.

"Does she say anything more?" Sophie asked carefully, trying to keep her grip on her emotions as Cameron's rage still roiled through the bond.

"Only that no one will come to any harm if you return to Anglion."

"I don't suppose that there is any assurance that statement extends to Cameron or myself?" she said.

"No," Aristides said gravely. "No such surety has been given." He folded the letter and handed it back to Colonel Perrine. "You can read it for yourself once our discussions are concluded."

"What discussions?" Sophie asked.

Aristides tapped his fingers against his thigh. Only once, before his hand stilled. "I rather thought, Lady Scardale, that you might wish to revisit our previous conversation. About what exactly needs to be done about the Queen of Anglion? In light of these developments, I would say she has only made my point for me."

The Queen of Anglion. Not "your queen." Aristides had moved Eloisa to a different place on the board, it seemed. Or maybe he was moving Sophie to a different side entirely.

"Your Imperial Majesty," Imogene said, tone protesting.

Sophie registered the objection through the rush of blood in her ears. She couldn't say that Aristides had surprised her with his suggestion. Part of her had been expecting it since they'd received his summons. And that part had braced even harder when he'd told them about the letter. But despite the sense of inevitability, she still wasn't resigned to the fact that he thought he could force her to this. The racing heart and sick feeling in her stomach had less to do with him, and more to do with the thought of what her family was suffering. What Eloisa was doing to them, or if not Eloisa, then Domina Skey perhaps. *She* loathed Sophie enough. Though how the domina had convinced Eloisa to take this action was unclear. But her family....

She felt herself sway slightly and took a half step before Cameron caught her arm as Domina Francis snapped, "Someone bring the girl some water. Aristides, you won't get yourself a queen if you kill the child with fear."

Sophie lifted her head at that, though she had to close her eyes again, as the room whirled around her.

Someone touched her arm softly. "Lady Scardale," a man said. She thought it might be Jean-Paul. Not Cameron. Cameron was snarling something at the emperor.

"Lord Scardale," Aristides snapped. "I appreciate that you are under some strain, but do not overstep your limits."

"Cameron, Sophie needs you." Imogene's voice.

"Lady Scardale, you need to sit down." It was the domina again.

Her immediate instinct was to resist, but she wrestled it away. This wasn't Domina Skey and the temple here in Lumia had left her alone

Until now.

Until she was being pushed to a point of no return, perhaps. She opened her eyes, looked at the circle of concerned faces around her.

"Sit," Jean-Paul said in a tone of unmistakable order. She sank into the chair that had appeared behind her and closed her eyes before the room could start spinning again.

"Perhaps Your Imperial Majesty could clear the room for a time?" Domina Francis said in a steely tone, and Sophie heard the emperor give the order. Though none of the people closest to her moved to obey him.

"Drink something," the domina urged, pressing a glass into her hand.

Sophie raised it automatically and sipped water. It steadied her, easing the dizziness. She took another sip, blinked, and then opened her eyes.

The Domina was crouched by her chair, looking up at Sophie's face with worried eyes. "Are you well, child?"

"Yes," Sophie managed. Well enough, at least. Eloisa was holding her family to ransom, and she would happily set cities on fire to relieve her anger. Or perhaps collapse into a weeping heap until she knew her family was safe. Either way, far from normal, but she could think again. Her family needed her to think. To keep them from paying the price for her choices. Though she had no idea how she was supposed to make that happen.

She stared down at the glass of water, her knuckles white where she gripped too tightly. What she wouldn't give to be able to see her parents now. To tell them that she was...she was...she didn't know what exactly. The light shining off the water turned its surface a strange shade of blue for a moment and the color caught her eyes and pulled her under before she could blink.

A whirl of images rolled through her mind, blinding her to anything happening in the room where she sat. The palace at Kingswell, still shattered and broken in part. The throne room there filled with smoke. Chloe, her face twisted in anger in a way that Sophie didn't think she had ever seen in real life. Her mother sitting on the floor in an empty room, pressed into a corner, her face tear-stained and exhausted. And then, as Sophie began to try to pull herself out of the vision, to get away from the images before they broke her, she was dragged even deeper. Around her, the vast tree began to grow, the enormous trunk rising only a few feet from her face, the light on her face shining dappled green through its branches. For a moment hope flooded her. The tree seemed healthy. Thriving even. But then the light began to darken, and she was yanked down, down beneath the earth, faced again with twisted blackened rotting roots and Eloisa's dead face lying so still. Until it turned toward her and smiled, showing teeth and bone through rotting flesh.

"No!" Sophie threw out a hand as though to ward Eloisa off, and the vision broke and shattered, dissolving before her eyes in a thousand sparkling shards. Leaving her staring into the domina's deep green eyes.

Nobody spoke at first.

The domina cleared her throat. "Lady Scardale, forgive my bluntness, but what did you just see?"

Sophie blinked and swallowed, wondering how she could avoid answering. She went to lift the cup to her lips and realized she no longer held it. Instead, her shoes were wet and the glass lay several feet away on the thick blue carpet.

"I—"

"I know the look of a vision, child," the domina said sternly. She looked back over her shoulder at Aristides. "You didn't tell me she could scry."

"I was unaware that she could," Aristides said. "Imogene? Did you know about this?"

"She's a water mage. Some of them can scry," Imogene said defensively.

"Lady Scardale is newly come to those powers though, is she not? I thought that scrying took training?" Aristides sounded displeased.

"It does," the domina agreed. "But the training for those who have the ability to learn control. And that didn't look particularly controlled to me." She peered up into Sophie's face. "So, child. Tell me."

Sophie hesitated. She didn't want to talk about what she had seen. Not with Aristides standing there, looking for any excuse to invade Anglion. But she had seen the same horrifying vision of Eloisa three times now. Seen the rot and decay surrounding her.

She had to ask someone about it. But only once she had decided who she could trust. And when she had time to come to terms with what had been in the queen's letter. Right then she had no idea about who to choose for the former and no idea about how she would do the latter. She needed a way out.

"I—" she broke off, flailing for an escape route. Recalled the image of her mother sitting in the corner, crying and tearstained and afraid. "I saw my mother," she said and let all her fear and anger and grief loose, bursting into tears.

It was a successful ploy. Though once she'd started, she lost hold of any intention to cry prettily and be excused. The sobs rushed through her. Choking and uncontrollable. Cameron and Imogene and the domina hovered around her, trying to soothe her and offering more water and handkerchiefs. None of it helped.

Eventually Cameron picked her up bodily out of the chair and then sat himself, holding her in his lap so she could cry on his chest while he murmured soft words that she didn't really hear until the tears started to dry up and she hiccupped and sniffed her way to silence, face buried in Cameron's chest.

Which left her tear-stained and soggy, her eyes and throat on fire from the weeping. Mortified that she had lost control so badly. She didn't lift her head.

"Lady Scardale appears overcome," the domina said. "Perhaps we should continue this conversation tomorrow, Aristides? The Scardales have heard the news from Anglion, they are aware of how the situation has changed. They need some time to deal with what has happened."

"I am not unsympathetic," Aristides said. "But time is also of the essence."

"If the queen was going to kill their families, they would be dead already." The domina's voice was blunt and Sophie flinched into Cameron. "Eloisa wants Lady Scardale to return, she's not going to overplay her hand early."

Meaning that the domina thought Eloisa might overplay it later on? It wasn't outside the realm of possibility. Eloisa wasn't acting entirely rationally. But, no. Best not to think about that. If Sophie started to think, she was going to start crying again.

"Lady Scardale," Aristides said. "I understand that this news is distressing for you and that you have been dealing with all manner of unpleasant things since you came here. I also appreciate that my proposal to you in relation to the Anglion crown is something you view as one of those unpleasant things, but this letter from the queen has done nothing to change my mind. This threat is not a rational action. She knows she doesn't have the power to compel you and that she is outnumbered if she chooses a war."

"By threatening your families, she wants to force you to return home. But she can't imagine that I will allow you to return on your own. Therefore she is asking for a war that she is unlikely to win. One that I am not certain her nobles would support her in. One that doesn't make sense. All to secure your return. When you are far less of a threat to her here, in Illvya. With you here, no Anglion would contemplate that you might be scheming to take her throne. No one who is—how do you Anglions say it? 'Thinking straight?' at least. Which makes me question, yet again, whether she is rational."

Sophie lifted her head, rubbing her stinging eyes. She didn't want to dissolve into tears again. It would achieve nothing. "You *are* scheming to take her throne," Sophie pointed out. Her voice rasped, and she sipped more water.

Aristides made a dismissive gesture. "Only because of how she is behaving. The sanity, or lack thereof, of the Anglion nobility has not been of concern to my family for several generations now. We had an understanding of a kind between our realms. But if your queen is not rational, if she will do this, then I am forced to consider that such an understanding no longer holds."

"She is the queen," Sophie said. "Her subjects will be loyal to her." Her throat burned with each word. She had to convince him.

"She is a new queen," Aristides said, shaking his head. "Her father was loved and respected, but she has come to power in a difficult time. If she falters, it would be easy enough for them to turn from her. If presented with a palatable alternative."

"With all due respect, Your Imperial Majesty, there is no way that to the average Anglion I would be considered a palatable alternative. I have a sanctii. I have broken pretty much every taboo our temple holds. I broke some of them before I even arrived here. On the day of my Ais-Seann, no less." She stopped, realizing that not everyone in the room needed to hear chapter and verse about what had happened between Cameron and her on the day of her twenty-first birthday. "You will not be able to convince them that I am a suitable queen."

"Maybe, maybe not." Aristides said. "But would you leave them to be ruled by madness?"

"I'm not convinced Eloisa is mad," Sophie said. Then shivered. Maybe not mad, but if her visions were anything to go on, the queen had to be in danger, at the very least. Worse, if she took the vision literally.

"If she is not insane, then she is taking bad advice or letting some other emotion guide her actions," Aristides said. "And to me, a young queen who will not be guided wisely is just as dangerous as a mad one."

Sophie stiffened. "Is that what you expect of me, if I agreed? That I would be a compliant young queen who you could guide as you saw fit?"

Aristides's eyes narrowed at her. "Not as I saw fit, but I would hope that you would take my counsel, and that of others you respect. I would hope that your country and my empire could enjoy a more fruitful relationship than has existed between us."

"You hope that we would join your empire," Sophie said. "In which case you don't need a queen. Why not take Anglion for yourself? Install a governor."

Aristides sighed. "Because that is not the best way. My empire has moved to a stage where it is mostly peaceful. Where people have accepted that we are better as one—or most of them have. But the Anglions have fought fiercely for their independence all these years. I do not think they would accept my rule so easily. I would rather work with your country than against it."

Sophie didn't think it could be quite that simple. Aristides sounded benevolent, but there had to some benefit to him from his plan.

"Perhaps this is a conversation for the morning," Domina Francis said, rising to her feet. "Lady Scardale needs time to consider. You have made your position clear, Aristides. She understands what you are offering her. You cannot expect her to decide here and now."

The emperor's mouth twisted. "That is fair. But, as I said earlier, there is a timetable in play here. You must understand this, Lord Scardale. I'm sure the Red Guard have to take hostages from time to time. You know how it works."

Cameron nodded. "I agree. There is a time limit to how long we can stall, but we do need time to consider." He turned to the domina. "I don't suppose you could raise a convenient storm or something that would mean that the Anglion ships would need to stay in the harbor a few days. That would buy us more time."

"Sorry. Magic of that kind may be within the realm of the goddess, but it's not something I wield." Domina Francis smiled wryly. "But I would like to help you in this choice, if I can. Offer such guidance as the goddess may have. We should speak further. Come and see me in the morning."

CHAPTER 14

They had barely walked through the door of the Academe when Mestier Allyn, the Master of the Ravens, stepped out of one of the doors into the entry hall. He halted at the sight of Sophie, a smile crossing his face.

"Lady Scardale," he said. "I thought you weren't returning for another few days."

"Her Grace was recalled to the city," Sophie said, trying to sound normal. Her throat still hurt, and she hoped her eyes weren't as red as they felt. She didn't want to deal with any well-meaning questions. But if her face still showed any traces of her emotion, Mestier Allyn didn't comment.

"I'm pleased," he said. "Tok has been fretting. I was starting to worry. But I can go and let him out now. He'll be happy to see you. Hopefully that will bring back his appetite."

Sophie's heart wrenched. She hadn't let herself think about Tok since they'd left Lumia. She hated the thought that he'd been in any distress because of her. She'd caused enough pain. "I'll come with you," she said.

"*Sophie*," Cameron said.

"What?" She turned back to him, ready to fight. "This is something I *can* do. A hurt I can prevent here and now."

"Are you going to take him as your familiar then, my lady?" Mestier Allyn asked, his voice cautious.

"Yes," she said. "I am."

Cameron made a soft noise. She glared.

He held up his hands. "Do you think that wise?"

"I don't care. It is *right*," she said. "I already have a sanctii, a petty fam can't possibly make the situation any worse." They hadn't yet spoken, but there was no way they could get away now. Not with their families hostage.

Bonding Tok could do no harm. Only good. Whether or not Cameron accepted her point or was simply unwilling to carry on this conversation in public, she didn't know. And she wasn't inclined to particularly care. This one thing was her decision.

"Let us go to the tower," she said to Mestier Allyn, not stopping to see if Cameron followed.

The climb to the tower didn't take long. As she stepped through the door to the rookery, there was a frantic cawing and the sound of something banging against metal echoed across the room. Behind her, Cameron made a startled noise, but Sophie was looking for Tok.

"Hush now," Mestier Allyn said, crossing the room and pulling back a curtain to reveal a large cage, where Tok was perched on a branch, banging a small metal tin against the bars. "Stop that fuss. Yes, yes, she's back. I will let you out if you can behave."

Tok cawed again, his bright eyes meeting Sophie's. She hurried over to the cage while Mestier Allyn opened the door.

"I don't like to confine them," he said. "But this was for the best. He tried to get out of the building. I'm not sure what he would have done if we'd left him free. Taken off after you, I suspect."

"How would he know where I'd gone?" Sophie asked as Tok leapt to balance on the small wooden stand by the door.

"They have their ways. Of course, no guarantee he'd survive a trip. Plenty of predators out there." Mestier Allyn stood back from the cage.

Tok launched himself toward Sophie with a final squawk, swooping up into the air to circle her head—so close she heard the air rustling through his feathers—before he landed on her shoulder and delivered another loud caw in her ear before rubbing his beak on her hair.

"What's this nonsense about fretting?" she said, reaching up to stroke him.

She looked back at the Master of the Ravens. "Do you have anything I can give him to eat?"

"Yes, I have food." His face turned serious. "But if you're not going to bond him, my lady, then you need to let me know. I'll send him away to one of the other towers before it's too late for him."

Sophie shook her head, resisting the urge to pluck Tok from her shoulder and cradle him to her chest. She doubted he'd appreciate it. "No, that won't be necessary. I can't do that to him."

Tok made a distinctly satisfied grumbling squawk.

"In fact," Sophie said. "I'll take him to Madame Simsa now. I assume, she can tell me what I need to do to arrange the bonding?"

Mestier Allyn nodded. "She can, my lady."

She blew out a breath, relieved. She didn't want any more trouble, so she needed to do this correctly in the eyes of the Academe.

"Are you sure about this?" Cameron asked. Sophie turned. He was still standing by the door.

"Yes. This is my choice." She knew she was being unfair. None of this was Cameron's fault.

"Then I will meet you back at our rooms. I have to speak to Henri. Bring him the emperor's message," Cameron said.

Chloe. Sophie's heart clenched. Someone else caught up in the trouble that she had caused. Henri would be furious. And heartbroken. All the things she still felt. But, as she listened to Cameron's footsteps descending the stairs, she knew she couldn't help Henri. Or Chloe. And thinking about that might drive her mad.

But she could help Tok. Could give him what he needed to be safe and happy. "Mestier Allyn, let's see if we can get Tok some food."

"Yes," Mestier Allyn agreed. He crossed to a metal cabinet, unlocked it, and withdrew a plate of meat scraps, holding it out to Sophie. "He'll want more later. Make sure you send him back here. Or ask the kitchen for some raw meat if he won't leave you. I'll send them notes on what you'll need."

Madame Simsa's apartment wasn't far from the Raven Tower, but Sophie's progress was slower than usual thanks to Tok. Full of energy after scarfing down the meat Mestier Allyn had provided, he kept launching himself into the air, circling her wildly before landing back on her shoulder, as though he couldn't quite make up his mind where he wanted to be. Repeated entreaties for him to behave didn't seem to have any impact. He was nibbling her hair when Madame Simsa opened her door.

At the sight of Sophie and Tok, her silver eyebrows shot upward. "I thought you were rusticating in the countryside?"

"We came back," Sophie said shortly. "The emperor needed his duq, apparently." She didn't want to say more than that.

Perhaps Madame Simsa read something in her tone. She didn't ask any more about Sophie's return. "Come for a lesson, have you?"

"Actually, I came to ask you about Tok. I've decided I will take him as my familiar. So I need to know how that works."

"You could ask your sanctii, she'd probably tell you." Madame Simsa's expression was as sharp as her voice.

"I'm asking you, Venable. You and Henri told me not to do

water magic." Not that the bond was water magic as she understood it. Petty fams were a tool of earth. Though one that Anglion earth witches didn't use. Or even know about. Imogene's words in the bain-sel about Anglion women being held back from their power came back to her. As did the image of the soap floating in the air. Which was almost definitely Sophie using the water magic that she was not supposed to.

Madame Simsa, however, didn't seem to be able to tell that Sophie had broken the rules. "I suppose that is a step in the right direction." She stepped back and beckoned Sophie inside.

Rikki was curled on one of the sofas seemingly asleep, but the monkey opened one brown eye briefly as Sophie came into the room with Tok on her shoulder, before closing it again as though satisfied that there was nothing to be concerned about.

"Have you told Elarus about this?" Madame Simsa asked.

"Not precisely," Sophie said. "Will it matter to her?"

Madame Simsa shrugged. "Maybe not. There aren't many earth witches who also are strong enough in water magic to hold a sanctii and the bond between each mage and their sanctii is similar but not identical. I was already bonded with Rikki when I bonded with Belarus. He didn't seem to mind." Madame Simsa settled down next to Rikki. "But your bond with Elarus is far from the usual kind, so perhaps it would be prudent to ask."

"I'm not sure she could change my mind." Sophie said. "Mestier Allyn said Tok was fretting already while I was away. I don't want him to be sent away."

"You must make your own decisions, of course. But still, when it comes to one's sanctii, it pays to keep things civil. And in your case, make sure there are no peculiarities in your bond that might play into this."

Sophie hadn't considered that aspect of the problem.

"I'll do it now," Sophie said. She barely had time to think [Elarus] before the sanctii appeared.

"Yes?" Elarus asked in her graveled voice.

"We have a question for you," Sophie said. "Do you understand about petty familiars?"

Elarus glanced down at the sofa where Rikki was curled up next to Madame Simsa. "Like that one? Yes." Her gaze returned to Sophie. Or maybe it was the raven she was watching.

Sophie stroked Tok's beak. "You've met Tok before. Well, I was thinking of making him my petty fam. Is that something you would mind?"

"Mind?"

"Would it upset you?"

Elarus' expression shifted. "Upset? No. But why need small one when have sanctii?"

"I'm an earth witch too," Sophie said. "And Tok has grown attached to me. The Master of Raven thinks it would be best if we formed the bond. I agree."

"Small one should be happy." Elarus was definitely watching Tok now. The bird was uncharacteristically silent and still under her gaze. "I bond?"

"Madame Simsa will show me how," Sophie said. "Unless it would be different because of the way you and I are joined?"

Elarus shrugged. Apparently not. Sophie looked across to Madame Simsa. "That seems to answer that."

"Good," Madame Simsa said. "When do you want to do this?"

"Is it difficult?"

"Not hugely. Normally it is something that a student would attempt after progressing further in their studies than you have, but there are precedents for bonding early when the petty fam has shown such a clear preference." Madame Simsa looked at Tok. "Silly creature. Hardly out of the nest and thinking that you should have a person of your own. Too smart for your own good, just like your mother."

Tok seemed to take this with no comment to offer in return. Or else he was still quelled by Elarus's watchful gaze. But he was going to have to get used to the sanctii.

Sophie waited to see if Madame Simsa was going to continue, but the older woman was looking down at Rikki, one hand stroking the monkey's head.

"How did you meet Rikki?" Sophie asked.

"At a party, of all things, "Madame Simsa said. "It wasn't unexpected. Our hostess was fond of strange pets and I had recently lost my previous petty fam. The bond extends their lifespan, but it can't stretch things forever, and I am quite old. Rikki wouldn't leave me alone at the party once she spotted me, and I realized I had found my next fam. It caused some consternation. Madame Petra was quite attached. Or so she claimed. Maybe she was trying to make sure that she wasn't left out of pocket. I handed over gold, and she didn't argue much against that. And Rikki has been with me ever since. Her species apparently can live thirty years or more in the forests where they roam, hopefully she will be by my side until my time is done." She nodded toward Tok. "These ones are long-lived, so that helps. Though you are young, child, so there will be loss in the end if you take this path. Does that worry you?"

Sophie shook her head. "I've grown up with dogs and cats. I know what it is to have to say goodbye. I also know that the love before is worth the price you pay. And I imagine that the bond with a fam will be even deeper." She wasn't going into this entirely blind. She knew that the bond with Tok would offer an extra source of power and linkage to the earth when she needed it. Not in the realm of how a water mage could work with—or through—a sanctii but enough to be helpful in times of need.

Not that she was doing it only for the power. Or at all, if she was honest. She simply didn't want to see Tok unhappy for something that was no fault of his own. She knew too much about how that felt, to want to inflict it on another when she had the power to prevent it.

Madame Simsa's smile at her words was definitely approving. Which made a pleasant change from the chilly attitude Sophie had been received since she had bonded with Elarus.

"What does the bond involve?" Sophie said. "A ritual?"

"That is the formal way, yes," Madame Simsa said. "But it can be easier than that if you wish it."

Sophie hesitated. "How easy?"

"We could do it here and now if you wanted." Madame Simsa cocked her head.

Was this a test? Sophie's bond with Cameron was irregular as was the way she'd bonded with Elarus. Was Madame Simsa wanting to see if she would take the unconventional path yet again if she was offered the choice?

She needed allies, not mistrust. "Perhaps it would be better to do things the usual way," she said. "But I'd like it to be done soon."

"Leaving again?" Madame Simsa asked.

No. Not anymore. Sophie looked away to hide her flinch. "No. But Tok has waited long enough, and if we do this, then we can get on with our lives. Maybe Tok will be helpful to me in my studies." This earned her a squawk and a gentle nip to her ear, as though Tok wanted to reassure her that he would definitely be useful.

She winced and smiled ruefully. "Maybe once we're bonded, he'll stop pecking me."

"I wouldn't rely on that, my dear," Madame Simsa said "Petty fams tend to get more independent, not less so. Though you will, of course, have the power to compel him to action if you ever really need to." She pushed up from the sofa. "Let me speak to Henri and we will see what can be arranged for later this evening. The bonding doesn't take long, and it doesn't need to be a public spectacle. Your husband should attend though. In case there is something we need to adjust to deal with your *augmentier*." Her mouth quirked. "I suggest this be the last bond your consider forming. Three should be enough for any woman."

"You have two," Sophie pointed out.

"True. But not a third. I was not foolish enough to lock my power up with that of a man's. Not that you have done that exactly." Madame Simsa's expression turned speculative, and she peered at Sophie as though considering. "But still. Three is enough. Any more and anyone who can see the ley lines will be tripping over you. You don't want to draw any more attention to yourself than necessary."

Too late for that.

Sophie thought of the eyes of all the counselors in Aristides's audience chamber. And remembered the domina's invitation. Or command. Whichever it had been. Yet another thing that she needed to attend to. But, first things first. Her stomach was starting to remind her that she hadn't eaten since she'd left Sanct de Sangre.

"Is there something I should read about the ritual? Something I need to do to prepare. Or to prepare Tok?" she asked.

"Do you have the *LivreTerre?*" Madame Simsa. "That has a chapter on petty familiars, which contains the basic ritual. As I said, there isn't much to it."

The LivreTerre was one of the small tower of books about earth magic that sat on Sophie's desk in their apartment. "I have it. I'm going to get dinner, and then I will be in my rooms with Tok. Send for me there once Henri agrees."

"I will," Madame Simsa said. "Make sure Tok eats. Petty fams can burn more energy when they're used in a working, so you need to get used to having to feed him up. I'm sure Mestier Allyn can advise you. At least he shouldn't have a fondness for exotic fruits like this one." She looked back over her shoulder to where Riki still slept. "She's cost me a small fortune over the years."

Cameron waited for Sophie to finish eating. She'd been pale and quiet, shrunk in on herself, on the journey back from Sanct de Sangre and quieter still on their return from the palace. He hated seeing her that way.

She looked somewhat happier now as she sat and ate, feeding Tok crumbs of toast between her own bites.

Damn bird. He didn't understand why she was suddenly in a rush to bond with the creature. But if Tok could help her cope with the emperor's news, then he was going to accept it and move on. She was right, after all. A petty fam was nothing when she already had a sanctii.

He'd stoked up the fire on his return from Henri's office. The maistre had been infuriated by Cameron's report that Eloisa had included Chloe in her hostages and angered further still that the emperor hadn't included him in the gathering at the palace to hear the news directly. But he'd kept his feeling in check, had offered no criticism of Cameron's and Sophie's decision not to return to Anglion. The maistre's restraint had done nothing to relieve Cameron's own anger. The coals had borne the brunt of his frustrations when he'd returned to the apartment, but at least the room had been warm by the time Sophie had appeared with Tok.

She sat near it now, the warmth returning some life to her cheeks.

The colors of the flames flickered over her hair bringing out the red sheen that was growing stronger every day and high-lighting the patches of black starting to form. She hadn't said anything about those, but he'd noticed them at Sanct de Sangre.

Water magic. Making its mark on her. Which only made the emperor's suggestion even more preposterous. Anglion wouldn't accept a water mage for a queen. Unless Sophie covered her hair every day and never spoke to Elarus, the powers she had embraced here in Illvya couldn't be hidden.

But as much as he didn't like the plan, somewhere deep in his gut, he was beginning to believe that Aristides was correct about one thing. That there was something wrong in Anglion. Some-thing wrong with Eloisa. The woman he'd known—who he'd shared a bed with-had been capricious and spoilt, perhaps, but she had never been cruel. Or overly power-hungry. Her position at the court had been clear. She was the Crown Princess. She would inherit after her father if she survived him. In fact, other than her desire not to remarry after she'd lost her husband, she hadn't made many overtly political moves that he could remember. It made no sense for her to challenge the empire now.

Not if she was in her right mind and exercising her own will and not someone else's.

The fact that Sophie had seen Eloisa in her visions seemed to only confirm his misgiving. Had she seen the queen again today? Clearly she'd seen more than she had told Domina Francis. Had it been Eloisa? That would be three times. He didn't know much about visions and water magic, but three times seemed like a message from the goddess.

One perhaps they shouldn't ignore.

"Are you going to tell me what else you saw?" he asked softly.

Sophie's head jerked up, her expression flashing guilt. "What do you mean?"

"You didn't tell Domina Francis everything, did you? I understand why you wouldn't, but I don't want you to hold back with me. You can tell me. Was it Eloisa again? The same vision?"

Sophie slumped deeper into her chair. "Yes," she said quietly. Too quietly. "This time she turned and looked at me." She shivered. "Three times. Three times I've seen her now. It can't be a coincidence."

Her words, so like his own thoughts, made him want to shiver too. "I think you need to talk to someone who knows more about this than we do."

"Like Domina Francis? You think I should tell her that maybe Aristides is right? That something is terribly wrong in Anglion? You think she wouldn't tell him immediately?"

"She probably would," he agreed and leaned forward to take her hand. "Madame Simsa, then. She's your teacher, and she has no reason to want to see you on the throne back in Anglion. I get the impression she's rather fond of you."

"Lately she's been mostly annoyed at me," Sophie said. "She

thinks I was foolish to bond with Elarus. That I'm overreaching. Though she was pleased about Tok."

"You have to ask someone. You need to know what it means that you have seen this three times now."

"You mean I have to know if it's true?" She put down the glass of water and curled her feet up into the chair. "What good does that do me? Unless I do what Aristides wants, and I—we—go back there."

"I'm not sure we're going to have much choice about that," Cameron said. He'd hoped she'd be the one to say it first. But it had to be said. "Unless you're prepared to sacrifice our families."

Sophie closed her eyes. "I'm not a queen, Cameron. I don't want to rule."

"Then we can find another way, perhaps. Make a deal with Aristides. But right now, using what he can offer us seems to be our best chance. He can't force you to take the throne once you're there."

"You think I could refuse? Does he strike you as a man who would take kindly to me turning around and saying 'no' after he's started an invasion for me?"

"There are other heirs, other options. We could return, retrieve our families, find out what is happening at court. If Eloisa is—" he broke off, not wanting to say it.

"What? Crazy?" Sophie's mouth was grim. "She could be. She changed after the attack on the palace; we both know that. Maybe the strain was too much for her, or maybe the domina didn't heal her fully."

Her eyes flared wide. "Or maybe," she said slowly. "It isn't Eloisa who is the problem."

Cameron frowned. "What do you mean?"

"Eloisa changed after the attack on the palace. After Domina Skey healed her. It's Domina Skey who hates me. Because I'm not bound like I should be. What if she did something to Eloisa when she healed her? Gained some sort of hold over her?"

"How could she? That's not something I've ever heard of."

"The temple knows how to do bindings. They form the marriage bonds, after all. Bindings can be used to give a degree of control. The water mages control the sanctii."

"The water mages use water magic," Cameron pointed out, trying to will his pounding heart to slow. "Last time I saw her, Domina Skey's hair was redder than the sun. No black. She's an earth witch, nothing more."

"Maybe not," Sophie said. "But maybe she found another way. You and I formed a bond with no water magic. The marriage bonds are earth magic. She could have found a way to twist an earth bond, somehow. But if it can be done, it can be undone."

"By you?"

She winced. "I don't know. Aristides has half an army of mages. Someone should be able to figure it out. If we can free Eloisa, then she can be queen. She would have no reason to pursue us further."

"I'm not so sure about that," Cameron said. "Right now you're her heir. You have powers that she can only dream of. Forbidden magic. She might still see you as a threat."

"Not enough of a threat to worry about," Sophie said. "Not once she knows I'm a water mage. She can exile me or disinherit me. Both."

"You'd be happy to return here? Leave Anglion behind permanently?"

Sophie hesitated. "Not happy, exactly. But it hasn't seemed likely that we could return to Anglion for some time now. I don't want to leave our families behind, but if they were safe and if Eloisa was restored, well, perhaps exile would be a price worth paying."

"But how do we get out safely? There's a price to pay for harming a domina," Cameron said. Those laws were as old as Anglion itself. The goddess protected her most favored children.

"The goddess has been sending me visions to tell me something is wrong. Or at least it seems as though she has. If she wants me to fix the problem, then surely she can't seek retribution."

"She may not. But I wouldn't count on the Anglion temple viewing things the same way. Eloisa's hands would be tied. The palace doesn't interfere in temple law, you know that."

"You're assuming that we'd have to kill the domina to reveal her. We don't have to hurt her. If we could break the bond, then she wouldn't have any power over Eloisa any more. Eloisa takes her power back. Eloisa punishes the domina. I'm sure there are temple laws about binding people against their will. The temple is supposed to help protect the crown and the country. They're not exempt from treason."

"Are you sure about that?"

"No, but I know someone who could tell us," Sophie said.

"You want to ask Domina Francis what happens if Eloisa has to depose Domina Skey?" That seemed unwise. Would a domina even be willing to consider such a thing? Let alone encourage someone on such a path? "Temple law here will be different anyway."

"Once upon a time, they were the same. Domina Gerrard told me that the temple at the palace has archives. Records. We had the same laws once, the same beliefs. They will know what has changed.

"They know what has changed here. Not at home."

"We know the temple banned water magic in Anglion. We know they've changed the marriage bonds. But they always tell us that the rituals haven't changed for a long time. If they are determined to maintain the status quo, I can't imagine they have changed the laws. Or that any of the monarchs would allow a change that would let the temple attack them. King Stefan wasn't under Domina Skey's control for a start."

"No," Cameron agreed. Stefan had been civil to the temple, and he had taken part in the rites and rituals as his duty dictated he needed to, but he hadn't been particularly devout.

And he was firm in his grip on power. There had been clashes with the temple at times over resources and other minor matters. Damage to temples when the Red Guard had been settling disputes and such. Stefan had paid for the damage—or made those who had caused the disputes to do so—but he hadn't given into any of the temple's more excessive demands for recompense and retribution.

Cameron's father had told stories of spirited discussions between the domina—and her predecessor—and the king. He'd used them as lessons in politics for Liam but didn't spare Cameron and Alec either.

They were expected to know what was happening at court, to understand power. They were tools for the erl to use as he wanted, and if Cameron was honest with himself, he imagined the erl had wanted to be sure that if anything had happened to Liam that either of his other two sons would be able to step into the role of the heir—and the erl eventually—with the appropriate skills they would need to continue the Mackenzie's legacy.

How exactly his father had thought he could control what they would do once he was dead was something of a puzzle, but the erl had never been a man who had considered his way could be anything but the right way. Or that he wouldn't live forever, possibly. The explosion that had killed him was not something that he would have imagined a possibility. No one had expected an attack on the court.

Other than those who had planned it, of course.

He stilled a moment. That was something they hadn't thought about. Domina Skey was a problem, and perhaps Sophie was correct and the domina was wielding some sort of influence over Eloisa, but she wasn't the only one. Sophie had felt the presence of water magic after the attack. Someone had supplied the scriptii to trigger the attack on the palace. Someone had sent Sevan to kidnap or kill Sophie if she didn't agree to return and provided him with the means to summon a sanctii.

Whoever that was, they had some access to Illvyan magic. If he had still been in Anglion, Cameron would have assumed it was the emperor, but now he knew better. The emperor could take Anglion if he wanted it. He didn't need to scheme and plot. He could send his armies over the ocean to overwhelm Anglion with sheer numbers whenever he wanted.

"I think—" he started to say, but the door wards began to chime.

CHAPTER 15

Sophie walked into Henri's office feeling both nervous about the bonding to come and relieved to have an interruption from her conversation with Cameron. She needed time to think. Willem's arrival at their apartment door with a note from Henri had been a welcome distraction.

Tok made a small grumbling noise as they walked into the room but stayed where he was perched on her shoulder.

Mestier Allyn stood near to Henri's desk. He peered at Tok and grunted something that might be approval rather than saying anything. Madame Simsa was seated by the fireplace, watching Venable Ettier, one of the earth witches who taught Sophie's classes, lifting coals from the fire into a wide iron brazier that rested on three tall, thin legs. Henri had been sitting at his desk, but he rose as Sophie and Cameron entered, murmuring a greeting. She braced herself for him to say something about Chloe, but he didn't. She didn't know whether that was worse.

But she pushed away the guilt. Time enough for guilt later. She had to focus now, make sure she did everything in this ritual correctly.

The four Academe staff wore their robes, glittering as rainbowed black as Tok's wings in the lamplight. Sophie had chosen to wear hers because its padded shoulder offered the most comfortable way to carry Tok. If he got much bigger—which he was going to do—she'd have to look at ways to reinforce all her clothing or she would need a wardrobe allowance far beyond what they could afford.

"Are you ready to begin?" Henri asked and Sophie started.

"Yes, Maistre," she said hastily, hoping she had covered her distraction.

Henri turned to Mestier Allyn. "And you, Master of Ravens, do you judge this bonding to be what the bird wants?"

Tok couldn't speak for himself so it seemed fair that he was to be allocated a voice.

Mestier Allyn nodded, the wrinkles around his dark eyes deepening as he smiled. "Yes, Maistre. He has made his choice clear for some time now."

"Then let us begin." Henri nodded and gestured at the brazier. Mestier Allyn and Venable Ettier grasped it by the legs and moved it to stand in the center of the room with careful movements. "If you would step forward please, Sophie."

She did so, Tok's claws pricking her as the bird shifted his stance to keep his balance. Cameron moved too and the others formed a rough circle around them.

"We are here to witness a binding of a witch and her petty familiar," Henri said, his voice measured, the Illvyan words hitting Sophie's ear at a different cadence, almost as though Henri was singing them rather speaking them. "Does anyone have any objections to this binding?"

No one spoke.

"Sophie, could you hold out your arm please?"

She extended her arm and Henri produced a small silver knife. The blade caught the light from the coals and the lamps around the room, a shimmer of gold and red and blue dancing along the edge. She took the flashing gleam as testament to its sharpness and turned her hand palm up, determined not to flinch. There hadn't been much time, but she'd managed to read the LivreTerre's pages on the ritual.

The binding required blood. Not common, in earth magic, but blood carried magic, and it made sense to use something to enhance the magic when binding a human and an animal.

The bite of the blade was quick and bright. Sophie caught her breath against the sting as she turned her hand over and held the wound steady over the coals. Madame Simsa caught several drops of the blood in a dish that gleamed as brightly as the knife before moving back. Sophie's hand continued to drip blood slowly, the drops hitting the coals with a sizzle and a flare of burned salt and copper.

"Do you know the words?" Henri asked.

Sophie nodded. "Yes." She'd tried to commit them to memory. It wasn't a long spell, but she was tired and reveilé or no, memorizing written Illvyan was still a strain. Hopefully her memory wouldn't fail her.

[I remember,] Elarus said suddenly in her head.

Sophie's hand jerked. [Are you here?] There had been no mention of bringing the sanctii to the ceremony, and if Martius or Belarus were in the room, they were keeping themselves as unseen as Elarus.

[Might need help. With bond.]

[You said we wouldn't.]

No answer was forthcoming. She bit her lip.

"Sophie?" Henri said. "Is something wrong?"

"No." She shook her head, turning her mind back to the task at hand. She had no way to force Elarus to leave. To be honest, she didn't particularly want her to leave. The sanctii was right. This bonding could be more complicated than others. Besides, neither Martius nor Belarus had raised any alarm so perhaps there was nothing objectionable to Elarus being there.

"Mestier Allyn, will you take Tok please?"

The master stepped forward and held out a gloved hand. "Tok, come here."

Tok squawked indignantly and his claws curled deeper into Sophie's shoulder, as though he was reluctant to give up his perch.

"It's only for a short time," she said, trying to sound soothing. "Go along or we can't do this. You don't want me to have to bond some other raven because you wouldn't follow instructions at this point, do you?"

The answering squawk was extra loud and extra annoyed. But Tok leaped and landed on the master's outstretched arm, shaking out ruffled feathers.

"Good boy," Mestier Allyn said and moved his arm over the brazier until Tok was level with Sophie's hand, the smoke moving over both of them.

Henri took the plate from Madame Simsa and dipped his thumb into the blood, pressing it first against Tok's head and then onto the wound on Sophie's hand. Sophie closed her hand into a fist, closed her eyes, and began to recite the ritual.

As she said the last word, Tok stepped from Mestier Allyn's hand to hers as if drawn there by a leash, and she felt a flare of power, a sensation akin to something within snapping into place. Nothing of the strength she had felt with Cameron or Elarus, but the feeling had familiar echoes.

"It is done, I think," she managed.

Tok cawed, a triumphant sound that Sophie both heard and felt inside her head and then launched into the air, circling the room and cawing triumphantly. He swooped exuberantly and Sophie laughed at the happiness she could feel in a small corner of her mind. She'd done something good today. She could hold onto that.

"Tok," she called, and he changed course so fast it was a wonder that he managed to stay in the air. He streaked back to

Sophie and landed on her shoulder with a thump and a rustle of settling wings.

"Sophie," he croaked distinctly.

She was so surprised she almost dislodged him craning her neck to see him.

"Sophie," he croaked again.

"He *spoke*," she said.

Henri and Mestier Allyn smiled in unison.

"Oh yes," Henri said. "The smarter ones can learn to over time. Those who are bonded usually develop quite good vocabularies."

In Anglion she'd heard of parrots who could talk but the birds weren't common, and she'd never actually seen one.

Madame Simsa cleared her throat and smiled. "You should have chosen a monkey, my dear. They can't offer commentary."

"Rikki makes quite enough noise," Venable Ettier said with a smile. "At least Sophie will be able to understand Tok."

"Sophie!" Tok repeated. Sophie couldn't see his face, and she wasn't sure if a raven could actually look smug, but he definitely sounded smug.

"Silly bird," she said, but she was delighted. "Do I need to teach him words?"

"If you want him to say certain things it can be a good idea to practice with him," Mestier Allyn said. "He will learn some things he hears regardless. You need to watch what you say if you don't want him to pick up less...desirable phrases."

"Are you suggesting I say unsavory things?" Sophie asked with a grin.

Henri shrugged. "We all say things we don't intend at times. There was a court case once where a man was arrested because his raven kept saying 'you killed me' after his wife disappeared. The truth seekers said the bird was telling the truth. His master went to prison."

"I'll be sure to make sure Tok isn't in the room if I ever plot murder," Sophie said. She didn't know if it was Tok's happiness infecting her, but she was feeling distinctly giddy. "Where will he stay now? Will he still sleep in the tower with the others?"

"That is usual while you are here. He may not want to for a time while you both adjust to the bond, but it is best for him to still spend time with other ravens. I've asked for a traveling cage to be brought to your rooms. He can sleep in that. We can talk about the rest of his care in the morning. The hour grows late, and I must settle the rest of my charges for the night." He bowed in Sophie's direction. "Congratulations, my lady. I wish you many years together."

The phrase was echoed by the others and still rang in Sophie's ears as she and Cameron returned to their apartment with Tok flying sentry above her. Many years. She hoped there would be, but part of her was afraid that she might be forced to choices that might cut them short.

"Now, you have to behave," Sophie said to Tok as the carriage turned into the forecourt of the palace temple the next morning.

Tok made a protesting noise, and she wagged a finger at him. "Don't pretend to be innocent. Look at the fuss you made when I tried to leave you behind."

The raven was perched on the sill of the carriage window, wings spread slightly against the jolting of the ride. He gave her a look through one beady eye that clearly suggested that leaving him behind had been a stupid idea, and he had merely pointed that out. Madame Simsa and the Master of Ravens had been correct. Tok had shown no desire to let her out of his sight in the ten hours that had passed since they had completed the bonding ceremony.

So much so that he had perched on the end of her bath earlier. She hadn't attempted breakfast in the dining room. Petty fams weren't supposed to go in there, and besides, she was in no mood for idle conversation.

Not when there had been a note from Domina Francis, reiterating the domina's request to speak to Sophie that morning. She had made no mention of Cameron, but he, like Tok, had refused to be left behind.

"You're going to have to learn to let her go some places without you," Cameron said to the bird, breaking the silence of their journey. "You can't sleep at the foot of the bed like a dog. Nor, I imagine, will the emperor want feathers in his ballroom."

"Sophie!" Tok said indignantly.

Sophie smiled, amused and relieved that Cameron was talking to the bird. He was right, but the raven's reluctance to be parted from her was oddly charming. Though she suspected the charm would wear off eventually. She hoped that Mestier Allyn had been right and that Tok wouldn't always need to be her shadow.

She had—with the help of a platter of fresh meat—managed to coax him into the cage Mestier Allyn had provided. There had been squawks of outrage when she'd closed the door, but she'd draped the cage as per the instructions that had accompanied it, and he had settled eventually.

Unlike her. She'd lain awake half the night, alternating between fighting tears and trying to figure out a way to rescue her family that didn't involve going along with Aristides's plans. She failed utterly in coming up with an alternative.

Cameron had slept as little as she. He'd lain still and silent, but his breathing hadn't sounded like he'd been sleeping. As much as she'd wanted to reach out for his comfort, the fact that he hadn't reached first stopped her. Maybe they'd finally reached a point where he wouldn't be able to forgive her for what she'd done to his life. Or his family. Maybe he should return to Anglion without her. But she suspected that was no longer an option. If he returned without her, it seemed likely he would only be seized as well to try and increase the pressure on her.

Eloisa was unlikely to believe him if he disavowed Sophie. The queen wouldn't have bothered to try and undermine their marriage on their wedding day if she hadn't been jealous of the affection between Sophie and Cameron. And, if by some chance of the goddess, the queen did believe him, it was highly likely that Domina Skey would step in and declare that he should be punished for being married to a water mage.

So, no. They were both out of options. Apparently Cameron was finding that as difficult to cope with as she was.

He'd been silent over breakfast, and as much as she'd wanted to believe it was only that he was not yet quite awake, she didn't. Relief had flooded her when he'd said he was coming with her when the domina's note arrived. Even if he was furious with her, apparently he was still keeping his oaths.

She didn't think he'd take kindly to her offering to release him from those oaths. He'd made his position on their marriage clear. He was sticking to her, sanctii and ravens and emperors be damned.

Perhaps he was crazy, but then again, if he was crazy, so was she. Perhaps a degree of insanity would be needed if they were to survive.

Tok pecked the window, making the glass rattle and Sophie realized the carriage had stopped moving. The door opened and Tok swooped out before she could stop him.

Cameron followed Tok, turning to offer Sophie his hand.

She climbed down and stopped to stare.

Unlike the temple in Isle de Angelique, there was nothing ordinary about this structure. It, like the palace, was designed to awe. It was a marvel of domes and columns punctuated by stained glass. The walls were the same dazzling white marble as the palace, but the domes and the many slopes of the roof were bronze, judging by their green-gold shade. The largest of the domes dwarfed the others, a plume of smoke rising from its apex. Presumably it sat over the main offering fire, but the shape and size of the many-layered building made it impossible to judge where exactly within the walls that may be.

The forecourt was planted with oak trees, massive gnarled things that had to be ancient. The broad paths between the trees were tiled in a pattern of soft greens and white. The mosaics didn't form the quartered circle outright, but they definitely suggested it.

"Shall we?" Cameron said, offering Sophie an arm.

"I guess we shall." She tucked her hand around his elbow, and they began to walk. A prior in pristine brown robes approached them as they neared the building.

"Good morning. Goddess shade you both. May I assist you?" the man asked, smiling at them. His hair was a reddish shade of blond and the shaggy eyebrows above deepest blue eyes much the same color. His deep brown robes were similar to the ones Domina Gerrard had worn. More tailored than the robes worn by the Anglion priors but similar enough that Sophie could tell the man's rank without asking.

Tok swooped in from above and settled on Sophie's shoulder. The prior's smile didn't falter though his eyes flicked to the raven.

Sophie ignored Tok. "I am Lady Scardale and this is my husband, Lord Scardale. Domina Francis is expecting me, I believe."

The man's eyebrows rose, but he nodded. "I will send word that you are here." He lifted a hand and waved one of the devouts standing near the temple doors over, bending to whisper a few quick words in the woman's ear. She hurried off.

"I am Prior Giarme," the man said, turning his focus back to Sophie. "If you would follow me, my lord and my lady, I will take you to Domina Francis." He paused. "Unless you would care to stop first in the sanctuary and spend some time in devotion." He tilted his head. "I do not think I have seen you attend here?"

"No, we are new to the city," Cameron said. His tone didn't invite further questions.

"We've been to the temple in Isle de Angelique to give our respects to the goddess," Sophie added. "We don't want to keep Domina Francis waiting for us."

Prior Giarme didn't comment on this but asked them to follow him. As they neared, the temple, Tok squawked and flew up to perch in one of the oaks.

"Tok," Sophie hissed.

Cameron took her hand. "He'll wait for you. Or he'll come find you. Let's go."

They entered via the main doors, but there was no time to gain more than a fleeting impression of the interior—more marble, bronze, and stained glass—before Prior Giarme led them to an unobtrusive door in the left wall just past the entry and into a corridor that was more functional than lavish in its decoration.

The floor was still marble, but the windowless walls were an undecorated stretch of plain white, broken here and there by bronze sconces supporting alternate rows of lanterns and earth-lights that were the only source of illumination. They walked for a few minutes until they reached a staircase and began to climb. Two flights before another door opened and they stepped into a second hallway.

This one was slightly more welcoming, the stark white walls edged by tiled borders weaving patterns of leafy green. Sunlight fell through the high windows, highlighting the same pattern painted along the edges of the wooden floor. The prior stopped at a set of doors about halfway down the corridor and knocked once before entering.

Two dominas looked up from identical desks set either side of a second set of doors in the far wall. One of them nodded at Prior Giarme.

"The domina is expecting you, you can go in." She turned her attention back to the stack of papers on her desk as though she had no more time to spare.

Prior Giarme advanced to the inner doors and knocked again, beckoning them to follow.

Domina Francis sat behind a vast wooden desk piled high with ledgers and papers and crowded with plants and vials of what looked like temple oil. Several inkwells, pens sitting in them, were perched precariously amongst the clutter. She didn't look up immediately, her gaze intent on whatever she was writing. She finished it and signed with a flourish, and then stood.

"Lady Scardale, Lord Scardale, welcome." If she hadn't expected Cameron, she showed no sign of surprise. She came around the desk smiling at them with what looked like genuine warmth. Her robes were the same temple brown as the others wore, but the quartered cross that hung around her neck was heavy gold, set with emeralds the size of a good pearl. She was *the* domina, Sophie reminded herself. Illvya's Domina Skey. Not someone to take lightly. Or trust on face value.

"Domina Francis." Sophie curtsied.

Domina Skey would have expected a greater obeisance, but Domina Francis merely waved a hand and said, "Don't bother with ceremony up here. There are not enough hours in the day to get through my work if I have to spend half of it watching people bob up and down." She held out the folded paper. "Adolphus, this needs to go to the mistress of halls, please. Quickly. Don't worry about a reply. Tell her this is my final word. I'll send for someone to escort Lord and Lady Scardale back to their carriage when we are done. You can get back to your duties."

The prior, Sophie thought, looked slightly put out at this succession of orders—hoping to remain and gather some gossip perhaps—but he took the paper and murmured, "Domina," before departing swiftly.

The domina gestured them toward the cluster of chairs arrayed in front of a small fireplace. It wasn't lit, the sunlight streaming through the windows enough to warm the room. "Let's sit. Can I get you anything? Tea, perhaps? Something to eat? We dine simply here, but there will be cake. Domina

Andreis, who runs our kitchens, knows I have a sweet tooth and thinks she can get on my good side if she indulges it." She seated herself in the chair facing the door.

"And can she?" Cameron asked as he took the chair that sat between the domina and the third chair, leaving Sophie no choice but to sit on his other side.

"Some days, yes," the domina said. "Running this place is trying at times, and generally, we do not indulge in alcohol. Cake is a reasonable substitute." She grinned; the expression more wicked than Sophie expected. It made her look younger—or less formidable perhaps—though Sophie wasn't sure what her true age might be. There were silver threads in the domina's hair, but her face was mostly unlined.

"It may not do my waistline any good, but the goddess gave us sugar, so I expect she does not mind the indulgence much," the domina continued.

Sophie laughed, startled. She had never had much of a friendly relationship with any temple representative she'd known. The small temple in the nearest town to her family's estate had been simple and welcoming enough, but she wouldn't have described Domina Greenleaf who was in charge there as having much of a sense of humor. Domina Skey rarely even smiled. But she steeled herself against the inclination to like Domina Francis too soon.

After all, charm was a weapon all of its own.

The domina had risen to a position of high power, even if the goddess wasn't the only deity recognized in the empire. She hadn't made it there by pure goodwill and being the sort of simple down-to-earth woman she was currently portraying herself to be. Temple politics—like any other kind—was too complex for that.

"I'm not hungry," Sophie said. "But you should eat if you wish, Domina. Your days here must be hectic. The temple is so large."

The domina nodded. "Yes. Close to three hundred serve

here, including servants. Of course, we have the school for acolytes and their teachers, and that increases the numbers. Usually we have fifty students at any one time. Not nearly so large as your Academe, but enough to keep us busy."

Fifty acolytes. Hardly enough to keep the empire supplied with future dominas and priors. There must be other schools elsewhere. Which made sense. There were other Academes di Sages in other parts of the empire, Sophie understood. But the Rookery was the most prestigious.

"The temple in Kingswell is not half so big," Sophie said. In fact, she didn't know exactly how many served there. She had never had much reason to concern herself with the inner workings of the temple before Domina Skey had taken an interest in her. And no opportunity after, given the speed with which events had moved following the attack on the palace.

"Well, Anglion is not so large a country as Illvya," Domina Francis said. "The goddess needs less of us to serve her people there. But I didn't ask you to here to talk about numbers."

"Why did you ask us here?" Cameron asked.

"I wanted to speak to your wife about her vision," Domina Francis said. She looked him up and down. "She may not have wished to tell the emperor what she saw, but it seemed distressing. And it is my purpose to ease suffering where I can. But I'm not sure if your wife wishes to discuss it with you present, my lord. I hope you take no offence, but if she does not, we can make you comfortable elsewhere."

"I would prefer that he stays," Sophie said. "There's nothing I could tell you here today that would be news to him."

Domina Francis raised an eyebrow. "Well, I commend marital honesty, of course." She peered at Sophie a moment as though considering whether she should say something else, but then merely shook her head. Sophie got the feeling that she doubted the truth of Sophie's words, and maybe she was right to. Sophie didn't tell Cameron everything. He didn't know every secret of her soul, but he did know the truth about her visions and every other important factor in the choice they were about to make.

"If we are not going to keep this between just you and I, my lady, then perhaps we should get started." Domina Francis settled back in her chair.

Sophie hesitated. "All right. But if I tell you about my visions, then I have some questions of my own. And I would ask that you keep what I am about to tell you to yourself for now. Treat it as though I am one of your congregation."

"I would have to share if one of my congregation told me something that endangered others or was otherwise illegal."

"I'm not planning to commit a crime." Not in Illvya, anyway. What the Anglions might make of her plan was another matter entirely. Perhaps, if the conversation got that far, she could ask the domina what the repercussions for attempting to remove Domina Skey might be under temple law. "Or hurt myself or anyone else. On the contrary. I'm asking for some grace, my lady. Some time to consider. The choice that his Imperial Majesty has laid before me is not an easy one. I want my family to be safe, but I don't want a crown."

"I should imagine not," Domina Francis said. "You were not raised to expect power, from what I understand."

"I wasn't raised to expect almost anything that has happened to me since my Ais-Seann—" She leaned into the word making sure she gave it the Anglion pronunciation. She wanted no chance of misunderstanding. The domina needed to be clear that her loyalties weren't entirely with Illvya. "—other than getting married of course. I expected that." She didn't look at Cameron. She had no idea if the domina knew much about the circumstances of their marriage, but she wasn't going to explain it. "I most definitely was not raised to expect power or desire it. I was thirty-second in line to the throne a few months ago. All I wanted was a quiet life with a family. Children. Peace to raise them in."

"And now?"

"If I'm honest that is still what I want. A quiet life. Children. Peace."

"That last part may not be so easy."

"So I am coming to see. But I'm not sure that the emperor's plan is the best one for me or my country."

"Is your country still Anglion, then?"

CHAPTER 16

W as her country still Anglion?
That was a question that was becoming more and more complicated to answer.

"I was born there. Raised there. Despite what they currently seem to think of me, it is difficult to see myself as anything but an Anglion, my lady." Difficult but not impossible. She was no longer just an Anglion. Her time in Illvya, and even what had come before, had changed her.

Domina Francis toyed with the quartered cross at her neck. "I see. Well, that may make no difference to your decision. Only the goddess knows how things will proceed. For now, I think it is simpler for us to start at the beginning. Why don't you tell me exactly what you saw in that vision you had in the palace? And what you are doing having visions at all. Have you always had the sight?"

"No, not even a hint of it," Sophie murmured. "But it hasn't been that long since I manifested. Less time still since I found out I had water magic."

The domina pressed her lips together, which made Sophie think that perhaps she knew something about how Sophie had come to that particular set of powers. "Go on."

"Madame Simsa and Maistre Matin have only begun teaching me to use those powers. You can appreciate that we are not taught anything of water magic in Anglion. Other than to fear it, of course."

"Of course." Apparently Domina Francis wasn't going to pause for a discussion about the theological differences between Illvya and Anglion. Well, there was time enough for that discussion once Sophie had told the rest of the story. Or as much of it as she decided to tell. She still didn't know how much to share. But she was leaning toward more rather than less. They didn't have time for secrets. Not if they wanted to be able to decide if what she and Cameron had discussed the night before was in any way feasible. If there was a way out of this mess that didn't end with the crown she didn't want.

"Anyway, they decided to start with a lesson in scrying. That was when I had the first vision."

"And what did you see then?"

"Much the same. My mother crying. Glimpses of home. It was...strange. Upsetting."

"And did Henri or Madame Simsa seem surprised that you had succeeded so quickly? I understand it is a skill that takes time to master."

"I don't think I've mastered it," Sophie countered. "So far I cannot control what I see. Or when."

The domina tapped a finger against her cheek. "I see. All right. Your lesson was the first time you had a vision. And then another at the palace. Have there been others?"

Sophie nodded. "One more. In the temple in Isle de Angelique. The same day as the first. I don't know what triggered it there."

"What does the temple have to do with a vision of your mother and Anglion?" the domina said sharply. "What else did you see? I will keep your confidence, but I think the stakes that you are dealing with are too high for deception. I cannot advise you if I do not have all the information, and it's not only your life at risk now."

That much was true. And the choice seemed clear when put so bluntly. But that didn't make it easy. She couldn't leave her family to suffer—or worse—but once she took this next step—once she told the domina what she had actually seen in her visions, then she would be saying "yes" to everything that came after. To Aristides having his way. To Anglion being invaded. To pain and death, even if she was trying to save people with her actions. It could even end with her death, or Cameron's, and the thought of that—of losing him—was one of the most frightening things of all. She reached for his hand, unthinking.

"Breathe," the domina said. "This is frightening, yes. You're in a place you didn't ask to be and faced with a decision that no one should be forced to make. But all you can do here and now is try to choose wisely. Tell me what you saw. After that, we find the next step to take, and then the next."

Breathing was easier said than done with the fear tightening her ribs like the clasp of a giant's fist. But she did it. Took a breath. Found her voice. "You're right. I haven't told you everything. I haven't told anyone other than Cameron. Because I don't know what it means."

"Leave meaning for later," the domina said, her eyes not breaking contact from Sophie's. As though she could will the truth out of her. Maybe she could. After all, as a domina she had to be used to coaxing the truth from those who didn't necessarily want to face it. She might not be Lord Castaigne, with magic to confirm what she heard, but Sophie, caught by that clear green gaze, didn't think she needed it.

"I saw the tree," she said. "Or *a* tree. Bigger than any I have ever seen. And at first, it looked strong and healthy, but then below the surface of the earth, the roots were turning black."

"Is that all?"

"No. There was a woman lying under the tree—buried beneath it, I guess. The roots grew through her and where they pierced her body, the rot was deepest. I couldn't see her face at first, it was covered by a veil, but then that fell away, and I saw Eloisa's—the queen's—face. Decaying."

The domina's expression didn't change. "Is that the only time you saw her? Or the tree?"

"No. Three times. I've had three visions, and every time I've seen her. It's been slightly different each time, but it's her. Yesterday, at the palace, she turned and looked at me. That's why I cried out."

"I see." Finally the piercing green eyes lowered, breaking the spell.

"What do you think it means?" Sophie said. "Is it a true seeing?"

Domina Francis exhaled. "I'm no water mage, and the goddess has not gifted me with the type of foresight that some of our earth sisters have. I cannot tell you for sure. Maybe no one can. But I believe that all magic comes from the goddess, from her earth and her grace, and that includes visions. The same vision sent three times? I must confess, that seems hard to disregard as coincidence. You had no reason to fear for Eloisa herself before you left Anglion?"

"No. She was injured in the attack on the palace, but she was...healed."

The domina cocked her head at the hesitation. "That sounds like a conversation we need to have another time. All right. The queen was healthy when you left. No reason the goddess would be sending you a warning that she had sickened somehow?"

"I can't be sure," Sophie said. "But not that I knew about. She was different after the attack. But not ill."

"Different?"

"More distant. More—I'm not sure of the word. Angry, perhaps though that wasn't quite it. More ruthless. Less kind. I assumed it was grief and the weight of her new responsibilities. And maybe—" she looked at Cameron who nodded as though to say, "Tell her if you must."

"There was a reason she might dislike you specifically?" Domina Francis asked.

"She wasn't pleased about our marriage," Sophie said.

"Why not?"

"For one thing, at one time, I was her lover," Cameron said bluntly. "For another, Sophie and I broke some rules. We weren't supposed to be a match, but then there were...circumstances."

"Circumstances that explain the bond I see between you? I have seen an Anglion marriage bond once before. This"—she swept her hand at the space between Cameron and Sophie"—doesn't look like that."

"Yes," Cameron said. "Those circumstances." He looked distinctly uncomfortable.

The domina sighed. "Perhaps the details of that are also a conversation for another time. All right, so the two of you were an unexpected union. One that foiled some plan, or other for Lady Scardale's marriage, perhaps? Lost the crown some advantage?"

"I don't know," Sophie said. "For royal witches, no marriage contracts are discussed formally until after our Ais-Seann. They wait until it's known whether we have power or not before they decide who might get to marry us. I don't know what happens behind closed doors, of course. We aren't consulted. I have no idea who King Stefan may have had in mind for me if I manifested. No one told me. Then the palace was attacked before my Ais-Seann. After we came through that, well, Cameron and I were bound. There were more pressing matters than anyone bothering to tell me who I had been intended for. For all I know, the prime candidate for my hand was killed in the attack."

Domina Francis looked from Sophie to Cameron and back again. "So the queen was displeased. Either because you, Lord Scardale, married another or because Lady Scardale was married to a minor lord when she might have been used to tie a more powerful lord more tightly to the crown. I understand your father was an erl, Lord Scardale? But you were not the heir?"

"No. My oldest brother, Liam, has children, besides which I am the youngest of the three of us and Alec, my other brother, also has a family. It would have taken a cataclysm worse than the attack on the palace for me to become the erl. And for that reason, also, I am not anyone that Eloisa was ever going to marry. We both understood that."

"Perhaps not. But that doesn't mean she didn't care for you."

Cameron shrugged. "Maybe. But I don't think she cares enough to drag me back to Anglion. After all, I would be no more acceptable as a consort to a queen than Sophie would be to wear the crown after spending time here." He gestured abruptly as though encompassing all of the empire in the sweep of his hand.

"Not to mention she would have to somehow do away with your wife," the domina said, one side of her mouth quirking.

"I don't think we can rule that out," Sophie said. "After all, there have already been assassins sent after me. Twice."

"Twice? Here in Illvya?" The domina looked startled. Perhaps she didn't know their tale in full after all.

"No. The first attempt was in Anglion. It was the reason we came here," Sophie said.

"You did not think you would be safe there? Or that your queen would protect you?"

"There were those at court who seemed uncomfortable with Sophie's power," Cameron said.

"Anyone in particular?"

Sophie bit her lip, feeling sick. But they had come here meaning to discuss Domina Skey. This was the opportunity. She breathed in, then out, pushing through fear. "Domina Skey comes to mind."

Domina Francis went still. Then her hand crept back to the quartered circle at her throat. "Why do you think that?"

Sophie looked at Cameron, and he nodded encouragement. She teetered on the edge of speaking. Her next words would either be a big mistake or their way out. All Sophie could do was hope that it would be the latter rather than the former.

"The man who attacked me in Anglion told us he was hired by someone he thought came from the temple. Domina Skey was furious that we escaped the marriage bonding. And Sevan— the man in the Anglion delegation who tried to kill me here—he was always devout."

"Anything else?" Domina Francis said. There was a wry twist to the words as though she thought what Sophie had said might be reason enough.

"I told you earlier that Queen Eloisa was injured in the attack on the palace. That she was healed." Sophie stopped, then rushed on before she could talk herself out of it. "I didn't tell you that Domina Skey used me to heal her."

"Used you how exactly?" Domina Francis said. Her voice has gone flat, and she sat rigid in her chair, her eyes suddenly a much darker shade of green. Like a hunting cat perhaps, intent on something small and vulnerable.

But who was the prey? Sophie or Domina Skey?

"I'm not entirely sure," Sophie said. "It was as though she tapped into my power somehow."

"Describe to me what happened."

Sophie took a deep breath. Those scenes in Eloisa's chambers were a memory she'd mostly buried away. Hard to recall. Which didn't lessen the fear they invoked in the slightest.

She laid out what she could remember as fast as possible.

Domain Francis didn't immediately respond when Sophie finished. Instead she closed her eyes, her mouth moving as though she was talking to herself and couldn't quite stop what she was saying from showing on her face. What was showing was anger. "Is this a usual practice in Anglion?" she asked eventually.

"Not that I am aware of," Sophie said. "But I'm hardly an expert. My mother's powers were small. I don't know what exactly the temple healers or earth witches who have the talent for healing are capable of."

"I don't think they usually feed off other people's magic," Domina Francis said. "Not without their consent at least. There are those who can form temporary bonds—a less binding form of an augmentier as it were—to share power, but as far as I know, it takes consent to enable such a thing." She paused and lifted her gaze briefly skyward before looking back at Sophie. "Of course, in Anglion, you do not necessarily follow the rules that we do. I do not know enough about the rites as they are performed there as I would like."

Sophie was somewhat surprised that she knew anything at all.

Her face might have betrayed her because Domina Francis smiled tightly. "We do not live in complete ignorance, child. We have ways of staying informed, though I will admit it is hard to get anyone inside the temple to pass information on. And rare that someone with any actual knowledge of the temple flees Anglion to come here. We get those with minor powers—and minor knowledge—at best." Her gaze turned thoughtful.

"But in this case, I think I need to know more. Even if it is only what you can tell me. You know about the marriage bonds for the royal witches at least. That is something we haven't been able to learn much about. Tell me about that rite."

"That rite would be part of the reason that Domina Skey is not fond of Sophie. Or me," Cameron said drily." I don't think it went to plan."

"Actually, no," Sophia said. "I think it was the earlier rite that went wrong."

"What earlier rite?" Domina Francis asked.

"The dedication to the goddess after my Ais-Seann," Sophie said. "The sigils were supposed to disappear, and they didn't."

The domina's eyebrows shot upward. "Sigils? Tell me more.

Sophie shrugged. "I don't know much. After the Ais-Seann, if we manifest, there are rites. I'm not sure what they do. But when it didn't work, Domina Skey was furious. She knew that—"

She stopped, glanced at Cameron who shrugged. "That Cameron and I had—"

The expression on Domina Francis's face became enlightened. "Oh. I see. You formed your bond before the wedding, so to speak. And the bond between you is not the usual kind?"

"No," Sophie said, glad that the domina seemed not to need a more detailed explanation of how they'd formed it. "Though I will confess, I cannot tell you what a normal bond should be. Or even how it looks. They don't teach us to see the connection to the ley line and other people's magic as you do here."

Domain Francis nodded. "That much I did know."

Sophie nodded. "From what I've gathered, marriage bonds are usually more one-sided. They are designed to somehow feed some of the wife's power to her husband. I don't know how much. Men married to royal witches seem to lead long and healthy lives. Though the same is not always true of their wives." She paused a moment, remembering Lord Sylvain warning her about the death of his first wife. "Not if they fall out of favor with the temple or those more powerful than their husbands, perhaps."

"I see. But there was a rite at your wedding?"

"Yes." She and Cameron spoke together.

Cameron nodded. "But it was done after the ceremony, and I suspect it was mostly for show. The binding is always private, but Domina Skey didn't waste much time on us. She knew we were already bound."

Domina Francis frowned. "That makes sense. But it doesn't explain how she was able to use Sophie in her healing of the queen. I could imagine if the dedication rite worked, that perhaps that would give her a channel to use. Maybe it was partly successful? Left her some thread of access. It would explain her anger, if she was expecting to have some degree of control over a witch of some potential, only to be locked out."

Sophie shrugged. "I wish I knew more."

"So do I," the domina said ruefully. "Regardless of how

exactly she achieved it, it is clear that your dominas—or Domina
Skey at least—have some skill at bindings and bonds. Enough to
let her use you in some fashion. "

She grimaced as though the idea was distasteful. Sophie had
to admit she couldn't blame her for that. The more she found
out about the way that the royal witches were treated in
Anglion, the more distasteful she found it too.

"Do you think other dominas may also have this knowledge?"
Domina Francis continued. "Is it always the highest of the
dominas who performs the rites for royal witches?"

"Yes," Sophie said. "I can't think of many circumstances
where a royal witch wouldn't be married at the temple in
Kingswell. There aren't so many of us that it is a burden. Only a
few in any given year. Such weddings tend to be elaborate cere-
monies, to reflect the status of the grooms. Unless the domina
who heads the Kingswell temple was unwell or, as with me,
something untoward happened around a witch's Ais-Seann, to
cut her off from the temple, and she needed to be married away
from the capital, I don't think it would be anyone else who
performed the rites."

"So maybe the wedding bond is a secret only entrusted to a
few?" Domina Francis tilted her head. "It is only royal witches
who are bound in this way, is it not? That is what we have been
able to observe, at least. From time to time, we have had earth
witches not of the royal line arrive in Illvya. Some with
husbands. Of those, some have had the rudimentary beginnings
of a bond between them, but that can sometimes happen
between spouses who both have some power without anyone
doing anything."

Cameron opened his mouth and the domina held up a hand.
"Not a bond like the one between you and your wife, Lord
Scardale. That is a different matter altogether. The bonds we
have seen are mostly love rather than magic." They may give a
more heightened sense of what the other is feeling or experi-
encing or a sense if they might be in danger but nothing reliable

and nothing that they even be aware of. I'd imagine if the two of you worked with the bond you share, you could do much more." She paused. "Or perhaps you already know this?" Have you explored what you can do together or have the maistres had you locked away studying your lessons as though you were just like all their other students?"

"Maybe not exactly like the others," Cameron said. "But we both have ground to make up."

"Me in particular," Sophie said. "There is a vast difference between what your earth witches are taught and what I learned before my Ais-Seann. And what the temple was willing to show me afterward. Again, I don't know if that is what was normal or whether it was the domina being cautious because she didn't trust me."

"Because you weren't bound in the usual way," the domina mused. "To the goddess or to your husband."

"What do you mean?" Cameron said, expression turning intent.

"I am suddenly minded to consider whether the temple takes two bites at a royal witch, as it were. Once during this 'dedication' rite and again when they bind a royal witch to her husband. There has to be some reason why they would agree to weaken royal witches to benefit their husbands when that is so clearly against the goddess's will. If there was also a benefit to the dominas who perform the rites, then that could explain why they may have been initially swayed to cross the line. It would explain why the temple has been growing strong while the witches of Anglion seem to be weakening over recent generations. Is that something that is acknowledged in Anglion?"

Sophie nodded. "That witches are growing weaker? There is some talk. At least, amongst the ladies of the court. Eloisa's great-great-grandmother was a strong witch, she could affect the weather apparently. There's been no one to come near her in the generations since then. And even in her time, she was rare."

"Rare like you?"

"Me?"

"You are strong. And unbound, that strength uncontrolled. It begins to make sense to me that your Domina Skey would fear you. Those who have gained power—or stolen it—can be ferocious in their attempts to defend that power."

"Spoken like someone who works beside a conqueror," Cameron said.

The domina flipped a hand. "Aristides is not so bad. Neither was his father. Yes, they conquered, but that is past, and since then, they have worked hard to bring peace and stability to the empire. They are not cruel rulers or capricious. I'm not saying it excuses everything the family has done, but I do not see them abusing their powers. They have the parliament to check them for one thing, and there are enough magic users who are not part of the imperial forces to present a serious challenge to an emperor who wanted to become a tyrant."

"Aristides doesn't strike me as a man who is easily checked," Cameron said.

"Perhaps not, but then neither is he a man who does the sorts of things that might inspire such checks to be activated. Our court has plenty of politics and game playing and jostling for power, but it isn't corrupt or working against the good of the empire. At least, not often. And when it is, then the emperor himself is quick to put a stop to it."

"Are you one of those checks?" Sophie asked curiously. "What would the temple do if the emperor turned rogue and started abusing his power?"

"The goddess sets the temple to guard the land," the domina said, a sudden thread of steel clear under her words. "We may not be the absolute religion in the empire in the way we are in Anglion, but we are still a power in our own right. We would do what was needed to protect the people in our care."

"Has that happened?" Sophie said. "Has the temple ever removed an emperor?"

"Not since there have been emperors. But kings and queens

before that—centuries ago, yes," the domina said. "And there have been, other, less drastic means by which we have intervened. We can influence, and we can make our views known."

"And what of the reverse?" Cameron asked. "What if the temple was the problem rather than the crown?"

"I think a domina who plotted treason would be unlikely to be successful here," the domina said. "The emperor, after all, has an army of mages at his disposal, more than a match for our earth witches, even if I hauled every woman or man with even the slightest hint of power to heed my call. That's before we consider the sanctii." Her gaze sharpened. "But that is not the case in Anglion, is it? Not in the same way. There are blood mages and illusioners but no water mages. No sanctii."

"No," Cameron agreed. "No sanctii. And the blood mages largely answer to the crown. If the king or queen wasn't aware that they were being manipulated, there would be little that anyone could do. Without staging some sort of palace coup on top of taking on the temple. I can't imagine anyone currently in the chain of command in the Red Guard attempting such a thing."

"Particularly if the temple was slow to grow their influence. It might go unnoticed if they were careful. If they took control one tiny piece at a time and bided their time for an opportunity to do more," Domina Francis mused.

"Like the one presented when a queen is made vulnerable. One who was inexperienced. Or injured," Sophie said, stomach churning. When she'd first had this idea about Domina Skey, she'd half convinced herself that she was being ridiculous. Jumping at shadows and building conspiracies out of air. A temple who wanted to remove her because, in their eyes, she was a rebel and a danger was different to one who was somehow plotting to take over the country or control the crown. But now, listening to the domina and feeling the pieces click into place in her head, she was no longer sure that she was being paranoid. Quite the opposite, in fact.

"So. An inexperienced, injured queen. A domina who perhaps is ruthless or playing to some grand scheme the temple set in motion a long time ago." Domina Francis closed her eyes again. "I can see why Domina Skey might indeed be desperate to be rid of you in that situation, Lady Scardale. You are a powerful witch, who she doesn't control. Who she, in fact, cannot control in any real way. One who has a claim on the throne."

"But one who has no means to act on any of that."

"Maybe not then. Maybe in Kingswell, it merely seemed prudent to try and get rid of you before you could realize your own power and moved truly beyond her reach. I suspect if she tried to use you now in a healing, you could resist if you chose. But now that you are here, now that there may be the fear of the emperor turning his gaze once more to Anglion and having you on hand to help his cause, then who can say what that might drive her to?"

"Which means what, exactly?" Sophie said.

The domina shook her head. "It means that you are not going to like what I have to say, but that I rather fear Aristides is right. Anglion may need a new queen. One who will deal with the rot creeping though its heart. And, considering this and your visions, it would seem that the goddess may be trying to tell you exactly this."

"Or she's telling me to save Eloisa," Sophie blurted. "Isn't that the better option? If it is Domina Skey behind this, then if we remove her, isn't Eloisa free?"

Domina Francis leaned back. "By 'removing' Domina Skey, do you mean breaking the bond?"

"If she has bound the queen without consent, then breaking the bond would only be a first step," Cameron said. "Attacking the queen is treason. But determining what else needs to happen after Eloisa was free from the domina's influence, would be Eloisa's decision."

"Perhaps," Domina Francis said. "And perhaps only time will tell if that is correct. But first, I think we need to make it Aristides's problem. I'm sorry, Lady Scardale, I know I said I would keep your confidence if I could but—"

"I know," Sophie said, holding up a hand. "You are loyal to the emperor. To Illvya. I understand, and I agree. We need to speak to Aristides."

~

"Are you sure you want to do this?" Cameron asked as their carriage clattered away from the temple and turned left toward the palace. He'd been relieved when the domina had called for a separate carriage. The journey would only take a few minutes, but it was, at least a small window for them to talk.

"I'm not sure. But I don't think there's another choice," Sophie said. She reached down to run her hand over Tok's back as though touching the bird soothed her. The raven had been waiting for them in the oak tree when they'd left the temple and had swooped back down to Sophie's shoulder. Cameron watched the bird press his head into his wife's palm, pleased with her touch.

Cameron knew how he felt. But right now he needed more than that to soothe him. He knew that Sophie's idea—to free Eloisa—was the best path for them, but he didn't know how they could do it. Or even if Aristides would agree to their approach. Fear and anger rode his gut. Swirling and stamping like fretful horses. His magic sparked, rising to the emotions. But his long years of training rose to counter it, and he held himself in check.

"Do you think Domina Francis will support us if you tell Aristides you want to free Eloisa rather than dethrone her?" There had been no further conversation once Sophie had agreed to talk to the emperor. Domina Francis had summoned minions from various places, and in short order they'd been back in the carriage. The gates to the palace grounds were already visible through the window. They didn't have much time.

"She seemed concerned with what we told her. I don't know how she will choose to act. But I'm not going to change my mind."

"I don't think you should," Cameron agreed. "But I do think you will need all the help you can get to convince Aristides."

"You think he's intent on a larger invasion?"

"He's an emperor from a line of conquerors. I think conquest is in his blood, and now he thinks Anglion is in his grasp."

"He hasn't tried for it before now."

"He hasn't had the opportunity," Cameron said as they clattered through the palace gates.

"You mean the excuse?"

Cameron shrugged. "It doesn't matter what we call it. But it does matter that he now thinks he has the means to his end."

"Me," Sophie said. She twined her fingers through his, her grip tight.

"Not just you. Us," Cameron said. "He may think he's dealing with you alone, but perhaps that's where he is underestimating things. We are a team, you and I. Always." He leaned down and kissed her hard. "If anyone wants this to go badly for you, then they have to go through me."

CHAPTER 17

"Have you come to tell me you have changed your mind, then, Lady Scardale? Do you wish to be queen?" Aristides leaned back in his chair and wiped his mouth with a napkin. They had been led to a golden pavilion set in one of the gardens, where the emperor and the crown price were having tea. Or a late breakfast perhaps.

Sophie straightened her shoulders. "Not exactly, Eleivé. I think there is another option."

"Why do we need another option?" Aristides asked. He crumpled the napkin and tossed it onto the table.

"Hear her out, Your Imperial Majesty," Domina Francis murmured.

Sophie waited to see if the emperor would object. Instead, he reached for his teacup and drank slowly. For the first time since Sophie had met him, he looked almost tired. A hint of shadow played under his eyes, as though he'd stayed up late into the night. When they'd first stepped into the garden he'd been yawning and calling for more tea.

Alain, on the other hand, was frowning, mouth pulled down. Sophie hadn't encountered the crown prince since the ball Aristides had thrown to welcome the first Anglion delegation. The one where a man had attacked the Anglion ambassador. Where she'd danced with Sevan and been called a traitor. Where Elarus had first appeared. All in all, it had been an eventful evening. Meeting Alain had been one of the least pleasant parts, which was saying something. He had forced her to dance with Sevan after all. She'd distrusted the prince on sight, and that had only sealed her first impression.

He didn't look any more pleased to see her than she was to see him. The deep green silk and linen he wore seemed to emphasize his discontent. Perhaps the heavy gold embroidery weighed him down. He was practically encrusted in it, his clothes nearly sparkling in the sunlight.

In contrast, Aristides was dressed relatively simply in a white shirt and breeches and long boots, as though he had been intent on going riding after his meal. Now he was intent on Sophie, and as he fixed his dark eyes on her, she forgot the sulky prince and focused her attention on the man who held the power.

She'd been hoping to speak to Aristides alone, but the emperor made no move to dismiss Alain, and Sophie could hardly request him to. Judging from Alain's expression, his father's offer hadn't warmed him to Sophie and Cameron.

The emperor put down his cup again, settled back in his chair. "All right, Lady Scardale. Speak to me of Anglion and your plan."

"I have come to speak to you of Anglion, yes," she began carefully. Aristides hadn't moved from the table and hadn't made any offer for them to sit. Even if he was currently out of patience with Sophie herself, she would have expected him to offer the courtesy to the domina. The table was only set for two but there were six chairs.

"Go on," Aristides said. He lifted his chin. "I take it from your presence, Domina Francis, that the three of you have been discussing Lady Scardale's...experience yesterday?" He glanced at Alain. "You do not need to stay for this conversation if you have somewhere else to be."

The crown prince smiled. The expression put Sophie in mind of a snake. Maybe that was because there were, once again, serpents embroidered on the prince's clothes. She shook off the sensation of dislike again.

"Oh no, Father," Alain said. "I am more than interested to hear from our Anglion friends. The politics on their little island have become quite entertaining."

The look he received from his father in response to this comment was unimpressed, but to Sophie's disappointment, Aristides didn't press the point and send Alain packing.

Domina Francis stepped forward. "In answer to your question, Your Imperial Majesty, yes, we did. It was an enlightening conversation."

"Oh?"

"I believe Lady Scardale's visions are true, Your Imperial Majesty. I am no water mage certainly, but I am a faithful servant of the goddess, and I believe that she has sent a message for us all."

The crown prince's expression turned sour again, but he didn't speak.

"And what might that message be?" Aristides asked.

"I think she is trying to tell me that Domina Skey has obtained some sort of influence over Queen Eloisa," Sophie said before the domina could answer. "And that if we free her of that influence, then Anglion will return to peace once more."

"Convenient," Aristides said. He reached for the delicate china teacup and sipped before settling it down. "I take it you think then that you can do this? Free your queen and then what...return here? Or settle back in Anglion in relative freedom?"

"I'm not sure what would come after," Sophie said.

"Other than you not being queen? That wasn't the offer I made, Lady Scardale."

"But this is a better one, Your Imperial Majesty," Sophie said. "If we're correct and Domina Skey is the true problem, then we can remove her, and you will have a queen who was raised for the job in place."

"With a temple in disarray presumably. What makes you think your queen would take kindly to that?"

"I know Eloisa," Sophie said. "She always knows her own mind. She didn't take politics lightly. I do not think she would be anything other than grateful to be released if the domina is indeed influencing her without her consent."

"Gratitude is not often an emotion that kings and queens feel when others meddle in their politics, Lady Scardale. Not, at least, in my experience. And I have met more of them than you, I believe."

"The queen is not unreasonable, Your Imperial Majesty," Cameron said. "She was raised to succeed her father. She will do what is best for her country."

"And what if what is best for her country in her view is removing an heir who has proved troublesome and led Illvyan forces onto her lands?" Aristides asked.

"I won't let her do that," Cameron said. His voice was like steel. Sophie stopped herself from reaching for his hand.

Aristides lifted one eyebrow. "And what if removing the domina fails to remove whatever influence you believe your queen is under?"

"You Imperial Majesty, that is one possibility. But don't you think it is worth trying my way? It would not take an army merely to subdue the domina," Sophie said. She glanced at Domina Francis, but she merely made a small "go on" gesture.

"Is that so? How exactly do you propose to get to Anglion and undertake this task, then, Lady Scardale? The temple and the palace in Kingswell are well protected. We cannot use the advantage the sanctii give us if we cannot take them with us. Which leaves us with a more direct assault. That usually involves an army."

Sophie steeled herself. "I have an idea about that, Your Imperial Majesty."

"So many ideas," Alain murmured.

Aristides merely glanced at him, then back to Sophie. "Go on, Lady Scardale."

"I was thinking, Your Imperial Majesty, of Imogene's navire."

Aristides's dark brows flew upward. Then he stood and lifted a hand. A blue-clad servant appeared within seconds. "Find out where the Duquesse du Laq is. If she is not within the palace, then bring her here. Or no, not here. I believe we will go to the war room. Fetch Colonel Perrine. Tell him to meet me there."

The servant bowed and scurried off.

"Lord and Lady Scardale, if you would accompany me?" The invitation didn't seem to include the crown prince, and Sophie tried not to look relieved as they followed Aristides back to the palace without Alain joining them.

Imogene arrived not five minutes after Colonel Perrine appeared in the war room. Aristides had directed Sophie and Cameron to be seated on one side of a long table. Domina Francis to the other.

The surface of the table was decorated with a map of the continent, the countries and their boundaries inlaid in shades of green and gray marble. Sophie didn't know what most of their names were, too tired to try and recall her Illvyan geography lessons. Cameron, on the other hand, bent forward to study the map more closely. Aristides made no effort to engage them in further conversation until Imogene joined them.

The duquesse curtsied to Aristides, then saluted vaguely at Colonel Perrine. She arched one eyebrow at Sophie across the table but focused her attention on Aristides.

"How can I serve you, Eleivé?" she asked.

"I was wondering, Major, if you had neglected to inform me that your navire project had been successful?"

Imogene frowned. "The construction is nearing completion, Eleivé, if that is what you refer to?"

"How much longer?"

"That entirely depends on the number of workers I have at my disposal."

"And the problem of how exactly you intend to fly it? Has that been resolved?"

Imogene shot a look at Sophie, lips pressed together. "Not...exactly, Eleivé."

"Then perhaps you would care to explain to me why Lady Scardale seems to think we can use it to effect an stealth mission to Anglion?"

"Sophie?" Imogene said, swinging around to face her.

Aristides snapped his fingers. Imogene turned back. "I asked the question, not Lady Scardale. I found it interesting that Lady Scardale has returned from her time at your estate with such an idea. Given how dear you hold this project, Major, I would have thought you would have informed me if there had been a break-through."

"Indeed I would have. If there had been. But there has not."

"Something must have happened to make Lady Scardale feel such a thing was possible."

Sophie winced. She hadn't intended to get Imogene in any trouble when she had mentioned the idea. She owed it to the duquesse to offer an explanation. "At Sanct de Sangre, I did something unexpected with my powers, Your Imperial Majesty. I floated some soap."

"You floated soap?" The emperor looked confused. "What does soap have to do with the navire?"

"It was not so much what she floated, Eleivé but the way she did it. It was not the usual method."

"And you think you can use this...method...to lift a navire and take it to Anglion?"

"I think I can try," Sophie said squaring her shoulders. "I expect it will take some time to practice."

"Time is of the essence in this situation," Aristides said. "Your queen's temper seems to be growing short. Were I you, I would not gamble the lives of your families on her having the patience to wait while you figure out whether or not you can do this thing."

"I know that," Sophie said. "But the lives of our families are at risk no matter what. If you lead an invasion, I'm not sure they have much chance of surviving past the first moments that the queen learns that an Illvyan force has made landfall." She pressed her lips together to quell the nausea that rolled a protest through her stomach at the thought. "I think a method that would perhaps provide an option of stealth is worth the attempt. A small force, one that included sanctii, might be all that's needed. But we need to be able to get the sanctii to Anglion. That's why you wanted the navire in the first place, wasn't it? To allow sanctii to move across oceans?"

The emperor exchanged a look with Colonel Perrine. Who failed to offer any enlightening comment. Aristides sighed. "Your grasp of our military plans is...unusually informed, Lady Scardale. But your logic is sound. So. As you wish. As you are the one with the greatest risk here, I will give you this time. But if it fails, then we will do this my way. Swiftly. With force. Whatever it takes."

He was saying "yes." Relief made her light-headed, but she managed a curtsy. "Yes, your Imperial Majesty. Thank you."

"Good. Then we have an understanding." He snapped his fingers quickly. "Colonel, you and I have plans to make. Domina, I thank you for your assistance. You are free to go. Major, I suggest you and Lady Scardale discuss this further. Let me know when you know more clearly if this could work. And of the likely timetable."

"It will take a few more days to complete the navire," Imogene said.

"And if I doubled your workforce?"

"Still a day at least," Imogene said. "The final stages are

mostly delicate work, and there is a limit to how many workers will actually be able to fit aboard the vessel and still have room to do what is needed. But more will be helpful. Do I have your permission to take them?"

Aristides nodded. "As many as you need. Report back when you can." He turned his gaze on Sophie. "And while Imogene is finishing her work, you have some time to perfect whatever it was you managed to do at Sanct de Sangre, Lady Scardale. A navire is much larger than a bar of soap. I would suggest you practice." His eyes lifted to Cameron. "Lord Scardale, do you wish to accompany your wife or stay here with the colonel and me? Your knowledge of Anglion will be more than useful to us."

Sophie watched a muscle in Cameron's jaw tighten. The emperor was asking Cameron to commit treason against Eloisa. Give Anglion's sworn enemy information they would use to invade. Even though she knew he was intent on saving his family and agreed with her plan, she couldn't imagine the emperor's request would rest easy with him. But after a pause, he inclined his head.

"I will stay, your Imperial Majesty. I agree with my wife. And I would prefer to achieve a satisfactory outcome with minimal losses."

Aristides nodded. "Let us proceed, then. Lady Scardale, go with Imogene."

[Elarus, are you here?] Sophie asked, staring at the bed in her apartment. She couldn't think of anywhere else in the Academe to practice without raising questions. Imogene had told her that there was no point trying anything like the navire until it was completed. The duquesse hadn't seemed terribly happy with Sophie, and Sophie had deemed it wiser to leave her to her work until the next day. Cameron had yet to return. It was the perfect opportunity to see if she could work out how to float something again, even though part of her didn't want to. If she couldn't, Aristides would get the invasion he wanted. That was quite the incentive.

[Here.] Elarus appeared near the foot of the bed. [Trouble?]

"No," Sophie said. "But I want to try something."

"What?"

Sophie pointed at the bed. "Do you remember when you helped me at the carriage?"

"Yes."

Sophie thought there was a hint of impatience in the sanctii's tone. "Well, I want to lift the bed."

"I can lift."

Sophie frowned. "Yes. But Imogene said that some water mages can do this. I want to try it for myself. I floated some soap in the bain-sel at Sanct de Sangre."

"Bain-sel?"

"The building made of salt."

Elarus' forehead wrinkled. "Not friendly."

"No. It was built to prevent sanctii from eavesdropping. To stop people from spying on discussions that they shouldn't be privy too."

"Maybe stop," Elarus said.

Maybe? Imogene wouldn't like that. "Do you think you could go inside that room?"

"Not for long but maybe," Elarus said.

"Salt doesn't bother you?"

"Hurts but can ignore pain. For a time."

Meaning that most sanctii would refuse to do it? From what she'd learned, a mage couldn't order a sanctii to hurt themselves through the bond. Not directly. It was after all, an agreement the sanctii formed. The water mage was in charge, but it was still an agreement. A mage could banish a sanctii back to their realm and break the bond that way, but they couldn't hurt one. That rule was strict. But Elarus didn't seem to have to stick to the usual rules. She hadn't been summoned by anyone the first few times they had met. Maybe she would choose to do something of her own free will that a sanctii bound in the usual way wouldn't.

But that was something to discuss another time. It wasn't as though she needed Elarus to go into the bain-sel.

"All right. What about salt water? Why don't sanctii cross it?"

"Hurts also. Makes magic strange."

"Strange how?"

Elarus made a vague gesture. "Thin. Difficult. Cannot explain."

"So being on a ship at sea is painful to you? And can break the bond?"

"Yes. Then most would leave due to the pain."

"What about a ship that was high above the water? A ship in the air?"

"How high?"

"That's a good question. I'm not entirely sure. Do you think there is a distance where the pain would become something a sanctii could stand?"

"Possible," Elarus said. "Might be better. Might still be weak. May not be able to keep doing magic. No lift," she added as though she wanted Sophie to understand what she meant.

"But if it was a human doing the magic...could you maybe help even if you were over salt water? If you were high enough?"

"Perhaps."

"Good. Then this may work. Will you show me how you lifted the carriage?"

Elarus tilted her head. "How did you lift...soap?"

"I'm not sure. I did it without thinking. The soap slipped, and it was heading toward Imogene, and I didn't want it to hit her. I wanted to stop it."

Elarus made a sound that was somewhere in the region of "hmmmm."

"I'm sorry, I really don't know what I did."

"I can show," Elarus said. "Like with the bond."

"Show me in my head? Like a reveilé?"

"Same. Maybe."

Not at all reassuring. But she was already breaking the rules that Henri and Madame Simsa had set for her in trying to use her water magic without their supervision. They might be able to teach what she needed to know to be able to make this work, then again, maybe not. Imogene had said this was not a common ability. Besides, she didn't have time to learn the slow way. "Can you show me by doing it while I watch? I'll try and see what the power does while you lift."

"Sanctii not do the same way. But watch."

Elarus turned to face the bed more directly. Sophie let go of her control over how she saw the ley lines and let the magic bleed through. Elarus shone with a cool silver light. But Sophie couldn't quite see how Elarus was connected to the ley line.

"All right, I'm ready. Show me."

Elarus lifted her a hand. The silver light flared, and Sophie had a faint sensation of focused power, but she couldn't tell if Elarus was using water magic or something else entirely. It didn't matter to the bed. It rose into the air and hovered a few feet above the carpet, as though it was designed to float. Sophie took time to look at both it and Elarus, but she couldn't tell how it was done. She sighed. "Put it down. I can't see this way."

The bed lowered again. Gently, Sophie was glad to see. She didn't want to have to explain a smashed bed frame. She studied the wood and the now rumpled covers as though they might reveal the secret to her. The silver glow was fading now, and she still couldn't see anything to hint at how Elarus had managed to raise the bed in the first place.

"All right, let's try this the other way." She braced her shoulders. "Is this going to hurt? Like the other times?"

Elarus shrugged. "Not big magic. Should be easy."

Sophie looked around a moment, then dragged a chair over to be nearer the bed and took a seat. Maybe Elarus was right and there would be no searing pain or dizzy nauseas after this particular sanctii lesson, but she would rather not fall to the floor if there was. Explaining such a mishap to Cameron would be as awkward as explaining a broken bed to the Academe's chatelaine. Worse, perhaps. The chatelaine probably wouldn't yell at her. Cameron wouldn't hesitate to if he thought she had done something foolish.

Elarus watched her silently. Sophie smoothed her skirt and then smiled, trying to look braver than she felt. "All right. Let us try."

Elarus moved closer and stretched her hand toward Sophie. She stopped before she made contact. "Touch?" she said in a tone that was as close to nervous as Sophie had ever heard from her.

"You need to touch me?" Sophie hesitated for an instant, then nodded. Elarus hadn't touched her since the night they'd bonded, but Sophie either trusted her or she didn't. If she was going to ask Elarus to help her fly a ship over the ocean using their magic, then there was no point balking at this. "Go ahead."

Elarus put her hand on Sophie's shoulder, the weight of it heavy but not as heavy as Tok, who was muttering at them from where he was shut in his cage.

"Ready?"

Sophie nodded again.

[Watch] Elarus stretched her free hand toward the bed. Sophie made herself focus on the flows of magic. The thread that stretched between her and Elarus flared brightly, then as the bed began to rise from the floor, a blurred rush of images and sensations tumbled through her head. Followed by a pinwheel of stars in front of her eyes that blocked the bed from view entirely. Her head throbbed once as though someone had punched her, but then the pain vanished, and the stars dissolved.

She stared at the bed. Saw how Elarus was using the flow of magic to hold it in place. And realized that she done it slightly differently back in Imogene's bathhouse. Her way had been a combination of magics. Water and earth and blood mingled together, which was why perhaps, she had been able to do it at all.

"Done?" Elarus asked.

"Yes. Put it down. Let me try."

The bed hit the floor with a solid thump. Sophie winced. She'd used the aural wards around the room but that didn't necessarily mean that whoever lived in the rooms below hers wouldn't notice their ceiling vibrating.

But she would worry about that when someone started pounding on her door. Until then she would see if she could avoid adding a thump of her own.

She rose from the chair slowly, wanting to make sure that there were no lingering after effects of whatever Elarus had done to her. Once she was sure that her legs were steady, she crossed to the bed.

It looked smaller now that she had seen Elarus lift it. But that didn't mean it would be easy. "Won't know until you try," she muttered to herself and stretched out her hand, reaching down to the ley line to tighten her hold on the magic.

Then she tried to remember what she had seen. What she had remembered about how she'd worked the magic in the bathhouse. Tried to recreate it.

The bed began to shake, then lifted a few inches from the ground. When Sophie tried to increase her efforts, nothing happened, and she blew out a breath in frustration. Which did nothing but result in the bed thumping to the floor once more.

Tok squawked, "Sophie!"

Sophie glanced over her shoulder at him. "Sorry."

"Not same," Elarus observed. "Why different?"

"I think this is what I did in the bathhouse. I know that works with salt water around me, so I want to try and do it that way."

Elarus nodded. "All right. Try again. I will watch."

Sophie did as asked. She was beginning to regret the fact she hadn't stopped to eat before attempting this. The appetite she'd lacked all day was returning with a vengeance now that she was using magic.

The bed wobbled into the air once more, this time, she fancied, higher than before. But, like before, she lost control of the magic and the bed crashed back down.

"Again," Elarus said.

Sophie repeated the exercise. Bed. Lift. Wobble. Thump.

"Unbalanced," Elarus observed.

"The bed?" Sophie frowned at it. It was a simple rectangle. Four posts. The weight should be evenly distributed.

"Not bed, magic. Too much earth. Need more blood. If not do it other way."

"More blood. Right." She tried to sound as though she understood. *More blood.* Maybe if she drew on her bond with Cameron? But he was still at the palace. She had no idea if she could use the augmentier in anyway when they were so far apart.

She flexed her hands and closed her eyes, preparing to try. Then opened them again as the door swung open and Cameron stepped through.

He spotted Elarus and stopped short. Then turned and carefully closed the door before joining Sophie. "Elarus, hello."

He bent and kissed Sophie's cheek. "Lonely without me, were you?"

"Elarus is helping me try to lift the bed," Sophie said. "Practice for the navire," she added hastily before Cameron could ask why.

Cameron sighed and shook his head. "My wife wants to float beds." He sounded as though he wasn't sure whether to be amused or alarmed. "Have you finished practicing? I was looking forward to lying down."

"No," Sophie said. "In fact, you've arrived just in time. Elarus and I were discussing why this wasn't working and she suggested I needed more blood magic. You blood mages can move things. You can lend me some of your expertise."

"We sometimes shove or break things, we don't make them fly," Cameron pointed out.

"Semantics," Sophie said, flipping a hand. "Anyway, I'm the one making things fly. I just need some of your magic to help me."

"You want to use the augmentier. You've never done that on purpose before."

"No, but people do. That's what they're there for, after all. And we know a little of the theory. We have to try this. If I can't fly the navire, then innocent people are going to die because of my failure."

Cameron shook his head. "Not because of you, because of Eloisa and the domina."

"Semantics again," Sophie said. "It's us—or me—that they want."

Cameron looked as though he was going to argue but held up his hands in surrender. "All right. What do you need me to do?"

She reached for him. "Just hold my hand."

His mouth quirked. "Sounds like an invitation to trouble."

"You like holding my hand."

"I do. But I like it more when we're not trying to do magic no one has ever attempted before."

"Where's your sense of adventure?"

"At this point, running for the hills," he said then grinned ruefully. "That didn't sound like something a Red Guard should say, did it?"

"I won't tell anyone." She tightened her fingers around his. "Now, let me concentrate."

She faced the bed again. This time, when she looked for the magic, she split her focus three ways, reaching for Cameron, Elarus, and the ley line.

Tried to gather them together as she pushed at the bed.

It floated up into the air. What's more it stayed there while she blinked at it, shocked that it had worked.

"I guess that answers one question," Cameron said, sounding

surprised.

"Yes. Now all we have to do is see if we can work it on something a lot bigger."

"We?" Cameron said absently. He stared at the bed warily as though he half-expected it to grow wings and fly around the room.

Sophie waved at the bed. "I couldn't do that before you arrived back. Well, not and keep it there."

"But I wasn't there at Sanct de Sangre when you floated the soap. And I didn't feel anything through the bond when you did."

"Soap is smaller. Maybe I didn't need you. Or maybe I used the bond without realizing it. And didn't need much. Maybe you weren't paying attention." She frowned. "Did you feel it this time?"

He nodded. "Yes. I can't describe it exactly. But I knew you were using magic. Like that time in the ballroom when you shoved that idiot who was harassing you."

"All right. We've learned something." She looked at the bed. "Elarus, is there a gentle way to put this down?" Floating was one thing. Delivering whatever she was floating safely back down to earth was equally important. Particularly once what she was lifting changed from a bed to a ship full of people who wouldn't appreciate a crash landing. And maybe wouldn't survive it either.

Elarus shrugged. "Let go of magic slow," she said, her tone vaguely amused. As though Sophie should have known that was the answer.

Well, that made sense. She focused on the magic flows. Thought about releasing them slowly, like loosening her grip on the reins of a fractious horse. Ready to take control again if necessary but easing off her power. Or their power.

The bed settled back down to the ground.

Sophie let out a breath she hadn't realized she was holding. Then turned to Cameron. "I guess you are coming with me to see Imogene in the morning."

CHAPTER 18

There were far more workers swarming around the navire than there had been on the night when Imogene had first revealed it, and it bore far more resemblance to a ship than it had then. In fact, it looked complete. It seemed that Imogene had put her extra workers to good use. Sophie stared up at the vessel and tightened her grip on Cameron's arm. The navire was huge. It seemed ridiculous to think that she could move it an inch, let alone fly it to Anglion.

A bed was one thing, but this was another game altogether.

But a game she couldn't afford to lose. This had to work.

"She's made good progress," Cameron said. He stared up at the navire, no doubt, cataloguing every inch of it.

"Yes," Sophie said. The air was dusty, filled with the scent of fresh sawn wood, varnish, and something more acrid. She squinted through the faint haze, looking for Imogene. She'd sent a note telling them to meet her at the navire at ten. There were many people wearing the black uniforms of the Imperial army on the navire's decks, but Sophie couldn't tell if Imogene was one of them.

"Almost as though she'd already increased her efforts before you came up with your plan," Cameron added.

Sophie glanced up at him and shrugged. "Anglion must have been always partly on Aristides's mind when he let Imogene pursue this project. They only lacked the answer to the problem of how to fly it."

"Which you have neatly provided."

"I'm sure someone would have figured it out eventually. Imogene told us the sanctii thought it could be done with the right combination of powers."

"I wonder," Cameron said. "You said Elarus lifted the bed using her magic. And told you to do it her way. Why would the sanctii think of mixing human magic?"

"I don't think Imogene would have given up. She's tenacious."

"Agreed. And now she has her solution."

Sophie sighed. One day she would find out exactly how much Imogene had known about Aristides's plans to put Sophie on the throne before he had made the offer. She doubted he had made that decision entirely on his own, despite the fact that some of his counselors seemed less than supportive of his announcements.

But there was no time to waste in recriminations, or accusations, or trying to understand exactly how far she could trust Imogene. The Illvyans wanted to use her magic, and she was willing to trade it to get back to Anglion to free Eloisa and their families with minimal bloodshed.

"Admiring my handiwork?" Imogene's voice came from behind them. Sophie turned on her heel in unison with Cameron.

"You have been busy," Sophie said. The words were sharper than she had intended. Perhaps she had time for recriminations after all. "It looks complete."

Imogene didn't flinch or look at all regretful. She met Sophie's gaze. "Time is of the essence, is it not? But no, it is not quite ready."

"Does it really matter if it is one hundred percent complete?" Sophie asked. "It's not as though it has to be watertight?"

"Actually, it does," Imogene said. "Or not watertight, exactly, but airtight. If the hull isn't properly sealed, and air flows through the gaps in the wood, then that affects my calculations of how the navire should move through the air. No one wants to plummet to the earth because it became unbalanced due to an unexpected force."

Sophie didn't understand most of the sentence. But Imogene was a Mage ingenier. She had all of the best minds and mages in Aristides's service at her disposal, Sophie had to trust they knew what they were doing.

"How long until it's done?"

"A day." Imogene stared up at the structure, her expression intent. "No more than that."

So fast. The thought was both encouraging and terrifying. "Then why are we here today?"

"Because the navire has taken a lot of time and money to build. I didn't think it was necessarily a good idea for the first thing you attempt to lift into the air was something of its size and weight. It would be an expensive experiment if you were to drop it, not to mention a significant setback to our plans. You seem to want to avoid an invasion, therefore, I thought it might be best to practice with something other than the final product first." She began walking back in the direction she'd come from, clearly expecting them to follow. They hadn't taken more than a few steps when Elarus appeared, taking up a position next to Sophie.

A few seconds later, Ikarus materialized and moved to Imogene's side. Imogene didn't stop walking or slow her pace. Ikarus stayed by her side but glanced from time to time back at Elarus as though he'd prefer to keep her within his sight.

They took a circumspect path, moving around piles of supplies and worktables and groups of workers to the farthest corner of the work room, where scaffolding hung with linen panels blocking Sophie's view of what lay beyond. The scaffolding was much smaller than the structures surrounding the navire, which was comforting.

When they reached the scaffold, Imogene lifted a flap in one of the panels and gestured for Sophie to go through. She did, Elarus and Cameron still trailing her. Ikarus grunted softly as they passed, and Sophie heard something close to a snort in her mind, but Elarus didn't say anything more.

[Is everything all right?] she asked.

[Males,] was all Elarus offered in reply. Sophie didn't press further. Sanctii relationships were not something she felt qualified to offer any opinion on.

[Ignore him, if you can. We have work to do.]

[Is not *my* problem.]

Sophie hoped that Elarus was referring to Ikarus's attitude rather than the work that lay ahead. Because there was definitely work to be done.

On the floor, cradled in support structures that looked as though they had been hastily thrown together were three boats. The first was a small dinghy of a kind Sophie had ridden on various lakes and rivers with Eloisa at palace entertainments. The second was more the size of the smallest of the fishing boats that worked the Kingswell harbor—a vessel maybe twenty feet long. The third closer to forty.

She sucked in a breath, trying not to panic. They weren't as big as the navire but still seemed huge.

Think. One step at a time.

All right. The smallest of the boats was larger than a bed but not by much. And the bed in her rooms was carved from solid hardwood. A boat would be lighter. If it was, she and Cameron—and Elarus, if needed—should be able to lift that one at least.

"Practice," Imogene said, sweeping a hand at the boats. "I thought it might be helpful to find out what your limits are. If you struggle with any of these, then we will need assistance. If," she added, "you've worked out how you did your trick with the soap in the first place."

"Elarus and I experimented last night," Sophie said. "We seem to have come up with something that works."

Imogene's face relaxed. She tilted her head at Cameron. "And are you part of this, Lord Scardale, or merely here to observe?"

They'd discussed whether they should tell Imogene exactly how they'd managed to lift the bed. That it had taken all three of them. Sophie had suggested it might be better if Cameron was seen to be uninvolved. If by some chance someone else decided to attack her on the navire, it would be useful if they thought that Cameron was with Sophie to guard her, rather than so she could use his blood magic. Of course, it would be more than foolish for someone to attack her while she was flying the navire —assuming she ended up being the one to do so—as that would result in everyone being plunged to their deaths. But Sevan had been willing to die for his mission. It didn't seem completely impossible that another assassin reconciled to the fact he might have to die to accomplish his task might be sent.

But Cameron had pointed out that if they told Imogene, then there might be time to find out if there were any other pairs of water mages and blood mages who could work together to help fly the navire. There hadn't been any rational argument to counter that.

"I'm here to help," Cameron said. "Turns out the sanctii were right. It does take a combination of magics to do this. Or, at least, that is true for us."

"All right," Imogene said. "Show me. I'll watch but afterward, you'll need to explain exactly what you're doing."

Sophie nodded. "I'll try." She turned her attention back to the three boats. "We'll start with the smallest."

Half an hour later, after each of the three practice boats had been successfully lifted into the air, Sophie leaned against

Cameron, while Elarus, Ikarus, and Imogene held a long conversation in the sanctii tongue.

"Tired?" Cameron asked.

Sophie shook her head. "Hungry. But no, not tired. Not yet. I'm not sure I'd want to do that for hours on end, but I think I could carry on for some time if needed." She shook her head. "I guess that's something else we will need to test."

"That seems wise," Cameron agreed.

"Are *you* tired?" Sophie asked, searching his face. She'd tried to limit the blood magic she'd drawn on through the bond, leaning more heavily into Elarus this time. She wasn't sure if that was smart or if it would work if the salt water proved troublesome to the sanctii, but she wanted to spare Cameron while she could.

"I'm fine, love," Cameron said. He raised his voice. "Major du Laq, we're going to have to try this over salt water. And do some trials to determine how long the mages can work the magic. We don't have much time."

Imogene turned back to them, frowning. "I agree. We need the ocean. But it can't be the harbor. If there are any Anglion spies left in Illvya, they'll surely be watching the docks."

"Not to mention the ship that brought the queen's message," Sophie said. "Are they still in port?"

"I believe Aristides sent them back out to sea to await any response," Imogene said. "Apparently they didn't argue. I imagine your delegation have carried tales of terrifying sanctii back with them."

Ikarus made a dry chuffing noise that Sophie thought might be laughter. Elarus sent him a look, and he quieted.

"Not terrifying enough if Eloisa turned around and sent someone straight back here," Sophie muttered.

"Be that as it may. We can't practice in the harbor in case we tip our hand."

Sophie nodded. "But it has to be salt water. There's no point attempting this if Elarus can't help once we're out to sea."

"Yes. From what I understand of what she told me, it is the combination of your magics that's working. But maybe we can replicate it. There are plenty of blood mages and water mages in the Imperial army."

"Bonded?"

"No, but a temporary bonding can be formed. Whether or not it will work the same way for a pair who don't have—" she stopped and gestured at them—"your level of augmentier is the question."

"Perhaps you should ask a few of the Academe mages to try. They have to be best at the theory of all of this," Sophie said.

Imogene's lips pressed together. "This is a matter for the army."

Cameron held up a hand, palm up. "It won't be a matter for anyone if no one else can do what we can or if we run into problems over water. A wise soldier uses all available resources, Major. And Henri's daughter is among the hostages. He deserves a chance to join the efforts to rescue her."

"I know you do not like the Academe, particularly," Sophie added. "But I am sure they would be willing to help."

Imogene grimaced, the expression drifting into a sad sort of smile. "You have that the wrong way around, Sophie. It is the Academe who is less than fond of me. Or, Maistre Matin, at least."

"Henri?" Sophie said, startled. "Why?"

"Chloe Matin and I were best friends. We studied together. And she met her late idiot of a husband at my betrothal ball. Henri, I believe, holds me partially to blame for all that came after that." Imogene looked down for a moment, then straightened. "But you are right, Cameron. This is a problem bigger than old wounds. Henri will want to lend what aid he can. I will send word for Academe mages along with some of the Imperial corps."

"Which leaves the question of where to practice."

Imogene frowned again. Then her expression lightened. "I

have the perfect place. As it happens, there is an old shipyard a few miles down the coast from the city limits. It isn't busy these days, but I'm sure it will offer sufficient options for our experiments."

"Do you think the owner will mind?"

"No," Imogene said, and she smiled. "Because the owner is me. Or Jean-Paul, I suppose, but he will not quibble if we break a few of the ships-in-progress. Aristides will make it up to him."

Cameron surveyed the gathered mages milling around Imogene's shipyard and tried to not to feel like they were doomed to failure.

Since arriving, there had been a lot of heated discussions about which mages might team up and how that might be accomplished and what the protocol for practicing would be but nothing resembling actual action. Sophie, standing in the middle of the group in her pale gray dress, was starting to tug at the end of the braid she'd pulled her hair into. Imogene, standing beside her, stern in her Imperial black, looked like she'd like to do the same.

Venable Marignon said, "It's like trying to get a gathering of cats to agree how one should best hunt a mouse. And whose mouse it is in the first place."

Cameron couldn't disagree. "Any suggestions? You're familiar with Illvyan mages."

"Not the Imperial mages," she said. "I have stayed clear of those."

"Any particularly reason?" She was one of the most skilled fighters and best blood mages he'd ever met. Yet she taught at the Academe.

She shrugged, face somber. "My father was an Imperial mage, and he died serving the emperor. Likewise my older brother. I saw what it did to my mother and my family when we lost them.

THE UNBOUND QUEEN 261

My family had more than paid any nebulous duty we might owe the empire. When I manifested and it seemed my talent lay in blood magic, I decided that I would rather teach people than kill them."

"Don't some of your pupils go off and join the Imperial mages anyway?"

"Yes," she said. "I can't stop them from making that choice. But I can give them the best chance possible of surviving before they go."

"Is being in Aristides's service still dangerous these days? It's not like he's waging wars across the empire."

She gestured at the scene before them. "We're here today because he wants to invade Anglion, are we not? Don't fool yourself that the empire is entirely peaceful. There's still plenty of death and misery to go around." Her mouth went flat as she pressed her lips together, perhaps hoping not to say more than she should.

"Yet you came here today to help anyway?" Cameron asked.

"You're a good student. And, from what I've seen of your wife, she's a good woman. She doesn't deserve to be put in the center of these games. Neither of you do. So I'm here to do what I do best. Help you be prepared. But I will not be joining you on Aristides's jaunt to Anglion."

"I can't say that I blame you," Cameron said. "I'd rather stay here myself."

"You don't want to return to your homeland?"

"My homeland is not the same place I left. Or perhaps Sophie and I are not the same people who left it. Either way, I don't think it's safe for us. If it was, we wouldn't have come to Illvya in the first place."

"Even if the emperor succeeds in making your wife queen?"

Cameron hesitated. They hadn't yet explained that the work they would be doing today would be serving a slightly different objective. The mages who learned to fly the boats would join them on the navire, but others would remain behind. For caution's sake, they wouldn't explain the mission until they had decided who would be going.

"If she is queen, then I will command the Red Guard. I will keep her safe if humanly possible. And if it's not humanly possible, well, she has a sanctii now." Elarus stood near Sophie, watching the humans around her with an expression that seemed somewhat disgruntled, though it was, as always, hard to judge what a sanctii might be thinking.

He had noticed, however, that the other sanctii who had arrived with their mages seemed to give her a wide berth. Even when their humans approached Sophie and Imogene, the male sanctii—he was assuming they were all male—hung back. Snatches of the sanctii tongue rumbled amongst the hubbub of human voices. The whole thing was beginning to give him a headache.

Someone needed to take charge and get things underway. Imogene was the ranking Imperial mage as far as he could tell. It should be her. The other soldiers would listen to her, but he didn't know if the Academe mages would take as kindly to her being in charge.

In the distance he heard a familiar chime. The du Laq shipyard, small and not particularly busy as it was, possessed a portal. Because goddess forfend, that the duq should be inconvenienced by having to ride between Lumia and the shipyard if he ever wanted to inspect it. It made Cameron wonder if there was a portal at Sanct de Sangre after all. One they'd missed. One they could have used. But it was too late for that now. If they had left, their families would have paid the price.

He turned in the direction of the chime. The portal was located in an unprepossessing hut, nestled back against the sandy hills that curved around the small cove that housed the shipyard. The door pushed open as it had many times already as the various mages arrived. To his relief, Colonel Perrine emerged from the darkness, and, in his wake, Henri Matin and Madame Simsa. A few seconds after Madame Simsa began to move carefully along the somewhat shaky wooden pathway laid over the sand, Belarus appeared behind her.

Between the colonel and Henri, they should be able to quell the chatter and move the mages towards cooperation. If that didn't work, then maybe Madame Simsa could scare them into obedience. She had to have taught most of the assembled mages at some point. Even if she hadn't, he wouldn't put it past her to start whacking people across the shoulders with her cane if she wasn't satisfied with their behavior. She was old, yes, and moved slowly, but he had no doubt that she could more than hold her own if she ever had to.

Colonel Perrine and Henri nodded greetings as they joined them, looking over the rest of the mages.

"What exactly is going on here?" Colonel Perrine asked.

"They're wasting time posturing, no doubt," Madame Simsa said as she came stumping up behind them. "Wasting time we don't seem to have." She pushed her way between Cameron and Colonel Perrine. "Your wife continues to exercise her talent for trouble, I see, Lord Scardale."

"My wife hasn't really chosen any of this," he said. Not entirely true. This was Sophie's idea after all.

"Well, she's chosen something because here we all are. Henri tells me that you have been putting your augmentier to some interesting use for once." She flapped a hand toward the group of mages. "You may as well show us what you have come up with. Put this lot to work." She glanced at Belarus. "You can stay up here if you'd rather." She turned back to Cameron. "Give me your arm, Lord Scardale. The du Laqs may have money, but they certainly haven't spent it on these paths. I won't be able to intimidate all these young fools if they see me fall on my behind on the way over." Her pale eyes twinkled.

He smiled back. "My pleasure, Venable." He offered her his arm, and they headed for Sophie. Belarus didn't follow.

"Won't you need Belarus?" he asked.

"He can be with me quickly enough if needed. It's not as

though I'm going to try to float one of these boats. I'm here to advise, not participate."

"And staying up there keeps him farther away from Elarus," Cameron murmured. "The male sanctii seem to be nervous...around her."

"Noticed that, have you?" Madame Simsa glanced up at him. "I'm not entirely sure why. The females are rare here, yes, but not unheard of. There used to be a mage with a female at the Academe twenty or so years ago, and Belarus had no issue with her. Maybe it's because your wife and Elarus didn't do things by the rules." She half shrugged one shoulder. "Whatever the reason, I haven't been able to get Belarus to explain. But no point upsetting him, if it's unnecessary. The sanctii who go with you are going to have to get used to her though. Let's hope their mages have a strong hand."

That would be all they needed. A sanctii rebellion. Was that even possible? Every small smattering of information on water magic he'd come across in Illvya was crystal clear on the matter that the mages had control over the sanctii. He hoped it was true rather than merely good propaganda.

Before he asked Madame Simsa, they reached Sophie and Imogene. Colonel Perrine and Henri had been faster in traversing the pathway and were already talking quietly with the two women.

"Do we have a plan?" Madame Simsa asked.

"Madame, we were just discussing that." Sophie bobbed a swift curtsy. Nervous. She fell back on court manners when she felt nervous.

Madame Simsa let go of Cameron's arm, leaning on her cane. "Talk faster. None of us are getting any younger, and I doubt your queen is growing any more patient either."

"We were discussing the best way to teach the technique," Sophie said.

Colonel Perrine cleared his throat. "Perhaps the simplest approach might be the most expedient in this situation, my lady.

If you and Lord Scardale demonstrate, the rest of the mages can watch. Then we can decide how best to attempt replicating what you do. Between the maistres, Imogene, and your sanctii, hopefully a solution will present itself."

Cameron looked at Sophie who merely shrugged as though to say she had no better plan. He nodded. "Let's get to work. Colonel, Major, if you want to call your Imperial mages to order and perhaps, Henri, you can do the same for the Academe mages. Then Sophie can explain what we are trying to do."

A few minutes passed as the mages bustled around and moved into pairs—one blood mage with each water mage—selected by the colonel and Henri. The pairs grouped themselves in front of the small unfinished hull that Imogene had offered up for demonstration. It sat in a wooden cradle near the center of the shipyard. The sanctii moved too, but most of them stayed to the rear of the sandy stretch of ground, away from the edge of the shipyard where the ocean lapped onto the beach. Apparently, they didn't like the prospect of salt water any more than they liked Elarus. When everyone was settled, and the hum of chatter had mostly died away, Sophie stepped forward.

"All right," she said. "You have heard what we are here to do. Lord Scardale and I will show you the technique we have been using. Then each pair can try it for themselves. Save the questions until afterward as we don't have much time." Her voice was clear and firm and rang out over the group with no hint of doubt. She may not want to be queen, his wife, but she had learned certain lessons from her years at court. She could do haughty-aristocrat-who-will-be-obeyed with the best of them.

To Cameron's surprise, none of the mages offered any argument. In Anglion they would have quibbled at taking orders from a woman. Or asked him to lead the demonstration. He was grateful not to have to waste any time in explaining that it was Sophie using his power rather than the reverse. On his own, he could no more float a pencil than he could float into the air himself. He tried when Sophie had been bathing. Tried and failed.

He took his place beside Sophie and wondered if Elarus would come closer. But the sanctii stayed where she was. So he simply reached toward the ley line that they had established lay slightly north of the shipyard and waited for Sophie.

She stood still a few more seconds, as though she wanted to ensure that everyone was focused on her, then raised a hand toward the ship they were gathered around. Her magic flared and he felt the no-longer-strange feeling of his own magic flowing to her, whether drawn by her will, or offered freely of his, he wasn't quite sure. He couldn't feel Elarus exactly, but Sophie's magic had a weightier feel he was beginning to associate with her working with the sanctii.

As the magic flowed, the ship began to rise free of its cradle. That broke the silence. The assembled mages reacted with noises ranging from gasps to cut-off cries of shock; more than one of them goggling as though they'd never seen magic before.

Sophie held the ship in the air while the mages around them whispered and muttered. The male sanctii didn't look entirely easy either, glancing between Sophie and Elarus warily. Ikarus and Martius were silent, but they'd had more time to grow used to Elarus than the others. Belarus remained near the portal hut farther up the beach. When Cameron noticed Sophie shifting her stance, he leaned forward and whispered, "That's enough, love."

One side of her mouth quirked up in acknowledgement and a few moments later the ship settled back into the wooden cradle.

CHAPTER 19

Almost immediately the mages broke into a babble of shouted questions. The result was incomprehensible chaos. They may as well have all been speaking the sanctii tongue. Indeed, there were sanctii voices mixed in amongst the noise. One of them was distinctly shaking his head.

"One at a time," Sophie yelled.

Cameron didn't know if perhaps Elarus was doing something to increase the sound of her voice, but the sound cut through the tumult and the mages fell silent.

"Thank you," Sophie said. She smiled tightly. "It appears that some of you have questions. Let's do this the civilized way. Raise your hand and we'll go through them one by one. This will go faster if we can actually hear what you're asking."

Cameron hid a smile. Several of the mages lifted a hand. Sophie pointed to the first and began to deal with the questions. This led to another quick demonstration along with asides from Imogene and Madame Simsa. This time the mages watched more closely, with less fuss, and after Sophie let the boat settle back into its cradle a second time no one else raised a hand.

Colonel Perrine and Henri went to work then, speaking to

each pair. Sophie took a step back to lean against Cameron as the other mages started trying to replicate what she had done.

"All right, love?" Cameron murmured.

"Hungry," Sophie said. She turned to Imogene, who hadn't paired off with any of the blood mages. "We're going to need to make sure there are plenty of supplies on the navire. This magic burns brightly."

Imogene nodded. "Noted."

"You don't want a turn, Major?" Cameron asked.

Imogene shook her head. "There will be too many other things for me to attend on a first flight," she said. But her eyes strayed over the pairs of mages and the ship itself with barely reined in excitement. Cameron didn't think she would keep herself from learning the skill for long. Though Jean-Paul wasn't a strong blood mage so Imogene would have to find another partner for that particular endeavor.

Around them the mages began to practice. Some of the other boats and ships in the yard wobbled in their racks, but none actually floated.

Sophie watched the nearest pair, a frown wrinkling her brow. When the ship they were working lifted on a few feet, her hands curled. But then it crashed back down again almost immediately, and disappointment flickered across her face.

"Can you see what they're doing wrong?" She flicked him a glance over her shoulder before focusing back on the mages.

Cameron returned his attention to what was going on in front of him.

"I'm not as good at seeing the flows as you," he said after a minute, "but the magic between them doesn't seem strong. The water mage seems to be working slightly more easily, he seems brighter." He shrugged. "Perhaps they need time to become more accustomed to each other and find their balance."

He looked at Henri who stood near Imogene. "Are there any pairs here who are used to working together in this way?"

Henri shook his head. "Of the mages we have who have

shared an augmentier, there are no blood-water pairings. In truth, it has become a rarer tool for us over the years. Water mages bond with their sanctii and others with the petty fams, but outside of married mages, experimentation with augmentiers has fallen out of fashion."

"Well, we need to reverse that trend," Sophie said. Her gaze turned to Elarus. "Can you see what they are doing wrong?"

"Weak," Elarus said.

"Any way to make it stronger? Are the sanctii helping?" Sophie said.

"Yes. But not same as you" Elarus nodded at Cameron. "You two have bond. Easier."

Sophie twisted her braid, still watching the mages. "Would it work if each pair had a temporary bond? Can the sanctii do that?"

Elarus nodded "Probably. If told."

Ah. Right. Yes. The other sanctii needed an order from their mages. Not to mention the fact that the mages themselves would have to agree to forming an augmentier. Figuring out how those might work just added another delay or complication.

He stared at the mages. "What if we used bigger groups?" Most of the mages were making some headway, but none of them seemed to have enough power. There were twenty pairs. That would make ten foursomes. With two sanctii each. "Henri, Colonel, get them to work in fours."

Colonel Perrine nodded.

"This will be complicated," Henri warned.

"Tell them that if they can't do it this way, we'll be introducing some augmentiers into the mix. Maybe that will increase their motivation," Cameron said.

Behind him, Ikarus said something to Imogene. Before she could reply, Elarus said something in reply, her words biting and rough. Ikarus took a half step back and held up one hand. Elarus just snorted.

"What was that?" he asked.

"Elarus told the boys to work harder, I think," Madame Simsa said. "Which is interesting."

Cameron wasn't sure he wanted to know why. He resumed his study of the mages. They had re-formed themselves into fours, gathered around the ten closest ships. There was a certain amount of jostling and discussion, and then they began to focus. To his surprise, the ships rose more steadily this time. Perhaps not quite as high as he and Sophie had lifted theirs, but each craft was definitely floating above its cradle.

"How high does the navire need to go?" he asked Imogene, realizing that they hadn't actually discussed that.

Imogene shrugged. "When I was designing it, I thought, maybe two hundred feet in the air. Enough to be clear of trees and hills and such, while being able to see a good distance around. Plus that height would put it out of the range of most weapons."

He understood that. "Out of range of Illvyan cannons?"

She nodded. "A rifle might hit a target that high, but it wouldn't do enough damage to make a difference. And those in the navire would be at an advantage retaliating. If you had illusioners on board you could, perhaps, disguise the ship, so it wouldn't be noticed in the first place."

"Does that mean less height would be required over the ocean? The ocean doesn't have landscape to dodge and hopefully, we shouldn't encounter any enemy forces," Cameron asked.

Imogene hesitated. Then shook her head. "The air moves differently over water. I'm not sure I would want to go any lower. There could be strange currents in the air. Plus lower would be harder on the sanctii." She frowned at the mages. "Do you think they will be able to reach those heights?"

"They seem to be improving. Sophie and I found that once we managed the first few feet, it seemed to take no more effort to go higher. The complicating factor will be the sanctii, of course." Even the briefest glance at the groups of mages and sanctii showed the bond between each sanctii and their water mage flaring brightly. There was no way they'd be able to sustain the navire without the sanctii helping.

"I agree," Imogene said.

"Yes," Sophie chimed in. "The sanctii and the stamina of the mages. As I said, this is hungry work. How long do you think it would take for the navire to travel to Anglion?"

"A ship takes a good day. If the winds are right, the navire could move faster, I think. Maybe eighteen hours. The mages could trade off. Have time to rest and refuel."

"That might work," Sophie agreed. "But we have to establish some limits. We need a stamina test."

She beckoned to Colonel Perrine who returned from supervising the nearest foursome. "Colonel, we need to progress. I want those ships as high as they can get them and then they are to hold them aloft for thirty minutes." She turned to Imogene. "I hope you have a watch?"

The next thirty minutes were tense. The groups of mages were silent as they worked to keep the ships, floating high above the yard like ungainly birds, in the air. Sophie gripped Imogene's watch as though she thought her life depended on it, the tips of her fingers turning white. Each minute took an eon to tick past but none of the ships came crashing down.

"All right," Sophie called when the time was up. "Put them down."

All around them, came audible groans of relief as the ships came back to ground.

"That was good," she said to the mages. "You can rest now." She turned back to the group of supervisors. "There. We know we can do shifts of at least thirty minutes. All we need now is to test this over salt water. What's the best way? We float one of these down to the mouth of the river and try it on the ocean?"

This started another rumble of voices. Not the mages, but the sanctii. Reading the body language of each of the tall gray males ranged around them, it was clear that none of them were enamored with the idea. Even Ikarus made a small noise of protest.

"What are they saying?" Sophie asked, and Cameron wasn't sure if she was asking Imogene or Elarus.

"They're nervous about the salt," Imogene said.

"The mages knew what we were coming here to do," Sophie said sounding somewhat exasperated. "Surely they explained to their sanctii?"

"Apparently they weren't clear enough," Imogene said.

"Can they actually refuse?" Cameron said.

"No, but most of the mages don't like to force a sanctii unless it's a matter of life and death."

"This *is* a matter of life and death," Sophie said.

"Not theirs," Imogene replied.

"It will be if the navire falls from the sky," Cameron countered. The rumbles from the sanctii hadn't yet subsided. If anything, the exchanges seemed to be growing more heated.

"What can we do to make it easier?" Sophie asked. Before anyone could answer, Elarus stepped forward and uttered a sentence in a blast of sound that echoed across the yard.

As one, the male sanctii shrank back. Elarus roared again, not quite so loudly, and they all nodded, looking down.

She looked at Sophie. "They will do."

It seemed that was settled.

"Interesting," Madame Simsa said with a smirk, as Colonel Perrine started issuing orders for the mages to assemble around the largest of the ships.

Cameron glanced down at her questioningly.

She grinned up at him. "I'd say your wife is not the only one with the potential to be a queen, Lord Scardale."

Cameron blinked. "Sanctii have queens?"

Madame Simsa shrugged. "We know little of their society. But they certainly obeyed her, didn't they? I'd pay attention to that, young man. It may come in useful."

Cameron nodded. He couldn't argue with that. Foolish to

ignore any possible advantage. He filed it away and turned his attention back to Sophie and the ocean awaiting them.

It had been an eternity of a day. Sophie sat beside Cameron on the end of their bed and tried to ignore how tired she was. Their tests of the ships over the ocean with the sanctii had been successful, though none of them had enjoyed it much. The ships were not navire, and not entirely steady in the air, their hulls not designed, as Imogene had pointed out, to fly rather than sail. It was more nerve-wracking than she had expected to stand on a deck that was bobbing over a few hundred feet of nothing. The sanctii had all been silent and watchful, clustering near the center of the deck. And they all vanished in an instant as soon as the ship landed back at the shipyard.

But the end of the practice hadn't brought the end of the day. Instead, they had returned to the palace and spent several hours with the emperor, various officers of the Imperial army, and assorted counselors. The upshot of which was that they would be leaving for Anglion in the morning. Imogene's workers had wrought miracles and finished the navire. All that remained was to provision it. And give everyone a night of rest before they set off.

She was exhausted.

But she doubted she would sleep.

Home. They were going home. Or were they?

"Do you think it's the right choice?" she asked, breaking the silence. Cameron had been gazing out the window, but he turned serious blue eyes back to her.

"I think we've reached a point where there isn't really a choice. We're in this now. The only choice is how we play the game."

She shivered, and his fingers tightened over hers. Offering warmth and comfort. Solid as always. She knew there was no choice. They couldn't leave their families to rot as hostages, but she couldn't shake the knowledge that she was risking what she had here with him, by returning. There was no guarantee either of them would survive. "We've had a few of these moments already. I was hoping we were done with them."

One side of his mouth lifted. "Sometimes you have to go where the goddess sends you. Besides..." He paused, thumb stroking over her wedding ring. "We haven't done so badly out of those choices so far. Have we?"

No. The first point of no return had been agreeing to their marriage—or being forced to agree. She'd had no reason to hope then that Cameron might come to care for her. No reason to hope that the heat that had flared between them wouldn't sputter and die, leaving them bored and indifferent like many court marriages. But that moment had led to this one. And he was still here, standing beside her. Standing with her. Loving her as she loved him. "No," she said, out loud this time. "We haven't." She tightened her grip. "You know I'll always choose you, don't you?"

His eyes were very blue. Her favorite color now in all the world. "I'm glad to hear that. Because there is no other choice for me either. Only you. Us." He brought her right hand up to his chest, ducked his head to kiss it.

She glanced toward the window. It was dark. Their escort would arrive not long past sunrise. But... "We still have a few hours. Before it all starts."

He smiled again. "That is true. Sensible people would sleep."

"I rather think that we've left sensible somewhere far behind us at this point."

"In that case, what exactly are you proposing, oh witch of mine?"

"I'm proposing that I take off your clothes and have my wicked way with you."

His smile grew into a true grin. The one that made her knees turn weak. What did it say about her—and him—that she was standing on the edge of a war, and yet, he only had to smile at her and everything grew brighter and hotter. She reached for his cravat, began to ease it from his collar. "Any problems with my plan?"

"Sophie, my darling, any plan that involves you and me and no clothes will always get my approval." He glanced down to where she was starting to work on his buttons. "My extremely enthusiastic approval." His hands came around her hips, tugging her closer.

"So I see," she said as the hard length of him pressed into her, pressing in all the right places and making her fingers tremble, so that the button slipped in her grasp and she had to bite her lip and try again to set it free.

"See? Or feel?" He moved against her. A gasp rose in her throat, stole past her lips.

"Now that's the kind of sound I like," he said as she tugged the last button free and pulled his shirttails out of his breeches.

"Maybe I want to be the one to make you make some sounds," she said. She slid her palm down the length of him, watching as his pupils flared hot and dark. Tightened her grip and slid again through the cloth until he moaned.

"A proposal I'm also fine with."

"Good. Then undo my dress." She turned on her heel, lifting her hair. Cameron's fingers moved faster than hers had. She stepped free of the cotton and lace and silk keeping her from him and pulled him down to the bed with her, wanting to let him fill her with light, even if it might be the last time.

Sophie stood on the deck of the navire and tried not to tremble, fussing instead with the collar of her heavy coat, trying to pull it tighter around her. Perhaps if people thought she was merely cold, they wouldn't see the terror gripping her. The deck rail of the navire was smooth under her hands, the scent of freshly varnished wood still strong despite the competing smells of salt, sour dock water, sailcloth, and the nervous sweat of the mages and soldiers aboard.

She gripped the rail tighter, hoping it would keep her upright. Her training as a lady-in-waiting, an occupation that involved hours of standing, had taught her some tricks. Including not locking one's knees against nerves—a lesson learned when one of the court ladies had fainted during a particularly tense night at court. A lesson Sophie had never forgotten, though, right now she wished that it wasn't true, unsure if her trembling knees would keep her upright in their current state.

But she wasn't going to fight not to let the fear rule her. She —or some part of her—had felt terrified since they'd first heard that Eloisa had taken hostages. Or maybe long before that. The fear wasn't going to leave until she knew that her family was safe. She had to work around it. Which she would do by focusing on the other emotion that simmered beneath the fear and the hopeless desire for things to be different.

It had taken her some time to recognize that other emotion and to see that she could use it to her advantage. It had flared when the sanctii had been difficult during the final tests with the ship last night and steeled her spine to take control. It had burned brighter while she'd sat curled up on one of the chairs in front of the fire in her apartment last night while Cameron had slept, trying her hardest not to think about all that she could be about to lose.

The opportunity she had at the Academe to be something more than the mild-mannered obedient earth witch that the Anglion would have her be.

Her husband.

Possibilities.

A life.

And her fury had burned.

Her time in Illvya had taught her that being an exile wasn't perfect, but it wasn't terrible either. She had changed here. She wanted her family to be safe, and she would do this to save them and to save Eloisa, but she still resented all the recent politics and pressures that kept dragging her to places she didn't want to be.

She'd prayed to the goddess then, even pricking her finger and sending drops of her blood sizzling onto the coals. She'd didn't have salt grass or oil, but her plea would be heard anyway. Surely if the goddess cared enough to send her visions of Eloisa and the future and ask, in her own mysterious way, for Sophie's help, she should be open to a simple request in return.

To let them survive this. To let them have a life together. The kind of life Sophie she longed for. Simple. Unencumbered. Happy.

Free.

Her prayers had been reasonable, she thought. Fair price for services offered.

And yet, there was part of her that didn't believe that they would be answered. She didn't want to examine what that part of her did believe—she'd never let go of this railing if she let herself think it was all going to end in chaos and disaster and death—but she had felt the anger that simmered inside at the possibility. The frustration and rage that no one would let her call her life her own, that they all expected her to do what they considered best with little thought for what was best for her. Or for her marriage.

She'd eventually crawled back into bed and wrapped herself around Cameron, managing an hour or two of fitful sleep.

And now, standing here and staring back out to the harbor entrance and the sea that lay beyond, the sea that stood between Illvya and Anglion, she reached for that anger again. Anger would help her survive.

She was steeling herself to let go of the rail when Cameron's arms came around her, his hands covering hers. She leaned back into the warmth of him, determined not to waste any moment they could steal.

Time would be short once they reached Anglion and the future uncertain. So she would take stolen seconds and store them up to keep leading her toward the future she hoped would come. When they would have time enough and more together.

Cameron breathed with her, and then, as she had known he would, his head bent closer, his breath brushing past her ear. "They're ready for us, love."

"All right." She was surprised that the reply came easily. Her fingers bit tighter into the railing. If her voice and head recognized what she had to do, the rest of her body didn't seem to have reached the same point of acceptance yet.

But her hands uncurled just as she thought she was going to have to ask Cameron to pull her free. He moved away from her as she lifted them from the railing.

It felt as though everyone on the ship was staring at her when she turned around. Imogene and Ikarus stood near the wheel of the navire—apparently the guidance of the craft was much like a ship, though the navire pushed against air, not water and there were other subtle differences that Sophie didn't entirely understand. But there was a captain—one of Colonel Perrine's Imperial mages who would steer them once they were in the air. She would trust him—and Imogene—to keep them safe.

But getting them aloft was her job. Their experiments yesterday had proven she and Cameron could sustain the lift for longer than any of the others so they would handle the takeoff. Cameron had insisted that there should be a strict schedule of shifts between the mages to keep the navire airborne. An equal share of the load, though Sophie suspected that he was attempting to ensure her power wasn't drained in case something went wrong and they needed some additional strength that no one else could provide.

Behind Imogene stood Jean-Paul who had insisted on coming to lead the small squad of soldiers accompanying the mages. More of Aristides's forces would follow by sea, but the navire was to travel alone at first, to see if they could indeed free Eloisa and the hostages without a show of force.

The emperor hadn't come to bid them farewell. Madame Simsa and Henri, however, stood in the yard below, watching the departure. Sophie made herself wave one last time at them. Henri had asked the emperor for permission to accompany the expedition, determined, it seem, to make sure that his daughter was safe. But Aristides had refused.

Henri had raged, and he was still furious, the tension clear in the way he stood. But he waved to her, jaw tight. Madame Simsa was more encouraging, smiling approval as she lifted her hand.

Two more reasons to survive, Sophie thought. She wanted to see Henri and Madame Simsa again. Wanted to learn more at the Academe. Wanted to see Willem and Lia and Mestier Allyn.

In her ear, as though sensing her emotion, Tok squawked, his claws biting into the wool of her coat and the padding on her shoulder beneath.

There had been no way to leave him behind. So she had one more companion on the journey.

One more reason to fight.

She moved to stand in the center of the deck. Imogene had hastily added benches and railings for the mages steering the navire to use as they chose. Sophie was sure she would welcome the opportunity to sit later but for now she wanted to stand. Cameron took his place on her left, Elarus to the right.

Imogene nodded once and Sophie squared her shoulders.

She lifted her arm, a gesture that probably did nothing to help the actual magic but that made her feel better and spoke a single word.

"Rise."

CHAPTER 20

"Land, I see land." The voice of the lookout was a soft call rather than a shout, but the sound was enough to jolt Sophie, half dozing, awake.

Around her, the deck of the navire began to fill with the sound of voices before someone said, "Quiet," in a harsh tone. Jean-Paul, perhaps.

She rubbed her eyes, trying to focus. They were still traveling in near-dark. The navire was operating with the minimum lighting possible, and they'd all been warned to silence once they had reached the point in the journey where Jean-Paul judged them to be far enough away from the Illvyan coast that they might encounter Anglion vessels below.

It should now be nearing dawn, and they had farther to travel before they could bring the navire down and continue on foot. They were aiming to land on a remote part of the Mackenzie estates, near a seldom-used hunting lodge high in the mountains. From there they could scout down to Alec's house and try to find out what was happening in Kingswell. It was a gamble. Eloisa could have seized control of all the Mackenzie properties, but Alec and his wife hadn't been listed as hostages, so they were rolling the dice.

It was telling that Eloisa hadn't taken Liam hostage either. The Erl of Inglewood was young, but his father had been one of the most powerful nobles in the kingdom. The title was old and respected, and the rest of her lords might object if a queen so new to her crown started throwing the most senior-ranked of them in prison. Even if the domina was attempting to subvert the power structures in Anglion she had to do it slowly and carefully. A rebellion by the lords of the kingdom would surely undo all the work she had put into Eloisa.

Sophie stretched carefully, easing the stiffness born of napping propped against a barrel. She'd been unwilling to go below deck to rest, wanting to be close if the other mages needed her. Thus far, they were managing on their own. The navire had flown smoothly, and she only served her scheduled shifts. Their intended destination had the added benefit of taking them through a part of the country that was far more sparsely populated than the south. The seas around the northern end of the country generally came to shore against high cliffs, so fishing villages and other coastal dwellers were scarce.

They had to hope that they weren't noticed by any stray Anglion vessels before they reached land or northern land-holders out for a night's stroll once they did. Hence the quiet and the caution. They had several illusioners on board, and they would put their skills to good once it grew lighter, but Jean-Paul wanted to conserve their energy for when it was most needed.

She rose and continued to move cautiously, trying to convince her brain she was actually awake. It was tempting to go straight to the front of the navire and see if she could see land— not just land but *home*—but no doubt others would already be there, doing just that. She didn't need to be distracted by the thought of being back in Anglion. Instead she made her way over to where the current group of mages and sanctii were working to keep the navire aloft.

This particular group consisted of two Imperial mages and two Academe mages, and if Sophie was keeping track correctly, it was their third shift. Their faces were pale blurs in the faint light of the moon, but as her eyes adjusted to the darkness, she made out lines of strain.

The mages' breath came fast and the sanctii were pressed as close to the center of the navire as they could be. Most of the others would be below deck. The sanctii may have agreed to help in this venture, and Elarus had insisted during their trials that the salt water was no more than uncomfortable when they were so high above it, but none of the sanctii but Elarus had spent any more time above deck than they needed to. And none of them had, as far as she could tell, blinked out to wherever it was that they went when they vanished.

She would have to ask Elarus about that, about whether their connection to the magic had grown tenuous here. They could obviously access enough of their powers still, to help the mages. But even Sophie had noticed that her bond with Elarus soften somehow once they were over the ocean. She'd tried to lean more on her own magic during her shifts, sending her sense of earth down from the ship, seeking the sea floor far beneath them. Ley lines ran beneath the ocean too, and she'd found traces of them strong enough to connect to, though they didn't offer much of a boost to her magic. Some of the other mages had used the ley lines once she'd mentioned it, but keeping the navire aloft was hard work, and the effort was beginning to show.

"You're awake," Imogene said, joining her.

"Yes," Sophie said. "Have you slept?"

"Not much." Imogene scrubbed at her eyes and ran a hand over her braided hair. "But I can handle lack of sleep."

"Do you know how much longer?"

"A few hours perhaps," Imogene said. "We could be faster or slower over land. It will depend on the winds."

Sophie looked at the laboring mages. "I was thinking maybe I should spell them for a time."

Imogene shook her head. "You should rest more. There are

other teams who have only done two shifts. I'd rather you and Cameron were fresh for the landing. You've had more practice than the rest of them, and you're stronger."

"They'll be stronger over land. It will be easier to find the ley lines and the sanctii will be able to help more."

"Still, I'd rather keep the best in reserve. You need to sleep, and I don't mean leaning against a barrel on deck. Cameron was talking to Jean-Paul earlier, but I think he went below deck. I gave him the keys to one of the cabins. Go find him. Rest."

"I'm not sure I can sleep again." Now that they were closing in on their destination, adrenalin had filled her veins again.

"Try. Elarus can probably help you to sleep if you ask her nicely."

"Sanctii can do that?"

"Not without permission, but yes."

Sophie wasn't sure how she felt about that, but she didn't think Imogene was going to drop the subject, so she went in search of Cameron.

She didn't realize that she had fallen asleep again until Cameron was shaking her awake. Pale sunlight drifted through the small round window in the wooden wall beside her head. It took her a few seconds to remember where she was.

"We're nearly there," Cameron said. "Ready to land this thing?" His jaw was stubbled and his clothes rumpled, but he looked wide awake.

"Ready as I'll ever be," she said. She smiled at him as though her stomach wasn't full of slow-twining lead snakes. Was he as scared as she was? They'd practiced this maneuver with the boats in the shipyard but not with a fully laden navire. And if they landed safely, then what came next was even scarier than the flight. "Is there tea?" She doubted she could eat, but tea might soothe her.

"Probably. Let's go above."

She patted her hair as she climbed free of the narrow bed. She'd worn it braided tightly and it didn't feel as though it had come adrift. Her dress was creased but that couldn't be helped. She let Tok out of the cage where he'd been sleeping and then followed Cameron up the narrow ladder and back out above deck, shading her eyes as she emerged. He led her over to the railing.

"Look," he said, pointing over the rail, and there was a hint of something close to longing in his voice.

Sophie grasped the rail carefully and peered over. Instead of rolling waves beneath the navire, the multicolored deep greens of a forest drifted by below. She hadn't spent much time in the north, and the time she and Cameron had spent with Alec and Lucy after the attack on Kingswell had been brief, but she still somehow knew that the land beneath her was Anglion.

"Home," she breathed through a throat suddenly tight. Up until a few days ago, she hadn't been sure that she would ever actually see Anglion again. True, the circumstances now weren't ideal, but she was here. Breathing Anglion air. Seeing the countryside flowing beneath her feet. Once they landed and disembarked, she would recognize the tree and plants and flowers. She would understand the voices.

"Let's hope so, love," Cameron agreed. "But enough sightseeing. We have work to do. We passed over Neavis Peak a few minutes before I woke you. It's only a few miles farther to the fields above the hunting lodge."

In other words, not much time to ready themselves to bring the navire down safely. She backed away from the rail, reluctant to relinquish the view. But after a few steps, she almost bumped into someone standing behind her and whirled to find Imogene looking sleepy and nearly as crumpled as she herself felt. It made her look far more human.

Imogene smiled as Sophie apologized for the near collision and gestured Sophie toward the benches where the current group of mages were working. They looked tired, but they were, she noticed, mostly silent. In fact, the whole navire was quiet, other than the snap of the sails and the creak of the wood. The

Illvyans weren't talking. Some were standing near the rails, peering down as she had been, but most weren't even above deck. Sleeping while they could? Or unnerved to be in a country they had never expected to enter? The Imperial mages at least should be used to being in unfamiliar parts of the empire. But Sophie remembered how strange her first days in Illvya had felt, and she hadn't arrived intending to try and free a queen. So perhaps it was merely nerves about their mission rather than their location.

She spotted Elarus standing near the wheel. The sanctii saw Sophie and made her way across the navire, taking up her position to Sophie's right.

Sophie looked at the mages. "Ready to hand over?" she asked.

The transition of power went smoothly. Sophie felt the now-familiar magic settle over her as she and Cameron and Elarus worked together to accept the weight of the navire. The other mages backed away, stretching and yawning, and she turned her attention to Cameron, who stood on one of the benches so that he could see beyond the prow.

They hadn't been flying long when he suddenly pointed. "There it is." A few minutes later they set the navire down on the ground, its flattened bottom coming to rest with only a slight bump and slide along grass still damp with morning dew.

Sophie and Cameron kept the ship upright as the first teams descended rope ladders and speedily set up the cunning system of props that kept the navire upright. It had a flatter bottom than an actual ship but still had curves to assist—so Imogene had said—with moving smoothly through the air.

Once the navire was stable, the next few minutes became a blur of orders and people grabbing gear and securing the gangplank-like ramp they would descend. Sophie ended up walking behind Imogene, among the first to leave, and then waited with her, a little distance from the first team, while everyone else disembarked.

Imogene ignored the bustle around the navire, focusing

instead at the forest that started at the edge of the valley, lips
pursed. "I think it's just as well your husband is a blood mage to
find his way through that."

She rubbed the palms of her hands down the front of her
tights, creasing the black fabric of the breeches she wore. Sophie
had donned trousers too. She hadn't worn them since childhood,
but she had been quick to accept Imogene's suggestion when
they were deciding what to pack. She would need to put a dress
over the breeches once they reached anywhere they might be
seen, but she couldn't argue with the ease of movement that
trousers offered for the scrambling journey through the forest
they were about to undertake.

"He grew up here. I'm sure he could find his way even
without blood magic to aid his sense of direction."

Imogene glanced back at the navire. "Let us hope so. And let
us hope he is right that no one will stumble across us here."

They were leaving one team of an illusioner and a water mage
with the navire to hide it. Cameron had deemed it unlikely that
anyone would be wandering the valley at this time of year. It was
the end of harvest, and most of the farmers who worked the
Mackenzie estates would be involved in bringing in the last crops
or preparing stores for winter. The mill would be working over-
time; the granaries had to be filled with the harvest not destined
to become flour, other crops needed to be preserved or stored or
sold, and seeds had to be put away for the next year's planting.
The northern summers were not as warm as they were in
Kingswell and once the seasons turned to fall, it grew cold fast
and hard. The people who lived on the estate worked to wrest all
they could out of the spring, summer, and early fall crops. Apparently the erl's house at Inglewood had a large green house that
gave those who lived there access to fruits and vegetables year-
round, but a greenhouse couldn't produce enough to feed
everyone.

Still, they were careful to be quiet and cautious as they
moved through the forest, picking their way down the hilly

ground slowly and staying within the depths of the trees rather than seeking the trails. Cameron took the lead, and even though she could tell he was wary about what lay ahead, she also thought that some tension she hadn't even been aware of had left him now that they were back on Anglion soil. She shared some of his relief, but the northern terrain was unfamiliar, which made the fact they were home not entirely real.

Not real enough to quell the fear or that quietly simmering anger she was leaning into more than any other emotion as she picked her way along the path the others were breaking, clambering over fallen logs and dodging around rocks.

It was good to have the terrain to concentrate on, but she was starting to flag. Flying the navire had taken a toll, and the few snatched hours of sleep and hasty breakfast she'd managed hadn't been enough to restore her.

So she wasn't quite paying enough attention and almost ran into Elarus when the sanctii halted in front of her.

[What is it?] Sophie asked silently.

Elarus pointed ahead. [Man stopped.]

Sophie peered around Elarus. Cameron stood about twenty feet ahead of her and about twenty feet farther on from him was a break in the trees. She jogged up to join him.

"The hunting lodge," he said, pointing.

Past the edge of the woods, sat a squat stone building that was larger than she had expected. Easily big enough to house all of them for a short time.

The hunting lodge was dark and quiet. The windows were shuttered and there was no smell of smoke. No human sounds broke through the birdcalls and rustling trees. But illusion could be used to hide activity.

[Elarus, can you check if anyone is in there?]

[Yes,] came the response in her head though Elarus herself didn't appear. All of the sanctii had blinked away as soon as the party had left the navire as though they needed some respite from the human world after so much time over the hated ocean.

Given the stories of salt breaking sanctii bonds, Sophie hadn't been entirely sure any of them would reappear when asked. Given that would make the rest of their trip through Anglion far more dangerous, she was relieved to hear Elarus's voice.

"I'm sending Elarus to check," she said softly.

"Ikarus can't see anything," Imogene said.

Ikarus then, had also returned. Sophie blew out a breath. They had the sanctii. Or two of them.

"I'd like Elarus to check as well," Sophie said. "She has some familiarity with Anglion magic through me. She might see something Ikarus would miss."

But within a minute, Elarus was back in her head, reporting no sign of humans anywhere.

Cameron made a dash for the building and unearthed a key from a hiding place below one of the windows. The door opened easily, and he slipped inside. Sophie held her breath while he was hidden from view, but he reappeared quickly, beckoning for them to join him.

It didn't take long for all of them to make the trip from trees to the lodge. Once everyone was inside, people set to their assigned tasks with practiced efficiency. Wards were reinforced, the fireplace in the main hall put to work—the Imperial mages promising no smoke would be detectable from outside, and bedrolls rolled out wherever there was space.

Sophie was assisting one of the water mages to hang a kettle of water to warm over the fire when she spotted Cameron drifting into the corner with Jean Paul and Imogene.

She wasn't going to be left out of any decisions and went to join them. "What's going on?"

"I was telling Jean-Paul that I should go ahead to make my way down to Alec's house. See if it's safe," Cameron said.

Oh no. He wasn't going anywhere without her. She shook her head vehemently. "You're not going alone."

"I know the way," Cameron argued. "I know how to blend in,

and besides, if I do encounter anyone, they will likely be loyal to my family. They won't raise an alarm."

"You don't know that," Sophie said. "For all you know, Eloisa has Alec's house surrounded and there are Red Guard waiting to pounce on you. I should come. That way Elarus can scout ahead. She will spot anyone long before we can."

"Perfect," Jean-Paul drawled. "That way they can take you both, and the rest of us will be in Eloisa's dungeons before we know it."

"You have sanctii. You can make it back to the navire and leave," Cameron said.

"Return to the emperor and let him know that I let the two of you be taken and that we didn't accomplish his orders? That is not an option, Lord Scardale. I am in charge of this mission after all."

"But Sophie and I are not part of your chain of command," Cameron retorted.

"Perhaps not. But I am here to keep you safe and help you succeed in what you came here to do. Do not be so quick to reject the assistance we offer." The duq's voice was sharp. He, like the rest of them, looked tired and rumpled. Not as drained as the mages but Sophie hadn't seen him go below deck at all during the journey. The last thing they needed right now was for him and Cameron to fall out.

"Not just the two of us then," she said. "We can take one or two others." She ran through the faces of the mages aboard the navire in her head. There were a few among them who shared Cameron's northern coloring. Even Imogene with her darker hair and pale skin would fit in. Better than Sophie herself who was more clearly a southerner. "Who speaks Anglion best?"

"Possibly me," Imogene said. "And I have Ikarus. If we take another of the blood mages, then we would look like two couples off to do whatever Anglions would be doing here in the woods, perhaps."

Jean-Paul glowered at her, clearly not liking this proposal.

Imogene shook her head at him. "We cannot stay together all the time, my dear. I can send Ikarus back to you easily once we know that the way is safe. Even a full squad of Red Guard would be hard pressed to defeat two sanctii. I can't imagine Eloisa would have set more than that to watch Cameron's brother if she has sent men at all."

Jean-Paul looked as though he wanted to argue, but apparently the military man won over the husband and he nodded reluctantly.

Half an hour later, after more hastily drunk tea and warmed soup, Sophie was back in the woods with Cameron, Imogene, and Michel, one of the Imperial blood mages who could have passed for Cameron's cousin. Tok swooped ahead, for once flying silent and intent, as though he understood the seriousness of what they were doing.

The journey down the mountain took them close to two hours before the woods opened up onto a field that was clearly cultivated.

Cameron stopped them inside the tree line once again while he studied the field. There was no one working it, but she got the feeling he was listening for something more.

She thought they were at the rear of the estate. The first time she'd come here, they had approached the entrance to Alec's estate up hill. That time they'd been on foot and unsure about what sort of welcome awaited them and what was happening in the capital too.

"Do you want me to send Elarus ahead?" Sophie asked. "She doesn't know what a Red Guard looks like of course, but she understands the idea of uniforms."

Cameron hesitated a moment. "I was wondering if Alec might be at the distillery. They would have brought the barley in a few weeks ago. It would be drying. He often checks it alone."

He looked back at Imogene. "It seems safer than the main house until we know if there are guards."

"It's your family," Imogene said. "Your land. You know best." She pushed stray hair back off her face, wiping her brow with the back of her hand. Her cheeks, like Sophie's, were flushed from the exertion of the journey. The sun had climbed higher, and the air drifting toward them from beyond the trees was warm. She ran a hand over her own hair, checking the braids and ribbons hiding the black streaks in her hair. Time enough to reveal what she now was once they knew they were safe.

"What does the distillery look like and what direction is it?" Sophie asked. "We can send the sanctii there to check if you prefer."

Elarus and Ikarus were scouting ahead still. She could sense Elarus vaguely at the other end of their bond and the sanctii seemed curious but not alarmed.

"It might be better for them to check the house," Cameron countered. "I can make my way to the distillery and back quickly from here."

"We already had this discussion about you going anywhere by yourself," Sophie countered. "It's not safe."

"She's right about that, brother. These woods are full of peril."

CHAPTER 21

T he four of them whirled.

Alec Mackenzie stood on the path, his gray and green clothing blending into the dappled light. He held a pistol in one hand and two large daggers were pushed through his belt.

At least the pistol wasn't pointed at them and he was smiling, although the expression was strained. The large red-and-black bane hound sitting at his feet was silent but straining toward Cameron, Alec's hand on his head keeping him in check.

"Alec!" Cameron embraced his brother. "You're safe."

The two men hugged for a minute before stepping apart. Cameron bent to pat Ludo, who was now dancing around the brothers.

"What in the name of ashes are you doing back here?" Alec said. "You're supposed to be safely out of the country."

"We were. Until Eloisa decided to inform us that she had gotten into the hostage business."

"Don't tell me you've come back to turn yourself in?" Alec's smile vanished.

"No. We're here to make sure everyone goes free. I can't tell you more than that," Cameron said.

Alec studied his brother for a long moment, through eyes of

the same steady blue. Then he turned to Sophie. "It's good to see you, Sophie. But it might have been smarter to stay away."

"My family are also hostages. Besides, your family is my family now," she said, raising her chin. "I'm not letting anyone suffer on my behalf."

"Have you heard from Liam?" Cameron asked. "He wasn't on the list of hostages that Eloisa sent to Illvya."

"No," Alec agreed. "We had a letter about a week ago. He's essentially under house arrest, but she hasn't outright declared him hostage. I don't think she wants to antagonize the other erls."

"She shouldn't want to antagonize me," Sophie said fiercely.

Alec's brows lifted. "Perhaps not. But apparently she wants you here anyway." He studied her a moment. "What exactly have you done to the queen, lass? We couldn't get any explanation that made sense when the two of you disappeared. They found a dead man in your rooms, and at first it seemed you were most likely dead too. But no bodies were found. Liam was informed that you were both in Illvya after a few weeks. He said Eloisa was in a rage about it. He has been working around the edges at court to try to find what happened. He got James onto the delegation and then we heard nothing. Their ship returned to harbor, and the next day Eloisa took her hostages. What happened?"

"Someone else tried to kill my wife," Cameron said. "He was no more successful than the first."

"The first being the dead man in your rooms?"

Cameron nodded.

"Which rather brings me back to the question of what exactly Sophie has done that people are trying to kill her."

"That's a long story. And not one we can explain now. Not all of it anyway." Cameron looked at Sophie. "But we should explain one part. Sophie, perhaps you should ask Elarus to join us for a minute." His gaze slid to Imogene and he said, in rapid Illvyan. "Not Ikarus. Two might be overwhelming."

"Who is Elarus?" Alec asked. "For that matter, who are these two?" he nodded his chin and Imogene and Michel who were sensibly staying silent.

"I'll explain all of that in a minute," Cameron said. "But there's something more important you need to understand." He held out his hand. "But first, pass me that pistol."

Alec's brows shot up again. "You want to shoot something?" His voice was faintly uncertain, as though he was perhaps concerned that the something might be him.

"No. But I don't want you to overreact to what's about to happen, either." Cameron said. "Trust me, brother. No harm will come to you, you have my word."

Alec's mouth twisted, but he reversed his grip on the pistol and passed it to his brother. Then stood, his thumbs tucked into the front of his belt where, Sophie realized, it wouldn't take him long to reach for a dagger. But she didn't think a dagger would hurt a sanctii even if Alec could move fast enough to actually reach Elarus.

"I'm about to ask Elarus to join us. She's a friend." Sophie said. "Focus on the friend part. Stay calm."

"She must be a formidable woman, this Elarus," Alec muttered.

Cameron grinned. "You are right about that, brother."

He nodded at Sophie and she called Elarus.

When she appeared, Alec stumbled backward, cursing and reaching for his daggers. Ludo began to bark but went silent when Elarus looked at him. He stepped between Alec and the sanctii, teeth bared, making it clear he would defend his master.

"She's not going to hurt you," Cameron said, his voice soothing. "She's on our side."

"That's...that's a *demon*," Alec said, half choking on the word.

"A familiaris sanctii," Sophie corrected. "It's not polite to call them demons."

"Goddess be damned to politeness," Alec said. He swallowed

hard. "That's..." His gaze swiveled to Imogene and Michel. "Illvyans. One of you is controlling that-that creature?"

They both shook their heads, expressions wary.

"Elarus answers to me," Sophie said.

"Water magic," Alec said. "That's forbidden. *Cursed.*" His eyes were wild.

"Not in Illvya," Sophie said. "I've had a long talk with the domina of the temple there. She has no problem with sanctii."

Alec looked like he didn't know whether to try and kill Elarus or run away screaming. She had some sympathy for his reaction, understanding the fear that the sight of a sanctii must be rousing in him. But they didn't have time to coddle his reaction for long.

"Alec, I love your brother, and I love his family," she said. "I would never hurt any of you and neither will Elarus or anyone else we've brought with us. We wouldn't have come back if we didn't value your safety over our own. We could have stayed in Illvya. Aristides would have protected us there."

"Aristides?"

"The emperor," Cameron said gently. "I understand you have questions, brother, and that this is a lot to take in. But we don't have time to waste. I need to ask you some questions, and then we need to make a plan about how we proceed."

Alec scrubbed a hand over his chin, his gaze raking over Sophie, eyes still wide. "Am I right in thinking your hair isn't all red underneath those ribbons, lass?"

She nodded.

"And you, little brother?"

"I'm no water mage," Cameron said. "I only have my blood magic."

Not strictly true, of course, but Sophie understood why Cameron didn't want to push his brother further.

"You can disown us later if you must," Cameron said. "But if you want to see James and Jeanne safe, if you think Sophie's parents deserve to be safe too, then you need to trust me now."

Alec took one slow shuddering breath and then raised his hands. "All right. I trust you. What do you need to know?"

"Are there Red Guard around your house?"

Alec shook his head. "No. I'm not supposed to leave the grounds, and they've sent a few men up a time or two to check that I'm still here, but nothing more than that. A patrol came yesterday and poked around for hours. I don't think they'll be back for a few days."

"Are they watching the portal near the village?"

"Not that I know of," Alec said. He clicked his tongue and Ludo moved back to his side, though the dog's gaze stayed fixed on Elarus. Alec's fingers curled into Ludo's fur. "But it's possible, of course. We haven't tried to go anywhere. We didn't want to make matters worse, and the harvest still needed to be completed." He lifted his chin defiantly.

"Of course," Cameron agreed. "You've done the right thing. Lucy and the children are safe?"

"Yes."

Cameron left out a breath. "Good. That's all good. Alec, there are others with us. More Illvyans. They're waiting at the hunting lodge. Can we bring them here? Not to the house if you don't want them that close, but we could house them in some of the farm buildings. Only for today. We'll move on tonight, but we need rest first."

"You're going to the capital then?" Alec asked.

"We're going to try," Cameron agreed.

"Using the High Rest portal?"

"It's the closest," Cameron said.

Alec nodded. "But that makes it more predictable." He looked down at Ludo, stroking the dog's head. "There's that old portal in the temple in the village."

Cameron looked confused. "That hasn't been used since they stopped sending a domina here. No one's been maintaining it, have they?"

Alec's mouth quirked. "Well, maybe we've sent it a little

power now and then. The temple doesn't pay it any attention. They wouldn't notice it was still working unless one of them tried to use it, and why would they?"

"I thought the temple portals only connect to other temples," Sophie said.

"Mostly," Cameron said absently. "But the ones in the remoter parts of the country tend to grow a branch or two over the years. Understanding priors and dominas turn a blind eye. They know it helps people to be able to travel more quickly if there is need and, in truth, there aren't that many people around here with the power to use one unaided. It's not much risk." He frowned, turning his focus back to Alec. "Does that one have a connection to Kingswell?"

"Yes," Alec said. "Though I've never used it, and I can't tell you where it comes out. I don't think anyone has actually used that connection in years and years. We've only used the portal a time or two to take things to Innersleigh when it was needed."

Innersleigh being the largest city here in the north. Sophie wondered if the things Alec were talking about included the odd barrel of iska destined to miss being recorded for the queen's tax collectors. Well, she wasn't going to blame Alec for that. Most estates kept a small portion of their earnings back for themselves when it was necessary. The crown mostly ignored it as long as they received roughly their share. Stefan hadn't needed to clamp down on his tax base during the last decade of his reign, because the country had been largely peaceful.

"Risky to emerge somewhere unknown," Cameron said.

"What choice do we have?" The portal will also be linked to public portal points, won't it? No easy cover that way, either." Sophie considered the problem. She didn't remember much of the details of the first few portal jumps that she and Cameron had taken out of Kingswell, but she did know where most of the public portals in Kingswell were. There were a few in places that might be safe enough to use if they left their journey until after dark. Another thought struck her. "We could try for Chloe's portal."

"Chloe has a portal?" Imogene, who had been silent up until now was apparently too startled by this piece of information to continue to hold her tongue. Her Anglion was clear but faintly accented, and Alec looked at her sidewise.

"Yes, beneath her store. No one knows it's there. Refugees aren't supposed to have such things," Sophie said. "Cameron, do you remember the symbol for it?"

He shook his head. "I wasn't paying attention. We were leaving both times. I wasn't thinking to return the same way. Do you?"

Sophie wracked her memory, trying to call to mind the small portal room tucked away in Chloe's basement and the symbols on its walls. She frowned. "Let me think."

Imogene looked around, then bent down and picked up a stick. She drew a quick symbol in the dirt, a cross with a circle at the end of each of the horizontal arms and a wavy line beneath it. "Was there a symbol like this?"

Sophie studied it. "No, I don't think so. What is that?"

"The symbol for Vert de Cite, where the Matins live. I thought she might have used something that reminded her of home."

Sophie stared down at the symbol. Tok suddenly swooped down out of nowhere and started pecking at the stick.

"Another friend of yours?" Alec asked, staring at the raven.

Sophie nodded absently, still thinking. "Yes." She smiled at Tok wondering what Mestier Allyn would think of one of his charges being loose on Anglion ground. Then blinked as the memory came clear in her head. Not the symbol that Imogene had drawn but there had been one unfamiliar symbol on the walls of Chloe's portal. Or rather, unfamiliar at the time, but now Sophie knew what it was. A stylized flying bird. A raven like the one Mestier Allyn wore on the collar of his robes. Imogene had been right. Chloe had chosen something familiar.

"I remember," she said suddenly. "It was this." She tugged the stick away from Tok and drew the raven in the dirt.

"The raven master?" Imogene said. Then she smiled. "Well, I suppose that makes sense. Chloe practically grew up in the Academe. Henri was a venable before he became the maistre. And she was always fond of the ravens. I suspect she would have bonded one if she hadn't..." she trailed off as though she didn't want to remember something unpleasant. "All right. Cameron, do you remember seeing this symbol?"

Cameron stared down at the symbol. "Maybe. I'm not sure."

"Well, it is worth an attempt if it lands us somewhere less public than other portals you know," Imogene said. "With the sanctii here, we should be able to forge a link easily enough."

Sophie had forgotten that part. That they would need to connect the path of the portal. "Is that safe?"

Imogene nodded at Alec. "If what he says is true and the temple haven't noticed the portal being linked to other places in the past, then it should be safe enough. It's a risk we have to take if Chloe's portal is the safest option."

"They have Chloe though. They may have searched her house. Found the portal," Cameron said.

Imogene shrugged one of her fluid Illvyan shrugs. "We cannot control every factor. We have to make some choices blind. You knew that when you chose stealth over—" She paused and glanced sideways at Alec. "Over a more direct approach," she continued diplomatically. "You need to decide which path to take, and then we will fetch the others."

Cameron stared at the stained and dusty portal door doubtfully, and then turned back to Alec. "Exactly when was the last time that you used this?" The portal looked like it had been undisturbed for a very long time.

"A few years ago," Alec said. He reached out and poked the door cautiously. "It worked then."

"Forgive me if I don't find that comforting." Cameron ignored the doubt in his gut and held out a hand. "Give me the key. You should go back to the house."

It was hard to see his brother's expression in the dim light of the single lantern they'd risked using. They'd waited until full dark to bring everyone down from Alec's house to the village and slip them inside the disused temple. Rats had squeaked and rustled in the debris lining the floor when they'd entered, but there'd been no other sounds of protest from the village. Not even a barking dog. Either the goddess was protecting them or Jean-Paul's illusioners were very skilled indeed.

He could, however, see when Alec shook his head. "I'm not leaving until I've seen you safely gone. You'll need my help if you have to find an alternative. And besides, someone has to cleanse the portal and lock up after you."

Alec had always been the most stubborn of his brothers, a trait he'd inherited from their father, though he lacked the erl's arrogance that had, at times, turned the tendency from obstinacy to delusional pig-headedness. Still, Cameron knew that trying to convince Alec to leave would take longer than actually just getting on with things.

"If you insist. But make haste once we're through. Lucy and the children need you." It was a low blow, but he needed to know that Alec would be safe. He and Sophie had caused enough trouble without bringing still more down on their families.

He gritted his teeth against the sudden thought that the trouble to date had been nothing compared to what might befall all of them if this mission to free Eloisa failed. But if it did, he and Sophie would probably be dead and free from seeing what came next. A grim comfort, perhaps. Better not to contemplate failure as an option at all. He flexed his fingers. "The key, brother."

Alec passed it over, along with a small bottle of oil. Cameron dripped oil over the key and then fitted it into the lock. It took some force and several more applications of oil before the tumblers yielded and clicked open. The portal door swung inward, letting out a waft of stale-smelling air. Cameron fanned it away from his face. Apparently, Alec had been telling the truth about not using the portal recently. Which was a relief. Smuggling iska was a dangerous game, and Alec should know better. The Mackenzie estates didn't need the money.

He raised the lantern and peered into the room beyond the door. It wasn't large, but it wasn't tiny either. He gauged that they could perhaps fit six or seven people inside at a time. He amended that estimation when he recalled the size of the portal at Chloe's. Half as big, at best. Only two or three of them would be able to travel at once. So he, Sophie and, perhaps, Imogene first. That would give them another sanctii as backup. Provided they could link the portals and make this work at all.

The portal room was strewn with cobwebs and layered with dust, but that was a good sign. No footsteps had disturbed the dust. Perhaps Alec was right, and the temple had forgotten its existence. Which should mean that the Red Guard were also unaware of it. Still, he couldn't be sure. Slowly, he waved his free hand from side to side, ready to leap back if the motion tripped any wards or other traps.

Nothing.

All right. He raised the lantern higher and studied the symbols arrayed around the portal stone. He recognized the one for the Kingswell temple and what he thought was the Innersleigh temple. The others, he had to assume were also for temples elsewhere in the country. But there was a blank space right above the stone, where another symbol could be written.

That was where they'd scribe the symbol Sophie remembered, and pray to the goddess that her memory was correct.

And that the portal still worked. He could sense the ley line that ran beneath the temple. It wasn't particularly strong but obviously strong enough. If there was a symbol for the Kingswell temple, there was no reason why they couldn't reach Chloe's house as long as the portal itself was still functional.

"Sophie," he called softly. She appeared in the doorway as though she'd been waiting for him to speak her name. In the lamplight her skin was pale gold and her hair, still braided to hide the betraying dark streaks was a deep shade of red. She'd donned a simple dark blue dress; one Lucy had produced after proclaiming the Illvyan dress Sophie had brought with her would stand out in the capital. Lucy had given a dress to Imogene too. The brown wool didn't particularly suit the duquesse, but Imogene had said nothing but "thank you" and changed.

He drank Sophie in for a moment, aware that once they set foot in Kingswell anything could happen. But she was already moving toward him. "What is it?" she asked.

"Can you tell if the portal is working?" He felt a faint pull from the portal stone, though it wasn't nearly as strong as the portals he was used to. But he didn't trust his judgment. Most of his day had been taken up planning with Jean-Paul and then snatching a few hours with his brother and Lucy. He hadn't slept. His magic was likely still drained from the journey from Illvya. Besides, earth witches were the ones who tended portals in Anglion. Imogene had said there were other ways to fuel them, but he trusted Sophie's assessment most.

"I know the theory," she said. "I can try."

Sophie pressed her hand against the portal stone and then closed her eyes, leaning in as though listening to it. The bond stirred, not with the usual flare of her power but something more cautious and controlled, sinking into the stone slowly. Then it seemed to almost...fade. Sophie opened her eyes.

"There's a connection. I can see if I can strengthen it before Imogene tries to make the new link," she said. "Or we can try it as is."

"What do you think is best?"

"Someone might notice if I try to strengthen it. If they

happened to be working on one of the portals that this is connected to."

The likelihood seemed low, given the lateness of the hour. But then again, the temple at Kingswell never actually closed, and he had no idea how often the devouts and priors and dominas used the portal there. "Do you think it will work if you don't?"

"It should. Everyone here is a strong mage. They have power to make the connections. Perhaps the sanctii can help. We should ask Imogene. She's the one who has to make the link."

Cameron nodded and called the du Laqs. There was a quick whispered conversation that resulted in Imogene agreeing with Sophie. So, a plan. All that remained was to make the connection.

They had decided to let Imogene scribe the symbol and attempt to join the portals with Ikarus assisting. She'd practiced with the other Academe mages until they'd all agreed that the drawing was as close to the Master of Raven's sigil as any of them could remember.

It didn't take her long now. With Ikarus at her side, she inked the symbol into the blank space and then cupped her hands over it. Magic flared around her, then faded as she stepped back.

They all stared at the black mark now limned with icy edges that glittered faintly in the darkness. Alec would clean it off after they left. If anyone came looking, they wouldn't be able to follow.

"No way to find out other than to try it," Jean-Paul said eventually. "Imogene and I can go first if you prefer."

Sophie shook her head. "No. It should be us. You don't know what Chloe's portal looks like. Give us five minutes. If we don't return, then follow."

She took Cameron's hand and squeezed it. "We should say goodbye to Alec."

He squeezed back, his throat dry. But no, he couldn't afford to let himself think that this could be the last time he would see his brother. Rather it was his chance to make sure Alec would be safe. Be free to go on with his life once more. Turning on his heel, he left the portal.

"Well?" Alex asked.

"We think it will work," Cameron said. "So, we will begin." He stepped closer, pulled his brother into an embrace. "Thank you," he whispered. "Stay safe."

"Heed your own advice, little brother," Alex said. "You may be a reckless idiot, but I am fond of you. And your wife."

"Me too," Cameron said, and Alec laughed quietly and let go of him to turn and kiss Sophie's cheek. Then he stepped back into the shadows.

Cameron took Sophie's hand. "All right, wife. Time for us to return to the scene of the crime."

CHAPTER 22

There was the usual stomach-wrenching sensation and then Sophie's foot hit a different floor. Ahead of her, Cameron was already lifting the lantern to examine the room. It was small and nondescript, but familiar. She closed her eyes a moment, breathing hard against the nausea, less strong than before but still present.

"There, that's Chloe's symbol," Cameron said.

She opened her eyes to find him pointing to a space above the portal stone, a grin spreading over his face.

"We're in the right place." He stepped forward, hand stretching toward the door.

"We should check for wards," Sophia said urgently. "Elarus can check if there's anyone in the rooms above."

Cameron pulled his hand back. "You're right. Sorry." He studied the door. "Do you see anything?"

She didn't but wasn't sure if that was a good sign or not. Chloe de Montesse was a cautious woman beneath her bold front. Sophie would have expected her to ward her escape route. Though, perhaps Chloe had decided it would be safer to have nothing that could draw attention to the fact that she had a private portal by not warding it at all. "I think it's clear." She paused a moment, to ask Elarus if she had found anything upstairs.

[Empty,] came the response.

"No one is here."

"Then we should move out into the basement," Cameron said. "We can wait for the others there, and then we'll make our plan. We don't have time to waste if we want to move tonight."

She knew that. But heard the nervousness beneath his words, so she put her hand on the door handle and pushed it gently open. She stood listening for a moment, but no sound came from above. No sound from outside either. Chloe's store and the apartment above it, where she lived were in Dockside. A busy part of the city, but more during the day, at least in the slightly more respectable part where Chloe lived.

The taverns and brothels and gaming halls nested deeper back in the warren of streets that wove around warehouses and business and houses. Right now that worked in their favor. But every minute that passed was time lost. The docks came to life early. Before the first hints of sunrise. They needed to make their attempt in the next few hours, to leave a window for those who could to return safely if something went wrong.

She and Cameron moved into the basement, and she began to count seconds off in her head as he prowled around. Tok flew up to the rafters and started preening. Cameron lifted the lantern and studied the ceiling above the bird's head. There was a trapdoor down to the basement; they'd used it the night they'd fled to Illvya. But the lantern also revealed a set of stairs in the far corner.

"The trapdoor's bolted from this side," Cameron whispered after he lowered the lantern. "I'll check the stairs."

Before Cameron returned, a soft thump came from inside the portal room, followed by a discomforted grunt.

"Sophie?" Imogene called.

"Out here," she said softly.

Imogene, Jean-Paul, and Michel filed out of the portal room, looking none the worse for wear. Jean-Paul and Michel both lit the small lanterns they carried, and Imogene pulled a tiny earth stone from the pocket of her dress, holding it in her palm as she looked around at the boxes and barrels piled against the stone walls.

"This is Chloe's house?" she asked.

"It's mostly her store," Sophie said. "But she lives above it."

"And she is not here?" Imogene's voice held a note of hope beneath the question.

"Elarus says it's empty," Sophie said. "If Chloe's been released, then she hasn't returned."

Imogene's lips tightened, but she didn't ask anything else. It took nearly half an hour for all of the Illvyans to traverse the portal, and by the time everyone was gathered in the basement, it was crowded.

Jean-Paul consulted his pocket watch. "It grows late. We should begin." He turned to Cameron. "Have you decided where the hostages are likely to be?"

Cameron reached into his jacket for the map he'd drawn of the city while they'd waited at Alec's. It wasn't perfect, but his knowledge of the city—hard-won through his years of patrolling as a junior guardsman—had provided them with more than enough detail. "There are still three main possibilities," he said. "The palace has a building for prisoners. Or there's the main city prison. Or the temple, of course."

Alec hadn't been able to provide them with any clues. Liam's letters hadn't given him any details of where Jeanne and James were being held.

"Or they could be in one of the houses the queen owns," Sophie said. "If she thinks we might try something, then she might put them somewhere less obvious."

"How do we decide?" Jean-Paul asked.

"I could try scrying. Or one of the others," Sophie said, waving her hand at the assembled mages.

"You have the best chance, you know the people you are

looking for," Imogene said. Then she looked up at the ceiling. "Though, if I had something of Chloe's, I could send Ikarus to search for her. He could get a sense of her if he has something she uses regularly. He knew her back in Lumia."

"No guarantee she'll be in the same building as the others," Jean-Paul said.

"No," Imogene agreed. "So, we let Sophie scry, and then we send Ikarus to look for Chloe, and he can tell us where she is. Then we will see if that matches up with anything Sophie sees." She glanced around the room, then pointed at several glass bottles stacked on one of the shelves. "Look, wine. Sophie can use that. We need something to put it in."

"I have that." One of the water mages stepped forward, holding out a small silver bowl.

Sophie took it and sank to the floor, sitting cross-legged with the bowl in front of her. Imogene grabbed one of the bottles and extracted the cork with a practiced flick of her wrist. She offered it to Sophie, who filled the bowl nervously.

It was difficult to focus with an audience, but she tried to clear her mind of anything but the thought of her parents. The wine shimmered and quivered, but no image formed. She reached for the ley line, feeling the hum of the familiar strength of it as it yielded its power to her. Another sign that she was home. Not that it was truly home until her parents were free.

The longing to see them and hear their voices bloomed deep within her chest, so fierce it almost made her gasp. But before she could, the wine shimmered again, and the vision rolled across her. She saw her mother, not crying as she had been in the visions of Eloisa, but sitting on a small wooden chair, by a fireplace, staring into the flames. She looked drawn but otherwise unharmed.

Sophie resisted the urge to try and reach for her and instead tried to focus on the room, looking for any clue as to its location. The walls were pale but papered and the chair, though simple, was elegant in its lines. Not the kind of chair you would expect to find in a jail. Then, on the fireplace mantel she saw the carvings and she knew. She fought her way free of the vision, pushing the bowl away hard, heedless of the wine spilling onto the floorboards.

"I think they're at Summer's Light," Sophie said.

"What is that?" Jean-Paul asked.

"One of the houses in the palace grounds where important guests sometimes stay. When Eloisa first came back to court after Prince Eric died, when I became one of her ladies, her rooms were being refurbished and she hated the smell of the fresh paint. We used to escape to Summer's Light. It has a view down to the harbor and catches the breezes on warm days. The fireplaces all have different carvings of sea creatures above them. I saw my mother sitting by one of them." She looked at Cameron. "You know it, don't you?"

He nodded slowly. "Yes, that time was before I joined her personal detail, but they make us memorize all the palace buildings."

"Then you could draw a map?" Jean-Paul asked. "Is there a portal nearby?"

"No portals in palace buildings," Cameron said. "But Summer's Light is way back in the grounds. You should be able to make your way there from the portal in the western end of the garden. Or the one outside the palace wall in Emmerhill. That may be safer. I know the guard patrol patterns, so you should be able to avoid them." He drew Jean-Paul away, the two of them leaning over a barrel while Cameron began to draw a map.

"You and I should go upstairs," Imogene said to Sophie. "See if we can find something of Chloe's to guide Ikarus."

It made sense. Sophie wasn't familiar with Chloe's apartment, but she knew the layout of the building. The door at the top of the stairs wasn't warded or locked, and Sophie opened it cautiously before stepping through.

Imogene took a deep breath when she joined Sophie in the

hallway. "This place smells of magic," she said, holding up her earthlight to provide a faint light.

"I told you that Chloe sells magical supplies," Sophie said. "You can smell those."

Imogene looked skeptical. "We should take a look, see if there's anything useful."

Sophie shook her head. "The shop has windows out into the street. Too risky that someone may notice the light. She nodded toward the other staircase. "We should go up there."

It didn't take them long to find Chloe's bedroom. Sophie watched Imogene bite her lip as she looked over the things laid out neatly on the small dressing table, swallowing hard before she reached for a silver locket threaded on black velvet ribbon.

"I remember this," she said softly. "Chloe wore it at school. Her mother gave it to her. This should work." Ikarus appeared beside her, and she held out the locket to him. "Can you find her?"

The sanctii nodded once and then vanished.

"Now what?" Sophie said.

"Now we wait." Imogene stared down at the dressing table. Stretched out a hand, then pulled it back without touching anything else. Then looked past it to the front of the room where two small windows were heavily draped. "I guess it would be safest to go back downstairs." Her hand crept forward once more, and she stroked a finger over one of the glass jars.

"You have missed her," Sophie said.

Imogene nodded, pulling her hand back. "Yes, she was my best friend. What happened to her wasn't fair. I'm not saying Charl didn't deserve his fate, but I refuse to believe that Chloe was involved in any way."

"If we get this mess sorted out, perhaps she can come home again," Sophie said. "So we should focus on what we came to do."

They made their way back downstairs and had hardly set foot back in the basement when Ikarus reappeared.

"Did you find her?" Imogene asked. Ikarus nodded and spoke a few short sentences in the sanctii tongue. One of these days Sophie was going to have to ask Elarus to teach that.

A smiled bloomed over Imogene's face as she listened to the sanctii. "He says she's in a building near the palace. And that there were big fish over the fireplace. It sounds like she too is in this Summer Light." She grasped Sophie's hand, squeezing it in excitement. "They're all together. That makes things easy."

"Good," Cameron said. "We can keep things simple. Sophie and I go to the palace to reach the queen. The rest of you to Summer Light to free the hostages and take them either directly to Alec's or back here. Each of you have the portal symbols to follow if you need to." He looked at Jean-Paul. "Agreed?"

Jean-Paul nodded, then gestured to his soldiers. They gathered around him to listen to his orders.

Imogene let go of Sophie's hand with one final squeeze. "Be careful." She held out a small stone. "Use this if you need help urgently."

Sophie felt the cold roiling off the stone before she even touched it. "A scriptii?"

"Yes. Hold it and say my name, and I'll hear you and we'll come. Ikarus will get a message to Elarus once we have freed the hostages."

Or if something went wrong. That was what they'd agreed. But Sophie didn't want to ruin their luck by mentioning that. She slipped the scriptii into the pouch under her skirt. "Goddess light your way."

"Goddess light your way," Imogene replied.

Sophie turned away, reached for Cameron's hand, and let him lead her up the staircase.

"This feels too easy," Sophie whispered as they reached the final corner in the corridor that led to Eloisa's apartments.

Cameron nodded, his face strained with the effort of keeping up the illusion surrounding them. "Maybe it is. But there's no turning back now." He reached for her hand. "Time to get Elarus to take care of the guards."

Sophie nodded. This time she barely had time to think the words before they heard three soft thuds ahead of them.

Cameron poked his head around the corner. "Yes, they're out." He set off at a run. By the time Sophie caught up with him, he had the first guard tied and gagged and was dragging him into the small office where the guard captain sometimes worked. Sophie bent to start work on the guard closest to her. Lieutenant Smythe-Stuart. Her hands flexed nervously. She hadn't thought about the guards being people she knew.

Smythe-Stuart was a twit, but he'd guarded Eloisa as long as Sophie had been one of her ladies. Longer, in fact. And now they were doing something that could ruin his career—if not his life—purely because he'd been in the wrong place this night. Twit or not, she bore him no ill will.

But little of what happened to her had been her fault either. If tonight's events fell in her favor, then she would try to help anyone she hurt in the process. If not, well, it was likely she would be in no position to help anyone. Or care. The dead didn't care.

Elarus was quiet in her head as Sophie helped Cameron move the other two guards into the office. Cameron locked the door with keys he'd lifted from one of them. So far no one else had approached, and no one had raised the alarm. Their luck was holding.

For now.

She rubbed her fingers over the pouch that held the scriptii, feeling the chill of it. There had been no word yet to indicate that the hostages were free and not knowing what was happening was driving her crazy. But she didn't want to ask Elarus to interrupt Ikarus and distract him at a vital moment.

She had to trust the Illvyans to do their part as they were trusting her to do hers.

All that lay between her and that now was the final door to Eloisa's apartments.

She licked her lips, had to swallow before she could talk. "Ready when you are," she said to Cameron. She could barely hear herself over the sound of her heartbeat pounding in her ears.

Cameron nodded and stepped forward. Eloisa's door was unwarded. It had wards, but they were only activated by the queen herself or her guards in case of an attack. The levels of security they'd already passed were supposed to make this final one unnecessary.

Sophie moved into place behind Cameron. They'd agreed that he would go first. He was armed. She was not, other than a small knife strapped to her thigh. Cameron had wanted her to take a pistol, but she'd thought it would be best not to come bearing something so clearly a threat. After all, she had Elarus if she needed a weapon.

[How many inside?] she asked the sanctii.

[One. Sleeping.]

Sophie tapped Cameron's shoulder. "She's alone." Cameron let out a soft sigh. There'd always been the risk that Eloisa would have some of her ladies with her. Or a lover, possibly, though that seemed less likely. A queen had to be more cautious than a widowed crown princess.

His hand tightened on the handle, the door swung inward, and they walked into the outer chamber.

The scent of roses and salt grass filled the air, the smell of it at once familiar and unfamiliar and so strongly entwined with Sophie's memory of the palace and her friendship, such as it was, with the queen that she nearly stumbled to a halt.

Cameron too, shook his head as though he wanted to clear it. But then he mouthed "bedroom" at her, and they crossed the room to open the inner door.

Eloisa had gone to sleep, in her usual fashion, with a fire burning and several earth-lights glowing on the walls. There was more than enough light for them to make out the slumbering form of the queen under the deep green velvet coverlet.

Cameron jerked his head toward the bed, one hand on the pistol. Sophie tiptoed closer.

There was no easy way to do this. Sophie studied the queen a moment but couldn't see any active connection to the ley line that might indicate Eloisa was awake and waiting for an attack.

"Your Majesty," she said in a tone that came automatically to her, pitched precisely loud enough to wake a sleeper without scaring them. A tone learned here at court. "Time to wake up."

The queen didn't stir at first, then she rolled over, tugging sleepily at the quilt. "What time is it—" She started to say, but then as she realized who was standing at the foot of her bed, she sat bolt upright. "*You.*"

Sophie bobbed a curtsy. "I believe, Your Majesty summoned me."

"How did you get in here?" Eloisa's green eyes were wide with outrage.

"That's not important," Sophie said. "But we need to talk, Your Majesty. Things have been difficult between us. But they don't have to be."

Eloisa straightened her shoulders, any lingering signs of sleep slipping from her face. "I didn't think you'd come. The domina said you would. It's good she's not a gambling woman. You would have cost me." Her eyes narrowed. "You've already cost me, Sophia."

Sophie held out her hands, palms up to show they were empty. "Your Majesty, I have offered you no harm. I offer you no harm now. And it's Domina Skey who I've come to talk to you about."

Eloisa opened her mouth.

"Don't bother shouting for your guards, Your Majesty,"

Cameron said from his shadowed position near the door. "They won't be able to hear you."

"You have returned too, I see, Cameron. Did you kill my guards?" Her tone was icy.

"No, Your Majesty. They are merely sleeping for a time." He bowed briefly. "Now, I suggest you listen to my wife."

"Do I have a choice?"

Cameron shrugged. "I imagine someone will notice that your guards are absent from their stations eventually, Elly. It would be better for all of us if things were settled before then."

"You came here to bargain with me? I'm your queen. Why should I bargain?"

"You are the queen," Sophie agreed. "And I have always been loyal to you."

"Then why did you not return with the delegation?"

"Because Sevan Allowood tried to kill me, Your Majesty. I am loyal, not stupid. I am here now, that is what matters." She didn't raise the subject of the hostages. She didn't think it would be helpful. "I'm here, and I need you to listen me."

"Why should I?"

"You don't actually have a lot of choice," Cameron pointed out. "I guess you could try to put your hands over your ears like a child. You could even try to use your magic on us, but I think you know that Sophie is more than a match for you. Even without my help."

Eloisa's eyes were flinty. "So much for loyalty, to threaten your queen."

"I have a pistol. I could have shot you already if all we wanted to do was remove the threat you currently represent to us. I am not threatening, Elly, I am merely reminding you of the reality of your current situation. You used intimidation to get us to return. Now you have to suffer a small taste of it yourself. Or, you can listen to Sophie."

If earth witches could kill with a look, Cameron would have

been a small pile of dust. Eloisa's eyes practically glowed with rage. "It seems I have little choice. Talk."

"You can't trust the domina," Sophie said flatly. "I believe she is trying to control you. No. I believe she *is* controlling you."

"Controlling me how?"

"Through a bond. Like the marriage bond." Sophie paused. "You do know how the marriage bonds work in reality, don't you? That they siphon some of our magic off to support our husbands? That's why we royal witches are so carefully guarded and married off fast. Why most women who show any sign of magic are taken into the temple or married too."

Eloisa frowned. "I don't believe you."

Did she really not know? Or was she stalling for time? Maybe Stefan had never told her the truth before his death. It was possible, given how he'd died. There was no benefit to Domina Skey telling Eloisa if she didn't already know. Not if she wanted to control the queen.

"Why do you think the domina was so furious that Cameron and I had sex?" Sophie said. "It was because we accidentally formed a bond, not because of my precious virginity. A bond that ruined whatever marriage plans she had for me."

"She? The crown chooses the matches for royal witches."

"With advice from the temple," Sophie countered. "I think you will find, Your Majesty, that the temple has been gathering power for itself for a number of years now. Decades, or more, perhaps. The royal women grow weaker. The men and the temple grow stronger. I suspect the temple is stronger than we know. And now the domina is seizing her moment. I believe she formed a bond with you when she healed you. I think she's using you. You changed after you were healed, Your Majesty. I believe that's due to the domina. She's trying to take control of Anglion. That's why she wanted me dead."

Eloisa started to open her mouth to reply, but Sophie held up a hand.

"Please. I need you to think. These are the facts. A temple-paid assassin tried to kill me. Someone suborned Sevan Allowood to try again in Illvya. Perhaps you didn't know Sevan, but he was notoriously pious, Your Majesty. If you didn't send him to kill me—"

"I didn't," Eloisa said. "I wanted you back here, not dead."

"Why was it so important for us to return?" Cameron asked gently. "We were no threat to you in Illvya. I'm a minor lord. Sophie is a lady-in-waiting. Neither of us is important to your court."

"The domina said—" Eloisa halted, her forehead creasing in a frown. Her hand drifted up to rub her temple where she'd been burned in the attack. "She said—"

"She told you we were plotting against you, I imagine," Sophie said. "That I wanted the throne. Believe me, Your Majesty, nothing is further from the truth. I want a quiet life with my husband. The throne is yours. It should be yours. Yours alone. Not the domina's to control. Let me help you. I know about bonds now. I can set you free."

"Illvyan magic," Eloisa said, sucking in a breath. She pushed herself back against the headboard, flinging up a hand as though to ward them off. "Lies. Heresy. You've come to kill me."

"No!" Sophie said just as Elarus said, [Soldiers. I come?]

[Stay hidden.] Sophie shot back desperately. [The queen will be afraid of you. Stay hidden unless you need to protect me. Please, Elarus]. She turned her focus back to Eloisa, lowering her voice. "I swear, Your Majesty, I'm telling you the truth. I have come back only to tell you this. To set you free to be the queen you should be. The queen Anglion needs you to be. Please, Eloisa. This is me. Sophie. You know me. You have to trust me."

From the outer chamber came a sudden hubbub of voices. Cameron sprang across the room to put himself between Sophie and the door, pistol at the ready. The door crashed open and Domina Skey strode through in swirl of brown robes, eyes blazing. "Stay where you are, traitors," she snapped. Then over her shoulder. "Captain, see, I told you the queen was in danger. Seize these two."

"Wait!" Eloisa snapped in response. She scrambled out of the bed and Sophie saw a sudden flare of magic as all the earth-lights in the room sprang to life. Sophie looked from Eloisa to the domina. The line of magic that threaded between them was as thick as the bond she shared with Cameron. She made herself look away, not wanting to give the domina any hint that she knew the bond existed.

[Elarus can you see that bond? The queen's bond?]

[Yes.]

[Could you break it?]

[Yes. Now?]

[Not yet. But be ready.]

Elarus huffed. [Will wait.]

Eloisa was staring at the domina, regal even though she wore only a plain white nightgown. "Wait, we were merely talking, Domain Skey. I am unharmed."

Sophie saw the bond pulse, saw Eloisa's hand fly to her temple.

"They come armed into your presence, sneaking through your palace at night to enter your rooms like thieves. Disabling your guards. No doubt bringing filthy Illvyan magic with them. They are traitors, Your Majesty, and they are a threat. A threat we should deal with right now. Captain, I order—"

"I think not, Domina," Liam's voice came from behind the domina, followed by the man himself pushing his way through the soldiers. Sophie's knees threatened to buckle in relief.

Liam stepped between Sophie and the domina. "If my brother and his wife are accused of being traitors to the Crown, then that is a court matter, not a temple one. And they are enti-tled to a trial before the court."

The domina's face twisted in fury. "Who do you—"

"I am the Erl of Inglewood, milady," Liam said, voice drip-ping ice and authority. "My family is as old as the bones of this country, and we have always been true to the crown and the laws of the land. I will uphold the law. My brother will be tried, if that is what is needed. But the law is needed here, not the temple. And I believe my fellow erls agree. Liam looked back over his shoulder. "My Lord Sylvain, Lord Airlight. What say you?"

Lord Airlight had been the chief judge of Stefan's reign. Sophie had always found him rather intimidating, but she was more than happy to see him. And she could have kissed Lord Sylvain, who stumped up behind Airlight, eyes crinkling at her.

"I agree, Lord Inglewood," the Erl of Airlight said, stony-faced. The iron look in his eyes matched the iron gray of his hair as he stared at the domina. Apparently he had not taken kindly to his son being held hostage. "The law is clear in this matter. Any member of the court accused of treason must be tried in front of the court."

"Liam, how did you know we were here?" Cameron demanded, seemingly ignoring the rest of the conversation.

"I received word," Liam said. "But that is a discussion for a later time."

"I'm about to be tried for treason, it seems," Cameron said. "There may not be a later—"

"Be quiet, both of you." Eloisa had snatched a robe from the end of her bed and was tugging the ends of its sash tight around her waist. "Lord Airlight, if you say that this is what must happen, then this is what must happen. Lord Inglewood, you will escort your brother and his wife to the audience hall, and I hold you personally responsible to ensure they will be there to face their judgment. Lord Sylvain, assemble the court."

Sophie was halfway down the hall before she realized that she may have made a mistake. She hadn't told Elarus to break the bond. She could send the sanctii back to do it now, but she felt safer knowing Elarus was with her. Liam had brought a few of the Inglewood guards with him, but they were all surrounded by a double squad of Red Guard as they were marched toward the audience hall.

"Who told you where we were?" Cameron asked Liam softly.

"That would be me," said the Inglewood guard closest to Sophie. The one who sounded distinctly like—

"Chl—"

"Don't give me away." The guard's face flickered briefly, revealing Chloe's face for a second before the mask of a young man fell back into place.

Sophie nearly stumbled. "How?"

"I know something of the Arts of Air. When I saw Ikarus earlier I knew something must be happening. I decided not to wait around any longer. I thought perhaps you might try to speak to the queen, and I didn't think I could make it quite that far through the palace. I decided to go to the erl instead. Fortunately, he believed me."

"You know Ikarus?" Sophie repeated, still startled. Cameron was staring at his brother, brows high.

"Yes. Imogene bonded with him before I left Illvya. Granted, I wasn't expecting to see him appear in the palace here, but sanctii are quite distinctive. He blinked in and blinked out before I could ask him anything. Annoying habit that. Now, be quiet, you're supposed to be a prisoner."

"So are you," Sophie whispered back. "What about the others? My parents?" There was still nothing from Imogene.

"I figured if Ikarus was there, then Imogene wasn't far way. And I didn't imagine Jean-Paul would let his wife jaunt over the ocean to Anglion without accompanying her. No doubt bringing more Imperial soldiers. With more sanctii. Your parents will be safe." Chloe tilted her head. "How did you get sanctii to Anglion?"

"Long story," Sophie said. The Red Guard were moving fast, and they were nearly at the audience hall. "But I think we're out of time."

CHAPTER 23

The court assembled rapidly. Sophie, Cameron, and Liam stood near the Salt Throne, surrounded by Inglewood men and Red Guards, watching the rows of seats in the audience hall fill swiftly and mostly silently.

It was a shock to see so many familiar faces after being surrounded by strangers in Illvya. A shock too, to realize again that there were missing faces in the crowd, the victims of the attack on the palace leaving holes that ached.

When the court was settled, the doors swung open again and Domina Skey stalked down the aisle, moving like a storm, her robes swirling around her. Three dominas trailed in her wake, carrying braziers that wafted the pungent scent of salt grass and temple oils. Reinforcing her power, Sophie thought. And also, perhaps, that the domina was rattled to be indulging in theatrics. Which could be a hopeful sign.

The domina took her time to lower herself into her usual seat in the front row before she fixed her gaze on Sophie.

Sophie ignored her and turned her attention back to the doors. Eloisa's ladies—her former friends—began to file down the aisle. They were all correctly dressed, but Sophie could see the signs of a rushed job in the odd wrinkled skirt or slightly crooked hairpin. They were all draped in as many pearls as women could possibly be. The queen herself followed behind them, her triple strand of pearls banding her throat and matching gems bobbing from her ears and circling each wrist.

The court rose and sank into bows and curtsys, staying down until Eloisa reached her throne, and sat, smoothing her golden skirts into place. The same color she'd worn for her coronation.

No accident, that choice.

Eloisa was reminding all of them who was in charge. Sophie hoped the queen was right in that assumption. The nobles, at least, obeyed when she gestured for them to seat themselves.

The queen nodded at Domina Skey who rose and stalked to stand in front of the throne. She shot Sophie one last furious glare, then began to speak.

"Your Majesty, charges of treason are brought against Cameron Mackenzie, Lord Scardale and Sophia Mackenzie, Lady Scardale." The domina began to list their supposed offences.

When she reached bearing arms in the presence of the queen, Cameron said mildly, "I am a lieutenant of the Red Guard, you know. We have permission."

"Not helping," Sophie said quietly as the domina glared again but didn't cease her litany.

"Can't exactly make things worse, now, can I?" He sounded far more confident than Sophie felt.

The domina eventually stopped speaking—it was impressive, really, the list of things they had supposedly done both here and in Illvya—and the queen rose from the Salt Throne.

"Your Majesty," Cameron said before Eloisa could open her mouth. "I believe my wife and I are entitled to a right of reply. Perhaps this will go faster if you let us say our piece first."

Eloisa raised an eyebrow, and, for a moment, Sophie thought she was going to refuse. But she saw no pulse of light between the queen and the domina, and Eloisa said, "So be it, Lord Scardale."

Cameron bowed. "I yield my right to my wife, Sophia Mackenzie, Lady Scardale."

He what? Sophie froze. What was he doing? She looked at Cameron, but he only nodded encouragingly. Panic twisted her gut, but if he wasn't going to plead their case, then someone had to. Apparently that someone was her. She stepped forward, and the soldiers moved apart. Not letting her past their circle but not blocking the queen's view of her either. She curtsied to Eloisa, then rose again, resisting the urge to twine her hands into her skirts.

"Your Majesty. Neither of us are traitors. We have been loyal subjects of yours for many years and will continue to be. The only ones who have been attacked in this court are my husband and I. Assassins have been sent against us. More than once. I believe the people responsible for those attacks are in this room now. But the threat to our lives is less important to me at this moment." She paused. Let her words sink into the silence as she had seen King Stefan and Eloisa and Aristides do. Then took a breath and began again. "Actually, no. I spoke in error. I said the only ones who have been attacked are myself and my husband. That was wrong. This entire court was attacked. Many died. You almost died, Your Majesty. The goddess kept you safe. But I am very much afraid that you are still under siege, my queen." She turned to face the court rather than the queen. "I accuse Domina Skey of unlawfully seeking to control the crown. Of binding the queen without her knowledge and consent and of seeking to silence us to hide her crimes. In short, the only one guilty of treason in this room is the domina herself."

"You *dare*," Domina Skey snarled.

"I do," Sophie said icily.

"Be quiet," Eloisa said. "I—" She paused, and Sophie saw the magic flare between Eloisa and the domina. Eloisa's expression went dazed. "I—"

Goddess. If only the Anglions could see magical connection as Illvyans did. But of course, if they could, then their society would be very different. And the domina would never have been able to do what she had done. Nor would Sophie need to do what she was about to.

[Ikarus says people safe.] Elarus's voice boomed suddenly in her head.

Relief flooded through Sophie. All right. Her family was safe. Whatever happened next, she had achieved that much. And she was free to do what was needed.

[Elarus. Break that bond between the queen and the domina!] Sophie pushed forward without thinking, breaking ranks so she stood alone in front of the court. She saw a bright flare of magic hit the bond and snap it. The queen and the domina both staggered backward, Eloisa's hands going to her head.

The court erupted in shouts of alarm.

Domina Skey recovered first. "They are using magic on the queen," she screamed and pulled a pistol, aiming it Sophie. "Traitor!"

"No!" Eloisa screamed and threw herself forward as the domina pulled the trigger.

"Elarus!" Sophie screamed herself, not knowing exactly what she wanted the sanctii to do. But it was too late. The bullet hit Eloisa and the queen crumpled to the floor as Elarus appeared, snatched the gun from the domina's hand and closed her other hand around the woman's throat.

The domina had shot the queen. She'd *shot* Eloisa. Sophie stared down at Eloisa, unable to make herself respond.

Cameron's hand came hard around her arm. "Move," he said, pushing her forward. "She needs help."

Sophie stumbled toward the queen. No one else had moved to help, the Anglions frozen in place by the sight of Elarus. "Chloe," Sophie called. "Help me."

[Don't kill her,] she ordered Elarus as Domina Skey made choking sounds. Sophie ignored her, turning her attention to the queen.

Eloisa's chest was moving. "Goddess, help me," Sophie

muttered. She rolled the queen onto her back and pressed her hands against the fast-spreading blossom of red on the gold silk of Eloisa's dress, just below her shoulder. "Eloisa, can you hear me? Healers are coming." She looked around wildly. "Fetch healers."

"Most of the healers are dominas," Chloe said quietly beside her. "You can't trust them. You have to do this, Sophie. If it can be done."

Sophie stared at the blood bubbling beneath her hands. She'd healed Eloisa once, but it had been the domina directing her power, and she didn't know how to do it herself.

"S-Sophie." Eloisa's voice was soft, but it carried through the room, which had fallen silent as a grave.

Sophie reached for the ley line desperately, gathering power to send into the queen. "Eloisa, hold on. You'll be all right."

One corner of the queen's mouth quirked up. "Too young," she said, her voice rasping. "But I believe you."

Sophie blinked, trying to see. When had she started crying? It didn't matter. She ignored the tears pouring down her face as she tried to pour power into Eloisa. The magic swirled around her, but Sophie didn't know how to direct it safely. None of her training had dealt with wounds this severe. Goddess be damned. What was the use of all this power if she couldn't do this?

[Elarus, I need help.] She craned her neck, to look at the sanctii, who didn't move.

[Broken.] Elarus's voice sounded in her head, and it sounded infinitely mournful. [Dying.]

[No!] Sophie turned back, flung a hand out to Chloe. "Chloe, I need more—"

Chloe put her hand on top of Sophie's, and Sophie pulled from her and from Cameron and the ley line and somehow knew that it wouldn't be enough, that she didn't know enough. She reached again, felt another bright spark somewhere distant. Tok. She pulled on him too, felt the light of him flutter in response and knew that he would send everything to her if she let him.

And that it still wouldn't be enough. She would kill him if she took too much. She pulled back, reached for Elarus instead as she tried to will the blood to slow and the wound to close. She thought it might be working, but the blood still flowed fast, her hands shining red with it.

Eloisa's hand lifted slowly. Oh-so-slowly. Came to rest on Sophie's cheek. "I believe you," she said again. "All as it should be." And then her hand fell and the soft thump it made sliding back down onto the queen's body broke Sophie's heart as she watched the life vanish from Eloisa's eyes.

For long minutes, there was no sound, but Sophie's own sobs and the distant noises she recognized as other women crying. She waited for someone to seize her, to carry her away, to kill her. The queen was dead. Dead because of her. Dead because she had this stupid useless magic that only seemed to cause hurt.

"Sophie." Cameron's voice sounded as distant as the sobbing. "Sophie, love. Let go of her now."

She hadn't even realized she was clutching Eloisa's hand. She watched as Cameron eased her fingers free. As he put his clean hand around her blood-stained one and helped her to her feet. The pain bouncing through her filled the world, turning it sharp edged and distant. Her eyes fell on Domina Skey, who was standing, perfectly still now, Elarus's hand around her throat holding her in place. And the pain burned away to rage.

"You—" Sophie lunged toward the domina.

"Sophie," Cameron caught her arm. "*No*. She has to face trial. She killed the queen. Everyone saw that. She's done, love. If you kill her now, it won't help."

She shook him off. Took another step forward.

The silence in the hall was broken by the doors flying open. A Red Guard private bolted through. "Ships!" He bellowed. "Illvyan ships on the horizon. Invaders!"

Goddess. Sophie's hand went to the scriptii in her pouch, and she called Imogene's name. And, as the Red Guard began to turn to her and Cameron, hands going to pistols and swords, all the sanctii who had come with them to Anglion suddenly appeared, surrounding Sophie and Cameron and Chloe and Eloisa's body, a living wall between them and the rest of the court.

A wall of sanctii was apparently enough to stop the court from descending into violence. In fact, it seemed to freeze it solid. For a time, the silence was deafening. So deafening, Sophie wasn't entirely sure she could even hear her own breathing.

Then Liam's voice, pitched to carry, broke the silence. "Cameron, perhaps things would be somewhat less...complicated if you could explain your companions."

Cameron cleared his throat, held up his hands. "They are familiaris sanctii. They are here to protect my wife and me. They will not hurt anyone here unless given cause."

He managed to lay a world of meaning in the word "cause." Perhaps he had missed his calling in diplomacy.

"And the ships?" Liam asked carefully.

"Also here for us. It is not an invasion."

Sophie hoped devoutly that was true. She had no idea what Aristides would do when he learned Eloisa was dead.

"All right," Liam said. "If the Red Guard stand down, perhaps some of your companions could do likewise, and we can discuss what happens next."

Cameron raised a brow at Sophie. She nodded. She had no idea what *should* happen next, but perhaps they could make it through this without further bloodshed if she and Cameron could talk fast enough.

"Agreed," Cameron called.

[Elarus, can you ask the others to move to stand behind me, please?]

[Not safe,] Elarus objected.

[Sanctii are faster than men. They can't get to me before you. The Anglions are scared of you. This will make things easier. Please.] She stared at Elarus.

Who folded her arms. [Not like.]

"*Please.*" Sophie didn't realize she'd spoken out loud at first.

But Elarus nodded, and the sanctii began to move. Which was better than them all blinking out and back again in a new position, she supposed.

With the sanctii out of the way, one of the first things Sophie saw was the grief-stricken face of Princess Margaretta.

"We should let the princess and the ladies attend to the queen," Sophie said, her own throat tightening.

"One thing before that," Cameron said. "Salt forgive me." He squared his shoulders. "Lord Airlight, will you step forward?"

The erl glanced at the sanctii, then took two quite small steps away from the line of other senior nobles at the front of the court.

"A point of order, my lord, that might make the rest of this discussion go faster. Could you remind the court of the line of succession for the throne?"

The erl glared. Behind him, Lord Sylvain cleared his throat. "My memory is perfectly good still if yours is failing, Jonah."

The erl transferred his glare to Lord Sylvain before turning back to Sophie. "The current line of succession by right of birth is as follows. Crown Princess, Margaretta Fairley. Lady Sophia Mackenzie. Lady Penelope Fairlight. And I believe, next would be the young lord of Farcairn."

"Thank you, milord," Cameron said. He turned his gaze to the Crown Princess and bowed. "Your Royal Highness, I am so very sorry for your loss. Please believe me that if I could do anything to change what happened here today, I would. As would my wife. Your sister was dear to both of us, and we will always mourn her. But I must ask a question of you, and you must answer here before you can be alone in your grief."

Sophie opened her mouth to tell him to stop, to leave Margaretta alone. A sudden rustling sound like winds through a distant tree filled her ears for a moment and she paused, knowing suddenly that she had to let this happen.

Margaretta's eyes were the same shape as Eloisa's but a far paler green. Though the color seemed brighter now, seen through the tears shining in her eyes. "Ask your question, Lord Scardale."

Cameron bowed, his face grave when he straightened again. "Your Royal Highness, do you believe you meet the criteria to wear the crown?"

Please say yes, please say yes, please say yes.

Margaretta stared down at her sister's body for a long time, before she lifted her gaze again. "No, Lord Scardale, I do not." Her voice was calm. "My magic is slight, and the healers have told me I cannot bear a child. My family has kept this secret, allowed me my privacy, because we believed there was more than enough time for Eloisa to bear heirs. But now we are out of time, and my family has given enough to this court." She turned to face the court. "I am not the heir to the throne of Anglion. The crown, by blood, belongs to Lady Sophia Mackenzie."

Sophie closed her eyes even, as she heard a sputtered gurgle of protest from the domina.

"She killed the queen!"

Sophie's eyes flew open again. She hadn't seen who had spoken.

"No. Domina Skey killed the queen," Cameron said fiercely. "For that, I believe her life will be forfeit. After she has provided us with the details of her conspiracy and treason. My wife is guilty of nothing but standing in the domina's path because of her birthright and therefore being another victim to her attempts to manipulate the court."

"She has a demon! The goddess will not accept her." A different voice.

Sophie shook her head. "The goddess has not abandoned me nor I her." She contemplated whether a display of her power would help or hinder her argument. "But I understand your concerns. But the temple here in Anglion has not been telling us the truth. They have lied to us. Kept us ignorant. The sanctii are not demons, and the Illvyans are not monsters intent on slaughter and domination. Or invasion. So, I suggest we wait for

the Illvyans to arrive, and then we can discuss the way forward."
She looked at Margaretta again. "Your Royal Highness, would
you like to take your sister now?"

Perhaps it was unfortunate that, when Aristides finally arrived at
the palace and walked into the audience hall, Sophie's black
dress matched all too well with the gleaming black uniforms of
the Imperial mages and guards surrounding him. But it had been
the dress that Lady Beata had fetched for her, when she had
asked to be allowed to change out of the one stained with
Eloisa's blood. It was even her own dress, one of the mourning
gowns she'd worn after the attack on the court. One that she'd
left behind when she and Cameron had fled to Illvya what
seemed like close to a century ago.

She'd left the hall, under escort, washed and changed, then
been escorted back. Domina Skey still stood at the front of the
court, bound and gagged and surrounded by guards. Elarus stood
a few feet from her, gaze fixed on the domina.

The crown princess—though perhaps that was no longer
her title—had declined the invitation to be here to meet the
emperor, choosing instead to remain with Eloisa's body. Her
husband, and several hastily summoned squads of Red Guards,
had accompanied her to the temple where Eloisa's rites would
be held in due course. The guards would ensure none of the
dominas and devouts and priors left the temple until Domina
Skey had been tried, so she should be safe enough. And Sophie
could not bring herself to cause Margaretta any more pain by
forcing the issue. She did, however, wish she could be there
with her, safely away from everything that was about to
happen.

The only thing that raised her spirits slightly was the sight of
Jean-Paul and Imogene in the emperor's retinue. Hopefully the
presence of the du Laqs here meant that Ikarus had spoken the

truth, and everyone was safe. She hadn't dared ask for the hostages to be released yet.

Behind the du Laqs, several brown-robed and hooded dominas walked. The hoods hid their faces, but she could tell from their clothes they weren't from any Anglion temple. Judging by the ripple of noise that passed through the room in their wake, so could most of the court.

Trust Aristides to set a cat amongst the pigeons and bring with him a clear reminder that the worship of the goddess was alive and flourishing in Illvya. And that the goddess hadn't destroyed his empire, despite its water mages and its sanctii.

When Aristides reached the front of the hall, Sophie inclined her head. She was under strict instructions from Liam and Chloe that it would be improper to curtsy to the emperor while she was a queen-to-be in her own kingdom.

"His Imperial Majesty, Aristides Delmar de Lucien, Emperor of Illvya," one of the court announcers bellowed.

Sophie fought the urge to giggle as the faces of the Anglion nobles seated grew noticeably stiffer. Nervous laughter wouldn't help.

"Your Imperial Majesty," she said, managing to keep her voice steady. "Welcome to Anglion."

"Thank you, Lady Scardale. It is still Lady Scardale?" he said in very good Anglish.

This time she did roll her eyes at him. "Yes, Your Imperial Majesty. As I'm sure you have been briefed. If you would be so good as to address the court and tell them why you have journeyed here?"

Aristides nodded. His entourage had fanned out to the sides of the court though eight guards still stood close. He turned to face the court, spreading his arms wide. "My lords and ladies of Anglion. I assure you I am here with only peaceful intentions. Though perhaps, before we deal with matters of the politics of man, there are other matters to dispense with."

Sophie started to open her mouth to ask what exactly he was

doing, but Aristides ploughed on. "You have been dealt a blow of treason and deceit in this country. A king and a queen lost. A temple perhaps, betrayed. I thought perhaps I could offer a service. I have brought with me, our own domina of the temple of the Goddess to provide counsel in a time of need. Domina Francis, if you please."

The domina standing closest to Imogene pulled back her hood, revealing the unmistakable red blaze of hair. Domina Francis came forward to stand with Aristides and bowed to the court. "My lords and ladies, I am here as a servant of the goddess. I believe there has been deceit in your temple and that the goddess demands that deceit be rooted out, and her temple made whole again." Her Anglish was excellent. Even better than Aristides.

"Illvyan magic," someone muttered.

Domina Francis shook her head. "You can see by my hair that I am an earth witch and nothing more. I offer only the truth."

"How can we know that?" the Erl of Airlight said gruffly.

Sophie's hands clenched. If they couldn't convince the erl, then there was probably no resolution to this situation, other than she and Cameron returning to exile in Illvya. Which wasn't an entirely unappealing option. Though, exactly what Aristides would do to Anglion at that point was anybody's guess.

Domina Francis turned to Sophie. "My lady, do you have truth seekers here in Anglion?"

"No, milady domina," Sophie said. "That is not a magic we are familiar with."

The domina smiled. "How fortunate then, that we brought one of our own."

Chloe, standing beside Sophie as a temporary measure given Sophie had no ladies to support her and it was as yet unsettled as to whether she had the right to any, hissed a startled breath.

Sophie expected to see the tall, blond Lord Castaigne emerge from the ranks of Aristides men, but instead a short, wiry, red-haired man she didn't recognize stepped forward and bowed to the emperor, then to the domina and Sophie, before turning and bowing to the court. Chloe sighed softly.

Domina Skey strained forward a moment, looking as though she might try to speak despite the gag, but the Red Guard closest to her pulled her back and she subsided.

Aristides nodded to the domina.

She pointed at the truth seeker. "My lords and ladies, this is Lord August Edouard. He is a truth seeker. It is a form of magic that is rare in the empire. It allows him to tell who is lying and who is telling the truth. I understand that you may be unwilling to accept this as fact from an Illvyan. But I propose a test. Ten of you to come forward. You will each tell Lord Edouard two truths and two lies. He will tell you which is which. If he gets all ten right, when he knows none of you and has been in your country less than an hour, perhaps we can agree his power is real. Of course, we can make it twenty or fifty or however many it would take."

Lord Edouard gave the domina a sideways glance at that but didn't protest.

Aristides folded his arms and smiled pleasantly. It was clear the emperor was willing for the process to take all day if necessary.

"I'll do it," Liam said. His offer was quickly echoed by Lord Sylvain. Then the Erl of Airlight also stepped forward, somewhat reluctantly. The next to volunteer, to Sophie's surprise was Barron Deepholt. After that more hands raised, and they had ten volunteers in seconds.

"Perhaps we can start with you," Domina Francis said, nodding at Liam. "You are?"

"The Erl of Inglewood. Lord Scardale's older brother."

"True," Lord Edouard said and a few members of the court laughed nervously.

"All right, my lord Inglewood. This will be a better test if your truths and lies are known to others in the court. Perhaps even better if some of those others aren't your best friends or allies?" The domina smiled out at the court. "Do you agree this is a fair test?"

There was a reluctant rumble of agreement.

Domina Francis nodded. "Good. Lord Inglewood, please begin."

"All right." Liam took his time, pulling an exaggerated, let-me-think face. "First. I once beat the Erl of Airlight so thoroughly at a game of five-handed Starion that he had to give me both his favorite stallion and half his year's production of iska."

Smart. Everyone knew that the Airlights and Inglewoods were more rivals than friends and that the current Erl in particular had disliked Liam and Cameron's father intensely, despite the link between their families that Jeanne and Liam's marriage had forged.

"True," said Lord Edouard. Liam then offered two more facts. A tale of falling from his horse in his first hunt at court after breaking into the King's cellar the night before to steal several bottles of wine, and the last of being ill after eating a whole pail of summerberries with his fellow students.

Lord Edouard gave his opinion again. Lie. Truth.

"Are there those in court who can confirm?" Domina Francis asked.

The Erl of Airlight nodded tightly, followed by several other noblemen.

"Then let us proceed." They cycled through the remaining nine men quickly. Lord Edouard did not get a single answer wrong.

After the tenth, the domina spread her hands. "Do you concede this is a true power?" she asked the court.

Lord Airlight waved an irritable hand. "Yes. It's not natural, but it seems to be real. Get on with it."

The domina bowed her head. "As you wish, my lord." She turned back to Sophie. "Lady Sophia, did you have a vision that led you to fear that Queen Eloisa was under attack in her own palace? That Domina Skey was somehow controlling her?"

"Yes," Sophie said. She put her heart into the word, willing the truth seeker to hear her truly.

"True," Lord Edouard intoned, his eyes fixed on Sophie.

"Did you return to Anglion intending to free Eloisa and return her to her rightful state of power and place as Anglion's sovereign unfettered by that control?"

"Yes."

"True."

There was a ripple of noise through the court. Sophie didn't move her gaze from the domina.

"Did you ever desire the throne for yourself?"

"No."

"True."

"Are you a loyal subject of Anglion?"

"I was loyal while I lived in Anglion," Sophie said. "During the time I spent in Illvya, I held to that loyalty though I did things that Anglions would consider wrong. Or taboo. I have learned water magic. I believe there is nothing harmful in that. As I believe that the temple in Anglion has been corrupted for a long time. That it hampers the powers of the most powerful mages and witches here. That it has weakened and subverted the powers of royal witches, in particular. I believe the temple has sent assassins against me, and my husband, twice. And I believe the temple, and those in this court who might support these aims, were behind the attack on the palace that killed King Stefan and many others. I believe that Domina Skey, most recently, formed a bond with Eloisa when the queen was injured and vulnerable. A bond she then used to shape the queen's views and actions. Starting with using her to try to kill me." Sophie clamped her jaw shut before she could say anything more.

"Truth," Lord Edouard said again.

This time the court didn't stay silent. There was a babble of protest that only stopped when Liam roared for silence.

"She may well *believe* it to be true," Lord Airlight said into the ensuing silence. "That doesn't make it true. She doesn't know for sure."

"No," Sophie said. "But Domina Skey does." She gestured to the guards surrounding the domina. They tugged her forward to stand squarely in front of the empty Salt Throne, her feet on the patch of marble where earlier she had watched a group of servants scrub away Eloisa's blood.

Domina Francis stepped close to Domina Skey, green eyes boring into brown, full of banked anger. "You are supposed to be a faithful servant of the goddess. You have betrayed that trust. I might have found some sympathy for you because the first crack in that trust happened so long ago here. But you have done your best to fracture it beyond bearing. So, I ask you, sister. Will you speak truth here before the court and before the goddess, or do you want me to drag you to the temple you have betrayed and use the vows you gave to the goddess to compel you? Because, believe me, I am more than willing to do just that."

Her last words had a strange shimmering echo to them, and Sophie was almost sure she heard the rustle of leaves again and a waft of salt grass far fresher than the lingering traces of Domina Skey's braziers. But perhaps it was only her imagination.

Domina Skey's eyes burned with hatred, but she nodded, slowly. Domina Francis removed the gag from her mouth.

"Illvyan devil spawn," Domina Skey spat.

"Lie," Lord Edouard said.

Domina Francis merely smiled. "Lady Sophie, do you have questions for the domina?"

Sophie smelt salt and flames again and felt a pulse of magic from deep beneath her feet roll through her. She smiled then, no longer unsure as to what she was meant to do.

"Domina Skey, did you cause an assassin to be recruited to kill me here in the palace at Kingswell?"

"No."

"Lie." There was a gasp. Aristides held up a hand. Sophie took a step closer.

"Domina Skey did you recruit Sevan Allowood to kill me if he got the chance and have him placed on the delegation that Queen Eloisa sent to Illvya to carry out that mission if he could?"

"No."

"Lie."

Another step. The hatred rolling off the domina now seemed to pulse against Sophie, but she felt no fear. "Domina Skey, did you form a bond with Queen Eloisa and use it to influence her, intending to subvert the crown of Anglion for your own purposes?"

"No!" It was a shriek this time. Half the court stepped back at the fury in the word.

"Lie."

The domina lunged toward Sophie. It was Cameron, this time, who caught her, wrenched her away, then held her arms and turned her back to face Sophie.

Sophie moved until she was no more than three feet from the domina, the anger she had been tamping down for so long now, free to blaze bright. "No one believes you," she snarled. "You have no power here. You have cost this country a king and queen and countless other losses. You have stolen from every witch here. But it ends now. You failed. Because you couldn't leave me alone. I would have served Eloisa happily and no doubt disappeared with my husband to the country to have a family and live my life. But you were stupid and arrogant and thought you knew better than the goddess herself. You came after me, and you failed. And you know, milady. I never wanted to be a queen. But because of you, this country needs a queen. Needs *me*. I will not let you and your lust for power ruin any more lives. I will not let you twist the words of the goddess. *I* will not let you. And no one else here will either. Because they obey their queen, Domina. And the queen you have given them this time is not bound to you or your temple or your lies. I am *free*, and I will use that freedom as the goddess needs me to. I will protect this country and its people, and I will, quite happily, dance on your grave for what you have done to us." The fury she felt as she spoke the words nearly consumed her, and she realized she was close to reaching out and using her power to kill the domina where she stood. That would not do. She needed to be questioned, tried, and eventually handed back to the temple who would strip her of her powers and then end her life.

She needed justice. Anglion needed justice. And they needed a queen who could give it them.

She sucked in a breath, made herself step back, drawing up her chin as she stared the domina down.

"True," Lord Edouard said. Suddenly her ears were full of the sound of applause. She turned and found the court on its feet, clapping. And then, Cameron bowed to her, more deeply than he ever had, and she saw behind him, all the nobles following suit.

"Long live Queen Sophia," Lord Sylvain said into the deep silence that followed as she stood and stared at her court.

"And that, I believe," Aristides said, deep voice full of amusement, "is that."

"This is the worst part, little brother," Liam said, as they stood outside the Salt Hall, waiting for the coronation ceremony to begin several weeks later. Sophie had flatly refused to be crowned in the temple and her counselors, after some argument, had given in when Domina Francis had declared there to be no reason the rites couldn't be performed at the palace. The rebuilding project had tripled its efforts to repair the Salt Hall and it had finally been completed several days earlier.

"That's what you told me before my wedding," Cameron said. "You may have been right then, but I'm quite certain you're wrong now. Neither of us wanted this." He jerked his head toward the door and the throne that stood inside.

"Maybe that's why you'll do a good job of it," Liam said grinning. "And think of how proud Father would be."

Cameron rolled his eyes. "Pleasing our father with my choices was never high on my list of priorities. And I don't think he'd approve the way this came about."

Liam's smile turned harder. "Perhaps not. But the throne is Sophie's by right, and if we are to move forward, then we need both of you. You've seen beyond the edges of our particular world. You've seen the truth. There are things that need to be fixed here. And I can't think of anyone else I'd trust more to fix them."

"You realize that you're going to be helping me do that fixing," Cameron said. "You and Alec both."

"Good luck dragging him away from his estate," Liam said. "But trust me brother, all is as it should be." Then he flinched as he realized he'd echoed Eloisa's last words.

Cameron hid his own instinctive wince. Liam didn't know the true weight those words held.

He'd told Sophie that Eloisa had said them to him once before, when she'd sent him to take Sophie to Dockside on that first fateful day. Less than a year ago, but it was difficult to believe it was the same world, let alone that so little time had passed. Sophie was convinced that Eloisa had had a foretelling, and the idea seemed to comfort her, so he hadn't argued. He'd asked the goddess a time or two if it could be true, but she had so far declined to send him any visions of his own to give him any certainty.

But whether or not Eloisa had seen anything, perhaps Liam was right. Perhaps there was a reason that he and Sophie had been brought to this moment and the work that lay before them. Not the life he'd imagined, but he knew that as long as he had Sophie, it was a life he would be happy in. And perhaps the only true way he could honor Eloisa was to keep her country safe and help it grow into a new future.

Sophie's father appeared beside Liam. He wore a smile, but a slightly wide-eyed, uneasy one. Cameron sympathized. He couldn't imagine that Ser Kendall—who had resisted his daughter's offers to elevate that title—had ever envisioned he would be father to the queen.

But the older man clapped Cameron on the shoulder and bowed briefly to Liam. "She's on her way. Are you ready?"

"As ready as I am ever likely to be," Cameron said. Behind him, bells began to ring out, and he turned to see Sophie coming toward him, glorious in a shade of green that seemed blessed by the goddess herself, so perfectly did it suit her. Her hair was loose around her shoulders, a defiant blaze of red and black that he could guarantee no Anglion queen had sported for centuries.

When their eyes met, he smiled at her and mouthed, "I love you," before moving to his place at her side, to walk beside her on her journey.

EPILOGUE

Sophie stood on the docks at Kingswell one month later, watching Chloe gaze hungrily at the ship currently headed into port.

The ship, bearing the Illvyan flag proudly on the tallest mast was Aristides's own personal vessel, arriving to carry the emperor home in slightly more luxury than he had arrived.

Chloe would be returning to Illvya with him. She had received his assurance that no one would be pursuing her for any of the matters relating to her husband's crimes.

As she'd never actually been charged with anything, let alone convicted, Aristides couldn't actually grant her a pardon, but he had offered her his word she was safe. Sophie didn't know if Chloe actually needed his protection, but she had seen the joy and relief that had flashed over Chloe's face when Aristides had told her she could return home.

Chloe had barely stopped smiling in the days and weeks that had passed since then, but now, watching the ship easing toward them, her excitement seemed tempered with apprehension.

"Are you sure about this?" Sophie asked. "You can stay."

"I want to go home, Your Majesty," Chloe said, and Sophie hid the instinctive wince that she felt every time someone called her that. Even standing here, with Elarus at her side and a semi-circle of grim-faced Red Guards at her back, it still didn't feel real.

"I told you to call me Sophie."

Chloe smiled. "In private, Your Majesty, your wish is my command. Or it will be when we meet again."

"Who knows," Sophie said, aiming for a little levity. Chloe felt like the closest thing she had to a friend here in Anglion, her near-constant companion through the whirl of Eloisa's funeral and the coronation and working with Domina Francis to begin the process of reforming the temple here in Anglion. Not to mention the final preparations for Domina Skey's trial. The woman had so far admitted her part in the attacks on Sophie and Eloisa, so the verdict was a foregone conclusion. But neither Aristides's truth seeker nor Domina Francis had been able to get Domina Skey to name any accomplices. Sophie suspected Domina Skey would be defiant to the grave. Which only left her with more work to do to uncover the truth herself over time.

She shivered and pushed the thought away. She was here for Chloe.

Who was possibly the only person who might understand the conflicted emotions Sophie was trying to navigate as she grappled with her new responsibilities. "Maybe they'll get tired of me here." Sophie summoned a lopsided smile. She couldn't deny that part of her wanted to get on the ship, return to Lumia and the Academe and become just Sophie once more.

But that was a choice no longer hers.

Chloe glanced at her quickly and smiled in return—though her expression was far more genuine than Sophie's. She shook her head, her gaze drawn like a magnet back to the ship that was growing larger by the minute. "I don't think so, Your Majesty. You will win them over in the end."

Sophie hoped Chloe was right. She could use some friends. The ladies-in-waiting, that she once would have named her friends were still distant, reeling from the grief of losing Eloisa and the revelations about the temple. She had to give them time. Perhaps they could be friends again if she gave them that. "I may yet be returning to Illvya sooner than any of us think." The court so far seemed accepting but she knew there would be unrest while she worked for the changes that needed to happen.

"I'm sure Papa and Madame Simsa would be happy to have you back. But you are needed here, Your Majesty."

"I know. There is plenty to do." Rebuilding the faith of a country for a start. And showing them what unbound magic could truly do. Imogene would be returning to Illvya soon, taking her navire and its crew of mages home but Aristides had pledged that, when Sophie judged it to be the right time, he would send more Illvyan mages to help establish new schools of learning in Anglion.

Domina Francis, however, had already sent for Illvyan dominas to help restore order in the temple. Some of them might even be on the ship Chloe couldn't quite take her eyes off. "Your family will be so happy to see you, Chloe," she said gently. "Don't be nervous."

Chloe dragged herself around to face Sophie. "Easier said than done, Your Majesty." She wrapped her arms around herself briefly before she straightened her spine. "So. You are an exile who has returned home. Do you have any words of wisdom to share?"

"Expect things to be strange," Sophie said. "Nothing will be quite as you remember." Chloe had been away from Illvya far longer than Cameron and Sophie had been away from Anglion. Of course, she wasn't returning as an invading queen, but time would have wrought just as difficult a change on everything she remembered—and all the memories she had left behind—as Sophie's coronation had.

"Your father has missed you," Sophie added, thinking of Henri's anger when he'd been told to stay in Illvya before the invasion. "Start from there."

"Good advice," Chloe said. "I have fences to mend, I think.

And other matters to pursue." Her face darkened, and for a moment, the red stripes in her hair flared a little brighter to Sophie's eyes. She resisted the urge to touch her own hair, which was beginning to look as varied as Chloe's. The first time she'd met Chloe, she'd been shocked by the clear marks of taboo powers on her body. Now she bore those same marks herself. And Chloe would have other scars of her own to endure when she returned to Illvya. She'd lost a husband there, after all. Left a life behind.

Sophie stayed silent, thinking of her own scars and losses, as Chloe turned yet again to watch the ship, which was starting to slow. It was too large to take a mooring at one of the docks and would remain anchored in deeper waters, with the few remaining ships the emperor had brought with him guarding it.

Aristides's ship came to as much of a halt as a large ship ever did, and they watched together as the anchors were dropped and a launch lowered from the decks. It started to move toward the docks, making good time.

"Are you sure you don't want to wait for the others?" Sophie asked.

Chloe shook her head. "I'd rather not draw attention to myself. Aristides can have his pomp and ceremony when you farewell him. I would rather not. I've had enough of standing out from the crowd here in Anglion. I want to go home."

"I understand." Sophie had done more strange things than she thought she ever would to find her own way back to Anglion. She hoped that Chloe might find an easier homecoming. "You know that you are always welcome in my house."

"And you in mine, Your Majesty. As I said, I'm sure my father would be happy to have you back at the Academe."

"Perhaps one day. Hopefully no one else will have to endure the same sort of exile that we have, now that things have changed between Anglion and the empire."

Both of them stared at the launch a moment.

"I think there will probably always be those who need to disappear," Chloe said, softly.

Sophie couldn't disagree. She hoped to change Anglion, but it would be slow. And even if she achieved everything she wanted to, there would always be those who were unhappy or in danger. She could make Anglion better, but not perfect. "But hopefully always those who get to return home again also."

The launch had almost reached the dock. She hugged Chloe close, then made herself let go. "Go on," she said, trying to keep her voice cheerful. "Go back to your new old life. I won't keep you any longer."

"Thank you, Your Majesty," Chloe said. "And you have your own new old life to get back to as well. One with more pressing demands than my own."

As though on cue, Tok, who had been flying around the dock, annoying the seabirds, wheeled back through the air to land on Sophie's shoulder.

"Queen!" he squawked. It was his latest word, one he seemed to take great delight in.

Chloe laughed, bobbed a curtsy, and then picked up her bag. The porter she'd hired to handle the rest of her trunks—fewer than Sophie would have thought she'd need to move a whole life across an ocean—followed her down the dock toward the launch.

Sophie watched her go, but Chloe didn't look back. And she had been right. Sophie did have more pressing demands. She turned away, to face the Red Guard and the man who stood in the middle of their semicircle, guarding her as he always did.

"All right," she said and reached for Cameron's hand. "I believe we have things to do."

"Body and blood, my love. I am yours to command."

"Spoken like a true King Consort."

"Spoken like a man who is deliriously happy to be spending the rest of his life with the queen he loves." Cameron smiled, and she couldn't help smiling back. Her crown was not what she would have chosen given a choice, but Cameron definitely was. Given a thousand lifetimes, she would not change the moments that had made him hers.

So, the queen of Anglion threw her arms around her consort in a very unqueenly fashion and kissed him.

"Body and blood, my love," she whispered eventually. And took his hand.

THE END

ABOUT THE AUTHOR

M.J Scott is an unrepentant bookworm. Luckily she grew up in a family that fed her a properly varied diet of books and these days is surrounded by people who are understanding of her story addiction. When not wrestling one of her own stories to the ground, she can generally be found reading someone else's. Her other distractions include yarn, cat butlering, dark chocolate and watercolor. To keep in touch, find out about new releases and other news (and receive an exclusive freebie) sign up to her newsletter at www.mjscott.net. She also writes contemporary romance as Melanie Scott and Emma Douglas.

You can keep in touch with M.J. on:
Twitter @melscott
Facebook AuthorMJScott
Pinterest @mel_writes
Instagram @melwrites
Or email her at mel@mjscott.net

EXCERPT FROM SHADOW KIN
CHAPTER 1

The wards sparked in front of me, faint violet against the dark wooden door with its heavy brass locks, proclaiming the house's protection. They wouldn't stop me. No one has yet made the lock or ward to keep me out. Magic cannot detect me, and brick and stone and metal are no barrier.

It's why I'm good at what I do.

A grandfather clock in the hall chimed two as I stepped into the shadow, entering the place only my kind can walk and passing through the door as though it wasn't there. Outside came the echoing toll of the cathedral bell, much louder here in Greenglass than in the Night World boroughs I usually frequent.

I'd been told that the one I was to visit lived alone. But I prefer not to believe everything I'm told. After all, I grew up among the Blood and the powers of the Night World, where taking things on faith is a quick way to die.

Besides, bystanders only make things complicated.

But tonight, I sensed I *was* alone as I moved carefully through the darkened rooms. The house had an elegant simplicity. The floors were polished wood, softened by fine wool rugs, and paintings hung on the unpapered walls. Plants flourished on any spare flat surface, tingeing the air with the scent of growth and life. I hoped someone would save them after my task here was completed. The Fae might deny me the Veiled World, but the part of me that comes from them shares their affinity for green growing things.

Apart from the damp greenness of the plants, there was only one other dominant scent in the air. Human. Male. Warm and spicy.

Alive. Live around the Blood for long enough and you become very aware of the differences between living and dead. No other fresh smell mingled with his. No cats or dogs. Just fading hints of an older female gone for several hours. Likely a cook or housekeeper who didn't live in.

I paused at the top of the staircase, counting doors carefully. Third on the left. A few more strides. I cocked my head, listening.

There.

Ever so faint, the thump of a human heartbeat. Slow. Even.

Asleep.

Good. Asleep is easier.

I drifted through the bedroom door and paused again. The room was large, walled on one side with floor-to-ceiling windows unblocked by any blind. Expensive, that much glass. Moonlight streamed through the panes, making it easy to see the man lying in the big bed.

I didn't know what he'd done. I never ask. The blade doesn't question the direction of the cut. Particularly when the blade belongs to Lucius. Lucius doesn't like questions.

I let go of the shadow somewhat. I was not yet truly solid, but enough that, if he were to wake, he would see my shape by the bed like the reflection of a dream. Or a nightmare.

The moonlight washed over his face, silvering skin and fading hair to shades of gray, making it hard to tell what he might look like in daylight. Tall, yes. Well formed if the arm and chest bared by the sheet he'd pushed away in sleep matched the rest of him.

Not that it mattered. He'd be beyond caring about his looks in a few minutes. Beyond caring about anything.

The moon made things easier even though, in the shadow, I see well in very little light. Under the silvered glow I saw the details of the room as clearly as if the gas lamps on the walls were alight.

The windows posed little risk. The town house stood separated from its neighbors by narrow strips of garden on each side and a much larger garden at the rear. There was a small chance someone in a neighboring house might see something, but I'd be long gone before they could raise an alarm.

His breath continued to flow, soft and steady, and I moved around the bed, seeking a better angle for the strike as I let myself grow more solid still, so I could grasp the dagger at my hip.

Legend says we kill by reaching into a man's chest and tearing out his heart. It's true, we can. I've even done it. Once.

At Lucius' demand and fearing death if I disobeyed.

It wasn't an act I ever cared to repeat. Sometimes, on the edge of sleep, I still shake thinking about the sensation of living flesh torn from its roots beneath my fingers.

So I use a dagger. Just as effective. Dead is dead, after all.

I counted his heartbeats as I silently slid my blade free. He was pretty, this one. A face of interesting angles that looked strong even in sleep. Strong and somehow happy. Generous lips curved up slightly as if he were enjoying a perfect dream.

Not a bad way to die, all things considered.

I unshadowed completely and lifted the dagger, fingers steady on the hilt as he took one last breath.

But even as the blade descended, the room blazed to light around me and a hand snaked out like a lightning bolt and clamped around my wrist.

"Not so fast," the man said in a calm tone.

I tried to shadow and my heart leaped to my throat as nothing happened.

"Just to clarify," he said. "Those lamps. Not gas. Sunlight."

"*Sunmage,*" I hissed, rearing back as my pulse went into overdrive. How had Lucius left out *that* little detail? Or maybe he hadn't. Maybe Ricco had left it out on purpose when he'd passed on my assignment. He hated me. I wouldn't put it past him to try to engineer my downfall.

Damn him to the seven bloody night-scalded depths of hell.

The man smiled at me, though there was no amusement in the expression. "Precisely."

I twisted, desperate to get free. His hand tightened, and pain shot through my wrist and up my arm.

"Drop the dagger."

I set my teeth and tightened my grip. Never give up your weapon.

"I said, *drop it.*" The command snapped as he surged out of the bed, pushing me backward and my arm above my head at a nasty angle.

The pain intensified, like heated wires slicing into my nerves. "Sunmages are supposed to be healers," I managed to gasp as I struggled and the sunlight—hells-damned *sunlight*—filled the room, caging me as effectively as iron bars might hold a human.

I swung at him with my free arm, but he blocked the blow, taking its force on his forearm without a wince. He fought far too well for a healer. Who was this man?

"Ever consider that being a healer means being exposed to hundreds of ways to hurt people? Don't make me hurt you. Put the knife down."

I swore and flung myself forward, swinging my free hand at his face again. But he moved too, fast and sure, and somehow—damn, he was good—I missed, my hand smacking into the wall. I twisted desperately as the impact sent a shock wave up my arm, but the light dazzled me as I looked directly into one of the lamps.

A split second is all it takes to make a fatal mistake.

Before I could blink, he had pulled me forward and round

and I sailed through the air to land facedown on the feather mattress, wind half knocked out of me. My free hand was bent up behind my back, and my other—still holding my dagger—was pinned by his to the pillow.

My heart raced in anger and humiliation and fear as I tried to breathe.

Sunmage.

I was an idiot. *Stupid. Stupid. Stupid.*

Stupid and careless.

His knee pushed me deeper into the mattress, making it harder still to breathe.

"Normally I don't get this forward when I haven't been introduced," he said, voice warm and low, close to my ear. He still sounded far too calm. A sunmage healer shouldn't be so sanguine about finding an assassin in his house. Though perhaps he wasn't quite as calm as he seemed. His heart pounded. "But then again, normally, women I don't know don't try to stab me in my bed."

I snarled and he increased the pressure. There wasn't much I could do. I'm faster and stronger than a human woman, but there's a limit to what a female of five foot six can do against a man nearly a foot taller and quite a bit heavier. Particularly with my powers cut off by the light of the sun.

Damned hells-cursed sunlight.

"I'll take that." His knee shifted upward to pin both my arm and my back, and his free hand wrenched the dagger from my grasp.

Then, to my surprise, his weight vanished. It took a few seconds for me to register my freedom. By the time I rolled to face him, he stood at the end of the bed and my dagger quivered in the wall far across the room. To make matters worse, the sunlight now flickered off the ornately engraved barrel of the pistol in his right hand.

It was aimed squarely at the center of my forehead. His hand was perfectly steady, as though holding someone at gunpoint was nothing greatly out of the ordinary for him. For a man wearing nothing but linen drawers, he looked convincingly threatening.

I froze. Would he shoot? If our places were reversed, he'd already be dead.

"Wise decision," he said, eyes still cold. "Now. Why don't you tell me what this is about?"

"Do you think that's likely?"

One corner of his mouth lifted and a dimple cracked to life in his cheek. My assessment had been right. He was pretty. Pretty and dangerous, it seemed. The arm that held the gun was, like the rest of him, sleek with muscle. The sort that took concerted effort to obtain. Maybe he was one of the rare sunmages who became warriors? But the house seemed far too luxurious for a Templar or a mercenary, and his hands and body were bare of Templar sigils.

Besides, I doubted Lucius would set me on a Templar. That would be madness.

So, who the hell was this man?

When I stayed silent, the pistol waved back and forth in a warning gesture. "I have this," he said. "Plus, I am, as you mentioned, a sunmage." As if to emphasize his point, the lamps flared a little brighter. "Start talking."

I considered him carefully. The sunlight revealed his skin as golden, his hair a gilded shade of light brown, and his eyes a bright, bright blue. A true creature of the day. No wonder Lucius wanted him dead. I currently felt a considerable desire for that outcome myself. I scanned the rest of the room, seeking a means to escape.

A many-drawered wooden chest, a table covered with papers with a leather-upholstered chair tucked neatly against it, and a large wardrobe all made simply in the same dark reddish wood offered no inspiration. Some sort of ferny plant in a stand stood in one corner, and paintings—landscapes and studies of more plants—hung over the bed and the table. Nothing smaller than the furniture, nothing I could use as a weapon, lay in view. Nor was there anything to provide a clue as to who he might be.

"I can hear you plotting all the way over here," he said with another little motion of the gun. "Not a good idea. In fact . . ." The next jerk of the pistol was a little more emphatic, motioning me toward the chair as he hooked it out from the table with his foot. "Take a seat. Don't bother trying anything stupid like attempting the window. The glass is warded. You'll just hurt yourself."

Trapped in solid form, I couldn't argue with that. The lamps shone with a bright unwavering light and his face showed no sign of strain. Even his heartbeat had slowed to a more steady rhythm now that we were no longer fighting. A sunmage calling sunlight at night. Strong. Dangerously strong.

Not to mention armed when I wasn't.

I climbed off the bed and stalked over to the chair.

He tied my arms and legs to their counterparts on the chair with neck cloths. Tight enough to be secure but carefully placed so as not to hurt. He had to be a healer. A mercenary wouldn't care if he hurt me. A mercenary probably would've killed me outright.

When he was done he picked up a pair of buckskin trousers and a rumpled linen shirt from the floor and dressed quickly. Then he took a seat on the end of the bed, picked up the gun once again, and aimed directly at me.

Blue eyes stared at me for a long minute, something unreadable swimming in their depths. Then he nodded.

"Shall we try this again? Why are you here?"

There wasn't any point lying about it. "I was sent to kill you."

"I understand that much. The reason is what escapes me."

I lifted a shoulder. Let him make what he would of the gesture. I had no idea why Lucius had sent me after a sunmage.

"You didn't ask?"

"Why would I?" I said, surprised by the question.

He frowned. "You just kill whoever you're told to? It doesn't matter why?"

"I do as I'm ordered." Disobedience would only bring pain. Or worse.

His head tilted, suddenly intent. His gaze was uncomfortable, and it was hard to shake the feeling he saw more than I wanted. "You should seek another line of work."

As if I had a choice. I looked away from him, suddenly angry. Who was he to judge me?

"Back to silence, is it? Very well, let's try another tack. This isn't, by chance, about that Rousselline pup I stitched up a few weeks ago?"

Pierre Rousselline was alpha of one of the Beast Kind packs. He and Lucius didn't always exist in harmony. But I doubted Lucius would kill over the healing of a young Beast. A sunmage, one this strong—if his claim of being able to maintain the light until dawn were true——was an inherently risky target, even for a Blood lord. Even for *the* Blood Lord.

So, what had this man—who was, indeed, a healer if he spoke the truth—done?

His brows lifted when I didn't respond. "You really don't know, do you? Well. Damn."

The "damn" came out as a half laugh. There was nothing amusing in the situation that I could see. Either he was going to kill me or turn me over to the human authorities or I was going to have to tell Lucius I had failed. Whichever option came to pass, nothing good awaited me. I stayed silent.

"Some other topic of conversation, then?" He regarded me with cool consideration. "I presume, given that my sunlight seems to be holding you, that I'm right in assuming that you are Lucius' shadow?"

I nodded. There was little point denying it with his light holding me prisoner. There were no others of my kind in the City. Only a wraith is caged by the light of the sun.

A smile spread over his face, revealing he had two

dimples, not one. Not just pretty, I decided. He was . . . alluring wasn't the right word. The Blood and the Fae are alluring—an attraction born of icy beauty and danger. I am immune to that particular charm. No, he was . . . inviting somehow. A fire on a winter's night, promising warmth and life.

His eyes held genuine curiosity. "You're really a wraith?"

"Yes."

He laughed and the sound was sunlight, warm and golden, a smooth caress against the skin.

"Is that so amusing?"

"If the stories are to believed, you're supposed to be ten feet tall with fangs and claws."

I tilted my head. "I am not Blood or Beast Kind. No fangs. Or claws."

He looked over my shoulder, presumably at my dagger. "Just one perhaps? But really . . . no one ever said you were—" He stopped abruptly.

"What?" The question rose from my lips before I could stop myself.

This time his smile was crooked. "Beautiful."

I snorted. Beautiful? Me? No. I knew that well enough. The Fae are beautiful and even the Blood in their own way. I am only odd with gray eyes—a color no Fae or true demi-Fae ever had— and red hair that stands out like a beacon amongst the silvery hues of the Blood. "That's because I'm not."

He looked surprised. "I know the Blood don't use mirrors, but you must have seen yourself."

"Maybe the Night World has different standards."

"Then the Night World needs its eyesight examined," he said with another crooked smile. "Gods and suns."

Silence again. He studied me and I looked away, discomfited, wondering what angle he was trying to work by flattering me. Did he think I could sway Lucius into granting mercy? If so, then he was in for a severe disappointment.

"What happens now?" I asked when the silence started to strain my nerves.

"That may well depend on you."

Liked it? Find out more about Shadow Kin and the other three books in the Half-Light City series at M.J's website (www.mjscott.net).

Lightning Source UK Ltd.
Milton Keynes UK
UKHW011108170520
363415UK00002B/320